Julia Fitzgerald was born in North Wales and attended school in Yorkshire. She has two children and her interests include history, health and medicine (especially new discoveries), Persian cats, mythology and astrology. Miss Fitzgerald also writes under the pen-names of Julia Watson and Julia Hamilton, and now lives in Chester.

SLAVE LADY

JULIA FITZGERALD

BART

NEW YORK

Reprinted by arrangement with the author

ISBN: 1-55785-072-0

First Bart Books edition: January 1989

Bart Books
155 E. 34th Street
New York, New York 10016

Manufactured in the United States of America

No disguise can hide love for long, nor simulate love when it is not there.

de la Rochefoucauld

Chapter One

A million diamonds sparkled on a sea of cerulean silk.

Although Cassia had her Vincent beside her, nonetheless, as their boat sped across the waters towards Algiers, which at this moment seemed to be haloed in diamonds, she could not help remembering Lucien who had welcomed her in Algiers the first time she had been and who had behaved towards her so warmly. Poor Lucien: now dead, like all those who had been devoted followers of Captain Vincent de Sauvage. The wicked Nathan Dash had seen to that, determined as he had been to wipe out Vincent and his men so that he, Dash, could inherit the fortune and the ships which were to have been left to Vincent by Dash's half-brother.

Not far out from Algiers, Nathan Dash and his men had attacked Vincent, slaughtering all his men, stealing his ship and the slaves he had been intending to sell in Constantinople, and leaving Vincent for dead, lying in a pool of blood. Then he had taken Cassia, who had been amongst those slaves, and had sold her himself to the Sultan of Turkey, Hamid I.

Cassia looked across at Vincent and squeezed his hand as she remembered those terrible days in the harem when she had thought her lover dead and had believed that she was condemned to spend the rest of her days as one of the Sultan's five hundred concubines. But Vincent had not been dead. Miraculously, he had recovered from his wounds, helped back to health by an Arab physician of brilliant talents who lived at the court of the Princess Jasmina. Jasmina had fallen wildly in love with Vincent and had tried to force him into marrying her, but his heart had belonged to Cassia and it always would, whether she was alive or dead — and at that time he had not known anything of her whereabouts.

7

And then the strangest thing had happened. A Turkish peasant had appeared at Jasmina's court to beg her aid in rescuing the young girl who had fallen into the evil clutches of Leo, Lord Marchington, an English nobleman. Jasmina had been absent from the audience chamber that day, to Vincent's great fortune, for he had been present to hear the Turkish man's story and to hurry with him to save Cassia from being raped and forcibly married by Marchington.

Since then they had been fleeing, riding at night, sleeping in hideaways by day, to escape the pursuing hordes of the Princess Jasmina. They had ridden through Turkey, and Greece, and obtained a passage on a chebek which was heading for Algiers where Vincent had his home — and where, he hoped, Nathan Dash's half-brother would be waiting to welcome him back. The old Captain had been crippled with rheumatism, but had long ago promised that he would leave his empire to Vincent, whom he trusted implicitly.

'Remember the last time we arrived at Algiers?' Cassia said, smiling at Vincent. 'Remember how you made me wear purdah, whether I liked it or not? What a struggle I had getting down the hempen ladder from the ship to the little boat which came to take me to shore. All those voluminous robes twisting round my legs.'

'Can you blame me for wanting to keep your beauty concealed?' Vincent grinned. 'I knew what would happen if Nathan Dash set eyes on you, and I was right, wasn't I?'

'Yes, darling,' Cassia replied, causing Vincent to glance at her almost suspiciously, knowing as he did that any pretence she made at meekness was feigned. His Cassia, whom he adored more than life itself, was a creature of flame, and sometimes sparks flew. She liked to have her own way, and indeed after thinking she was lost and suffering long months without her, Vincent was more than willing to give her her head now. Cementing their alliance was vitally important. Not that it took much conscious effort on either part, for, having found out that they were made for one another, it needed

8

nothing more than for them to be together, deeply and passionately in love as they were.

Vincent had vowed with all his strength that nothing was going to separate them again.

He was a changed man now. Gone was the slave-master bordering almost on villainy who had spent his months scooping up women wherever he found them and taking them to the slave markets of Algiers and Constantinople. It had been on one of his night forays for slaves that he had abducted Cassia. Seven years condemned to the galleys for a crime he had not committed had driven him to that life. But now he had forsaken such callous activities. Now, with Cassia's help and through their love, he had been reborn. His aim in the future, wherever he went, whatever circumstances he encountered, would be to free, not to enslave. There are few more virtuous than the converted sinner.

The chebek was running up against the mole which ran down into the sea to enable ships to land safely. A small rowing boat was waiting to take the passengers from it. Vincent looked around, but saw no familiar faces; nor did Cassia. They had hoped to see some of Captain Dash's men waiting for them, for Vincent had sent messages earlier on a small merchant vessel.

Taking Cassia's hand, he helped her down the hempen ladder into the rowing boat. They had no baggage with them, only the clothes which they wore, just as they had fled from the island of Poseidon where Marchington had been keeping Cassia a prisoner. Cassia's white robe was now tattered and grubby. It had been the robe in which Marchington had intended to make her his bride; a simple affair on classical lines with black cord criss-crossed over her breasts and round her waist. Marchington was dead now, slain in a duel with Vincent.

Cassia did not know why he had spun into her mind as they rowed towards Algiers, but she had learned from past experience that the horrors she had undergone could not easily be exorcised from her mind, but insisted upon springing back

9

into her thoughts, often when she least expected them. Into her dreams, too. It was a state of affairs to which she would just have to become accustomed.

A conversation flittered back into her mind. It had taken place the first time she approached Algiers in a longboat with Lucien.

As they had neared Algiers, seeing the banks of white-washed houses before them, he had said, 'They look something like a Roman amphitheatre, do they not, mademoiselle?'

And she had looked from the houses to Lucien, speaking to him in French, saying, 'An amphitheatre, monsieur?' enjoying the surprise on his face, for he had not known that she could speak his language.

'Why yes, do you not think so? All those houses built so close together, elevated one above the other just like a classical theatre – myself I have always thought so. Of course the spires of the Mosque and the Janina – that is, the Dey's Palace – rise higher, but that only serves to make the scenario more interesting, would you not agree?' He had pushed back the blond hair which had fallen into his eyes, and she remembered that she had wondered how he avoided being burned by the scorching sun, for he had such a fair skin. Poor Lucien. She would never forget him, or the other brave and valiant men who had served her Vincent and who had been cruelly attacked and murdered by Nathan Dash.

They were now out of the rowing boat and walking up the harbour promenade and they still had not seen a familiar face. She could see that Vincent was concerned, for by now they should have seen at least someone whom he knew. It was true that Vincent had been thought dead for many months, but, all the same, the men he had known in Algiers would not *all* have left, surely?

'No one to welcome us. It is strange.' Vincent gripped her hand more tightly.

'Perhaps they did not get your message, darling. Perhaps

those merchantmen who took our money had no intention of delivering the letter.'

'Perhaps. And yet I had the feeling that they were honest enough. Well, we shall see. Come, follow me.'

This time Cassia did not notice the crowds of staring, gabbling onlookers who watched them pass. Beggars and sailors, gaping, chattering, pointing; the smell of dirty clothes and bodies; the beggar children with hands outstretched. There would be time to notice all these later when they had sorted out their affairs in Algiers.

Through streets, the square, a vast gateway, and into the serpentine passages which riddled the centre of the city . . . Past food stalls, heaped with exotic fruit and vegetables, fish, grain, leatherwork and woven materials of every hue, gaily coloured beads and crudely made bracelets, all vying for attention . . . Cassia noticed none of this, for memories were again crowding in on her. Along an extremely narrow, twisting street which was overhung with wooden houses and into a pretty square with white-washed walls and baskets of lattice-work, filled with brightly flowering shrubs and miniature trees with delicate fronds for leaves, in the centre of the square a fountain edged with tiles of gold and green, and more tubs of the fronded ferns . . . She remembered the last time she had walked through this square. How she had longed to stop and sit by the fountain to let its spray cool her face and palms. But she had been in purdah then, and Lucien was eager to get her to his master's house in safety. From the square it was only a short walk to the Street of the Golden Moon and the white house owned by Vincent.

Now they stood together, facing the house for a few brief moments before Vincent lifted the heavy brass knocker and rapped on the door.

'Why do you knock?' Cassia stared at him. 'It is your house, after all.'

'I want to see who answers the door. I have a feeling that all is not right, that something has gone wrong while I've been away.' His words were interrupted by the door swinging open. A bent old crone stared up at them, her eyes black and fierce like a dog's. On seeing Vincent and Cassia she hastily made as if to close the door, but Vincent's boot put a stop to that. He said something to the woman in Arabic, the harsh, guttural language all the terser for the anger in Vincent's voice as he spoke.

The woman looked at him with fear in her eyes, replying haltingly, hunched down into her dirty, ragged clothes as if she expected a beating.

Cassia peered into the tiled hallway. The last time she had come to this house the walls and floor were sparkling white, there were beautiful trellises in each corner, and magnificent flowers with heads of gold and scarlet so vast that she could hardly believe they were real. The sensuous scent of lilies had reached her nostrils. A young girl had come towards Cassia to greet her. She had been exquisite; a Turkish girl with glossy black hair, dressed in a chemise of fine linen dyed in blue and red and with baggy silk trousers gathered at her waist by an elaborately embroidered belt, and a yelek, a bolero sewn in red and blue silks, buttoned just below her breasts. Her name had been Fleur. She and Lucien had been about to discover that they were deeply in love with one another. Now Lucien was dead; Fleur would never see him again. All these thoughts crossed Cassia's mind as she listened to the exchange going on between her lover and the old woman.

Finally, Vincent lost patience and forced his way into the hall, gesturing to Cassia to follow him. It was not just the lack of light which had made the hallway look grey: it had been sadly neglected in the past year or so, and now the gleaming white tiles were covered with dust and filth. There were dirty streaks on the walls. The marvellous blossoms had died and there was nothing left except neglected tubs which had once housed their roots. One of the trellises had been broken at some time and had been left barely hanging together. Over all there was a sadly neglected air.

When the first shock had receded, Cassia looked at Vincent.

'What did she say? What has been happening?' she asked him.

'She says her master bought the house off Nathan Dash, that he paid fairly for it, a good sum, that the house is now her master's, that the Captain who owned it before is dead.'

'Have you told her that you are the Captain and that you still own the house?'

'Of course. She does not believe me.'

'Where is her master? We must speak with him at once.'

'He is at sea, just to complicate matters even further.'

'Has he no relatives, someone we can speak to, here in Algiers?'

Again Vincent spoke to the old woman in Arabic, at which she shook her head, lifting her palms upwards in a helpless gesture.

'No, her master has no relatives here.'

'What shall we do?' Cassia looked around her. How she had looked forward to coming back to this house in the Street of the Golden Moon with Vincent beside her, now her devoted lover. How different it was going to be from her first visit when she had been nothing more than a captive slave. She had dreamed of coming here and sharing Vincent's apartments with him, being mistress of his home, until they had collected his money in readiness to set sail for Cornwall. For both were adamant that they must return there to see what had become of Cassia's Aunt Julitta.

'There's nothing we can do. We'll have to go to Captain Dash and find out from him what has been happening while we've been away,' Vincent said, thanking the old woman and leading Cassia out of the house.

Captain Dash's house was four streets higher than the Street of the Golden Moon: a magnificent white house surrounded by verdant gardens, tiny trellised balconies framing the upper windows. Again Vincent hammered on the door, again a servant opened it, Vincent asking for entry. The servant looked up at him, astonished. He spoke in French, so Cassia understood what he was saying. As she listened she felt a coldness clutching at her which even Vincent's proximity could not dispel.

Captain Dash was dead. His half-brother had returned to Algiers many months ago and murdered the poor Captain as he struggled to defend himself in his bed. Crippled by rheumatism as he had been, he had little chance of fighting off his attacker. Before the next morning when the Captain's servants had discovered the murder, Nathan Dash had made off with all his half-brother's jewels and money, the treasure in his vaults beneath the house and his most prized servants. His ship had been well out to sea with all his booty and the abducted servants before anyone in Algiers had known what was happening.

A voice from behind the servant interrupted their exchange. Cassia saw a tall, very dark man looking at her with slumbrous, acquisitive eyes which made her shrink inside herself. She was all too familiar with the black Turkish gaze, full of lust and naked admiration. She moved a little closer to Vincent.

'Come in, come in,' the tall Turkish man said, waving his servant aside and frowning at him as if he had committed some sort of social crime. 'Come in, come in. You are French, yes?'

'Yes,' said Vincent. 'I have been deeply shocked to hear about Captain Dash's death. He was a dear friend of mine.'

'And you are . . . ?' The Turkish man looked enquiringly at Vincent.

'I am Captain Vincent de Sauvage. Perhaps you have heard of me?'

The man's face plainly showed that he had not. He gestured them inside, taking them into a cool sitting-room and ordering his servant to fetch them mint tea and wafers. When the tea had arrived and they were sipping its refreshing coolness, Vincent began to ask the Turk some pointed questions. The man told him that he knew very little about Captain Dash except what he had heard from his own servants. He knew that a murder had been committed in the house and, for that reason, for many months it had lain empty, gathering dust, with no one willing to buy it. He had come along, and, not being in any way nervous of the thought of buying such a property, he had moved in immediately and was very happy there. He was a merchant, he said, dealing in jewels and gold. As if to confirm what he said, he lifted his arms for them to see. His hands were extraordinarily long and thin, and on each of the bony fingers there were at least four fabulous rings — rubies, emeralds, pearls, sapphires, amethysts, stones which flashed blue, then pink, depending on how the light struck them. Previously the man had kept his hands encased in his sleeves, so they had not seen the jewels. Surely even an extremely successful merchant would not possess quite so many fabulous gems, Cassia wondered. Perhaps the man was of the blood royal? She realized that they had not yet learned his name.

Vincent must have read her thoughts, for he said, 'I'm sorry but I did not catch your name,' at which the man rose from his chair and gave him a courteous bow.

'I am Prince Kahmet abn Ahmoud Ahima, cousin of the Bey of Algiers.'

At this Vincent re-introduced himself and explained to the Prince that he had been Captain Dash's beneficiary, that the Captain had left all his property, treasure and shipping empire to him, Vincent Sauvage, when he died.

'I see. A situation totally lacking in fortuity.' The Prince, lifted his thin, plucked, black brows. Again he glanced at Cassia, and she wished for once that she was wearing purdah and not the flimsy gown which revealed her curvaceous figure. She pulled her cloak closer around her so that it overlapped across her breasts. How dare the man look at her like that, even if he were a Prince! His eyes stripped her of clothes, she could almost feel his long pointed hands on her body. He continued,

'You must find it disarming, to say the least, to return to what you believed to be your home and to find the Bey's cousin in occupancy.'

'I have already been to my home in the Street of the Golden Moon,' Vincent explained, 'to find that it has been sold by Nathan Dash and is now owned by a sea captain who is at present with his ship. So you see, I have no home in Algiers, when I had expected to find at least one.' He gave a wry half-smile.

'You must be my guests, of course. You must stay here until you have managed to despatch your affairs to your satisfaction. I could not think of turning you out onto the streets without a roof to put over your heads. It is getting dark, you must stay here for the night. My servant will take you to a room. You must have the one over the jasmine courtyard, it is a room for lovers.' The man again darted a glance of total sexual frankness at Cassia. She was pleased to be offered a room where she had thought they would have none for the night, but she did not like the idea of sleeping under the same roof as this man. She had had enough of Turks and their lascivious ways to last her the rest of her life. They had not intended to stay in Algiers long, only giving themselves enough time to collect Vincent's money before they left for Cornwall, and she had thought they would be sleeping in Vincent's house, not in this man's. She wondered if the Prince knew the Princess Jasmina. She wondered if word had reached him, as word is apt to do between those of royal blood, or of any affinity, of the escape of the Princess's most unwilling captive, Vincent Sauvage. She wondered if, at any moment, black slaves would enter the room with curved swords in their hands and bar their exit so that they would be prisoners once again. She tried to quell her fears, realizing that the long months of imprisonment and suffering had permanently scarred her where such matters were concerned. She really must fight such fears or else she would be persecuted by them.

A servant showed them to the room overlooking the jasmine

courtyard, where they were brought refreshments: pilaf, that most popular of Turkish dishes, comprising rice, mutton and onions, raisins, currants, oil and garlic; a dish of large, luscious fresh fruits, and a deep bowl of sculptured silver filled with *Rahat Lokum*, Turkish Delight, some the colour of roses and some white as snow. A carafe of beaten metal inlaid with coloured enamels stood on a tray with two matching goblets. In the carafe, to Cassia's surprise, was a delicate French wine.

The food smelt most appetizing, but Cassia had little taste for it after hearing of Captain Dash's murder and more of the evil crimes of Nathan Dash, who had once come so near to raping her and whom she had fought off with a knife.

'*Doucette*, I can see you've been deeply upset by what we have learned today,' Vincent said, taking her in his arms, 'but you can be assured I will not let things rest as they are. Wherever Nathan Dash has gone I'll find him, you can be sure of that. If it takes me the rest of my life I'll find him and make sure he pays for his crimes! He's not going to get away with kidnapping and ill-treating you, murdering my good friend, and taking my inheritance. The man must think he is invincible the way he behaves! Does he really believe that he can go through life behaving so despicably and that no one will catch him? If I could get my hands on him now!' Vincent's emerald eyes glittered. He clenched his hands furiously.

'But we have no idea where he has gone! He could be anywhere, how could we *hope* to find him again?'

'There's bound to be someone who knows where he's gone. One of his crew, who has got drunk in some orgy and blabbed about their destination. One who has a grudge against him. I shall make enquiries tomorrow, and when I find out where that swine has gone I shall be after him.' Vincent gritted his teeth.

'And I with you.' Cassia snuggled against her lover, encircling his slender, hard waist with her arm. 'Do not forget that I am going everywhere with you. You're never leaving me behind again, *ever*!'

'If the going becomes dangerous, *doucette*, I might have to.'

'*Never!*' Cassia cried. 'There is no way that you are *ever* going to leave me behind again, whatever the dangers!'

Vincent looked at her quizzically. 'Your devotion, my darling, is most moving. I do not deserve such love.'

Cassia pressed her lips to his chest, to his neck and face, kissing him and nibbling and darting out her tongue to lap at him like a kitten. As always, he responded instantly, scooping her up in his arms and carrying her to the bed, which was draped in sumptuous green and gold shot-silk, with bed-hangings of the same rich fabric.

'*Doucette*, how can you continue to love me now that I am penniless, now that my fortune is gone? I have not even a home to offer you.' Vincent interwove his words with kisses.

'But the last time I stayed at your house in the Street of the Golden Moon I was your slave and I loved you then, did I not? And did I not also love you when you insisted that you were going to sell me to Sultan Hamid? Through all those long, long months in the harem I went on loving you. When Marchington had me a prisoner on his island I loved you just as strongly.' She shuddered at the memory of the acquisitive and lustful English Lord, whose mind had become unhinged by his strange worship of the god Poseidon.

'All the time that you were loving me you believed that we had a future together, even if I was stupid enough not to see it. But then I was no pauper –' There was bitterness in Vincent's voice.

'I certainly did not consider your money when I thought of our future together, darling. I thought only of you, that is *all* I wanted, all I cared about, and nothing has changed that, nothing could *ever* change it.' Cassia spoke emphatically, pressing her head against Vincent's chest and squeezing him tightly. She had never seen him in such a bitter mood. She shared his mounting fury and frustration over losing his fortune to the villainous Nathan Dash, but instinctively she knew that angry brooding would serve only to increase his

18

bitterness. She pulled his head down to her and covered his face with kisses:

Soon their emotions were overcoming words as they clung to each other fiercely, their kisses growing more fervent, Vincent's knees slipping between Cassia's thighs as he moved on top of her. Their lovemaking, from the very first, had always been ecstatic, and it was so again now, as Vincent slipped inside her body and began to move gently backwards and forwards, their eyes holding one another in a passionate glance. Outside, a myriad stars pullulated in the sky, each one like a tiny throbbing silver heart in the dense black velvet, while a sharp sliver of ivory silk moon dominated the night.

Behind the concealed spyhole in the ornate tapestry which covered one wall of the room overlooking the jasmine courtyard, Prince Kahmet stood watching all that went on between his guests. He had spied on his visitors before in a similar way, but never one so voluptuous as the gorgeous red-haired Cassia Morbilly with the striking hydrangea-blue eyes. Had she been alone the sight of her would have been enough to arouse the Prince; as it was, the combination of her curvaceous white velvet body, the heavy breasts, slender waist and rounded hips, the long shapely legs, next to the hard, tanned and masculine body of Vincent Sauvage inflamed the Prince's lust.

The room in which the Prince stood was tiled in sky-blue, buttercup yellow and ivory; it was a cool, tasteful room, not in any way revealing its purpose – it was the room which the Prince used regularly when he had visitors. Lamps of gold filigree work were suspended from the ceiling, but at this moment they were not lit. The Prince must have absolute darkness for his favourite pastime of voyeurism, otherwise a stream of light would shine through the peephole and betray his presence. His thoughts ran back in time as he watched the lovers on the bed. He was remembering the Princess Muniza who had slept in his guest-room a few months before. She was his third cousin, a voluptuous woman of immense wealth, who dyed her black hair to a shade of rich chestnut with henna and who had the most fabulous collection of emeralds in Turkey, some of which he had been proud to give her himself. Muniza was in love with her Nubian slave, who shared her bed every night. The man was six feet six, with a body of polished ebony, rippling muscles, a gargantuan figure with appetites to match. Over and over he had made love to the Princess on the nights she slept in the room overlooking the jasmine courtyard, and each morning at the breakfast table she had asked the Prince why he seemed so listless and pale. Was he sickening for some illness? Smiling secretly to himself, the Prince had replied that he did not think that he was.

Shortly, he would be inviting the Princess back to stay with him, telling her that he had acquired a massive and beautiful emerald which she would adore. The stone, which was called the Eye of Allah, would surely be enough to tempt her back to Algiers? She was, of course, totally unsuspecting of how her third cousin spent his nights, but he fancied that he might, in all innocence, give her one of his own black slaves, and then she would perhaps let both the men make love to her while he watched in secret.

The lovers on the bed were becoming more ardent with each moment that passed. The woman's head was thrown back, her vibrant Titian hair flung across the silken pillow, her eyes half closed in ecstasy, her lips slightly parted, revealing pearly teeth. Her throat, smooth and white, was that of a swan, curving down to meet her rounded shoulders, beneath which were the generous, pink-tipped breasts, the most beautiful the Prince had ever seen. His breath now was coming in short gasps, a flush of heat was coursing over his skin; he slipped a hand inside his robe to finger his own flesh, imagining that it was the white beauty of Sauvage's woman. If only it were. He breathed heavily, a constricting feeling in his chest. He would have liked to make the woman his own, to add her to his harem, to make her his chief wife, for Ariasita, his premier wife, had died some months before and he had not yet replaced her. If only he knew more about the man and the woman. But he knew enough to have heard that Sauvage was admired and respected by the Bey himself and that he, Kahmet, must behave impeccably towards the Captain.

Sauvage was beginning to make love to his woman for the second time. The Prince could barely stand the torrent of passion searing him. He leaned heavily against the trellis which surrounded the peephole, struggling to fill his lungs with air without making a sound which might alert the lovers. His hand was aching, the fingers stiff, his skin was red and sore, but he would not stop – how could he, while he was staring on that radiant, milky body? Sauvage was the luckiest man in the world: he would have given anything to change places with him, anything. He would even have given his most prized possession, the enormous and legendary emerald called the Star of Destiny.

The man and the woman were lying still in each other's arms now, exhausted by their lovemaking, satisfied, but only temporarily. Prince Kahmet closed the peephole and let the trellis-work fall back into place to conceal it. He sank onto his bed, wiping the sweat from his forehead.

'The Prince's eyes,' Cassia shuddered, 'they made me nervous. They reminded me too much of the Sultan's. Black, and sharp as gimlets, boring right through me, full of lust. These Turkish men have only to see my white skin and they become animals.'

'They're not the only ones,' Vincent grinned, kissing her tenderly. 'Haven't you noticed how I turn into a ravening wolf the minute you begin to discard your clothes?'

'Now you come to mention it,' Cassia giggled, kissing him back. 'But having you undress me with your eyes is a totally different matter from being virtually stripped to the flesh by that Prince. Promise me we won't stay here long, darling.'

'I have no intention of lingering, *doucette*. As soon as I have found out exactly what is happening here, as soon as we know where Nathan Dash has gone, we shall be on course for his destination.'

'After we've been back to see Aunt Julitta in Cornwall, of course?'

'Of course. I cannot wait to meet her. She sounds a fascinating woman.'

'That's if she is still alive.' Sadness misted Cassia's eyes, but she said no more, for she knew how Vincent had bitterly regretted snatching her from the beach by her home. She had been nursing her sick aunt at the time and Julitta had depended upon her entirely, wanting no one else, ever since she had suffered the stroke which had partially paralysed her. Anything Cassia said to Vincent would have been like recrimination, so she said very little, but only voiced her longing to return to Penwellyn, her aunt's house, to see how Julitta was, and to let her know that she was still alive. They planned to marry while they were there, for of course she wanted her aunt at the wedding. They would have a beautiful ceremony in Morbilly church, surrounded by her aunt and her friends.

Cassia had planned her wedding dress, the jewels she would wear, and now they had no money to buy her wedding clothes, or Vincent's; the gold and jewelled ornaments which he had stolen from Princess Jasmina's palace had nearly all been sold to enable them to get back to Algiers safely. They only had enough now for the voyage to Cornwall.

Soon the lovers were drifting into sleep, the Prince likewise. The beautiful house, which had belonged to the late Captain Dash, became silent and still as night deepened around it, while the sliver of ivory moon glowed eternally on.

Chapter Two

They had been in Algiers exactly two weeks when Vincent tracked down one of Nathan Dash's ex-crewmen, an Arab who had taken lodgings in a dingy street down by the mole.

When Vincent entered his room the man shrieked with terror, screaming out, *'No, no! You are dead! Get away from me, you devil!'*

Calmly Vincent said, 'I am far from dead, and I am here for one reason and one reason only: to find out where Nathan Dash has gone.'

The sailor continued to huddle against the pillows of his filthy, crumpled bed, where he had lain for months now, ever since a fall from the crow's nest which had left him with both legs and his hip broken. They had healed badly and he could not walk; that was why Nathan Dash had left him behind when he had fled Algiers.

It took Vincent some time to convince the Arab that he was indeed alive, very much so. It helped when he produced some coins from his pocket and spread them out on the bed, promising the man that there would be more when he had told him all he knew of Nathan Dash's destination. At first the man seemed reluctant to speak, but more coins quickly loosened his tongue. Very soon he was telling Sauvage all that he knew of his ex-master. It was plain that he loathed Nathan Dash, and once he began to speak of the man, Vincent learned far more than he had hoped. Dash had fled far from the waters where he was now infamous, the most notorious man on the Barbary Coast, wanted for hanging by more than just Vincent and Cassia. When Vincent heard where he had gone he could barely believe it, but he paid the man more of the coins as he had promised and hastily left the foetid room.

'Liverpool!' Cassia cried when he told her. 'But why

Liverpool? I would have thought the Colonies, the New World. Some place where he could begin afresh, thinking as he does that you are dead and that I still languish in the Sultan's harem, a prisoner for life.'

'Perhaps it is because he thinks I am dead, because he feels so safe, that he has gone to England and not farther afield — but think how convenient this will make things for us. Instead of going to Cornwall and then on to America, as I had half planned to do, we need only remain in England. You can stay with your aunt while I search for Dash.'

'Now what did I say to you when we first arrived here two weeks ago, my darling?' Cassia faced her lover, hands on hips. 'If you have any wild ideas about running off and scouring the countryside for that villain while you leave me behind like an old maid, then you can put them aside now, once and for all. You are *not* going to leave me behind. You are *not* going to search for Dash on your own. I shall be with you wherever you go, *whatever* you do.' She tossed back her mane of rich auburn hair, her blue eyes flashing.

'A slip of the tongue, *doucette*,' Vincent grinned, clasping her round the waist, 'nothing more than that. Of course you will be with me. How could I leave you behind? How could I survive without you?'

'How indeed?' Cassia smiled up at him. 'But just in case you think you might be able to, I shall not be giving you the chance, my love. Remember what the marriage ceremony says, *Those whom God hath joined together, let no man put asunder.*'

They had spent only one night in Prince Kahmet's house, although the Prince had tried very hard to persuade them to stay longer, offering them the full hospitality of his home for as long as they wished. He had tried to tempt Cassia by telling her that she might be allowed permission given to few others to view his jewel collection. She did not rise to the bait, however, wanting only to get away from those lustful black eyes of his, the uneasy sensation she experienced within his presence.

With each day that passed, Cassia's desire to get away from the Barbary Coast increased. She had had more than enough of strange ports, even stranger customs, the barbarous men who peopled this country. She yearned for her homeland. Vincent, who could never return to France, the place of his birth, because there was a price on his head for his past exploits as a pirate-slaver, understood exactly how she felt.

They had taken lodgings in the house of one of his ex-seafaring colleagues, Barnaby Cadge; a bluff and ruddy-faced man with a rotund figure, who was the exact opposite of Prince Kahmet, much to Cassia's relief. Cadge was jolly and hearty and he was also English, all of which helped to make Cassia relax in his presence.

When they had arrived on his doorstep he had been unable to believe his eyes, for he had thought Vincent dead. Ushering them in, he fed them with torn-off hunks of fresh bread, possets of milk and wine, and a rich pilaf liberally flavoured with garlic. It was a rich and hearty meal, and Cadge barely stopped speaking during it. He told them all he knew about Captain Dash's murder, that Nathan Dash had crept up out of the sea in the middle of the night, slaughtered his half-brother, put Vincent's and the Captain's houses up for sale, and disappeared into the night with the Captain's ships laden with his treasure and possessions. On discovering what had happened next morning the Captain's friends had been horrified, naturally, but they were helpless to bring the dead man back to life. For months they had kept watch on the seas for Dash or any of his ships, but nothing had been sighted. It was commonly believed that he had gone to the New World to begin a fresh life. Those who had contacts in the Colonies sent messages there with a description of Dash, but there had been no response from any quarter.

'We know he didn't go to the New World,' Vincent said, having managed to find a space in which to speak while Cadge's mouth was crammed with bread and pilaf.

'Not gone to the New World?' Cadge spluttered, half choking on his food and going crimson in the face. 'So you've had new information? How have you done that? We've been trying unsuccessfully for many months to trace the man, and here you walk up and within a few days you've found him!'

'I wouldn't say we have found him, but at least we know the direction he went. Probably thinking that we would all believe he had gone to America, he set sail for England.'

'England? Well, stab me through the vitals! And what can the man get up to there? He'd have had a far freer hand if he'd stayed on the Barbary Coast trading, slaving, smuggling, and so on.'

'I imagine that a man like Nathan Dash would do exactly what he wants wherever he is,' Cassia said drily.

'The lady has obviously fallen foul of Dash,' Cadge grinned, glancing from Vincent to Cassia and wondering what relationship they bore, for Vincent had not enlightened him regarding that. The woman looked a lady, and a grand one at that, yet she wore no wedding ring, so she was unlikely to be his wife and, indeed, would such a beautiful, highly-bred creature look at a slave-captain?

'You'll stay, the two of you?' Cadge asked. 'Make my house your own for as long as you wish. Tell me more of how you found out Dash has gone to Liverpool. Let me know what you plan to do, my boy.'

Vincent proceeded to tell him everything, including their plans to go to Cornwall to see Cassia's aunt and then on to Liverpool on Dash's trail.

'So you'll go after him? Well, and I wish I was coming with you. That's a man who should be found and dealt with. I've never been a bloodthirsty man, which you might find strange coming from the lips of someone who lived by piracy, but whenever I think of that man my hand goes to this knife hanging here at my waist, and I have the most overwhelming urge to plunge it into his neck — if only he were here!'

'You're not the only one, Mr Cadge,' Cassia said. 'In fact, I once did try to knife the man, but unfortunately I failed.'

Cadge's bushy, wheat-coloured eyebrows rose. 'Tried to knife him, did ye? Well, stab me through the vitals, so you're a lady of spirit!'

'I can vouch for that,' Vincent grinned.

'So you're going with Captain Sauvage?' Cadge asked, eager to know exactly what the relationship was between these two. For as long as he could remember, Vincent Sauvage had been very much anti-marriage, but she was a comely wench, voluptuous enough to make a priest forsake his vows, and although Sauvage might be against wedding he was certainly not against bedding.

'The lady is to become my wife,' Vincent said, he and Cassia exchanging warm glances. 'As soon as we get to Cornwall we are to be wed.'

'Marriage, eh? Now that's a state which is not for the weak, the selfish or the lazy. So, you're going to wed at last, Captain Sauvage? Well, between you and me, I never thought I'd see the day.' Cadge spooned his mouth full of pilaf and munched happily.

So they had stayed at Barnaby Cadge's house, and virtually every day he had said how he wished he could come with them to England to bring Dash to justice, if only he were not such an old man and now retired from the sea.

'Come with us anyway,' Vincent coaxed.

'Voluntarily go back to a diet of ship's biscuit? Never!' exclaimed Cadge, searching in his pocket for a twist of marchpane sweetmeats. He always had his pockets full of tasty morsels of food, usually ones with a high sugar content. He reminded Cassia of her Aunt Julitta, who also had a sweet tooth.

'If you change your mind let us know,' said Vincent. 'You'll be more than welcome to come with us.'

'Stab me vitals, that I will,' grinned Cadge, offering round a twist of sugared plums before filling his cheek with them.

*

It took Vincent only a few more days to find a respectable merchant vessel which would carry them to England. Neither of them had any wish to travel on one of the pirate chebeks, for that would bring back too many unsavoury memories to them both.

The merchant vessel, the *Berengaria*, was free to sail safely in the waters of the Barbary Coast because she was personally protected by the Bey, to whom she brought foreign silks and velvets, spices, rare and unusual curios, jewels, ornaments, *objets d'art*, and valuable paintings. This time she had arrived in Algiers with a cargo of lustrous pearls, luminous as the moon, alabaster and porcelain figurines with jewels for eyes, crimson cloth-of-gold to make flowing robes for the Bey's chief wives and his favourite concubines, and some dozen chests of priceless old books for his library. Now that the hold was empty and the sailors rested it was time for the *Berengaria* to set sail once more, her Captain more than pleased to have two voyagers on board, for he usually travelled from Algiers with an empty hold and the money Captain Sauvage had paid for the trip would go into his pocket – his masters need never know that he had taken two passengers on board.

The Mediterranean was at its most brilliant and beautiful the day they set sail, the prow of the *Berengaria* curving out into the shimmering waters like a stately queen. Remembering her previous experience with rascally pirate sailors, Cassia was swathed in a concealing cloak and hood as she stood beside Vincent on the forecastle, watching Algiers diminish in the distance.

The sun was like a fire in the sky, its heat beating down on them; there was no shelter on board and soon Cassia said that she would have to go below to the cabin reserved for them. Vincent smiled and promised to join her in a few moments. When she had gone he stood watching Algiers becoming a dot on the horizon, thinking of his past, the years he had spent as a pirate-slaver, years when he seemed to have lost his conscience entirely. But he was no longer the famed pirate captain who had spent his life abducting women from the coasts of England and Europe so that he could transport them to Constantinople, where he would sell them to Sultan Hamid for his harem. The Vincent Sauvage who had committed such despicable deeds was no more. Cassia's love had purified him. Her sufferings at his hands and at the hands of Nathan Dash had made Vincent determined that he would try to put right the wrongs he had done her and all the others. Now more than anything he wanted to free those who were in bondage.

Already an idea had begun to take root in Vincent's mind. He knew that slavery was endemic, not only on the Barbary Coast and Turkey, but in England and America too. He himself had helped for years to swell the ranks of slaves. Now he and Cassia were the first members of the society which they had decided to call The Children of Liberty. It would be a society which, he hoped, would grow rapidly in membership and influence so that the lot of slaves might be made easier and, eventually, all of them freed. As yet he had no idea what the political climate would be like in England, whether slavery there was nurtured as much as it was on the Barbary Coast, or whether there would be others like-minded who dreamed of freeing slaves.

Before she had been kidnapped off the Cornish coast, Cassia had led a comparatively sheltered life, raised in the drawing room and boudoirs of her father's London home. She had then spent only a few months with her Aunt Julitta at Penwellyn before Vincent had snatched her from the Marriage Cove and taken her on board his ship, *The Poseidon*. She could say little concerning the political viewpoint regarding slaves in the Isles of Britain, but between them they would find out all that was necessary and react accordingly.

In the cabin below, Cassia was divesting herself of the cumbersome cape and hood and splashing cool water on her face and hands from the bowl which stood on the dresser in the corner. It was a very plain cabin, designed for men who made little observation of their surroundings: a narrow bunk bed, edged with a frame of dark brown wood, the dresser, a small table, two chairs, a desk which folded up against the panelling when not in use. The bunk looked barely wide enough for one, and Cassia had eyed it with amusement. She would not have minded sharing a hammock with Vincent, even in the heat of the Mediterranean night.

She had donned a cool white dress, purchased in Algiers, with small panniers of pale blue sprigged muslin, and blue forget-me-nots embroidered round the neck, when Vincent stepped into the cabin, smiling appreciatively at her outfit.

'You're not thinking of going on deck wearing that, are you, *doucette*?' he grinned. 'These may seem to be peaceable merchantmen, eager to go about their regular business, but I vow that if they see you in that attire they will forget what they are about and make for you like pins to a magnet.' He took Cassia by the shoulders and kissed her soundly.

'No, darling, this dress is entirely for you,' Cassia replied when her mouth was freed from his kisses.

'But, *chérie*, I had hoped to see far more of you than that during the voyage,' Vincent teased, tilting up her chin with one forefinger, his emerald eyes twinkling into hers.

'I expect you shall,' she teased back, 'but is there a good, sound lock on that door?'

'Indeed there is,' Vincent patted his pocket, 'and I am the owner of the only key which fits it. I saw to that before we embarked.'

Gradually, as the weeks passed, the searing heat of the Barbary Coast diminished. Days became not too unbearably hot, and the nights were balmy. Cassia found it a marvellous experience to walk on deck at ten at night with Vincent's arm around her. The air was velvety soft and warm. Out at sea the moon seemed even larger and more luminous, spreading its rays for thousands of miles all round them.

'A lovers' moon,' said Vincent, his eyes glowing like a cat's in the night, 'made specially for us alone.'

'Perhaps for just a few others, too,' Cassia smiled, blissfully content to have Vincent's arm around her, to be safely beside him again. She was a good sailor; it came of being the descendant of two seafaring families, the Morbillys and the Joliths. Even in the squalor and privation of the slaves' hold in Nathan Dash's ship she had not been overwhelmed, not even seasick, and whether the *Berengaria* hit calm seas or stormy, Cassia never lost her equilibrium, nor felt so much as faintly nauseous, a quality in her which Vincent plainly admired.

Or so it was until they hit cooler waters, the healing rays of the sunshine less benevolent. Grey clouds and torrents of rain became more familiar, and then a violent storm blew up, attacking them suddenly and unexpectedly, arching the ship up and down, up and down, so that everything not lashed for safety was flung about wildly.

Cassia knew quite early on in the storm that she was going to be very seasick. She lay gripping the sides of her bunk, her face ashen, pale green tints around her mouth. The storm continued unabated, savaging the ship mercilessly, pounding, drenching the decks. All hands were scurrying about protecting the ship, but Cassia just lay still, feeling her stomach churning. It confirmed a suspicion which had been mounting in her mind for some time.

Vincent, returning to their cabin, heard her retching and thought that she must be ill, that the ship's diet did not agree with her. He placed a hand under her forehead to support her while she leaned over the bowl he held, and he soothed her with sweet words until the nausea passed. Then he pulled her onto his knee and gave her some water to sip.

'I never thought the day would come when I would see you suffering from the *mal de mer*,' he teased, but he could not hide the look of anxiety in his eyes.

For a few moments Cassia said nothing, then, when she spoke, her words were in no way related to what had gone before, or so it seemed.

'The sooner we marry, the better — now,' she said. 'As soon as we reach Penwellyn.'

31

'But of course, *ma mignonne*,' Vincent grinned, and then, slowly, realization dawned. 'You are with child?'

'Yes I am.'

Vincent threw back his head and gave a great roar of joyful laughter. A father − he was going to be a father! He hugged Cassia soundly, then asked her how long it would be before the baby's birth.

'We have about six and a half months, my darling.'

'Six and a half months to get used to being a father!' Vincent laughed again from sheer happiness. '*Doucette*, would you like Captain Manley to marry us now, on board?'

'Yes, if it were not for Aunt Julitta's sadness when she knew she had missed my wedding. I want her as my major wedding guest.'

'Will you want your father to be present?'

'No, I most certainly will not . . . but I expect we shall have to send him an invitation,' she added reluctantly. 'The sight of his face would quite spoil the ceremony for me, I am sure.'

'And yet, if he had not sent you to Penwellyn we would never have met, would we, *doucette*? So in a way you owe him a great deal. Perhaps you could offer him a little sympathy out of that thought.'

'Perhaps, but I doubt it all the same.' Cassia sipped more of the water. It was luke-warm and she longed to drink fresh, icy spring-water. Towards the end of a voyage water was always running short, and had become murky, sometimes foul, and then it was dangerous to drink. This water tasted clean, but it was too warm to be refreshing, and it had a faint tarry flavour to it.

She voiced her longing to Vincent, who reminded her that they had only a few more days at sea, and that if the wind sprang up they could in fact be on the beach by Morbilly Cove within the next two days.

Cassia's eyes lit up. 'So soon? That's marvellous, I can hardly wait. Truth to tell, my thoughts have been turning inward of late to the baby. I was wondering how to tell you, and if I could really be sure that I was with child. Well, now I am, and you know. It does not change anything between us, does it, darling?' She looked at him earnestly.

'Change anything between us? You do get the strangest ideas, *ma mignonne*. How could anything ever do that? When we have six fine, bouncing, healthy children we shall still be looking at each other with exactly the same amount of love in our eyes.'

Cassia leaned against his shoulder. 'Perhaps not, perhaps you are wrong, Vincent.' She twinkled up at him. 'Perhaps we shall be looking at each other with a great deal more love by then.'

The Captain of the *Berengaria* was sorry to see his passengers leave. He had enjoyed their company tremendously. The woman's beauty was a feast to look upon and she was intelligent, too; her conversation always lively and interesting. Sauvage plainly doted on her. They were a very fortunate couple. He thought of his own sour-faced wife at home in London; Polly had a pert and pretty name, but there such qualities ended. He had hoped as the years passed that his long absences from home would improve her temperament, making her eager to see him and responsive to his caresses, but it had not been so. If anything she had grown worse: petulant and complaining, always finding fault with the generous gifts he brought her from his voyages. He had once brought her an exquisite music-box carved from scented sandalwood. When the lid was opened a lilting dance tune was heard in tinkling tones. Instead of being delighted with it, as he had hoped, Polly had closed the lid with a snap, snorting, 'When are you ever at home to take me dancing? Am I meant to play this music-box while you are away and think of all the happy times we are missing together?'

'Dear heart, I am home now,' he had said in desperation. 'Shall we go dancing on the morrow?'

'How can you be so cruel,' she had snapped. 'How can I go

dancing when my back aches so? Did you not get my last letter telling you about my fall?'

Next time he had brought her the handsomest gift yet, a superbly comfortable carved armchair with soft, downy cushions. She had taken one look at it and snapped, 'I'm not yet in my dotage, you know, Henry, ready to sit slumped in an armchair like your old father does all the time!'

Small wonder that now when he chose gifts for his wife, as he continued to do despite all her discontented remarks, he anticipated complaints about them all, however beautiful, however rare and exquisite.

He knew instinctively that when Captain Sauvage gave a gift to his dear Cassia, whether it be a tiny present or a large one, she would welcome it with delight and a smile and a hug. The couple, in their happiness, had underlined to Captain Manley all that he had been missing for years, all that he would never have while he was married to Polly.

When the rowing boat beached in the Marriage Cove Cassia looked round expectantly, her eyes lapping up the picturesque scene which she had not seen now for two years. Here she had ridden Printemps, the horse which her aunt had given her; here she had secretly met Charles Billings, her first love, who had shown his true colours by trying to rape her on the day that Vincent had sailed up to the Marriage Cove and abducted her, thereby saving her for himself. Charles. In retrospect, she saw him for exactly what he was — a scoundrel, a fortune-hunter. How could she ever have thought she loved him? How weak and insubstantial he was beside her dearest Vincent.

Dusk was descending, beginning to obliterate the beauties of the Marriage Cove: the plumed and creamy surf, the silvery sand, the shiny rocks sparsely dotted with marsh grass, scarlet pimpernel and sea convolvulus. She adored every tiny inch of it. Oh, it was good to be home!

They left their trunks on the beach, pulled up under the shelter of the overhanging rocks, said goodbye to the two sailors who had rowed them ashore, and walked hand in hand up the rough, shingled track to where cove met moorland. These were the moors which had enchanted Cassia during the months she had lived at Penwellyn with her aunt. In the half light they were eerie, places where one imagined one might be assailed by fairies or goblins, where an evil old wizard or two might walk at dead of night.

Cassia held Vincent's hand very tightly for the next thirty minutes or so until they came in sight of Penwellyn, its beautiful white facade glowing in the dusk. She could not wait to see the house by daylight, knowing that it would be haloed by thousands of spring flowers, that the trees and bushes and shrubs would all be in bud in preparation for summer.

Penwellyn, which had been more of a home to her than her father's house had ever been.

Vincent hammered on the front door and they stood waiting. They were still there some five minutes later and no one had replied. Where was Aunt Julitta's housekeeper? Where were the servants? Stepping back, Cassia gazed up at the house. She could see lights in some of the upper windows, so she knew someone must be in.

'Knock again, Vincent, I can see lights up there. They cannot have heard us.'

Vincent had knocked three times before the sound of movement reached them. A scratching, scraping noise, like something dragging along the hall floor; a hoarse, rasping cough, and then a croaking voice calling out, 'Who be it, who be it?'

'I don't know that voice,' Cassia said. 'Tell him who we are, Vincent.'

'Mistress Cassia Morbilly is without, awaiting entry to her aunt's house,' Vincent cried.

'Morbilly? Morbilly? Who be she, who be she?' the croaking voice asked.

'Oh, this is ridiculous!' Cassia stamped her foot. 'He must know who I am. Open this door at once!' she shouted. 'I have come to see my aunt, let me in at once!'

There was a shuffling sound in the hall and the clanking of chains and then, suddenly, whispered voices, voices which sounded tense and frightened.

'Something is wrong, Vincent, I can feel it. Oh, what if –' Her words were interrupted by the door creaking slowly open. A strange man stood there, one whom Cassia had never seen before. He was smartly and cleanly dressed, fashionably too, and gold rings sparkled on his plump fingers.

'Yes? Can I help you?' he snapped crisply, looking from Cassia to Vincent, then back to Cassia, his expression disdainful.

'I am Cassia Morbilly and I have come to see my aunt,' Cassia explained.

'She is not here.'

'Not here? But where is she then? Please tell me and I shall go to see her at once.'

'She . . . she went away on holiday. To visit relatives. I have no idea where she is.' A slight stain of colour marked the man's cheeks.

Cassia felt instinctively that he was lying. Her first thoughts had been correct. Something was very wrong.

'Has she gone to visit one of her daughters? Or perhaps my father in London?'

'I told you, I don't know. I have no idea where Mistress Julitta has gone, and if I had why should I tell you?'

'I am her only niece,' Cassia said, her anger beginning. 'I lived with her here for some months.'

'And then disappeared.' The man's lip curled. 'We all thought you were dead.'

'So you do know who I am?'

'Everyone knows the story of how Mistress Julitta's niece deserted her in her hour of greatest need.'

Fury hardened Vincent's face and he stepped menacingly towards the man, who shrank back nervously.

'You will retract those words!' Vincent growled.

36

Immediately the man rushed to shut the door, but he could not for Vincent's boot was in the way.

'Mistress Morbilly would not want you to turn away her niece under any circumstances. My future wife has a room here, and in it are her clothes and some of her possessions. She will wish to collect them and so we intend to come in.'

'B-but –. but –' stammered the man, as Vincent swept past him in one powerful movement, thrusting open the door and pushing the fat little man aside.

'This is my home and I am coming in!' Cassia cried, following Vincent into the hallway. 'If my aunt knew what you were doing, she would be very angry indeed. She would not wish me to be shut out of my own home! And anyway, who are you to try and prevent our entering?'

'I am Benjamin Sneely. Not that it is any business of yours, mistress.' The man cowered as Vincent looked about to lunge at him again. 'I – I am Mistress Julitta Morbilly's son-in-law.'

'Well, why did you not say who you were at the beginning?' Cassia said. 'Instead of standing here like this we could have come straight in. Aunt Julitta would not be pleased if . . .'

'She left me with strict orders not to let anyone into the house, visitors or otherwise,' Benjamin Sneely said, looking flustered and sorry for himself.

Cassia put her hand on Vincent's arm and whispered in his ear. 'This man could be telling the truth, darling. It is possible that Aunt Julitta was so upset when I disappeared that she doesn't ever want to see me again and left orders accordingly. I would hate to intrude if that is how she feels.'

'But you will want your clothes, will you not, and your jewels?'

'Of course.'

'Well, we can collect them before she returns.'

Sneely was watching them, eyes narrowed. He had a big, broad shiny face which seemed to go redder by the minute. Seven brown hairs had been carefully brushed across the bald patch at the front of his head and a fuzz of brown hair had been carefully brushed at the back. He had fat, wet lips and his eyes were pouched, which gave them a sinister look. Cassia noticed again the preponderance of heavy gold rings which decorated his rubbery fingers. Now that she was closer to him she smelled patchouli oil and it reminded her, sickeningly, of her months as a prisoner of the harem. For an Englishman to use scent! She wrinkled her nose in distaste.

At that moment, the door at the end of the hall swung open and two women entered. One of them Cassia recognized as Alicia, Julitta's eldest daughter who had visited Penwellyn when her mother was ill. Presumably the second woman was Melody, the third daughter. Both of them were extravagantly dressed, their faces heavily painted, and they exuded an over-powering clash of scents.

'Ah, there you are,' Sneely said, sounding relieved.

Alicia, the taller of the two women, approached Cassia and Vincent, eyeing them coldly. 'Cassia Morbilly . . .' she began. 'So you thought you would return to Penwellyn.' There was no welcome in her voice. 'Has Master Sneely not told you that your aunt is not staying here at the moment? She is away visiting relatives. She will not be back for some time. It would not be worth your while to wait for her. We shall tell her that you have been, but I know that she will not be interested.'

'Not interested?' Cassia sounded dismayed.

'That is correct. She was deeply hurt when you deserted her. Her heart was broken, so she said, and often. She has not recovered from it. She has expressed a wish that she never wants to see you again, under any circumstances. She has told us this on more than one occasion.'

'We have no reason to believe that she has changed her mind,' the second woman, Melody, added.

'I see.' Cassia felt Vincent's hand slip into hers and squeeze it tightly for comfort. 'Well, I am sure my aunt would not turn me out into the night. We have nowhere to stay, we have only just arrived in Cornwall, and I shall need to collect my belongings anyway. If you would just let me go to my room I shall not trouble you further, and in the morning I will leave without disturbing you.'

The two women exchanged a glance which might have been of fear or fury, it was hard to tell. Sneely swallowed. His gulp sounded very loud in the hallway.

'I will leave a letter for my aunt; I will write it tonight, and I will leave it here on this dresser in the hall so that you can give it to her when she returns, if you would be so kind.'

'We will do that, but I doubt if she will read it. And I think I ought to tell you now that there is no way you can inveigle yourself back into her favours,' Alicia said with a sneer.

Cassia would have retorted, but she did not think the remark deserved an answer. It was a despicable thing to say. She turned her back on the trio and led Vincent up the stairway to her room. When they were inside it, the door closed behind them, she said, 'What horrible people! How such a dear, kind woman as my aunt ever gave birth to such gorgons, I have no idea. And I don't know why they are here, behaving as if they own Penwellyn. They were always very distant with Aunt Julitta. They did not seem at all troubled when she was so ill. They did not offer to nurse her, you know. I did, of course. Oh, if only I had not left!' Cassia put her face in her hands, sinking down onto the bed.

'I am sorry, *doucette*, for all the misery I have caused in your life. So very sorry. How can you ever forgive me?' Vincent said, sitting down beside her. 'If I had only known – but I never thought. Believe me, I am a changed man now. I think you have guessed it.'

'Oh, yes I know it, my darling, but what happened that night could not be helped; it was Fate, Kismet, we both know that, do we not? Just imagine what our lives would have been like if we had never met . . .' Cassia forgot her own dejection in comforting her lover.

In distant parts of the house they heard footsteps, whispered voices, doors closing and then silence. 'Well, I suppose we'd better settle down for the night. Lock the door, darling, I don't want anyone bursting in on us.'

Fortunately the bed was the larger variety of tester and there was plenty of room for two. The room had not changed at all since Cassia had last seen it, but when she looked in the wardrobes she found her clothes had been packed into boxes at the bottom, and these tied up with string as if they were to be despatched somewhere. On the dressing-table her jewel box stood and when she lifted the lid she was relieved to see all her precious gems inside, including the pearls which her father had given her. At least they had not been touched. She knew that her aunt would not sell them, but she did not trust the daughters and Sneely. If Aunt Julitta now hated her so much and never wanted to see her again, she wondered why she had left her dressing-table exactly as it was, with her jewel-case there, her comb and beauty implements, her tiny silver rouge pot, powder jar, and phials of rose and orange-water.

'What are we going to do about our belongings down in the cove?' Cassia said as she suddenly remembered about them.

'It is too late now to send a servant down to collect them, and anyway I rather imagine that we might further offend our host and hostesses if we try bringing them into the house at this time of night. They are quite safe in the shelter of the cliff. We can send a man from the village for them in the morning.'

'But I would like to send one of my aunt's servants. There's no need to hire a man from the village.'

'I think we are rather treading on tender ground there, *doucette*. If your aunt truly has said that she no longer wishes to see you and does not want you under her roof, then we really have no right to expect her servants to do anything for us.' He placed his hands on Cassia's shoulders. 'Come to bed now, my darling.'

Listlessly Cassia began to unfasten her gown, helped by her lover.

'If only my aunt had been here, I'm sure that when she saw

me she would have changed her mind. I would have persuaded her, I would have told her the truth, what really happened, that I didn't desert her.'

'And will you also tell her that it was I who carried you off?' Vincent's eyes twinkled.

'I shall say pirate-slavers. I shall say that you saved me from them. That is not a lie.' She lifted her hand to touch Vincent's cheek, looking deep into his eyes. 'When she knows that we are to be married I am sure that she will come round. What shall we do?'

'Wait in the village until she returns. There is an inn there, isn't there?' Cassia nodded. 'Well, we shall stay at the inn, and when your aunt gets back you can send a message to her, tell her briefly what happened to you and then await her reply.'

'What if she says no? What is she has really hardened her heart against me?'

'From what you have told me I do not see her like that at all. She loved you, did she not? You said that you were like a daughter to her. Indeed, I find it hard to believe that she has said that she never wants to see you again. In my mind's eye I had pictured her grieving for you, longing for your return, whatever the circumstances.'

'So had I, I must admit. But she was so ill when I left, perhaps her sickness has changed her.'

'Myself I do not see it. If it were so she would not be well enough to go visiting. People do recover from strokes, you know. They learn to talk and walk again; it is a long, hard business, but they do. She could talk a little, could she not?'

'She could say my name, but haltingly. Certainly there was understanding and intelligence in her eyes, her mind had not gone, I know that. She just lacked the power of speech and limbs, and she depended on me utterly. Oh, Vincent, what am I going to do if she won't take me back?'

Vincent folded her in his arms, dropping kisses on her head. 'I am ready and willing to vow that she will. That whatever she said about not seeing you again was spoken in haste, and that

41

she will long ago have repented it. But what is the point of making yourself ill over this? We will stay in the village, we will have a holiday. The fresh air will do you and the baby good.'

'Yes, when Aunt Julitta hears about the baby she will be so pleased. You realize it will make her a great-aunt? I wonder how she will take that.'

'Perhaps we had better tell her about our marriage first?'

'Oh, she is not narrow-minded, Vincent.' Cassia sighed. 'I was so sure she would be thrilled to see me again.'

'She will be, she will be — give it time, my love. Now come to bed.' Vincent turned back the sheets. They were chilly but spotlessly clean. Wearing only her lace chemise, Cassia slipped between them, Vincent beside her. They lay back on the pillows, cradled together.

'This is a beautiful room. You are lucky to have such a handsome family home.'

'It is better than the museum in which I was raised. There I dared not put a finger or a foot out of place for fear of shattering some priceless ornament. My father should never have had children. They need a free place to roam, a relaxed atmosphere, freedom from the fear of beatings should they break anything accidentally.'

'My feelings exactly, *doucette*. I want our children to be strong and healthy, to walk on the moors, to learn to ride when they are very small, never to fear horses — or the sea.'

Vincent began to kiss her, thinking back over the months when they had been separated, when she had been a prisoner of the harem and he had believed her dead. His life had been a hollow shell to him at that time, a parody of living. The burden of struggling through the hours had been intolerable. They had sworn never to be parted again, but now that he knew she was expecting their child he was full of misgivings about her coming to Liverpool with him. Dash was a dangerous man and travel at the best of times was hard on a woman. He had wanted very much for her to be reunited with her aunt and for her aunt to beg her to stay here at Penwellyn with her, while he was free to go to Liverpool on his own. He would waste no time in tracking down Dash and bringing him to justice and getting back his lost inheritance, and then he would return to Cassia in time to see their son or daughter born.

His most prized possession at this moment was Captain Dash's will, duly witnessed and signed. For security's sake, the Captain had left a copy of the will with a lawyer friend in the Street of the Silver Horseshoe in Algiers, telling Vincent what he had done but no one else. No doubt when Dash had ransacked his half-brother's home and taken all his treasures he had also taken what he believed to be the only copy of the will. Well, one day, and soon, he would learn otherwise.

Cassia's kisses were beginning to distract Vincent from his memories in the sweetest way, he responding with passion, until their lips seemed to be moulded into one entity. He slipped his hands down to her breasts, caressing the soft white velvet flesh, palming her nipples, which sprang to life beneath his hands. Then, when she was roused, he kneeled over her, gazing down at the white Venusian form lying on the bed beneath him. There was no body in the universe lovelier than hers; no wonder the Sultan had been obsessed by her.

'If I had left you in the harem, *doucette*, you would have been the first Khadine by now. Perhaps the mother of Hamid's only son. You would have had thousands bending their knee to you, calling you Great One, and revering your name.'

'I would rather be queen of your heart, Vincent, my darling, than queen of any harem,' Cassia said earnestly. 'I shall miss my life in the harem as much as you will miss abducting and selling your slaves,' Cassia grinned, teasing him.

'The matter is settled, *doucette*. You are happy with me?'

'Have you heard me say otherwise?'

'No, but what do I have to offer you now? Nothing, not even enough to buy you a wedding gown.'

'You are still fretting over that, my love? But you must not. I

43

know it was a mortal blow to you to find your inheritance gone, but the last thing I fell in love with was your money, if at all. It is *you* I love.' She took him by the wrists and squeezed his arms tightly. 'Now who is making worries for themselves? Come, my love, and let us forget our problems for a few hours.' She pulled him down on top of her, feeling his hard, lean, brown body covering hers, joy thrilling through her as his arms curved round her back to crush her close.

When he took her the breath caught in her throat, making her twist her head from side to side on the pillow, scarlet rushing to her cheeks. It was unalloyed ecstasy to be in his embrace, to know that he was her lover and she his, and that nothing was ever going to part them again. They were so close that his heart seemed to be beating inside hers and hers inside him.

'We have exchanged hearts,' she whispered. 'I can feel yours as if it is mine, it is thudding against your ribs – my ribs – as if you – I – have been running.'

'If I have, it is the most beautiful race in the world, and what a prize at the end,' Vincent whispered, smoothing back the auburn hair which had become tangled across her face and planting a gentle kiss on the tip of her nose, then on her chin, and on each cheek, her brow.

Soon all their fears were vanquished by the escalating bliss of their lovemaking, as Cassia's passion mounted to such a frenzy that she felt that she could not contain it. Grinning, Vincent placed a gentle hand over her mouth.

'Sshh, our charming host and hostesses might be listening.'

Cassia giggled. 'Do you think so? If they are, let us give them something to hear, shall we? We do not want them to have their ears pressed to the panelling for nothing!'

Later, when Cassia's breathless little cries were echoing round the room for the third time, Vincent said, 'I think they will be satisfied now, but, more to the point, are you, *doucette*?'

'Yes,' Cassia gave a half-smile, 'for the moment, anyway.'

Then they lay back in one another's arms, revelling in the

luxury of their first comfortable double bed for weeks, not having to battle against an extreme of heat or cold, crushed together in the narrow bunk-bed that had been their berth on the *Berengaria*.

Cassia's last thought before she drifted into sleep was what had happened to her maid, Bessie, who had come with her to Penwellyn from London. She would not have returned to John Morbilly's house, for he had no need of a lady's maid. It was far more likely that she would have remained here to care for Aunt Julitta. If that were so, why was she not here now? Or possibly she was, but asleep in one of the rooms. Anyway, Cassia would find out tomorrow.

Chapter Three

It was strange to wake without the creaking, grinding noise of the ship's timbers, without the lapping of waves against wood, the shouts of sailors intent on their work, the screech of gulls high up in the blue, circling round the mast as they came into land. There was something else missing too, and for a moment Cassia could not remember what it was, and then she did — the raucous, screeching cries of her aunt's peacocks, George and Charlotte, named for the King and Queen of England. Before, they had always either woken Cassia or split the air with their noise shortly after she awoke. Why did they not do so now? Sun was glinting into the room, it was not too early for the birds to be up and about.

'The peacocks,' she murmured.

'Peacocks? What peacocks?' Vincent said, still half asleep.

'My aunt's. George and Charlotte. They're in a pen not far from the house, they usually deafen everyone early in the morning, demanding to be fed.'

'Perhaps they were fed this morning before they got a chance to make any noise.'

'I suppose that could be it, but usually we have our breakfast first.'

'Perhaps things are different now. Routines, timetables, do change you know, *doucette*. You have been away a long time, two years in all.'

'Yes, I know. I longed for Penwellyn to be exactly as it was when I left here. I *need* it to be just the same. Do you understand, Vincent?'

He kissed her face, her lips. 'Of course I understand, *ma mignonne*. We all have a deep need to have a home, to think of it as a place which can never change, which will always be the same happy, secure background that we need.'

'Forgive me, darling,' Cassia said. 'Here am I complaining because the home I remembered is not exactly as it was, when you have not had a proper home for years and years. How cruel of me! I had hoped you would be able to make Penwellyn your home.'

'When I have tracked down Dash we shall have enough money to build our own little house near Penwellyn, the finest place in the world for raising a family.'

'You speak as if you are quite sure my aunt will be reconciled with me. Oh, Vincent, what if she won't be? What if she will never speak to me again? She was the only mother I ever had, I couldn't bear it if she rejected me.'

'It is no good going over and over your worst fears, *doucette*. You must put it out of your mind until we have spoken to your aunt. As I have said before, I am sure that when she sees you are to be married and when she knows that she is to become a great-aunt she will be more than willing to be reconciled with you. Infants have a marvellous way of reuniting people.'

Before they went downstairs next morning, Cassia gathered together her rouge pots and jewellery and bits and pieces and tied them all in a shawl. She looked round at the boxes of clothes in despair. Where on earth was she going to take all these? A room at the village inn would not have space for them. She would just have to leave most of them here and take some of her dresses, the ones that were most serviceable. Having unfastened some of the boxes, she extracted some half a dozen gowns which were suitable to village life in Cornwall, and chose shoes, wrappers, gloves and bonnets to match. Packing up the boxes once more, she felt a sweet nostalgia as she looked at her favourite clothes, their pretty pastel shades and dainty flowered material bringing back her happy months with Aunt Julitta. Folding up the clothes into as small a bundle as possible, she wrapped them in her largest shawl, which Vincent picked up, and they then proceeded down the stairs.

Just as they entered the hall the front doors crashed open and a small evil-looking man burst in. He was red-faced, seemingly flustered, his black oily hair like drips of tar around his face. His eyes were uneven, one being set at least an inch higher in his face than the other; his tongue showed between his lips, as though too large for his mouth. His clothes were shabby and tattered, the breast of his jacket a patchwork of food stains. He gave off a rank smell, which, even from across the hall, Cassia could detect, and she wrinkled her nostrils.

Vincent stepped forward, thinking the man was some ne'er-do-well who had intruded and must be put outside. He had his hand on the man's shoulder ready to eject him, when the drawing-room door opened hastily and Sneely stood there, an outraged expression on his face.

- 'Sir, sir!' the evil-looking man gabbled. 'Sir, sir, this man be attacking me! 'E's put 'is 'and on me and I don' want it.'

Sneely stepped into the hall. 'That's quite all right, Botch, the man isn't going to harm you. He is going to take his hand off you this instant, is he not?' Sneely raised his face and glared at Vincent.

'I was merely defending the house against an intruder,' Vincent said casually, as if he did not care one way or the other how many intruders burst into Penwellyn.

'The man works for me,' Sneely said. 'He's not an intruder. Botch, go into the drawing-room immediately and wait for me there.'

Cassia, who had been watching the exchange with a startled expression on her face, almost winced at the thought of the evil-smelling Botch in her aunt's beautiful, spotless drawing-room. If he did indeed work for her cousin's husband, then surely it would be the most menial labour possible, not the sort which brought a man into the drawing-room?

She noticed Sneely's eyes on her bundle. He looked at her suspiciously. Did he imagine that she was stealing Penwellyn's silver? If he did then the man was a fool.

'You are going now, I see,' said Sneely unnecessarily, at which Cassia stepped across the hall to join Vincent, catching a fleeting look of immense relief upon Sneely's fat face. She did

48

not know which of the men repulsed her more: the sickeningly obsequious Sneely, or the malodorous, crooked-eyed Botch.

At the door Vincent turned to Sneely. 'We shall return when Mistress Morbilly is at home,' he said, and then he and Cassia were outside in the fresh April air and more than glad to be so.

'I never thought I would be relieved to leave Penwellyn!' Cassia exclaimed as they took the road to the village. 'What on earth can that dreadful man be doing, working for Sneely? He's too dirty even for a groom.' She paused, picking her way over the ruts in the road. 'And anyway, who is Sneely married to?'

Alicia had been married to a nobleman, Cassia explained to Vincent. She remembered when Julitta was sick that Alicia had arrived at Penwellyn in a grand coach with a flourish of servants. Cassia shivered as she recalled her cousin's coldness, even to her own mother. And Elizabeth, who had such a gentle name, was the most restless, dissatisfied creature Cassia had ever met.

'I cannot imagine either of those two married to Sneely,' Cassia went on. 'So that leaves Melody . . . But she wasn't at the house.'

'She might have been there,' suggested Vincent, 'and simply avoiding us.'

'Yes,' Cassia agreed, 'that's possible. It's all so mystifying.' Odd, too, she thought sadly, that her aunt had gone away visiting while her daughters who so rarely came to see her were in residence at Penwellyn.

But it was difficult to be downhearted for long with the crisp April air to be inhaled, the urgent cries of the gulls overhead. The path across the moors towards the village wandered through bracken and fern; here and there lay scatterings of granite rocks, some large, some small, some merely pebbles. The darker shades of bracken and moor-gorse were brightened by brilliant yellow wild daffodils, purple sea peas, bright-hued mallow and cowslips.

For centuries Cassia's ancestors, the Morbillys and the

Joliths, had been seafarers. For sixteen years Cassia had been raised at her father's home in London, with nothing more natural than a man-made park to brighten her days. She remembered again, with a fresh surge of exquisite delight, her first emotions on seeing the Cornish moors, the brilliant turbulent sea which caressed the cliffs and rocks nearby. Flinging back her head and breathing deeply, she drew in the intoxicating Cornish air which was like wine to her parched spirit.

'You really do love the moors, don't you?' Vincent said, gripping her hand.

'Yes, oh yes! Almost more than life itself. I did not truly begin to live until I came to stay at Penwellyn. I thought I was such a sophisticated young miss, knowing everything, until I came here and realized that there was far more to existence than stuffy drawing-rooms and the noisy dirty streets of London. You love the sea too, don't you, Vincent? You know what I mean. The call of the sea.' She sighed. 'It is like the call of a long-lost lover.'

'I had thought I was your long-lost lover,' Vincent grinned, twinkling at her. 'Do not tell me that I have a rival.'

She grinned back, knowing that no answer was necessary. Despite her misgivings about Aunt Julitta, despite the fact that they were penniless, Cassia was heartened by their long walk to the village. They saw no one but a very old man riding a donkey which looked just as old, and which was laden with firewood. They called out a greeting to the man, but he did not seem to hear them, for he did not look up.

'Probably deaf as a beam,' Vincent commented.

Morbilly village was larger than its name suggested. One might have been forgiven for thinking it was nothing more than a quartet or two of fishermen's cottages. It was here that there was a thriving market once a week, and Morbilly Fair once a year in May. Here, too, was the Three Feathers, the inn where Cassia and Vincent intended to stay until Aunt Julitta's return. The village street was narrow and twisting, circumscribing the cottages, village green, the village pump and pond, the sprinkling of larger cottages, the village stores, and the Three Feathers itself.

The inn was small but picturesque, having been built in Tudor times of black and white half-timbering. The innkeeper was standing on the doorstep, sleeves rolled up, a massive white apron almost totally blanketing him. He had carrot-orange hair, an enormous bulbous nose and cheeks to match: his breeches were shiny with wear, his hose wrinkled and splashed with beer stains, and his shoes buckled with odd tin buckles. He gaped at the handsome couple before him as if they were a Prince and Princess who had appeared out of the clouds.

'Why, Mistress Morbilly, we thought you wuz dead!' he exclaimed, throwing up his hands.

'But I am not, as you can see, Master Tomkiss. Do you have room for Captain Sauvage and myself? We wish to stay with you a few nights until my aunt returns. She is away visiting, you know.'

'Away visitin', be she? Well, I do net know anything o' that, Mistress Morbilly.' Master Tomkiss shrugged. 'Net seen your aunt down 'ere fer a mighty leng time. Used to ride down 'ere reg'lar, she ded, would come in 'ere and enjoy a drink with the fellows round about, ask them 'ow they wuz doin' and 'ow their families wuz doin'. Took a right interest in us, she ded, but not o' late.'

By now they were inside the inn, the smell of oak panelling, vigorously beeswaxed, overladen by the odour of ale. There was a massive hearth in one corner, which was big enough to take a spit and a haunch of venison, and by the roaring flames lay a mangy grey cat. It looked up as Vincent and Cassia entered, eyed them balefully for a few moments, then, having decided they were not worthy of its interest, went back to sleep.

'How long ago was it when you last saw my aunt?' Cassia asked the innkeeper.

He half closed one eye and pursed his mouth, deep in thought. Then, having tapped his foot a couple of times and scratched his head, he said, 'My memory ain't that good these days. Martha would know. *Martha!*' His sudden cry in the peace of the inn disturbed the cat again; it stared at them in disgust, as if to say 'Those humans are going insane', then dropped its head on its grey paws to doze restively.

Martha, the innkeeper's wife, was a very short woman, well under five feet in height. Rounded and pleasant looking, with grey frizzled hair pushed carelessly inside a mob cap, she was swathed in a massive apron, like her husband, and in one hand she held a clutch of dusters, in the other a pot of beeswax.

'Yes, Jake, what can I do for 'e?' Then she saw Cassia and Vincent. 'Why!' she exclaimed. 'Visitors this early en the year? My goodness me, whatever next? Why, I can 'ardly believe it, visitors *thes* early!'

'Martha!' Jake Tomkiss cut his wife short. 'We're not 'ere for prattlin'. This be Mistress Morbilly from Penwellyn, niece of Mistress Julitta Morbilly. This young lady 'ere wants to know when we last saw 'er aunt.'

Martha Tomkiss folded her arms thoughtfully. 'Six months past, I reckon it wuz. She came ridin' through 'ere on that 'orse o' 'ers, Satan, nodded to me, asked me 'ow I wuz and how the children wuz, then rode off, she ded. 'Appy as a lark she looked, same as allus.'

'So she was truly well again after her illness?' Cassia said, relieved.

'Oh yes, got over that, she ded. Still 'ad a little trouble with 'er speakin' and some days worse than others, so she told me, but she wuz up and about and well again and ridin'. Thought you wuz dead, she ded. Smitten to the 'eart by your goin' off like – took 'er that much longer to get better, it ded.' Mrs Tomkiss's voice conveyed an accusation.

Cassia explained what had really happened, and both the innkeeper's mouth and that of his wife hung open wider as they listened.

'Pirates! Pirate-slavers!' gasped Mrs Tomkiss, huddling closer to her husband as if terrified. Cassia wondered what the woman would do if she told her that the very pirate-slaver who had abducted her was actually standing not two yards away. Faint, probably. She smiled to herself.

'You don't happen to know where my aunt has gone to stay, do you?' she asked.

Martha Tomkiss folded her arms again. 'Gone away, 'as she? I didn't know thet. Last I 'eard, she wuz expectin' 'er daughters to stay. Didn't know whether to look forward to it or dread it, she dedn't.'

'Expecting *all* her daughters to stay?' Cassia asked.

'Not Melody. Poor Mistress Melody, 'twere very sad about 'er.'

'Something has happened to her?'

'Died, she ded, poor girl. Truly sad. That on top of you disappearin' upset your aunt mighty proper it ded.'

At the woman's words Vincent put his arms round Cassia, as if knowing she would need extra comfort.

'What happened to Melody? How did she die?'

'Reckless rider, she allus wuz. Came a tumble many a time when she was a young 'un. Used to ride through this village as if the devil and all his 'ordes wuz after 'er. Well, one day while she was out ridin' alone 'er 'orse stampeded. Must've stopped sudden at the edge of the cliff like, because she wuz found down on the beach quite dead. Must've died instantly. The 'orse went back 'ome alone, riderless, you see. That's 'ow they knew up at the 'ouse.'

'How terrible,' Cassia breathed. 'How dreadful for my poor aunt. What an awful shock she must have had — I wish I had been here to comfort her.'

'Miss Melody wuz allus a wild girl, but 'twere a tragedy she wuz took when she wuz. Mistress Morbilly 'ad been startin' to get 'er 'ealth back, and though there wuzn't no love lost between 'em, it took 'er right badly it ded.'

Again Tomkiss interrupted. 'Don't go passin' comments on

folk what be above 'e, Martha,' he said sternly, his red bulbous nose and cheeks belying the gravity of his tone. 'Mistress Cassia 'asn't come 'ere to listen to what us villagers do think.'

Martha Tomkiss opened her eyes wide in indignation. 'And if *you'd* been on a long journey, snatched away from your 'ome, Jake Tomkiss, wouldn't you be wanteng to know 'ow things stood when you got back? Now, mistress,' Martha turned to Cassia, 'if there's any other way I can 'elp you, you jus' ask me. Wish I could tell you more, but don't see 'ow I can unless we 'ears the gossip amongst the villagers who comes in 'ere for their ale. We don't get any time fer finding out about thengs.' She frowned. 'Now something's coming back to me . . . 'Oliday? Now I do seem to remember somethenk about an 'oliday and your aunt. Yes, don't 'e remember, Jake? Master Sneely came in 'ere some months back, spoke sort of pointed, like, 'bout Mistress Morbilly going away to visit relatives. Now, mercy me, 'ow could I have forgotten that? Stared at me 'ard, 'e ded, while 'e was speaking.' She turned to Cassia again. 'Trouble is, so many folks come in 'ere and say so much, you tend to forget what you 'ear after a time.'

'I don't suppose he said where my aunt was going, did he? Please try and remember, Mistress Tomkiss, it's so important.'

Mrs Tomkiss folded her arms, unfolded them, then folded them again in her efforts to think back, but at last she had to say that she could not remember.

'But I will think on it, mistress, and if anything comes ento my mind I will tell you straightaway, yes indeed I will. Now, Jake, this young couple will be wanting their room. 'Tis fine, and all, to see you married, mistress,' the innkeeper's wife beamed.

Cassia felt the pink rush to her cheeks. 'We're not married yet, Mistress Tomkiss, but we intend to be as soon as my aunt returns. We have delayed the wedding till she can be present.'

'Oh, so not wed yet? Well, and it is the right thing you hev done, mistress, for your aunt will be thrilled to 'er boots to know ye are to wed. Not one grandchild she hev yet, and she hev waited eagerly such a long, long time.'

'Martha!' exclaimed Jake Tomkiss, at which his wife darted him another reproving glance before beaming again at the young couple, then return to her polishing.

'So it's two rooms you'll be wanting?' said the innkeeper.

'Indeed,' said Vincent, as if shocked that anyone could suggest anything else. Flashing a private smile at Cassia, who fought to suppress a grin. Vincent took her arm and they followed Jake Tomkiss up the creaking oak stairway to the upper rooms of the inn.

Within a day of their arrival at the Three Feathers, their luggage had been collected from the cove by two of the villagers with their cart, and Cassia and Vincent were comfortably installed at the inn with nothing to do except await news of Julitta Morbilly's return to Penwellyn.

Despite the beauty of their surroundings, however, and the solicitous way in which Jake Tomkiss and his wife cared for them, Mrs Tomkiss cooking extra specially tasty meals, both Cassia and Vincent were growing restive after a week had passed without news of her aunt. Neither of them found relaxation easy, and at the back of their minds was the thought of Nathan Dash with his stolen hoard of money. At the moment Vincent had very little money left. Shortly he would have to go to the nearest town to sell the last of the gold ornaments which he had taken from the Princess Jasmina's palace to finance his escape. There was, of course, a second urgency. Cassia wanted her child to be respectably born in wedlock. Yet nothing was going to rush her into a ceremony without the presence of her Aunt Julitta. Whether or not her aunt was speaking to her, somehow, some way, she would persuade her dearest relative to attend. Surely Julitta would let bygones be bygones for such an important and happy day?

Three days later, Cassia and Vincent, having hired a light-weight cart from the innkeeper, set off for Helston, across the moors. Splashes of yellow heralded buttercups and wild mustard, the golden saxifrage creeping along the ground. The gorse had not yet produced its five-petalled yellow flowers, but when it did it too would add to the golden hue of the moors. They passed low mounds gleaming like gold with broom flowers; there were coltsfoot and celandine, too, and pale purple lady's smock scattered amongst the yellow. Here and there were the small low bushes of the burnet rose, now in bud in readiness for their early summer blossoming of white, and everywhere the tiny blue speedwell flourished.

It was a fine spring day of lucid golden light and tiny lint clouds. Cassia had a cushion at her back and a rug over her knees to protect her from the discomfort of the bumpy cart. They passed a farmer on horseback, also on his way to Helston, and a young lady in a dogcart who waved to them; she had a sketchpad propped by her on the seat.

'I promised my aunt that I would sketch Penwellyn for her. I never did get round to it,' Cassia said guiltily.

'Why not do it now, and have the painting ready for her when she comes back, a sort of peace offering?' Vincent suggested.

'That's an excellent idea, my love. You are right, I will do it. At one time I used to paint and sketch constantly. I could paint some of the flowers, there are so many here. Why, I could start a portfolio of all the flowers that grow around Penwellyn, as well as the house itself. That would surely please Aunt Julitta.' She beamed at Vincent, delighted at the thought of the project.

It was time for lunch. They had planned to select a particularly pretty spot and picnic there, which is what they did, Vincent reigning in the sturdy horse.

Mrs Tomkiss had packed them a marvellous repast: succulent pink ham which she had cured herself, cut into thick juicy slices; homemade barley bread; local pilchards in a pie with a crusty, wheaten lid; and a flask of fresh creamy milk from Jemima, the Tomkiss's cow. It was thanks to the staple Cornish diet of barley bread, potatoes, vegetables, wheaten pastry and broth, a little pork with flavouring, and fish, that the local people had such beautiful white teeth. Their diet could not have been more opposite from the one favoured in the harem where Cassia had spent so many months a prisoner. There, sickly sweet sherbets, Turkish delight and sugared sweetmeats were nibbled almost constantly throughout the day.

As they ate, Cassia said, ''Tis a shame Mr and Mrs Briscoe are away. I am sure they would have known where my aunt is.'

Cassia had gone to Polmaen House to ask Mrs Briscoe if she knew where Julitta had gone and when she would be back, only to be told by the Briscoes' servants that their master and mistress were in New Orleans, America, visiting their only son, who had emigrated the previous year. The couple had been away now for something like eight months and were expected back before the end of spring.

Cassia had felt very downcast at the news. She had visited other friends of her aunt's, people who had frequently visited Penwellyn two years ago, but everywhere she heard the same story: they had been told Aunt Julitta had gone away, but no one knew where.

With each negative response Cassia elicited, the deeper her feeling of unease grew. For her aunt, who so loved her home that she had never gone further than Helston Down, to disappear not leaving any word as to her destination nor when she would be back, seemed totally out of character. But in case it was London that she had visited and Cassia's father, John Morbilly, that she was staying with, Cassia had written there. It had been one of the first things she had done on arriving at the Three Feathers. Supposing that her father might have been worried about her disappearance, she had put in a few lines regarding her abduction and her safe return. She had received a terse, one line reply: *Your aunt is not visiting here, nor expected*, her father had written, signing himself 'John Morbilly, Esquire' in the most formal manner.

Had she not had Vincent nearby Cassia would have been

stricken afresh by her father's coldness, for however unnatural he had been as a parent, not caring one jot what became of her, he was, after all, the only father she had. She could imagine him being sent news of her mysterious disappearance two years ago, the knowledge that he no longer need be responsible for the daughter he considered recalcitrant and ungrateful smoothing out his features, a look akin to contentment passing across the stern face with its haughty Morbilly nose and the heavy hirsute brows which gave him the cruel look of a falcon.

But she had no need now of regret or bitterness, for she had her Vincent, who was everything to her — lover, friend and father.

She looked at him with tender eyes as he lifted the picnic basket up into the cart and carefully arranged the cushion in readiness for her to take her seat. When he stepped down to lift her into the cart, she coiled her arms round his neck, planting feather kisses on his cheeks and mouth.

'If you do that,' he warned, 'we shall not arrive in Helston before dark. Then we shall have to stay the night.'

'We shall have plenty of money after our visit to the goldsmith's, surely we can afford a room at the Angel? Its reputation is well-known in these parts, their cooking is famous.' Cassia was continuing to plant kisses on Vincent's face as she spoke, her arms not loosening their tight hold on him. Soon he had surrendered. He collected the rug from the cart and spread it down on the ground for them to lie on.

Wild birds chorused and the carthorse took another deep drink at the pool nearby as Vincent unbuttoned the pink satin buttons of Cassia's gown, gently pulling aside the soft white book-muslin so that he could kiss her breasts. She sighed, throwing back her head, putting a hand across her eyes to block out the dazzle of the sun. Her hair was fiery against the dark green of the rug, her skin fair as white roses. The spicy scent of the gorse, the song of the birds, the heat of the sun, all served to make their union sweet ecstasy. They had made love in the open in Greece when they had been fleeing from the

Princess Jasmina, but there the air had been humid and heavy.

'How rapturous it is to be able to lie here in each other's arms without fear of being attacked by Turkish hordes or Nubian slaves with scimitars,' she sighed happily. 'How safe we are in Cornwall, nothing could happen to us here. It must be the safest place on earth. After Turkey and our flight through Greece it is paradise, just paradise.'

'As I said, the finest place on earth to raise children.' Gently Vincent stroked his lover's stomach, mindful of the baby within, their future daughter or son. When Cassia had buttoned up her bodice and straightened her skirts, they kissed again, then Vincent lifted her up as if she weighed no more than a child and deposited her on the seat of the cart before taking his place beside her.

The horse, which had waited patiently, seemed eager to be off, and soon they were bowling along the moorland road towards Helston. They passed Pen Castle, a ruined fortress which was said to be haunted, a shiver coursing over Cassia's skin as she looked in the direction of the ruins.

'The locals say that Pen Castle is haunted by the ghost of a girl who fell in love with a man her father despised. She tried to elope one night, the man waiting for her at the bottom of the Castle walls as she crept down the ladder. The father came out and caught them and he had them taken prisoner and walled up together, telling them that they had wanted to be joined for the rest of their lives and now they surely would be. The girl's screams rang out for days, they say she took over a week to die. After the first two days the man's cries were not heard any more. The father did not relent.'

'What a mournful tale. It is best not to brood over things like that while you're expecting a child, *doucette*.'

'Oh, I shan't be brooding on it, Vincent. It all happened many, many years ago.'

'Only the silly and the credulous believe in ghosts,' Vincent said, trying to reassure her.

'Then I am both,' she smiled at him. 'I have seen a man's

face change completely when he was talking of Pen Castle. No one will go near it, not even in daytime. They say that to hear the screams of the dying girl is to bring death or disaster on oneself.'

'That's all nonsense, of course,' Vincent smiled. 'We shall come here and we shall picnic by Pen Castle just to show you that such superstitions are absurd.'

They rode on, and it seemed that Pen Castle was forgotten. Coming to a little dell ringed by elder trees, they paused to drink from the spring issuing from the earth. The water was delicious, icily pure, tinglingly fresh. Then they drove on and within the hour they were in Helston.

They went straight to the shop of Michael Polwheal, where Vincent was going to sell his gold. Cassia had met Polwheal before, for he had been a visitor at her aunt's. He was a quiet little man, neatly dressed, with dove-grey hair tied back with a black ribbon bow and rolled into a fat sausage on either side of his face. The shop was crammed with ornaments and antiques, jewellery, clocks, smaller items of *chinoiserie*. Many of the items looked dusty and lay jostling together in heaps, while others stood on proud display and were beautifully polished.

'Why, Mistress Cassia, we thought you were dead!' Michael Polwheal hurried forward at the sight of her. 'And what very sad news you have returned to hear. I offer my felicitations. How upset you must be to know you were too late.'

Michael Polwheal pulled forward a chair, ushering Cassia to sit down, and it was fortunate that he had, for when he explained himself Cassia turned white as a sheet and seemed about to faint.

'Dead? My aunt dead? But I don't understand. Master Polwheal, surely you have not heard aright? She is not dead, only away visiting.'

'Oh, but surely . . . that is —'

He was interrupted by Cassia's gasp. 'That clock! That clock over there on the shelf, the one with the roses and the cherubs, surely that is my aunt's clock, the one that stands on the drawing-room mantelpiece?'

'Why, indeed it is, Mistress Cassia.'

'But how did it get here? Surely my aunt would not sell that? It has been in the family for generations. It was one of her favourite pieces.'

Michael Polwheal looked highly uncomfortable. 'But it was sold to me. You see, now that your poor aunt has, well, has passed on, Mistress Alicia and Mistress Elizabeth, wishing to sell some of the ornaments at Penwellyn, came to me.'

'They came to you in person?' Cassia gasped. 'Bringing things from Penwellyn to sell?'

'Oh, not in *person*, Mistress Cassia. Poor Mistress Melody's husband brought them.'

'Melody's husband?'

'Yes – Master Sneely. Have you not met him, have you not been to Penwellyn yet? Oh my dear, if I am the bringer of this bad news and you did not know before, forgive me! I am truly sorry if I have upset you.'

Cassia was still deathly pale. She felt sick and faint, the room was spinning round her. So Sneely was Melody's husband and Melody was dead, and so was her aunt. Her poor, poor aunt was dead. And Sneely for some inexplicable reason had lied to her. She could not understand it. She felt dazed. Vincent was speaking now, his tones firm and authoritative.

'We were told that Mistress Julitta Morbilly was on holiday visiting relatives. Sneely himself told us, and this was verified by his sisters-in-law.'

'Verified? But I do not understand.' Michael Polwheal looked truly mystified. 'Sneely has been in here numerous times in the past months to bring objects he wishes to sell. Once or twice I have seen Mistress Alicia or Mistress Elizabeth outside awaiting him in the carriage. Even if I had not seen them thus, it would never have occurred to me that the man was selling property which was not his, for he came in here dressed in black from head to foot, looking utterly miserable and dejected, full of grief for his mother-in-law's demise. That was the day, why yes, that was the very day I glanced out of the window and saw Mistress Alicia, also robed in black from head to foot, sitting outside in the carriage, looking similarly mournful.'

'They were not dressed in black when we saw them at Penwellyn less than a fortnight ago,' Vincent said. 'How long ago was it that Sneely came in and told you this news?'

'Now, let me think. Why, it must have been five or six months ago. If they are not wearing mourning now, perhaps they have decided to come out of mourning early, although I admit that is a little strange, to discard black so soon . . .' His voice trailed off.

'Master Polwheal, something extremely disturbing is going on.' Vincent glanced at Cassia, who looked up at him in distress. 'We shall get to the bottom of this mystery, believe me. But until we do, I must ask you something.'

'Anything I can do to help, sir.'

'I must ask you not to sell any of the items which Sneely has brought in here.'

'But – but I have paid good money for them, sir.'

'I am sure you did, Master Polwheal, but we do not believe that Mistress Morbilly *is* dead. And if she is –' he glanced again at Cassia, taking her hand and patting it tenderly, 'then there is the matter of the Will.'

'The Will? Yes, yes, of course, the Will – but surely her daughters would inherit?'

'She told Mistress Cassia most firmly and decisively on more than one occasion that she would be leaving Penwellyn and all her belongings to her, for she had shown her more love than her three daughters put together. Now if you would be so kind as to fetch some water for Mistress Cassia?'

'Of course, of course.' Polwheal bustled away to do as he was bid, while Cassia looked up at Vincent.

'If she is dead – oh, Vincent, if she is dead, and they have been keeping it from me because she left everything to me! Oh, this is terrible, how can I bear it?' She pressed a hand to her stomach, a twist of pain rising within her.

'My darling, try not to upset yourself. Think of the baby, our child.' Vincent stroked her forehead, his eyes full of empathy for her plight.

'Oh, but I can't bear it, I just can't! If she's dead, if I am too late . . .' Tears gathered in Cassia's eyes and rolled down her cheeks.

Master Polwheal returned with a glass of water, which Cassia sipped in a half-hearted fashion. Had she not been with child, had she been her usual self, she would have been filled with fury and anger, getting into the cart and whipping up the horse and returning post-haste to Penwellyn to tell her cousins and Sneely what she thought of them. But the baby had made her more vulnerable, and tears and grief were her reaction. She felt helpless. Thank God she had Vincent to take command.

And take command he did. Having completed his business with Master Polwheal, Vincent took Cassia to the Angel, where they hired a room for the night. Immediately he put her to bed and ordered their supper to be sent up to them. He ordered roast goose with potatoes and green peas, and, to follow, chocolate pudding.

At any other time, Cassia would have relished the food, but tonight she could hardly bear the smell of it. Vincent propped her up in bed, stoked the fire, put on a fresh log as the April night was becoming cold, and rang the bell for a servant. When the girl came he ordered milk, wine and spices to be heated together and brought up at once. Bobbing a curtsey, the girl did as she was instructed.

'Do not waste the food, my love. Even if I am not hungry, you must eat,' Cassia insisted.

When the posset arrived he broke off from his meal and supported Cassia's head while she sipped at the warm, spicy liquid.

'This will revive you, *doucette*, like nothing else, I can guarantee it.'

Halfway through Cassia pushed the glass away. 'Oh, Vincent, I can't drink any more. I keep thinking of my poor aunt all on her own, dying, thinking I didn't love her, thinking I had left her and run off rather than nurse her back to health.'

'But we don't know that she is dead, do we, *ma mignonne?* Sneely told us she was away visiting relatives. He must know that if he is telling lies the day will come when he must face us, when we will *insist* on knowing the truth. He can only delay the inevitable by lying.'

'We must find out the truth now, as soon as we return to Morbilly. Things can't go on like this.'

'No, I agree that they cannot.' Vincent's voice was soothing. He looked down at her tenderly, stroking her hand. A little colour had returned to her face — she was recovering from the shock. Perhaps, he thought, the posset had helped after all.

Cassia raised her eyes to him. 'Vincent . . .' she said slowly. 'If my aunt had died the villagers would have known, there would have been a funeral. Sneely could not hide that from us, could he? She *cannot* be dead, Vincent, everyone would have known. She is so friendly with the villagers, everyone loves her. Yes, of course, there would have been a funeral. How stupid of me not to realize that. And there hasn't been, has there, Vincent, or Tomkiss at the Three Feathers would have told us, would he not? So she *must* be away somewhere visiting relatives. Oh, I feel better already,' Cassia sighed, leaning back against the pillows.

Vincent said nothing, placing his hand on her brow and stroking back the silken auburn hair until her eyes closed in deep relaxation. He did not tell her of the suspicions which had been developing inside him for some time now. He had not liked Sneely. The man, even if he did not look like a villain, had a villain's mannerisms; he had been hostile, he had behaved in a jumpy fashion. Vincent was sure he had been lying all along, but common sense had told him that if Julitta had died, the whole village would have heard. The death of a Morbilly of Morbilly was not something which was passed over. So, somehow, somewhere, Julitta was still alive, and Sneely was lying. Those two facts did not seem to hang together, and yet . . . For the moment Vincent put his fears aside, nursing Cassia as he had nursed her before, now gently taking a pillow away so that she could sleep peacefully. In a few moments he slipped off his clothes and slid into the bed beside her, gently, so as not to disturb her, his body curving lovingly round hers.

The creaking of the inn's old timbers punctuated the silence. The night grew dark, the fire died to ashes, everyone slept.

Chapter Four

Next morning they made an early start. Cassia was feeling much stronger and could not wait to confront Sneely and her cousins. Now that she knew Sneely had been Melody's husband she wanted to know why he was living at Penwellyn, now that Melody was dead. But first and foremost she wanted to know why he had lied to Michael Polwheal. Now that her suspicions were aroused she would not rest until she had got to the truth.

They were within some two to three hundred yards when they saw the rider; the terrain being flat, they had a clear view. He bolted out of Pen Castle as if pursued by the hordes of Hell, riding with his head lowered in a hunched position over his horse's mane, not looking to right or left of him, his ill-fitting clothing flapping behind.

'There's one of the locals who doesn't seem to be frightened of going near Pen Castle,' Vincent mused. 'It looks as though he's been in there.'

Looking up, Cassia stared hard at the disappearing rider. 'I know that man. Isn't he the one we saw in the hall at Penwellyn? What was his name? Hotch, or Cotch, or something odd like that.'

'Botch. Yes, you are right, *doucette*, it is he. And what would such a man be doing in Pen Castle? Hiding smuggled brandy or gold, perhaps. Shall we see?'

Cassia flung a doubtful look at Pen Castle. 'Do we have to?'

'I think we do. I have a suspicion this might in some way be connected with Sneely's strange behaviour.'

'You think he is hiding some of my aunt's belongings there in readiness to sell them? Oh yes, that could be so!' Cassia cried. 'Oh, if that is the case then we must certainly go in and look.'

'I have every intention of doing so, *doucette*. Will you wait here, or come with me?'

'I will come with you,' Cassia said bravely, alighting from the cart which Vincent had pulled to a halt a few feet from the entrance to the crumbling castle.

Pen Castle was every bit as eerie as it had seemed from afar. Cassia shivered, walking close to Vincent and holding his hand as they approached the doorway. Once, Pen Castle had stood proudly, staring out across the rolling downs. In the past, the Pen family had lived here happily, tending their estates and raising children. But, in the reign of Queen Mary Tudor, one George Pen had remained stubbornly a Protestant, and for that she had sent him to his death; his wife, never having recovered from the shock, had taken her own life. Their seven daughters had been put out on the parish, and none had ever returned to Pen Castle which, over the years, had fallen into ruin. The aura of tragedy and doom hung about it, even now.

As Cassia touched the rough stone with her fingers she was overwhelmed by a feeling of empathy for the lonely castle which had been meant to house a jolly family of laughing children, a loving wife and husband. Clutching his arm, she followed as Vincent stepped through the doorway and into the empty circular room of the main tower. Decades of dust, leaves, debris, and dead swatches of gorse and bracken littered the beaten earth floor. Worn stone steps rose up one side of the room, circling up the tower, past another floor level where the wooden floor had long since rotted away, and on to what looked like a dark and heavy oaken door, firmly shut.

'It must be up there where he hides his treasure, whatever it is,' Vincent mused, looking up at the firmly closed door.

'It will be locked, of course.'

Vincent began to ascend the stairway, Cassia calling out to him to take care. Having reached the stout wooden door, he tried to push it open. It was, indeed, firmly locked.

'I'll need some tools to get this open,' Vincent called down.

'Have we the right to force it?' Cassia called back.

'What if it has nothing to do with us, after all?'

'That is not like you, my love, to take defeat so easily,' Vincent grinned down at her.

'This place is so creepy, darling, I don't want to stay here longer than necessary.'

'Then I shall return alone tonight and force the door,' Vincent said firmly.

'Oh no you won't, I want to be here when you find whatever's inside that room.'

'Have patience, *doucette*.' Vincent put his shoulder to the door once, twice, three times. It gave a little. 'We need something strong, a metal bar or something, to force it open,' he called down.

'What about those tools under the old sacking at the back of the cart?'

Vincent hurried down the stairway and they went out to the cart to lift back the covering of sacking. Beneath it were implements for maintaining and repairing the cart, including two or three long iron bars which could serve as a lever. Snatching one up, Vincent went back into the castle with Cassia. Within moments he had levered open the wooden door.

After the bright sunlight outside, the room was dim and murky, and Vincent had to take time to adjust his vision. The room looked as if someone had used it as a storehouse for rubbish, mainly mattresses and old rugs. He glanced about him, frowning. There did not seem to be any loot here: no brandy kegs, no smuggled treasure, liquid or otherwise. He went to the door and called to Cassia.

'We were wrong, after all. I think this must be Botch's living quarters. There's an old mattress or two flung in a corner and some rags, a broken bench, one or two tools. This must be his home, his lair,' Vincent said. He turned back into the room for one more quick glance round, just in case he had missed anything. Seeing one section of the wall which looked as if the stones had been loosened at one time or another and pushed back carelessly, he went across to it, gently tugging at the stones to pull them out to see if anything was hidden behind them. Something was. A dirty stained little leather bag with twelve coins in it. Botch's treasure. If the man were not so repulsive Vincent would have felt pity for him and his little store of money. Carefully replacing the bag, the money and the stones, Vincent stood up and turned round.

When he saw the patch of white amongst the filthy old blankets on the mattresses he immediately thought that Botch's woman must be asleep in the bed. If that were so, she must be a very heavy sleeper, he thought.

As he stared, he pondered on the locked door. Could Botch be some sort of demented creature who kept a woman locked up here for his own evil purposes? If so, Vincent could not in all conscience re-lock the door, leaving her here. He walked over to the bed. Looking closer in the gloom, he saw that the patch of white was a fragile, immobile hand virtually devoid of flesh. Alarmed, he gently lifted back the covers. The rest of the woman was as deathly white and skeletal as the hand. She lay quite silent and still, as if dead, and for a few seconds he thought she was. Surely nobody could be quite so motionless and yet still be alive? Her lips were parched and cracked, her hair lank and greasy, her eyes had sunken into her head and looked like dark bruises, her lids were closed. Taut, parched skin stretched across the bones of her jaw and cheeks, which stood up like ridges. He glanced round. There appeared to be no water jug or food in the room. Taking one of the fleshless hands in his, he chafed it, trying to rouse some life into the woman. It was hard to determine her age, the state she was in. Perhaps fifty or sixty years old – certainly too old for Botch to be using her as a bedmate.

'Vincent, my love, have you found something?' Cassia was halfway up the stairs, eager to see what was keeping her lover in the tower room.

'Be prepared for a shock,' he called out. 'There is a woman in here, some poor starved creature, she looks near death. That Botch shall answer to me for this.'

Cassia walked into the room slowly, a little scared at the thought of what she might see. 'Is she . . . too near death? Are we too late to save her?' she whispered, walking slowly towards Vincent, taking her time before looking at the woman on the bed. When she did she felt as if all the breath had been punched out of her body, as if there were no air in the room, and she was gasping for breath. She put out her hand, and instantly Vincent was beside her, supporting her.

'No, no, I am all right,' she gasped. 'It is . . . it is . . . my aunt – that is my aunt in the bed!' she finally managed to say.

'Your aunt? *Mon Dieu*, but how can that be?' Then realization dawned on both their faces. Vincent swore beneath his breath. Cassia was bending over her aunt, pulling back the covers, looking closely at her face for signs of life.

Her eyes filled with tears. 'Oh, Vincent, Vincent, they have been starving her. She has been shut away in here for a long time, look how thin she is. Those brutes, those *pigs*!' Her voice broke on a sob. 'This bed is filthy. Her clothes are no more than rags. Oh, Aunt Julitta –'

A slight stir of movement, a fluttering of the eyelids, greeted Cassia's cry. A faint moan issued from between the blue lips, but that was all; no other response.

'She needs water, wine, nourishing food, and she must be bathed. She is so weak, Vincent, so fragile. She could not survive a ride to the house. And if we took her back now we would have those villains to contend with. Could they, oh could they stop us from taking her into her own home? Oh, Vincent, what fiends they are, what cruel and inhuman fiends!'

'I agree, *doucette*. They need to be taught a lesson, and we shall be the ones to do it. But first we must care for your aunt. Will you be all right staying here on your own while I fetch food and milk for her?'

'I shall have to be, even though the place is so eerie. Don't be long though, will you, Vincent?'

'As soon as I get to the village I will send one or two of the most able-bodied men I can find to stand guard over you until I return. As soon as I have shut the door, stand those stools against it, and the bench. I know they are not very heavy, but they will give you a little moral support.'

'I want them shut away, *all* of them, even if they are her daughters! How *could* they have done this to her?' Cassia's fury gave her courage.

The moment Vincent had shut the door behind him she banked everything she could find against it for safety, then began the long wait. She sat on the filthy rugs of her aunt's bed, stroking her hands and rubbing them and speaking to her lovingly, even though there was no response. Over and over she told her aunt how she loved her, how she had never wanted to leave her and that now she was back to take care of her.

'I'm going to have a baby, Aunt Julitta,' she said, 'and I want you to be fit and well so you can teach him or her to ride when the time comes. No one knows more about horses than you do, Aunt Julitta. We just cannot manage without you. You're going to be a great-aunt very soon, did you know that?'

The half-starved woman's eyelids seemed to flicker on hearing those words. For a moment they lifted, partially revealing the rich brown velvet eyes which were Julitta's greatest beauty.

'Cass . . . Cass-ie,' her aunt managed to whisper before sinking back into unconsciousness.

A sound outside jolted Cassia into action. She stood up, crept to the door and listened. Was it that foul Botch, or the men Vincent had promised to send? Hearing jovial voices, she knew that it must be the latter.

'Mistress Morbilly, it be we, sent by the Cap'n to take care of 'e until the Cap'n comes 'ere 'imself.'

Immediately Cassia began moving the wooden furniture to allow the men to push the door open. They had brought two warm blankets, a flask of mulled red wine, a flask of milk, some fresh white bread, and honey.

Gaping at the bed and then at Cassia, both the men seemed stunned. 'Why, 'tes your poor aunt! What be she doing 'ere? Why 'tes a crime!'

'She's been kept here, a prisoner, by that odious man, Sneely,' Cassia explained. 'He has a helper – Botch. Do you know the man?' As she spoke she was divesting her aunt of the filthy, ragged covers and flinging them into a corner in disgust, before covering her with the warm, clean blankets the men had brought. She pushed back her aunt's hair, away from her face, and raised her head slightly, supporting her with her own cloak rolled into a ball. Julitta stirred a little and moaned again. Gently Cassia held the flask of milk to her lips and some of the fresh clean liquid trickled into her mouth. She gulped, as if to swallow was painful, and then opened her mouth wider to drink more.

'Aye, we know that Botch,' one of the men was saying. 'Made advances to my young daughter, 'e ded. Dirty, nasty, animal of a man. Gave 'im what fer, I ded, told 'im if 'e came near my 'ome again I'd crack 'is 'ead with my shovel and a few more things besides if I got the chance.'

'Aye,' agreed the second man. 'Arrived 'ere a few days after that Sneely, 'e ded. Said 'e was 'ere to 'elp Sneely, but dedn't say what 'e was 'elping 'im do. Now we know,' the man said wonderingly. 'Criminal it is. That poor good lady shut away 'ere ter starve.'

Cassia looked from the second man's face back to her aunt, to find the beautiful brown velvet eyes were open and staring at her. They were full of something like awe and delight and love all rolled into one.

'Cass-ie . . .' her aunt whispered, one of the thin, frail hands reaching up to touch her niece.

'Save your strength, dearest Aunt, don't try to move. Here, have some more of this milk and then a little wine to strengthen you. There's bread, too, and honey, if you can manage to eat.'

'My . . . teeth . . . are loose,' Julitta managed to mumble.

'No . . . food, no water. Been . . . here for . . . weeks. Thought . . . they could . . . do what they liked with you gone. Wanted . . . my money. I was foolish . . . stupid old woman. Told them I had left all to you . . . and would not . . . change my Will . . . even though . . . you had vanished.' Julitta paused, exhausted, her eyes looking pleadingly into Cassia's.

'Dear Aunt! Oh, how I have missed you! I *didn't* run away, you know – I didn't want to leave you. I was captured by pirate-slavers; they snatched me up from the Marriage Cove and took me away. You wouldn't believe the adventures I've had! I've been to Algiers, to the Barbary Coast, I've lived in pirates' houses, sailed on their ships. I spent months in the harem of the Sultan of Turkey – I was his favourite! It all seems like a dream when I talk about it now, but I am back safely. And I am to be married, dearest Aunt. We came back here to get married so that you could be at our wedding.'

'Who is . . . the man?' There was a ghost of a smile on Julitta's parched lips.

'Oh, you will like him, Aunt. He is French, a sea-captain. He saved me from the Sultan.' Later she would explain the more complicated details of her adventures. 'He has gone to report what has been happening to you so that . . .' Here Cassia paused. How could she say, 'so that your daughters will be put under arrest?' She began again. 'So that those who did this to you will be brought to justice.'

'Sneely . . . he did it,' Julitta whispered. 'Married Melody for her . . . money. Then found she was . . . not to . . . get any. Angry. Greedy . . .' The effort of talking was too much. Julitta sank back into unconsciousness.

Cassia felt that to leave her in absolute peace would be the very best thing, now that she had had some milk and a few sips of the wine. She whispered to the men to stand guard outside the doorway of Pen Castle and to tell her should they see anyone approach. Vincent seemed to be taking a long time. She wondered if he was reporting Julitta's mistreatment. In a way she would have liked to have dealt with Julitta's daughters

73

and Sneely herself. She could, quite cheerfully, crack all their heads together: her hands itched to do so. They were vermin, the lowest vermin – that they could do this to their own mother! And they had been in league with that revolting Botch – how could they have stooped so low? And all because of greed. To someone who had always put love first and foremost, it seemed the most incredible motivation.

She was bowed with guilt. All this was her fault. If she had not been away so long they would never have dared do this to Julitta, not in a million years. Her poor, poor aunt! She paced up and down the room, wringing her hands together, making no sound which might disturb her aunt. There was a little colour in the thin, drawn cheeks and Julitta seemed to be in a more natural slumber. Cassia sent up a prayer for her recovery.

Some thirty minutes later one of the men popped his head round the door to tell Cassia that Vincent was approaching the castle on horseback. Thanking the man, she went on silent feet down the stairs and out of the door to greet her lover.

'They will be brought to justice, *doucette*. I have done all that is necessary, now it is in the law's hands. Judge Benchley has been informed and he is deeply mortified to think that such a thing could happen to such a loved and respected lady.'

Cassia announced her intention of staying at Pen Castle to care for her aunt until she was strong enough to be moved back to her home. She would leave the treatment of Sneely and her cousins to Vincent and the Justices.

Once the villagers knew what had happened, knew that Julitta Morbilly was lying sick and half starved in the tower at Pen Castle, they showed what good hearts they had. Gifts arrived daily: homemade broth, fresh barley bread, milk puddings, calves' foot jelly, herbal possets and brews, milk and chickens and hams, pilchards made into every conceivable dish. Martha Tomkiss, who was never happier than with a mop or duster in her hand, arrived in the cart with two of her friends and they set to, scrubbing the tower room. The filthy old mattresses were taken out and burnt, as were the dirty, tattered rugs. Even the stone walls were scrubbed. Two of Vincent's helpers brought two soft feather mattresses and Aunt Julitta was carefully placed on these, with clean linen sheets and warm woollen blankets. Behind a pile of rubble in one corner of the room they found an old hearth with a chimney hole, and a fire was kept burning in there at all times, for the invalid had no way of regulating her body temperature while she was in such a vulnerable condition.

The most difficult task was getting Julitta to eat and drink, for she was so very weak. Tenderly, and with infinite patience, Cassia fed her spoons of calves' foot jelly and broth, or milk heated in a pan over the fire. Each night Cassia slept beside her aunt on a single mattress which the men had brought her, so that she could be on hand when Julitta needed her.

Everyone who called in from the village was shocked to see Julitta's condition, to realize that all the time they had thought her away visiting, she had been a prisoner in Pen Castle tower, being slowly starved to death, so that her son-in-law and her two unnatural daughters could inherit her fortune and Penwellyn.

If the villagers had hitherto been cautious of approaching the castle which they considered to be haunted, they did not show it now.

As the days passed and Julitta slowly grew strong enough to talk, she told Cassia everything that she had heard Sneely saying. Apparently it had been his plan to let her die in the tower. They had talked of chaining or tying her up, but had decided against it because marks might be difficult to explain away on her body. Their story was to be that she had returned home in the middle of the night, complaining of severe stomach pains, and had gone straight to bed. Next morning, so they would say, they had gone to her room to see how she was, only to find her dead. As they would all tell exactly the same tale, who would have cause to doubt them?

It had been a nefarious plan, and one which only fiends could have employed. Sneely was condemned as evil, but what most horrified everyone was the wickedness of Alicia and Elizabeth.

'They be monstrous witches!' exclaimed one of the villagers' wives, out of hearing of Julitta of course, and these sentiments were echoed by all.

Chapter Five

For six days Julitta and Cassia remained at Pen Castle. Cassia stayed by her aunt's side almost constantly, only yielding to Vincent's demands that she should catch some sleep occasionally in order to maintain both her own strength and that of her unborn child's. Martha Tomkiss and other women from Morbilly village brought them food, and cleaned the tower room for them, and the men carried up logs for the fire and water from the well for them to wash in. But mostly they were alone together, and aunt and niece found comfort and happiness in each other's company.

As Julitta's health slowly improved, she was able to tell Cassia more about the iniquitous crime which Sneely and her daughters had planned.

Sneely and Botch had captured Julitta one day when she was out riding. They had brought her to Pen Castle, locked her in the tower room and left her for a week. There had been a little bread and water left for her in the room, but that was soon finished, and quickly Julitta's strength faded – as Sneely had planned. He knew she would be unable to escape from the tower room, and he was equally aware that few locals ever ventured near the castle for fear of the superstitions in their minds. Sometimes Sneely would send Botch to replenish her meagre rations, but eventually, after months of imprisonment, Julitta's health had broken down.

'I thought I would go mad,' Julitta confessed wryly to Cassia one day. 'The only living soul I ever saw was that fearful Botch – and he seldom came more than once a week.'

'Oh, Aunt!' Cassia cried. 'How you must have suffered! And while you were locked up here Sneely was telling everyone you were away visiting relatives!'

Cassia knew, for Vincent had heard it from the Justices, that

Sneely had meantime dismissed all Julitta's loyal old servants. Their mistress, he told them, had written and ordered him to do this. Alicia and Elizabeth had soon installed themselves at Penwellyn and then their greed had increased; they wanted money. So it was that Sneely began to sell Julitta's possessions. This had been a foolish risk to take because Sneely had been obliged to explain his right to sell Julitta's things by prematurely reporting Julitta's death. Michael Polwheal would thus have been suspicious when her actual death was announced, but by then it would have been too late to help Julitta.

Cassia shivered. They had almost arrived too late: another day, another hour – who knew how much longer Julitta would have survived?

'But y'know, m'dear –' Julitta's words caught Cassia's attention. 'More than anything else at Penwellyn, I shall be glad to see my horses – Satan and his foal.'

'He was all right when I saw him,' Cassia reassured her. 'He was cropping grass in the field by the house, looking very perky and fine.'

'Oh, that is good to hear, so good,' Julitta sighed. 'Did – did you happen to notice the peacocks?'

Cassia put her hand to her mouth. 'Why no. I remember now that that was one of the things that puzzled me. I did not hear their screeching in the morning.'

'Then I fear Alicia carried out her threat. I knew that she had always hated them and the noise they made, saying that it disturbed her sleep. I heard her say that she would put paid to their squawkings once and for all. But that was just before they carried me away on the cart all bundled up at dead of night, bringing me here to Pen Castle.' Julitta's eyes filled with tears, for she was still very weak. 'Those poor birds, I wonder how they suffered? I wonder what they did to them?'

'We shall get more, Aunt,' Cassia said. 'Perhaps the next ones will breed and we shall have young.' Julitta had always been disappointed because George and Charlotte, the peacock and peahen, had never produced any offspring despite all her attentions.

It was inconvenient remaining at Pen Castle and having to have everything brought out to them, but Cassia did not wish to move her aunt before she was sufficiently strong. Julitta seemed to be recovering surprisingly well, and had only a slight stammer occasionally when she spoke, which was, she told her niece, her legacy from the stroke she had had two years before. Cassia said she was amazed and delighted at how well her aunt had got over the stroke, for when Cassia had last seen her she had been barely able to speak her niece's name.

'Determination, m'dear,' Julitta said. 'Although I thought you'd left me, eloped with that young man — and Bessie told me all about that, you know, so that's what I thought you'd done — I still felt hopeful. I thought to myself, although at the time I couldn't be sure, that once you had married and had children you would be back, and I wanted to be hale and fit when you returned with the babies. I wanted to dandle them on my knee and be a great-aunt ye'd be proud of. I didn't want you to come back and find me still lying there in bed mumbling and muttering like an old beldame.'

Cassia's eyes misted over. 'You *will* be a great-aunt, you will be. And you will not have so long to wait,' she added, with an impish grin.

'Why . . . you mean — ? Oh, my dear!' The thin, pallid cheek flushed a cheery pink, and the brown velvet eyes widened. 'Then the sooner I am up and about again the sooner we can have your wedding, m'dear. When is the babe expected?'

'In the autumn, Aunt.'

'Then likely it'll be a little love-child born under the sign of Venus. How ideal that will be for Vincent and you.'

'Love-child by temperament but not by birth, I hope, Aunt Julitta,' Cassia grinned. 'I want to be married as soon as possible. Not everyone will be as tolerant as you.'

'Versity Mackles produced her son five months after her

wedding, m'dear, and Angelica Banton had her twins only a few hours after the ceremony, so you see it's not altogether unknown. Such things do happen hereabouts.'

'Nonetheless, dearest Aunt, I do not fancy spending my honeymoon in the company of twin babies.'

'I know, I know, m'dear. Don't you fret, I'll be well before you can say jackanapes. Christmas tidings, m'gal, I've got a lot of life left in me yet and I mean to let everyone know it.' A shadow passed across her eyes. 'When I think of those two daughters of mine! Why could they not have been like other girls? Why could they not have settled down to marriage and produced grandchildren for me? Alicia had not been married more than a few months when she elected to have a separate bedroom, and 'twas not that her husband was in any way physically repulsive: indeed not, he was passably handsome. They split up, you know. Didn't tell me, thought I'd be angry, and quite right too — I was. Now Jeffrey is off somewhere in the Colonies, carving out his own fortune.'

'I was dreadfully sorry to hear about poor Melody,' Cassia said, touching her aunt's hand.

'Yes, 'twas tragic. Terribly upset we all were. A setback for me; felt as if I were ill all over again. Do you know, Alicia would not come to her funeral? Said black did not suit her, so she would not come. Heartless, cruel, selfish girl.'

'I am so sorry, Aunt.'

'I know you are, m'dear, ye've a tender heart and I love ye for it.' Julitta paused, then said, 'Your Vincent has been a sea captain for years, has he not?' Cassia nodded. 'Will he fret after the sea? I know from my own experience of the Morbillys and the Joliths how the sea takes hold of a man and dominates his soul, calling to him when he is on land.'

'But Morbillys and Joliths were born to the sea. Vincent was not. Circumstances forced him to it, Aunt. Now he wants so much to help the Reformers — as do I. We have even named the society we are starting — we are calling it The Children of Liberty. We want to free the slaves,' Cassia explained. 'It will be a great challenge and Vincent loves a challenge, whether it is on sea or land.'

'Reformers, eh? Well, a task like that should certainly fill your time, child. But it won't be straightforward. So ye'll not be staying long in Morbilly?'

Cassia took her aunt's hand. 'We are staying here until you are fit and well again, Aunt, and then we are going to find someone reliable to take care of you just for the short time we shall spend in Liverpool. Then we shall be back, do not fear.'

Julitta sighed, leaning back against the pillows. 'We have never had a Reformer in the family before,' she said thoughtfully. 'Children of Liberty, eh? Well that doesn't surprise me after what you've been through, m'dear.'

A few days later Julitta was carefully borne down the stairway of Pen Castle on a soft sling made of canvas. Then she was placed on a mattress on a covered cart, which was gently and carefully driven to Penwellyn. The entire house had been scrubbed from top to bottom by the village women, who could not do enough for Mistress Morbilly. The larder was filled with freshly baked food; and a widow, Mrs Ankers, was ensconced as housekeeper. She had said that if it was all right with Mistress Morbilly she would remain in that position. Satan had been carefully groomed, and the cart pulled to a halt within sight of the stables, one of the village men leading the horse out so that Julitta could see him before she was gently carried into the house.

Recognizing his mistress, Satan jerked his head up and down by way of greeting, finally lowering his muzzle into the cart and affectionately nuzzling Julitta, who went pink with delight.

'He has not forgotten me,' she said to Cassia, who was sitting beside her holding her hand.

'If he could talk he would be telling you how much he has missed you now,' Cassia smiled.

'And his foal? How is Satan's foal?' Julitta asked.

'As healthy as his father,' Cassia replied. 'He's out in the fields enjoying the sunshine. When you are stronger one of the men will bring him here to the house so you can look out of the window and see him.'

'That will be just marvellous,' Julitta sighed.

Mrs Ankers was waiting at the door, her face swathed in smiles. She bobbed a curtsey as the canvas sling bearing Julitta went past her, the men slowly ascending the stairway to Julitta's room.

"Tis bliss to be back in a real bed after all this time,' Julitta said as Cassia tucked her in. 'What is Mrs Ankers giving us for lunch?'

Cassia hid a smile. This was the first time her aunt had shown a proper interest in her food for some time. Normally she had a very hearty appetite indeed, and an insatiable sweet tooth. Before Cassia could reply she said, 'I hope it is not more of that chicken broth. 'Tis invalid food. What I need now is some roast beef, or a capon.'

Now Cassia could not hide her smile. 'Actually, I think we are having roast lamb.'

'Roast lamb, eh? That sounds more like it.' Julitta licked her lips. 'And iced pudding for afters? Are we having iced pudding?' There was something of the old sparkle in the brown velvet eyes.

'I will see what the cook can do.' Today the cook was Mrs Ankers, for until the local women had got a proper household organized, they were taking it in turns to do the heavier tasks. There was talk of contacting the servants who had been dismissed, for they had been faithful men and women who had been with their mistress for some time. If it was possible to trace them then it was felt that this should be done, so that they might return if they wished. Oliver, Aunt Julitta's loyal, rust-haired coachman, had gone into the tin mines at Penwith and he could be contacted reasonably easily compared to some of the others. Mrs Rowse, the one-time housekeeper, a short plump woman who had always seemed short of breath, had gone to her married daughter in Truro and rumour had it that she had accepted a post in Lady Bletchley's country house.

'I do not wish to get them into any trouble,' Aunt Julitta said. 'If they have been accepted into posts elsewhere, then they must remain loyal to their new employers. People get such a bad name chopping and changing about.'

'I feel the option should be open to them to return, Aunt Julitta. You had such a happy, well-run household, and everyone seemed so contented here. And did you not have two excellent stable-men who knew everything there was to know about horses? Were they not helping you with your plans to breed more of Satan's foals? Such knowledge would take years for a new man to learn.'

''Tis true, 'tis true. All that you say is true,' Julitta nodded her head. She smiled tremulously at her niece. 'The rest of the truth, m'dear, is that I am so happy to have you back with me again that I do not notice anyone else missing.'

Tears had sprung into Cassia's blue eyes. 'Oh, Aunt, you are a dear, and I do love you.' She dropped a kiss on Julitta's forehead. She had thought to herself, somewhat guiltily, of their plans to go to Liverpool. Before then, it would be better to have some of the old household back, so that there would be familiar and loyal faces around her aunt when she and Vincent left.

She was feeling much stronger now that she had got the first three months of her pregnancy over. The morning sickness had not lasted very long and now seemed to have gone for good. She had never felt better: her cheeks glowed, her eyes sparkled, and she felt light of spirit. But nonetheless, she was aware that Vincent was growing restive. He had no gentlemanly occupation here. Oh, he could superintend the villagers and watch over the horses to see that all was going well in the stables, and he faithfully visited Julitta every day to chat to her. He had even ridden Satan, which had certainly astonished Julitta, for no one else had ever been able to find favour with the black-coated stallion whose temper at times matched his colour.

But there was so much Vincent wanted to be doing: tracing Nathan Dash for one, and beginning The Children of Liberty movement. Slavery was flourishing in Liverpool, which was growing rich on the proceeds. That must be the reason why Nathan Dash had been drawn there. Because of that, it also seemed an eminently suitable place for the convoking of the movement which in time, Vincent hoped, would change men's minds about slavery and all its attendant evils. What a challenge it would be to start his work there!

In the past eighty years or so Liverpool's population had grown from a mere five thousand people to around fifty thousand. The aggressive French Navy had been an ever increasing threat to the southern ports and so, from the second half of the seventeenth century onwards, more and more people had made their livelihood in Liverpool. In 1715 the first dock had been opened there, an invitation for further industrial and commercial investment and expansion. Coal-mining and glass-making were also expanding at a rapid rate. Communication, which was of prime importance, had been tremendously eased by the building of new roads, development of canals, and stage-coach services, the modernization of the navigational systems on the Mersey, the Weaver, and Douglas rivers.

Wealthy local families, such as the Norrises of Speke, the Tarletons, the Williamsons and the Moores of Bank Hall, frequently invested their excess money in various commercial schemes. Trading overseas had never been at a higher peak: coal and salt and other commodities went out to Europe, the Colonies and the West Indies. With this growth had risen an urgent need for ships, and so ship-building, too, was a flourishing industry now. A majestic new Town Hall had been built in 1754, the declaration of Liverpool's success.

From what Vincent had read of the city, he believed that enough fortunes could be made from ordinary commercial and business activities to eradicate the need for trading in human flesh.

Chapter Six

Despite his restlessness, his longing to be away in pursuit of Dash, Vincent never failed to be tender and understanding with Cassia. He had spoken to the local vicar and their marriage was arranged for the end of May, in two weeks' time. The ceremony was to be at Morbilly church, and Julitta was to be taken there in a sedan chair supported by two strong Morbilly men. Sewing women and tailors were calling at Penwellyn daily, bringing swatches of material and fitting Cassia, her aunt and Vincent for their wedding finery.

Vincent was to wear splendid new black top-boots and white hose, with ivory kid breeches and frilled shirt, and a wine brocade jacket which set off his ebony hair and emerald green eyes to perfection, making Cassia fling her arms round him and kiss him soundly when she saw him in the outfit.

Julitta was torn between plum and mustard, so she finally decided on cerise silk brocade for her gown. It was to be the most ornate outfit she had worn since her own wedding, and when she first tried on the two cages, one on either hip, which were the fashionable panniers, she pronounced them bulky and uncomfortable and said that doorways would have to be widened for her.

'I think that is something of an overstatement, Aunt. Once you become accustomed to panniers you forget you are wearing them. They certainly make the waist look smaller and emphasize the bosom.'

'Bosom? I have no bosom to speak of!' Aunt Julitta exclaimed, patting her flat chest.

Mrs Hawkins, the seamstress, declared that she could soon put that to rights, if only Mistress Morbilly would give her a freer hand.

'What was that, what was that?' Julitta said. 'I can't hear

what you're saying, woman, through that mouthful of pins.'

Mrs Hawkins carefully removed the pins from her mouth and said, 'If ye gave me a freer 'and, Mistress, then I could give ye a bosom of sorts. Miracles can be wrought with a little padding and expert whaleboning.'

'Now what would the people of Morbilly think if, after seeing me all these years without a bosom, I arrived at Morbilly church with one? 'Twould take away all the attention from the bride and that would never do. No thank ye, Mrs Hawkins, I'll stay as God made me.'

Cassia giggled at the mind-image of her aunt arriving at Morbilly church with a huge padded bosom, and all the villagers turning to gape in astonishment at the sight.

Having pinned the cerise silk brocade hem for Mistress Morbilly, Mrs Hawkins turned to Cassia with a smile.

'Now, Mistress Cassia, have you decided yet which material ye are to choose?'

Cassia fingered the swatches of gauzy silk which were on her knee. 'I just love the pale lemon silk with that silver thread running through it, but then I also love the ivory lace with the pattern of lilies, and I just adore the white silk taffeta. In other words, Mrs Hawkins — no, I haven't decided yet.'

'Then why not have an underskirt of the white taffeta, Mistress, and over it a gown of the ivory lace, with a lace veil? That will go with the white satin shoes you chose last week.'

'Yes, that sounds ideal,' Cassia said. She glanced at the dainty little satin shoes which a merchant from Helston had brought her, along with other samples of his wares. They had tiny Louis heels bejewelled with diamond chippings, and diamond chippings flashed on their toes.

Julitta said bluntly, 'Imagine where we would have been if they'd starved me to death before ye got back, m'dear. Sneely had destroyed my Will, you know, the one where I made everything out to you. As soon as I was dead they would have put their plan into action and got their hands on all my money, then there would have been nothing left for ye, m'dear!' She darted a loving glance at Cassia. 'No money to buy jewelled shoes and furbelows for the wedding.'

''Tis a chastening thought, Aunt, and one which will haunt me for the rest of my days,' Cassia said.

Mrs Hawkins, whose ears were flapping, looked from the thin face of the old woman to the glowing face of the younger one. Strange how two women could be so unalike in colouring – the young mistress with her white skin, blue eyes and flame-coloured hair and the older mistress with her jet-black hair and deep brown eyes – and yet there was such a similarity between them. Mrs Hawkins could not quite pinpoint what the similarity was, she just knew that even in a crowd she could have picked them out as kin. Was it the nose? Certainly their noses were similar; the straight lines of the autocratic Morbilly nose were here roundabouts. Was it the shape of the eyes, wide and full? No, she could not come to any sensible conclusion. She decided that she would ask her husband that night.

Jim Hawkins was not given to fanciful frames of mind. He had little imagination, being a somewhat grim and taciturn man, but he was faithful and devoted, so Mrs Hawkins could forgive him for what he lacked. When she put her question to him he looked at her as if she had asked him why green goblins jumped out of the earth. Then he gulped down a mouthful of barley bread, followed by a generous swig of weak tea, and said tersely, 'Way they walk. 'Old 'emselves both the same. 'Eads too, 'old 'em the same way.'

'Why, Jim, ye're right!' exclaimed Mrs Hawkins, staring open-mouthed at her husband, seeing him in a new light after all these years.

Three days before the wedding Julitta took Cassia aside.

'M'dear, I am very conscious of the fact that ye had no mother, and I know that ye have been kind enough on many occasions to say that I have been like a mother to ye, and nothing has ever made me prouder. But at a time like this a gal needs a true mother's advice. And there again, child, I feel as if

87

ye have lived more in your short life than many of the folk round here who are three times your age.' Julitta's eyes twinkled. 'Nonetheless, I felt that I ought to have something important to tell ye before the ceremony, so I came to a decision a while ago. You know that I have made a Will in your favour — no, not the one Sneely destroyed, but a new one. Remember Lawyer Timkins's visit a while ago? Well, that was so that I could make out a fresh Will in your favour. Thinking that I would kill two birds with one stone, as the saying goes, I decided to leave something in trust for the babe when he or she arrives. Now I know that Vincent has nothing of his own at the moment but that he hopes to recoup his stolen fortune eventually, and knowing him I've no doubt he will, but I thought it would be unseemly to allow a Morbilly to be born without a penny to his or her name. So, as I say, I have put a small amount in trust for the girl or boy, whichever God decides it will be.'

'Oh, Aunt Julitta, you are a dear!' Cassia exclaimed, hugging her warmly.

''Tis all tied up, perfectly legál and unchangeable. And Master Timkins has a copy safely shut away in his vaults so that whatever happens nothing can change my wishes. Not that Sneely will be out of gaol for a very long time, but one never knows how Fate conspires against one. And those two girls of mine, well, they are strange creatures, even though I say it myself, and who knows what scheming they might get up to in the future.'

Alicia and Elizabeth, on Julitta's instructions, had been let off with a caution. Alicia had gone back to her husband; Elizabeth had gone to Europe. Botch, who had done much of the dirty work for Sneely, and delighted in it, said Julitta, had been deported for his crimes.

The wedding day dawned, fresh and silvery with sunshine. Cassia awoke alone, for something of her puritan upbringing had returned to her, causing her to think that to sleep with her lover the night before the wedding would be somehow improper. Consigning Vincent to one of the spare bedrooms, she had felt full of empathy for him. He had looked so unhappy going off to his room alone. But she had a yearning to wake up on her own on the morning of her wedding day, like a virginal young bride.

Her eyes fell first of all on the sumptuous sight of her wedding gown hanging on the wardrobe door. The sleeves and hem were of white taffeta frilled with rich cream lace, the underskirt matching; bodice and overskirt were in heavy ivory lace. On the floor beneath the gown were the dainty white satin slippers with the jewelled heels, and over a high-backed chair in the corner was spread the cream lace veil, yards and yards of it.

Giving her hair a quick brush and slipping on a peignoir, Cassia tiptoed to her aunt's room to see if she was awake yet. Normally Julitta was an early riser, and she was slowly getting back into her old routine as her strength returned.

The brown velvet eyes glowed as they alighted on Cassia.

'Now have you not stayed in bed, child? 'Tis the custom of Morbilly brides to lie abed till they are brought a dish of tea.'

Cassia clapped a hand to her mouth. 'Oh I forgot,' she said, 'and I think I can hear Mrs Hawkins on her way up now.' She turned to the door, then glanced back. 'How do you feel, Aunt? You are sure you'll be strong enough for all the excitement?'

'Try and keep me away, m'dear, just try!' exclaimed Julitta.

Cassia was lying innocently in her bed when Mrs Hawkins pushed the door open and, beaming broadly, placed a tray with tea on it beside Cassia's bed.

''Tes a day made specially for brides,' Mrs Hawkins said. 'Now I'll just take in this tea to your aunt and help her to dress.'

'Don't get her up too early, Mrs Hawkins, or she'll just be sitting around and feel tired before the wedding begins.'

'Now don't you worry about that, Mistress Cassia. I know

how to look after invalids, that be why I'm here. Nursed my own mother for nigh on fifteen years, I ded. Then, soon as she 'ad gone, what 'appened but my father fell ill, so ye see, I 'ave 'ad plenty o' experience.'

Later, when the hip-bath had been filled with steaming water, herbs and rose-oils, Cassia climbed in with a ball of rose scented soap in her hand. She had washed her hair the previous day, because Julitta had said firmly that a girl was asking for trouble washing her hair and then going out too soon afterwards. So now she only had to bathe, and that was a delight, in the foamy, delicious smelling water. She sang to herself as she lathered her body, tucking a stray curl back into its pin, and seeing in her mind's eye herself and Vincent standing before the altar in a few hours' time. Lathering her hands, she smoothed them over her stomach. There was only the very slightest of protuberances there, nothing that could be seen unless being deliberately looked for. And she was feeling so well these days that it was hard sometimes to remember that she was with child.

She knew the time was coming when she no longer dared ride, and she would regret that very much, but she had been very fortunate with her health so far. She was regularly drinking raspberry-leaf tea, as her aunt had suggested, because it was well known that this made childbirth easier. And she went for a long walk with Vincent every day across the moors, breathing deeply and revelling in the scenery, which was as beneficial to her as any medicinal tonic. Frequently they would stand together, hand in hand, in the Marriage Cove and look at one another, grinning, remembering that night two years ago when Vincent had abducted Cassia and taken her away on his pirate ship to Algiers.

She wondered what Vincent was doing at this moment. Would he have finished in his bath and be putting on his wedding suit? She imagined him pulling on his hose over shapely calves, the soft silk material of his shirt moulding against his muscular back and shoulders, the ivory kid breeches tight across his narrow hips. Then she thought of tonight, when they would be alone after the wedding feast. She hugged herself at the thought. When she had her handsome husband alone with her tonight she would tear off his clothes and cover his body with kisses, then she would rouse him with her tongue, and when he could not bear such ecstasy anymore she would climb on top of him, slide him inside her, and then smile down at him as if to say, 'Now you are my captive.'

Her blissful reverie was shattered by the arrival of Mrs Hawkins, who bustled into the room, saying, ''Tes ten o' the clock, Mistress Cassia. If ye don't hurry ye'll be late for the church.'

'Is Captain Sauvage ready yet?' Cassia wanted to know.

'He may be, and he may be not,' Mrs Hawkins said mysteriously. ''Tes not proper to think of your groom before the ceremony. Not see each other, nor think of each other, that is 'ow it should be on the wedding day.'

'That is very hard on the bride and groom, Mrs Hawkins. I'm sure we are allowed to think of one another.'

'Well, maybe just a little.' Mrs Hawkins held out a fluffy towel to wrap round Cassia as she stepped out of the bath.

When she was dry she sat at her dressing-table and pulled the pins out of her hair.

'I really should have a maid with me today, a proper lady's maid. The best ones are trained in France, you know, Mrs Hawkins. They can change a disaster into a victory in just a few moments' work, and at the moment my hair looks as if something disastrous has happened in it.' Cassia brushed and brushed at her hair. She was not going to give in and wear a wig or powder, however fashionable that might be. She had tried powdering once and had nearly choked on the powder. It had festooned her skin, got into her clothes and, so it seemed, into every nook and cranny in her room. She had spent the rest of the day sneezing and blowing her nose, and that would never do on her wedding day.

Mrs Hawkins's daughter, Ginny, had come along specially

for the day to help Cassia dress. She was a slight girl, with brown hair and brown eyes and sallow skin, unnoticeable in a crowd. She stood now by the wedding dress, running her hands delicately over the soft, exquisite material as if it were pure gold she were touching. She was thinking of Bev, her own betrothed. He was a fisherman. They had been saving up to get married for two years. Ginny was making her own wedding dress. The material was nowhere near as fabulous as this, but she would be wearing a veil which her grandfather had brought back from a far-off foreign country when he was away on one of his long trips at sea. The veil was of Spanish lace, fragile and light as gossamer. Ginny felt no envy because her wedding gown would not be as sumptuous as Mistress Cassia's. It did not occur to her to compare herself with Mistress Morbilly's niece, for the Morbillys were gentry and she was just an ordinary girl of sturdy fisherstock.

Cassia slipped on the delicate silk chemise which she would wear next to her skin, and then a flounced petticoat and stomacher, which was laced tightly at her back to draw in her waist, but not too tightly, for she did not want to harm the baby. Over this went another petticoat with more flounces, and then another, and white silk hose with ivory silk garters embroidered with pink rosettes. Next was the underskirt, and then the wedding gown itself.

'Ye look like a princess, Mistress Cassia,' Mrs Hawkins exclaimed. 'Ye'll take the Captain's breath away.'

Cassia blushed and thanked her. She was beginning to feel nervous now, which, if she thought about it, was highly illogical. It was not as if she was rushing into marriage with Vincent: they had known each other for two years, even if they had been forcibly parted for much of that time. She felt fluttery inside and light-headed; her lips kept going dry and she had to lick them; her throat felt parched. Ginny brought her a drink of water and she sipped it while sitting on the edge of the bed, careful not to crush her gown.

'Now ye stay there, Mistress Cassia, and don't crease that

beautiful material, while I go and help your aunt to dress. Then I'll be back to put on your veil for you. Come along, Ginny.'

Cassia sat on the bed, sipping the water and thinking back over the past two years. During that time she had nearly been pressed into marrying an English Lord, Leo Marchington, an eccentric, obsessive man who had terrified her; and she had spent some months in the harem of Sultan Hamid I, where she had become his favourite and he had fallen deeply in love with her. She had felt nothing for either of those men except, perhaps, pity for the lonely and introverted Sultan who had spent the first decades of his life shut up in the Princes' Cage so that he would be no danger to the then Sultan. During all her adventures she had never stopped loving Vincent; she had never stopped wanting him. She loved him passionately. She believed that she could forgive him anything, accept anything from him; she would give him all she had. She longed to hold his child in her arms, to look down at the little face which would be a cross between hers and his. In one more hour they would be man and wife, tied to each other for the rest of their lives, for better or for worse. She had no doubt that it would be for better.

Mrs Hawkins returned, interrupting her reverie.

'Are ye ready, my dear? The carriage is ready at the front door and the men are waiting with the sedan chair for your aunt.'

'My aunt feels well? She is all right?' Cassia asked.

'I haven't seen her looking so bright and breezy for many months, Mistress Cassia. Anyone would think it was *her* wedding day.'

When Julitta had been carefully borne down the stairs in a comfortable armchair and lifted into the sedan, which was padded with cushions placed at her back, and a fur rug over her knees, and Cassia was sitting in the carriage, they set off.

Vincent had left some twenty minutes earlier and would be waiting at the church. For the groom to see the bride before they reached the church was considered to be highly unlucky.

Mr and Mrs Briscoe, Julitta's oldest friends, had recently returned from visiting their son in the Colonies. They had been mortified when they learned of what had been going on in their absence. Mrs Briscoe had said that had they been in Morbilly still, Sneely would never have dared to do what he did.

Mr Briscoe was going to give Cassia away at the altar. He was an uncommunicative man who favoured dun-coloured clothes, whose boots always looked as if they had been carefully covered with polish but never been polished to a shine. He had mouse-brown hair, thin and dull like his boots, and mouse-brown eyes to match. His long narrow nose peered over thin dark red lips. Although he said very little without forceful prompting from his wife, he had shown himself to be more than delighted to assist Cassia on her wedding day.

Mrs Briscoe was the exact opposite of her husband. In fact, Cassia thought of a peacock and a peahen when she thought of the Briscoes, for he was dull and brown and unnoticeable, like a peahen, and she was showy and brash in her style of dress and never stopped talking. A smile curved Cassia's lips as she rode along in the carriage. She was thinking of Mrs Briscoe's wedding day finery. She wondered what the small, plump woman would have conjured up for today. She was apt to dress as if for a court occasion when she came visiting for tea, so heaven knows what she would don for her oldest friend's niece's wedding day.

The quaint little church came in sight. It had been built during the wave of religious enthusiasm which had swept through Cornwall in the fifteenth century, and although it was small it was elaborate. It had pillars and arches, known as arcades; delicate window tracery; a beautiful ornate marble font; impressive carving; a lofty tower up to the parapet, and carved pinnacles at its four corners. It was built of good Cornish granite. The fishermen of Morbilly paid a regular sum each year to have the spire of the church whitewashed, in order to make it more visible at sea where it acted as a landmark. And the church contained one of the rare stained-glass windows which had been left in Cornwall by the Reformation. It showed the Annunciation in glorious scarlet, deep gold, and rich purple-blue.

There was a bustle of villagers at the church's doorway, all watching eagerly, faces alight, to see the bride arrive in her carriage. Julitta by now being safely ensconced in the church and warmly tucked up, Cassia stepped down from the carriage and walked slowly into the church. A hush fell among the villagers as she walked past them. They could barely see her face because of the heavy lace veil which she had pulled down to conceal herself. Some were holding bunches of flowers: the children had their arms laden with blooms, and they were gaping up at her as if she were an angel who had dropped from heaven.

It was dim and cool inside the church, and the scent of lighted candles filled the air. Halfway down the aisle Cassia smelt the most distinct odour of musk, and a little smile tilted her lips. Although she could barely see through the veil, she knew exactly who was sitting in the seat she had just passed: Mrs Briscoe. There was silence as she completed her walk to the altar; a reverent silence.

One or two of the younger guests let out a gasp of admiration as they saw the bride. Then Mr Briscoe was handing her to Vincent, who took her hand in his and squeezed it warmly, whispering, 'Welcome, *doucette*,' to her as she took her place beside him.

A massive smile splitting his flushed red cheeks, the vicar of Morbilly church began the ceremony.

Cassia felt as though her heart was overflowing with happiness. Though her eyes were lowered, she was conscious of the May sunshine streaming through the stained-glass windows, filling the church with light. She was conscious of the man of God reciting the words of the marriage ceremony, conscious of the presence of her beloved aunt and all the good people of

Morbilly, and of Vincent standing close beside her, holding her hand. This was the public proclamation of her love for him and her commitment to him, and she could tell by the warm grip of his hand and the melting light in the emerald green eyes that he felt the same way.

When she lifted back her veil at the end of the ceremony there were tears of joy in her eyes, and she could hear someone behind her amongst the guests trying to suppress noisy sobs. It sounded suspiciously like Mrs Briscoe. She heard Julitta's voice whisper, 'God give ye both happiness,' for her aunt had pride of place at the front of the altar, and she flung her a brilliant smile before lifting her head for Vincent's kiss. His kiss seemed to last forever. Finally they broke away, glancing somewhat apologetically at the vicar, who was even redder cheeked, for he had been watching them in unabashed admiration.

The organ leapt into joyous music. Cassia and Vincent were legally man and wife.

Chapter Seven

The honeymoon passed in a blur of loving ecstasy. Days were spent talking and walking, hand in hand, and tiptoeing upstairs when the servants were busy elsewhere to make love in the privacy of their room. At night they would make love again, and sometimes they would wake in the darkness to rush into each other's arms. They had both felt a spiritual satisfaction from the wedding ceremony, although Vincent had long ago given up any claim to religion. Cassia wanted the days to go on just as they were, for ever and ever, but she knew at the back of her mind that there were important things which her husband must do soon.

'Time is slipping by, *doucette*, and all the while I think of Nathan Dash spending our money and trading in my jewels and treasures,' Vincent said one day, as they were picnicking in the Marriage Cove. 'As you know, I have written to various prominent people in Liverpool to see if I can trace him, but no one so far has come up with his name. I have had nothing but denials from the people who contacted me. No such man of that name has been or is in Liverpool, they say. It is very mysterious, and I want to get to the bottom of the mystery as soon as possible. I want to know what that villain is up to.'

'I know you do, darling, and so do I,' Cassia sighed, knowing that their blissful honeymoon must be broken. She consoled herself with the thought that they would return to Cornwall eventually, that they would be together again here with her aunt. If they left now they could be back before she became ungainly with the baby, so she hoped.

Vincent seemed to follow her thoughts. '*Doucette*, I do not want to think of you being flung about in a coach on the public roads when the baby is nearly due.'

'I do not relish that either, my darling,' she grimaced. 'Yes, you are right, we must begin to prepare.'

'I feel that I must ask you once more if you would not prefer to remain here in peace with your aunt?' Vincent said gently.

'*No*, emphatically not!' Cassia declared. 'There is no way that you are going to leave me behind again *ever*. I have as much right to go with you as you have to go. We are man and wife now and we must not be separated. That, of course, is not the whole reason: I love you, Vincent, and I don't want to be left on my own without you. I don't want to think of you in possible danger and alone somewhere in a strange city without me. My worries as I thought about you miles away would do me far more harm than being with you, and that's an end to it,' she finished firmly.

Vincent could not help but smile. 'Sweetheart, with you beside me I could take on a whole band of Nathan Dashes,' he teased, at which Cassia shuddered.

'The very thought of more than one of that villain is too much for me to bear,' she said. 'I wonder why no one has heard of him in Liverpool? Surely his name should have come up somewhere? If he is trading or shipping or becoming involved in slavery again, his name should have become known to *somebody*.'

'I agree. It makes me wonder exactly what he is up to, and naturally I cannot wait to find out. Your aunt grows stronger every day and Mr and Mrs Briscoe are here to look after her now. Things are as they used to be in the household. I do not see any reason why we should not leave fairly soon.'

'As you say, Vincent. It is true that I will be pleased to have some money back again. I have not liked being the poor relation, although Aunt Julitta has been so kind.'

'Your father did send you a wedding gift.'

'Yes, and that was kind of him — though I am pleased in a way he did not come for the wedding. It would have made the ceremony more stilted — I would have felt embarrassed with him there, with his fierce eyes always staring at me disapprovingly. But I feel we should not touch much of that money until we know exactly how our fortunes stand. It would be foolish to spend it all, then to find out that we had no more forthcoming.'

'If the worst came to the worst and we could not trace Dash, you know that I would not sit around here twiddling my fingers, and spending your aunt's money. I would find work at once, and I would hope to support us all.'

'Oh, Vincent, you are a dear!' Cassia flung her arms round him and squeezed him. 'How very lucky I am!'

Julitta took the news tolerably well. She had recognized long ago the restlessness in Vincent's nature, his longing to be off after the villain who had stolen his gold, and she wished him all good fortune.

'I will write regularly, dear Aunt Julitta,' promised Cassia. 'Do not fear that I shall keep you waiting for letters. I will let you know everything that happens to us, and I am sure that we shall be back very soon.'

'Take care, Cassia m'dear. Look after that baby, get plenty of rest, and no horse-riding, now. And if ye have to go on a bumpy, rutted track on a coach, sit on plenty of cushions and pad yourself at the back with cushions and a rug over your knees. And don't forget thé raspberry-leaf tea every day without fail.'

'I won't forget,' Cassia smiled.

'You take care of her, Vincent, for if anything happens to her you'll have me to answer to.' Julitta sounded stern, but her eyes were twinkling. She had every trust in Vincent Sauvage, and thought him a splendid man.

They were packed and prepared in a very short time, and the carriage was ready to take them to the main coaching stop at Truro. They could have joined the coach earlier, but they had decided that it would be better to ride in their own because of Cassia's condition. She could relax in privacy with Vincent for the first leg of the journey which, even if all went smoothly, would take them well over a week. They planned to stop each night at a coaching inn and rest, and break their journey for two days or so whenever possible.

One of their longer stops was at Ludlow. They visited the castle, where those star-crossed lovers, Katherine of Aragon and Prince Arthur, had spent the six brief months of their married life. Nestling in a lush green valley, the castle was like a fairytale palace, and Cassia could imagine the petite Spanish princess with her flowing auburn hair and dark blue eyes, her adoring prince beside her, as they were serenaded by Welsh minstrels.

Shrewsbury was another attractive place where they broke their journey; it had been recommended to them by one of the coach-drivers. But it was Chester which totally captivated them. They shopped in the Rows, the fifteenth-century wooden arcades where one could visit the shops and stay free from the rain. They wandered through the Cathedral with its haunting atmosphere and beautiful red stone, and they saw the grave of Hugh Lupus, who had been interred here by his nephew Randle I, who had built the Chapter House. It had been not so long ago, in 1724, that the Earl Palatine's remains had been discovered there in a stone coffin, on which was engraven a wolf's head, representing his name, *Lupus* – wolf.

They walked on the city walls and stood on the Phoenix Tower, where Charles I had watched one of the battles of the Civil War, Rowton Moor. On being told something of the history of Chester by a helpful guide, Cassia was incensed to hear of what had happened on the death of the seventh Earl of Chester. Believing it to be improvident that the Earl's daughter should possess Chester, where the English army was preparing for the invasion of Wales, the King had said that he 'cared not to parcel out so great an inheritance to distaffs' and with that he had given Chester to his soldier son, Prince Edward, the future Edward I.

Pleased by the lively reception which Cassia and Vincent had given to his recitation of that tale, the guide told them one of his favourite stories.

In the year 1558, he told them, the Dean of St Paul's was sent by Queen Mary to Ireland, where it was intended that he should procure the oppression of the many Protestants in the north. The Dean stopped at Chester on his way, staying at the Blue Posts Inn, and there he was visited by the Mayor. Being a garrulous man, he told the Mayor what he was about, showing him the leather box in which he was carrying his orders from the Queen, and saying to the Mayor, 'I have that within this box that will lash the heretics of Ireland.'

'But,' said the guide with a sly smile, 'there was an Irish lady at the inn, and she overheard the Dean's words. She grew afraid, for her brother was a Protestant in Ireland, and secretly she managed to look inside the Dean's leather box. When she found the fateful royal commands that it contained, she resolved to act. Removing the Royal Commission from the box, she replaced it with a pack of cards, with the Knave of Clubs uppermost.'

The guide paused to chuckle, knowing that his audience was by now anxious to hear the end of the story.

'And then what happened?' Cassia pressed him.

'Well,' he continued, 'it was a cold December when the Dean arrived in Ireland, there to be greeted by the Lord Deputy Fitzwalter and the Privy Council. Reverently explaining what he was about, he gave the box to the Lord Deputy, who opened it and there –' the guide paused to chuckle again, his stomach heaving, 'there inside it was none other than the Knave of Clubs.

'Never was a man's face more stricken than was that Dean's. "The Commission has been stolen!" he cried. With great presence of mind, the Lord Deputy said, "Then you have nothing to do but to return to London and get it renewed. Meantime, let us shuffle the cards."'

Vincent and Cassia looked at each other and laughed out loud. 'And did they spend the rest of the winter playing cards and waiting for the new Commission?' Vincent wanted to know.

The guide guffawed. 'Well, sir, very nearly. The weather being bad, it delayed matters. And then, before they knew what had happened, Queen Mary was dead, and thus thousands of lives were saved by the wit of the mistress of the Blue Posts Inn here in Chester. And when the next Queen, Elizabeth, came to the throne, she gave that lady a pension of forty pounds a year.'

'Well done,' said Vincent.

Next, they saw God's Provident House, which was a memorial to the plague of 1662, gazing up at the carving on the old oak front, which said 'God's providence is my inheritance'. And they visited Bishop Lloyd's House in Watergate Row, with its sculptured wooden facade showing groups from the Scriptures, from the Garden of Eden to the Crucifixion.

The following day they went to look at the Water Tower at the north-west angle of the city walls, their guide telling them that it had been built in 1332 by a mason who had been paid one hundred pounds for his work. This Tower had been badly damaged during the Great Siege of 1645 when the Parliamentarians had battled to take Chester, which had remained staunchly loyal to the King.

Afterwards, they did more shopping and took refreshment at the Old King's Head in Bridge Street. Then they went back to their room at the coaching inn and fell into bed exhausted.

They had both been captivated by the pretty little city and by its friendly people. It was truly a city for lovers, with the picturesque River Dee winding its way along the lower part of the city and the red stone walls which had kept so many invaders out. It was a city of vivid and colourful history as well as romance, and when Cassia pulled Vincent's arms tightly round her waist and began to kiss him she was thinking of all the beauty they had seen together in the past two days.

'Shall we stay longer in Chester on our way back?' Vincent asked her.

'Oh yes, darling. I would love to stay here and really explore the whole city. We've had such a happy two days here, like a second honeymoon.'

'A second honeymoon? But we have barely finished our first honeymoon yet, *doucette*.' Vincent curved his palms beneath her chin, gently lifting her face to look at him.

'But if we have a perpetual first honeymoon, darling, then we cannot have a second, a third or a fourth, can we?' Cassia teased. She cuddled against him, revelling in the feel of his clean, hard flesh, knowing that he made every other man around seem unmanly by comparison. She ran her fingers through his silky black hair, gently caressing his eyelids. He grasped her fingers and rained kisses on them, then slid his hands down to her breasts.

'They are fuller now you are with child,' he said appreciatively.

'So you did not like them before, they were too small for you?' Cassia pouted.

'Certainly not,' he grinned. 'They feel so firm, they taste like honey.' To illustrate his point, he lowered his head and began to nip at her flesh very gently with his teeth, his tongue darting out to caress her nipples. Immediately she sighed, arching her body against his, pulling him closer to her. They were soon oblivious to everything but one another. They did not hear the birds' song outside the windows, the shutters of which they had pulled closed for privacy. Nor did they hear the bustle of the people outside and the passing carts and horses. They were shut out from the city sights and sounds.

'*Doucette*,' Vincent whispered, sliding his hands down Cassia's waist and over the rise of her shapely hips. She sighed again, opening her thighs to his touch, clinging to him as his hand curved against her body to press gently, exploringly.

'You are soft and warm, like a kitten,' he murmured in her ear as his fingers gently searched then found what they were looking for, and paused before continuing to move. Cassia gave a little whispered moan as a thrill swept through her body, taking control of her sensibilities.

'Vincent,' she whispered, her voice sounding hoarse. 'Oh, Vincent!' Then her hands slid down his body to hold him as he was holding her. There was no delay, he was ready and waiting for her. In a few sweet seconds they were one, forged together as if welded into one being, body, heart and soul.

'My dove, my heart,' Vincent whispered. 'You are everything to me. The sun and the stars.'

'And you to me, my beloved,' Cassia responded readily, rejoicing at the sensation of him deep within her, where she knew, irrefutably, he belonged.

Next morning they breakfasted on succulent roast kidneys, scrambled eggs, toast with quince marmalade, and fragrant Indian tea to drink, before the last leg of their journey, which would take them to Liverpool. They had not booked rooms in advance, for they decided they would select the place which most appealed to them and stay there. Whatever happened, Cassia knew that she would not forget Chester, with its Rows and Groves and the serpentine Dee against which it nestled.

The distance from Chester would be comparatively short after the earlier part of their journey, for there were now only about thirty-five miles to go. They had taken a private coach for this last part of the journey, and they were eagerly pointing out objects of interest and freely discussing all the vistas. Cassia was a little tentative; she thought the thick forests looked the sort of scenery where brigands might lurk, for there were so many places of concealment. Vincent just grinned at her words.

'Be thankful you're not travelling in winter or autumn, *doucette*. Without turnpikes the holes and ruts in the road would be filled with mud and we would not see them until it was too late.' As he spoke, the carriage swerved to avoid a particularly deep pit in the road, Cassia clinging onto her seat.

'Liverpool being such an important city, I would have

thought there were turnpikes leading in all directions,' she said.

'These things are left to the local people, I imagine, and if they neglect their duties or are ignorant of how to make good the roads, it is we travellers who suffer.'

'Perhaps we should add reforming the roads to our list of future activities, darling,' she teased.

'I have a suspicion we might find more supporters if we did that,' Vincent grinned.

'And we could make our rallying call "Take the new road to freedom"!'

'It is good to see you able to joke about such things, *doucette*, for truth to tell, at times I have felt that you would never be able to speak lightly of anything connected with your past experiences.'

'Oh, Vincent, you are still feeling guilty. You should not, you know. It was Fate, we have both agreed that. A stronger hand than ours had a part in our destiny. Just think, what would we have been doing if we had not met as we did? You would still be a pirate-slaver and, heaven forbid the thought, I might have been married to Charles Billings, the mother of his children! I can imagine what life with him would have been like: an eternal imprisonment, with him only biding his time until I was twenty-one so that he could get his hands on my inheritance! It does not take very much to guess that he would have spent it all within a very short time.'

'But you would not have had to leave your aunt . . .'

'But I *would* have had to lose my virtue to Charles Billings and I cannot think of anything more detestable now! Oh, he was my first love I know, but what I felt for him was a mere shadow compared to what I feel for you, Vincent.'

'I am glad to hear it,' he said kissing her hand.

The coach lurched again, flinging them together.

'The road seems to be getting worse instead of better the nearer we get to the city.' Cassia leaned out of the window. 'I can see why. Look at all those carriages and carts, all those packhorses carrying merchandise towards Liverpool. Look, that cart is laden with copper pans and kettles. I am sure those packhorses are carrying coal. Yes, they are, and that one is laden with cloth.'

'Liverpool has been built on trade, *doucette*. Salts, clocks and watches, hats, shoes, stockings, crockery, candles, textiles, even nails and hinges and locks leave here in the holds of merchant ships daily.'

'Where do they go?'

'I am told that they work what is called the Triangular Trade: that is, they set sail for the west coast of Africa, where they sell or trade their Merseyside cargo for slaves which they take to the West Indies to sell in Jamaica or Barbados. There they load up with sugar, tobacco or molasses and come back to Merseyside. At each stage of the triangle they make a substantial profit. It is much more remunerative than the direct Merseyside–Caribbean route.'

'I see. So slaves are exchanged for provisions and kitchen utensils and cloth? Human flesh is traded for everyday items like those.' Cassia's voice was sad. She was thinking of herself, shut in the noisome hold of Nathan Dash's ship on its way to Constantinople to be sold to the Sultan. She and the other women with her had been half-starved, left in their own filth, treated with contempt. One of them had bled to death in childbirth with outside help refused them. Nobody cared, nobody seemed to see the stupidity of half-starving, mistreating and neglecting women whom they wished to sell for a good price when they got to their destination. She imagined that the slaves bought and sold on the Triangular Trade were treated in a similar way to that. She was yet to find out the real truth, the full, horrifying, sickening details of the trade in 'black gold'.

After having booked a room for the night at the Golden Lion in Liverpool's Dale Street, they decided to spend the afternoon looking at the city sights. It was a crowded, bustling town, in many ways like London. The narrow cobbled streets were packed with wagons and carts, horses and riders, men and women on foot, everyone looking as if they were in a great hurry. There were many smart and elegant houses, tall, and built in brick and stone, just as there were in London. Cassia was surprised to see few beggars, but indeed the people seemed extremely well turned-out and many were highly fashionable.

Vincent showed particular interest in the Liverpool docks, and when they stopped at an inn for refreshment, he struck up a conversation with two men seated near to them. From the men they learnt that Liverpool's docks and the slave trade were dependent one upon the other. The Old Dock on Liverpool's north shore had been built early in the century after a wild storm had wrecked most of the ships anchored in the Mersey, and that had marked the birth of the now-thriving ship-building industry. Salthouse Dock had been added in 1753, and a third, George's Dock, had opened only a few years back, in 1771.

Liverpool's docks, boasted the men, were far superior to those of London, and this was in a large part because the slave trade flourished in Liverpool. Were it not for the slave trade, they said, Liverpool would probably still be but a minor port, harbouring a small number of ships carrying salt, textiles and household wares as their main exports to be traded for rum, raw cotton, molasses and tobacco. There would be no rich Triangular Trade, no expanding ship-building industry, no prosperity for the people of Liverpool.

'Well,' said Cassia as they bade the men farewell and left the inn. 'It looks as if we were right to come here to begin our mission against slavery.'

'Yes,' Vincent agreed thoughtfully. 'We have a challenge here, *doucette*. Slavery is the very foundation of this city's prosperity and we shall face grim opposition, of that I am sure.' He paused. 'But more than that, I am now convinced that this is where Nathan Dash will have come. Slaving, ships and great wealth — Liverpool has everything to attract a greedy man.'

'Oh, Vincent! Just think — he may be anywhere in the city! He may be in that house, or round this corner!' Cassia stopped, as though expecting to see the man's vicious face leering at her.

'Liverpool is a big place,' Vincent grinned, taking her arm. 'Come, shall we explore further?'

They began to walk back into the city. On their way they passed the Tower of Liverpool, glancing up at the red sandstone building with its Norman-style crenellations. It was now used as a gaol, and inside the quadrangle the prisoners took their exercise.

Everywhere they walked they saw sailors, and they were both struck by the preponderance of public-houses. During their days ashore the sailors would spend all their money in amusing themselves, searching out prostitutes, boar-baiting, going to cockfights and dog fights and matches between bare-fisted pugilists. But most of all they drank, for there was an unending supply of cheap rum.

Cassia noticed that the number of sailors were increasing, that the area through which they were walking was growing dingier. Vincent had noticed, too. When they saw a gaggle of heavily-painted women on the street corner, one of whom, ignoring Cassia, thrust out her hips provocatively at Vincent, they knew it was time to turn and retrace their steps. And this they did.

They passed a stall selling water in bottles, and stopped to read the sign. *'Liverpool Spa Water,'* it said, *'cures Headaches, Ricketts, Weak Eyesight, loss of Appetite, nerve Disorders, lowness of the Spirits. Specially Favoured for diseases of the Eye.'*

'But, will ye buy?' urged the eager little woman who was sitting behind the stall. She had a round, flattish face and dark brown eyes, and was swathed in shawls despite the heat of the day.

Cassia and Vincent smiled, but did not respond. Walking on, they passed yet another liquor house, with a sign outside saying in large black letters, *'Drunk for one penny, blind drunk for twopence.'* It was time to return to Dale Street, for they were both hungry.

And then they heard hysterical screams, the sound of dogs snarling, the loud splash of water.

'Someone's in trouble!' Cassia cried as they both hurried towards the water's edge.

Two children, neither older than ten, were in the Mersey, having been pursued there by a pack of mad dogs which were foaming at the mouth. One of the dogs had plunged into the water with the children and was snapping at their arms as they struggled to remain afloat. It rapidly became obvious that neither could swim.

Vincent did not hesitate. Tearing off his jacket and boots, he dived into the Mersey, making straight for the dog which was about to bite one of the children's arms. He gripped the dog, which was frothing at the mouth, squeezing its throat until its struggles ceased and it sank down beneath the surface of the water. Then, he turned to assist the two children. One had disappeared beneath the surface, the other was white and shocked, but still afloat.

Instantly, Vincent dived out of sight, in search of the drowning girl. Cassia watched in terror as long seconds passed and he did not reappear. Then he leapt back into view but without the child. Taking a deep gulp of air, he dived again. This time, he had the child tucked beneath his arm. Her face was white and still. She is dead, thought Cassia, tears in her eyes. Vincent placed the girl on the edge of the quay where Cassia rushed to attend to her, and then he went back to retrieve the little boy.

Out of the corner of her eye Cassia watched what was happening as she massaged the wrists of the unconscious girl and pressed against her back to help her to breathe. The boy was struggling, panicking wildly, and Vincent had to clamp his arms tightly round the child to enable him to lift him to safety. Then he climbed onto the quay and at once began to move the girl's arms up and down repeatedly to make her vomit the river water. It seemed an age before she responded, and then finally she coughed and water gushed out of her mouth, and Cassia knew that she was going to be all right.

Meanwhile, the mad dogs had been beaten off by passers-by with sticks, and someone had fetched the children's mother. She was hysterical and fell to her knees weeping loudly at what she saw.

'Oh my children, my beloved children!' she wailed, plunging her face in her hands and sobbing.

'They are both well. My husband saved their lives,' Cassia said proudly. 'Mad dogs chased them into the water – I imagine they had no choice but to jump.'

'Oh, sir! Oh, mistress, how can I ever thank you? Surely they would both have drowned but for you. Oh, sir, what can I do by way of repayment?' The woman took the girl into her arms and rocked her back and forth.

'We wish no payment, mistress.' Vincent gave the woman a warm smile. He pulled on his boots and jacket, and then he and Cassia continued on their way to Dale Street.

The inn was peaceful again after the departure of the Manchester coach which had just left, the innkeeper greeting them jovially but looking askance at Vincent's drenched appearance. Hastily, Cassia explained what had happened, and, after Vincent had changed into dry clothes, they headed for the dining area of the inn where the innkeeper bade them be seated while they selected their meal. They decided on mutton pie with fresh vegetables, spiced apple tart, and Cheshire cheese, which had a very pale colour, almost white, and was crumbly and possessed a delicate but pronounced flavour. They had tasted it in Chester and enjoyed it very much. While they were eating, they perused some of the posters pinned to the wall nearby; all were coaching advertisements.

One said:

> ### WATER STREET, LIVERPOOL.
> *The London Royal Mail Coach, every evening at half-past nine o'clock in Thirty Hours, to the Swan with Two Necks, Lad Lane, London, passing through Prescot, Warrington, Knutsford, Newcastle, Lichfield, Coventry, Daventry, Stony Stratford, Dunstable, St Albans, Barnet, and to London.*

Another said:

> ### THE MANCHESTER, LEEDS AND YORK ROYAL MAIL.
> *Every morning at three o'clock, passing through Prescot, Warrington, Manchester, Rochdale, Halifax, Bradford, Leeds, Tadcaster and York.*

There were posters, too, for the London Commercial Post Coach, which left every day at three o'clock, taking forty hours to reach the 'Swan with Two Necks' in London. Then there was the Birmingham to Plymouth Post Coach, which left every day at three o'clock, and the Preston to Carlisle coach, which departed every morning at seven o'clock, and every afternoon there was a coach to Manchester at two o'clock, which arrived six hours later to connect with coaches for Buxton, Sheffield, Derby and Leeds . . .

'A veritable hubbub of activity,' Vincent commented. 'And if there is not a coach to take you there, there will be a ship. Liverpool has certainly got itself well organized.'

'Except for keeping its mad dogs under control!' Cassia said wryly. 'I wonder where Nathan Dash is hiding out?'

'Wherever he is it will not take me long to find him, *doucette*. Remember how quickly I found that crewman of his in Algiers? Sailors talk, they cannot help it: they drink too much and the sight of a gleaming coin always loosens their tongue. I can now begin making my own enquiries in person. I feel quite confident that when I have asked some questions here and there I will find out where the man is.' Vincent smiled grimly.

'It should be easy to trace him if he has a ship registered here,' suggested Cassia.

'To register a ship he would have to have turned honest. Can you see him doing that, my love? Only genuine merchants and traders are allowed to register in the port. I wonder . . .'

'What do you wonder, darling?'

'The war with France affected the slave trade and merchant shipping; the docks lay idle. I believe it was a very anxious time for Liverpool.'

'There is no sign of idleness now,' Cassia said, looking puzzled.

'No, things have picked up. But as well as that, men started turning their ships to other uses when they could not get the slaves: in other words, my love, they became privateers. In such times as those, men who are far from honest can flourish. They prey on those who are fighting against their countries and, unfortunately, also upon their *own* ships. Now would not such activities appeal immensely to Nathan Dash? He would have a semblance of respectability, and yet he would be able to behave in his accustomed evil fashion. Another alternative would be that he had hired out his ships to merchants: some men do this, of course, their entire business being the loan of ships.'

'He is a monster.' Cassia fingered the stem of her wine glass thoughtfully. 'But let's not talk about him now.'

'I cannot prevent myself from thinking about him,' Vincent replied. 'I cannot tolerate the thought that he may be somewhere close by, spending my money, and here am I unable to do anything about it . . .'

'But we only arrived here this morning,' Cassia said sensibly.

'*Ma mignonne . . .*' Vincent reached across the table and took her hand. 'You are not only beautiful — you are also wise!'

The next day Vincent had an appointment to keep with one Paul Peacock. Peacock was a merchant of Liverpool to whom Vincent had written earlier regarding the whereabouts of Nathan Dash. He had also asked Peacock a number of other questions about the city and what he thought was the potential for a Slave Reform Society. He had not asked Peacock this until they had corresponded a number of times, because he did not want to alienate somebody who was making a living out of slavery, thus alerting others in Liverpool before he even arrived. He had questioned Peacock carefully regarding the articles in which he traded, and only when he had satisfied himself that they did not include flesh, nor ever would, had he put his final query to him. Surprisingly, Peacock had seemed highly amenable to the idea. His sister, Joanna, did many works for charity, he said, and she frequently expounded on the very same precepts. Then, to Vincent's surprise, he had revealed that he himself had once dealt in black gold, but now no longer. He promised to help Vincent in every way possible with his reform work.

With Vincent gone, Cassia decided to look through her clothes. She missed having the company of a maid. Not for the first time she thought of Bessie, the lively little Cockney girl who had been her servant in London and who had come to Cornwall with her. Bessie had been dismissed by Sneely, and had probably returned to London. Cassia often missed her cheery, robust presence. Perhaps she would find a Liverpool girl to be her maid? They seemed a sturdy race and not frightened of work, from what she had seen and heard.

After a time, when she had finished pottering round the room, she took a seat by the window, looking out on the busy street which was never empty of carriages or coaches of one kind or another, and people either alighting or stepping into them, ostlers tending to horses, servants fetching or carrying luggage. From here, coaches threaded their way all over

England in a vast tapestry, as she had seen from the posters downstairs. It seemed, compared with her memories of London, an even busier, more industrious place, but possibly that was just her first impression. No doubt there would be quieter residential areas where the wealthy lived. She was looking forward to seeing the rest of the city.

She had already realized that her wardrobe was somewhat outdated. What was all very well in Cornwall certainly would not do here if she wished to be associating with the well-bred people whom Vincent wished to win over to their Society. Julitta had given her a generous gift of money as they were leaving, so she had enough to buy herself some new gowns. She would need to find the name of a good dressmaker and perhaps a store where she could buy suitable material.

Loud shouts in the street below made her peer out curiously. A carriage wheel had narrowly missed a lady's pet dog as she was walking across the street. The dog was yelping and screaming and the lady looked as if she were about to faint, but a handsome young gentleman had appeared and was taking control of the situation. Soon the lady was recovering from the swoon and blushing beneath the admiring glances of the gentleman, while the little dog, seeing that his yelps were being ignored, sulked at her feet.

Cassia smiled to herself, glad that the scene had not ended in mishap.

When Vincent returned later that afternoon, he was looking very pleased with himself, and could not wait to tell Cassia all that had happened. He told her, too, that they had been invited to the Peacocks' home, for Paul Peacock, having heard that they were staying at an inn, had insisted on inviting them both to stay with him for as long as they felt it to be necessary.

'You will like his sister, *doucette*, she is a very solid, down-to-earth lady. She speaks out and says what is in her mind, and she has some very firm views on the slave trade with which I know you will agree.'

'And the younger brother — what was his name — Andrew?'

'Yes — Andrew,' Vincent said slowly. 'At first I did not think he was going to take an active part in the proceedings. He was merely polite, bidding me greeting, offering me wine, and sitting at the far side of the hearth with a book on his knee, and a hound by his feet. He listened to us speaking for some time and then he looked up.'

'And what did he say?' Cassia demanded.

'He said he was delighted that somebody was at last going to do something positive to help the slaves. He said that he had no grudge against men earning their fortunes, but that the mere thought of slavery totally nauseated him. He said that when he had learned there were twenty thousand black slaves in London alone, he felt ill for days.'

'A man of true sensitivity,' Cassia said happily. 'And what of Paul Peacock and his one-time trade in human flesh?'

'He is reluctant to speak of it, which is understandable. The trade was inherited from his father and he merely carried it on, without thinking, until one day he visited one of his ships unexpectedly.'

'Did he give details?'

'No. But I gather it was the sort of thing one would not speak about willingly in front of ladies — or even men. Perhaps he will tell me another time. I gather that whatever it was, he found the same conditions on each of his other ships, and that was when he abandoned slavery. Some very disturbing and bestial happenings have taken place on slave-ships, *doucette*. I do not think that even I know the half of it yet, but the more I do find out, the more I am determined to work for The Children of Liberty.'

'Yes, I think we shall have to be fully informed, however unpleasant that will prove to be. I can hardly seek to convert ladies if I am ignorant on the subject. Oh, I can speak from my own experiences as a slave of course, but that would not necessarily apply to the Liverpool trade.'

'I shall get you some books tomorrow. In fact, Paul Peacock has an extensive library; he said I can borrow any books I might need. We're invited to their house for lunch in the morning.'

'Oh, Vincent, is it a very fashionable house? Is Joanna Peacock a modish lady? I fear the gowns which I thought extremely stylish two years ago are now hopelessly out of vogue.'

'I expect Joanna Peacock can give you the name of a good sewing-woman. I would not say that she was highly fashionable. In fact, her gown looked very similar to the one you are wearing now.'

'Oh well, that is not too bad, then. Did she seem the sort of lady who would place great importance on one's attire?'

'No, I would have thought that an animal-lover would have a far greater chance with her than a follower of fashion.'

'So she loves animals? Does she have dogs?'

'Five of the most lively hounds you have ever seen, and she spoke of horses, too. I believe she follows the hunt.'

'Well, I hope that subject does not arise,' Cassia said tartly, 'because if so I would have to speak my mind about so-called adults who ride in pursuit of a poor little fox with the intention of killing it as brutally as possible.'

'Yes, that had not occurred to me. She speaks against slavery with such conviction and talks of the misery of human beings in shackles, yet in the same breath she spoke of the delight of the hunt. I know how you love wildlife, *doucette*, so let us hope the subject does not arise, for it would be unwise to alienate our first allies in the city.'

'I shall be circumspect — never fear, darling. Although I have strong views about people who go hunting, I have equally strong views about people who are rude to those who have shown them hospitality.' She tucked her arm through Vincent's. 'Which gown do you think I should wear tomorrow? Your favourite blue one, or the one with rosebuds? That one is probably better, it is that little bit more suitable for city wear.'

'Yes, the pink one. I like the way the panniers are decorated with flowers; they look real from a distance.'

'Very well then, the pink one it is. I shall need to buy some pink ribbon for my hair, though, and I really need a new sash for the gown.' She thought of the new mode in coiffures. When she had lived in London, hair styles had been so fantastic that specially constructed sedan chairs had had to be made so that ladies could sit inside them without bending forwards, but all that had changed while Cassia had been spending her long months on the Barbary Coast and in Constantinople. A Parisian milliner had invented a much lower headdress, intended originally to be worn at theatres so that people could see the stage better, and now everyone wanted to wear the new *Mignonne*, as it was called, which was selling in Paris for the sum of six to nine *livres*. As for the panniers with extended skirts on either side, on wide hoops, these had increased and become flatter, necessitating in some cases a sideways entry through doors. Necklines were lower, but a fichu was worn now, a white triangular scarf of some delicate material. Decoration on gowns had become very elaborate, embroidery, lace and garlands everywhere to be seen. Hats were also large and elaborate, and embellished extravagantly with flowers, silk roses, feathers and bows.

Cassia could not wait to go on a buying spree. The desire to purchase the styles she loved was intoxicating. During her months in the harem she had been forced to wear the Turkish style of clothes: gauzy trousers gathered at the ankles, called *shalwar*; jewel-encrusted caftans; *entari*, a gown which left the breasts naked; or a *yelek*, a bolero sewn with silks and buttoned just below the breasts; and, on her head, a *fotaza*, the pert little harem cap like a pillbox with a long tassle swinging from its centre. It had not been easy to stop the pillbox from sliding off, and the effort of trying to keep it on had frequently given her a stiff neck. What was more, she had been heavily painted with black kohl and her palms and feet had been painted with henna to make them a terracotta colour. To someone like Cassia with very definite views and preferences regarding clothes and jewels, the enforced wearing of harem dress, even if it had been exquisite and sumptuous, was an interference with her personal liberty, which never failed to irritate her. She knew that she would feel differently about wearing such beautiful robes if it were of her own choice and if she were free, as she was now. But to be imprisoned in the harem, to be painted and hennaed, and force-fed sugared foods and sherberts to increase her weight, had been intolerable.

After supper that evening they sat together looking out of the window on Dale Street. It was dark now, the only lighting in the streets being that of the occasional linkman illuminating the way for his master. The links were stiff lengths of tarred rope, thick as an arm, and an inadequate method of lighting the darkness. However, they were the only means apart from the occasional guttering oil lamp. They were smelly and smoky and a marvellous enticement for footpads who would leap out of the shadows and divest their victims of purses before they knew what had hit them.

Night drew in, and Cassia and Vincent remained sitting close to each other, holding hands, looking into each other's eyes, then down at the street and back again, until an increasing urgency prompted them to make ready for bed.

When they lay in each other's arms, Vincent kissed Cassia very tenderly, coiling his fingers in her hair and looking down at her adoringly.

'I am glad you came with me, *doucette*,' he said huskily, before their kisses became more passionate and they no longer had the need for words.

Later, dreamily, they began to discuss their plans.

'Peacock is going to assist me in my investigations. He has men who are going to be put on Dash's trail,' Vincent said.

'As long as you make sure that you are safe, darling. You cannot blame me for feeling fearful. Do not forget, sweetheart, how I saw you left for dead on the floor of that cabin after Dash had finished with you. You were lying there covered in blood and I thought that you had been murdered. I can never forget that sight: for the rest of my life it will haunt me. All that blood, and your deathly white face. Then being carried off by Dash and all those long, long months in the hold of his ship and in the harem, thinking that you were dead, that I would never see you again. That has been branded on my memory. Possibly, in time, I will relax more and feel happier when you are out of my sight for any length of time, but, for the moment, darling, I ask your tolerance. Please try to understand how I feel!' Cassia ran her finger down Vincent's cheek, looking deep into his emerald eyes.

'Forgive me if I sound restive, *doucette.* I want to be out searching for Dash, I want to be converting people to liberating the slaves.'

'We must compromise, my love. We must agree to tolerate each other's foibles. We have been through so much together, so very much. Nothing must part us now, nor drive a wedge between us. We must agree that in some cases we must disagree. Is that agreed?' she grinned.

Vincent laughed. 'Agreed, *doucette.*' Then he took her in his arms again and soon his kisses were obliterating every thought except the ecstasy of his naked body against hers, his hard muscular form against her soft white flesh.

'*Chérie,*' he whispered, 'how could you ever think that I would want to leave you for more than a few brief hours? Every minute we are apart is like an hour, stretching on and on, and all I do is long to be back with you, to see you smile with happiness. There is nothing else in the whole universe worth half as much as your presence to me. When I was Jasmina's prisoner the only thing which kept me alive was the thought of you, of finding you again. I dreamt of you at night, I thought of you by day. I knew all the time that my only hope of happiness, of salvation, was to find you again. I felt as if I had stepped into a vortex, a black, grim, hollow place which made my footsteps drag and my heart a leaden weight inside my breast. To be separated from you would be like the loss of my arm, my heart. I am not complete without you, *doucette*. I am empty, life is empty, without you.'

'Oh, Vincent, I do love you so,' Cassia whispered, her voice catching in her throat. 'I fear losing you so very much!'

They talked for a little while longer and then desire arose again. Vincent cupped her breasts in his hands and began to kiss her throat, working his way slowly and sensuously down her body until he reached the auburn triangle between her legs. There, it was like freshly woven silk, soft and warm, and he laid his head against her stomach for a few moments, inhaling the sweet scent of her flesh.

'You smell like roses,' he said, 'dew-splashed roses.'

'Kadine Mimosa named me Briar Rose when I was in the harem. Turkish girls like to take the names of flowers, did you know that?'

'I do not see what the briars had to do with you, *doucette*.' Vincent looked at her quizzically.

'They referred to my reluctance to adapt to harem life. I put up quite a fight, you know. Mimosa was frequently at her wits' end over my intransigence. She kept telling me over and over why I should be grateful for having been chosen to be in the harem, how fortunate I was to be one of the royal concubines. I was supposed to spend all my time giving thanks to Allah for my good fortune.'

'And you complained instead, is that it?'

'That is exactly it.'

'Then I am very lucky that I only see the rose part of you, my love. If the thorns are still there, then they are certainly well sheathed.'

'Oh, they are still there,' Cassia dimpled, 'always ready to show themselves over injustice or cruelty of any kind.'

'Then it is a good job that I have no wish to be anything but very kind to you, *doucette*.'

'I do not believe it is in your nature to be unjust or cruel to anyone, Vincent. Certainly I have never seen any example of that.'

Vincent frowned suddenly. 'Alas, *doucette*, you are being unkind to me now.'

'I am? How? Tell me how!'

'By talking when I want to make love to you.'

Chapter Eight

Straight away after breakfast Cassia went in search of a milliner's to buy her ribbon. The innkeeper's wife had said there was a very fashionable shop in Dove Street, which was not difficult to find if one kept to the main street until turning left, then left again. She had left Vincent dressing. He was polishing his boots and taking special care with his appearance, for he wanted to make an impression on the Peacocks.

Cassia had been so intent upon looking at the stalls and shops, and staring at the people who passed her by, that she realized after a time that she had lost her way.

Standing by a stall which was selling gulls' eggs for tuppence a dozen, she looked back the way she had come. She was sure that she had followed the instructions correctly, and yet she could not see Dove Street anywhere. She asked the boy who was selling the gulls' eggs. He seemed to have difficulty understanding what she was saying, and she certainly found it difficult to translate his broad Lancashire accent. Finally she said, 'Ribbon. I want to buy a ribbon. Do you know where I can get any?'

The boy looked as if he didn't know what she was talking about. Then, scratching his scrubby hair, he pointed to the right. Thanking him with a smile, Cassia followed his directions.

There was plenty of time yet before they had to leave for the Peacocks, it would not hurt her to get some exercise after all those days in the coach. It was a narrow, cobbled street, overhung with shops. She saw a cat chasing another cat, and a large, hungry-looking hound stood eyeing her. She wished she had some food to throw to it. Finally she saw a window filled with hats. They were not what she would have called fashionable, but no doubt she would be able to purchase her ribbon there. Inside, the shop was tiny and dark and cramped. It smelled of dust and chalk. Seeing some rolls of ribbon on the counter, she walked over to them and began to finger them in anticipation of making her purchase.

When she felt someone's eyes boring through her back, she turned. A slight woman with damp-looking skin was surveying her disapprovingly. She had a dark, shabby dress, with large sweat stains under the arms; beads of sweat stood out on her brow, and her eyes bulged quite frighteningly.

'May I help you, mistress?' she asked.

'I wanted some ribbons, please. Do you have a rose-pink sateen, and perhaps ribbon for a wide pink sash? And could you please tell me, also, where is Dove Street?'

'That's all the ribbons we got, mistress. I'll be getting more in on Monday.'

Cassia must have shown her disappointment, for the woman said, 'My sister has a shop selling caps and ribbons and such-like in Dove Street. Was that the one you were looking for?' Cassia nodded. 'Go down here, turn right, you can't miss it. It's just before you get to the Piazza.'

'Thank you.' Cassia went out, again following the instructions carefully, and this time she found Dove Street and a shop which was similarly small and dark, but far more fashionable than the first. She bought some ribbon and rose-pink material for her sash and tucked her packages in the pocket of her cape, then she stepped outside the shop, turned the corner and saw a scene which numbed her to the core.

The Bedestan in Algiers! The sight brought back terrible memories. On the steps of a large red-brick house beside the quay, slaves were lined up to be sold — men, women, poor helpless children, all in chains, waiting to be bought, some wearing ragged clothes, some virtually naked. Babies and children were crying. One child was clinging to its mother for it had been bought by a man who wanted a fashionable black pageboy, and the mother was screaming as the boy was torn from her arms.

Cassia stood watching, paralysed, unable to tear her eyes away. Here, in England, where she had thought such things could never happen, the happy place she had dreamed of when she had been sold as a slave in Constantinople! England, her home, her haven – but it was no haven for these poor slaves.

As she watched, one of the men suddenly doubled up, as if in terrible pain, his face contorted. By way of response, the slave-auctioneer kicked him hard in the side, cursing him and ordering him to get up and stop his pretence. The man's eyes opened wide, the whites huge. It was plain that he did not understand what was being said to him, and that he was not pretending. The auctioneer kicked him yet again. The man gave a high animal scream and then lay still.

A feeling of stunned disbelief swept over Cassia. This was like a dream, a monstrous nightmare. She had known that slaves were sold in Liverpool, but this – ! These brutal conditions, naked blacks chained up here in public, being ill-treated, just as the Christian slaves were in the Bedestan in Algiers and in Constantinople itself. She could not believe it. The auctioneer sounded like a stout man of Lancashire, for he had the same accent as others she had heard in the city since her arrival. Had she seen him in any other situation she would have thought him a solid, kindly family man.

The dead negro was unceremoniously carted away. No one appeared to pay any attention to the incident. Someone in the crowd called out, 'I will give you five pounds for that youth with the scar on his cheek.'

'Why, he's worth fifty!' sneered the auctioneer. 'Who was it who dared to offer only five pounds? Lift up your head, Scarface, show how strong you are.'

The negro seemed to understand his instructions, for he straightened his head and pushed back his shoulders. More bids were given – seven pounds, eight pounds, nine pounds, ten pounds, till finally the scarfaced negro was sold for fifteen pounds.

'Any advance?' cried the auctioneer. 'Going for fifteen

pounds, going, going, gone!' He crashed down his hammer with unnecessary aggression.

The woman who had had her boy torn from her was standing sobbing quietly. Cassia's heart went out to her. The boy had been taken off in a cart with his new owner. Because he had struggled so much, his hands had been manacled behind his back.

Next to be sold was a negro boy of fourteen years old, with a straight back and handsome features. The auctioneer said that he was just from the Coast and would make an excellent pageboy.

'What shall I say for a start?'

'Three pounds,' one man offered. 'Five!' shouted a second, after which came bids for six pounds and ten shillings, then seven pounds and ten shillings, then nine pounds, for which sum the boy was finally sold. The boy's face split in what looked like a grin, but then Cassia saw that there were tears in his eyes and the grin was in fact a rictus of grief.

Next ushered to the front was a woman who was heavily pregnant. She had a ragged cloth tied round her head, but no other clothing, not even shoes on her feet. She looked terrified, glancing round at the other slaves, at the auctioneer, at the audience of bidders. Her price was higher, for whoever bought her would be getting a free infant, and although babies were despised in slave-ships coming to Britain and were frequently thrown overboard at their birth, here, on dry land, a pregnant woman was an altogether better proposition.

The auctioneer and the bidders had been so intent upon their business that they had not seen Cassia. The first shock having slightly receded, she glanced round her. She was the only white woman in view, and she realized that she must have come to a place where no proper lady would wish to tread.

Cassia felt faint and sick by now. There was a pain deep in the pit of her stomach. She wanted to be away from this place. She wanted to pretend it did not exist. Such things as these could surely not go on in the country she loved so much?

Turning on wooden legs, she retraced her steps, finding the milliner's in Dove Street again and going inside the shop to sit on a chair and recover herself. The woman was sympathetic at first, but when Cassia voiced what she had seen, her face closed as if shutters had come down on it.

'Decent folk don't ought to go near the Custom House,' she said sternly. ''Tis not for respectable ladies to see savages being bought and sold.'

'Oh, but they are *not* savages,' Cassia began to explain.

''Course they be savages, what else? They certainly ain't Christians. Barbarous customs they have back in their homelands, brutal, savage customs.'

'I cannot answer as to that, but it seems to me far more brutal and savage that they are torn from their homes where they have lived all their lives to be transported over here and sold.'

''Tis a great service done them, taken from their savage land where they know nothing of God and brought here to a good Christian land where they can learn about Him. What could be more fortunate for them than that? Lucky they are, luckier than the ones what get left behind.'

Cassia was stupefied by the woman's words. 'But I saw a child torn from its mother, sold to a strange man and taken off in a cart!'

The milliner peered at her as if looking for some outward evidence of her insanity.

'They have no souls, you know,' she said, enunciating each word clearly. *'They have no souls.'*

Cassia had the strongest desire to retaliate, to tell the woman that she was being wicked and ignorant. How could the colour of a man's skin deprive him of his soul, make him a victim, a slave? She had thought that the Turkish were monsters for making non-Moslems into their slaves, but here were 'good Christian' men selling negroes and ill-treating them. Her own countrymen behaving fiendishly towards those who were helpless, and, to diminish their guilt-feelings, taking unto themselves the belief that negroes had no souls!

There was so much she could say to this woman, but what would be the use? She was a milliner not a slave dealer; words would be wasted. Getting up, Cassia thanked the woman for the loan of her chair and then she left the little shop in Dove Street and headed back towards the Golden Lion. She still felt strange, as if she had suffered an appalling waking nightmare or had woken from a bad dream which still hung over her. Her stomach felt unsettled and her head was beginning to throb. She hoped that her unpleasant experience had not had a bad effect on the baby lying within her. She had heard of a woman who had been frightened by a rabbit and consequently her baby had been born looking just like a rabbit; another woman had eaten too many strawberries and had had a baby born with two strawberry marks on its face. It was well known that a mother's experiences could be transmitted to her unborn infant.

Vincent was ready, wearing a jacket of dark blue embroidered in dull gold, with a matching dull gold waistcoat edged in blue, ivory stockings and a frilled white shirt. When he saw Cassia's face he flung his hat to one side and took her in his arms.

'*Doucette*, what has happened? Are you ill? You look so white!'

She told him what she had seen and how she had felt about it. The man being kicked and dying on the ground where he lay, the boy being snatched from his mother.

'It was like the Bedestan, Vincent, just like the Bedestan in Algiers. And like the time I arrived in Constantinople and the Kislar Agha came along to buy me and the other women. Oh, I could forgive them – they were pagans, they did not know what they were doing, they cannot be judged by our standards. But these men I saw just now were Christians, Christians like you and me, Vincent! Englishmen, behaving every bit as savagely as Turkish ones. Oh, I knew that slavery existed, after all isn't that one of the reasons we are here? But this has really brought it home to me, Vincent.'

'My darling, you are trembling. Come and sit down, I will send a messenger to the Peacocks and tell them that we cannot come, that you are not well.'

'Oh no, you must not do that, Vincent. They will have everything ready and waiting for us, I do not want to disappoint them, nor to give a bad impression when we need them as allies. No, I shall be all right if I just sit here for a few moments and get my breath back.'

Vincent sat with her, holding her hand, while she talked about what she had seen, getting some of the agony out of her system. After a while, the threatened headache thankfully began to recede, but she still felt queasy, as if she had eaten rotten meat. She would dearly have liked to lie down, but she was not going to spoil Vincent's chances of making friends and getting his first recruits for The Children of Liberty.

Just before they were ready to leave, Cassia picked up a newspaper which Vincent must have been reading before she returned. It was a copy of a local paper, the *Williamson's Advertiser*. Glancing at its pages Cassia saw numerous adverts for slaves, those who were thought too fit and healthy to be sold by public auction but would be sold privately. She read the adverts with a feeling of loathing rising inside her.

'To be sold by Auction at George's Coffee House betwixt the hours of seven and nine o'clock a very fine negro girl, about eleven years of age, very healthy and hath been some time from the Coast. Any person willing to purchase the same may apply to Captain Arthur Porters at Messrs Garnley, Horridge and Sales near the Exchange, where she may be seen till the time of Sale.'

Beneath that was an advertisement for a runaway black boy, who was wearing a heavy metal collar on which was engraved the words *'My Lady Partington's-Black, in Norris Green'*. A generous reward was offered for his capture.

Beneath that advertisement was one by a goldsmith, Matthew Morton, who declared that he made *'silver collars and padlocks for Blacks or Dogs; and etc.'*

Cassia flung aside the paper in disgust. Vincent looked at her with a wry smile.

'We are finding out the facts, *doucette*. It is not always pleasant to discover the truth. I had not realized things were ⁊s bad as this. Liverpool's fortunes are now so firmly founded on the slave trade that when there was war with France, the whole city ground to a halt and men became paupers and had to beg on the streets.'

'So they are hardly likely to tolerate our reforming zeal!'

'We may fail, my love, but at least we must try to awaken men's consciences. At the moment, they are dormant. They see money, nothing else. Like that woman in the shop in Dove Street, they think blacks have no souls and that they are doing them a tremendous service by bringing them from a pagan land to a Christian one. We must try and change their way of thinking. There are many even now in London who are forming societies and working for Abolition. The Peacocks and I shall be linking up with them as soon as possible; we will all be working together, forming a great link throughout England. The main slaving cities, Liverpool, Bristol, London, must all become a part of the Abolition work.'

'But we must leave now, *doucette*, or we shall be late for lunch. Are you ready?'

'Yes, I am ready, Vincent.' Cassia had put on the rose-pink sash and tied the pink ribbon in her hair, fastening it with a rosette bow above one ear so that her auburn curls coiled round it prettily. They stepped out of the Golden Lion just as the Peacocks' coach arrived to collect them, and soon they were bowling away along Dale Street and out of the hubbub of the city towards the pleasant, verdant scenery of Speke, where Peacock Hall lay.

Peacock Hall was beautiful, with a white stucco facade and white colonnades on either side of the main doorway. It stood in gardens arranged in the Italian style, ornate and beautiful.

Joanna Peacock was standing on the top step awaiting them. Cassia looked at her with interest. She was sturdily built, large boned, with a square face, broader at the ears then the forehead. There was a deep groove in her chin, and faint semi-circular lines running from her nose to the corners of her mouth. Her eyes were very dark, and her lashes heavy and thick, as were her brows. She wore a powdered wig in the new low style, with ringlets clustering on either side of her face, and her panniers were somewhat excessively wide for everyday wear. Her gown had long, tight sleeves and a heavily frilled fichu of powder blue voile edged with silk ribbon. She was very tightly corseted, so that her waist seemed improbably small for the rest of her bulk, this being accentuated by blue flounces around her hips. The hem of her gown was ruched in deep blue satin and matching blue satin slippers peeped out from beneath her skirts. She wore fine drop sapphire earrings, and a sapphire on a slender gold chain round her somewhat mannish neck. On seeing Cassia she beamed at her, revealing strong white teeth, also of a mannish effect, then hurried down the steps towards her, arms outstretched.

'My dear, how delightful to meet you! Your husband told us so much about you, and I see that he did not exaggerate your beauty. Why, what beautiful skin you have, and what a superb shade of red is your hair! I see that you do not powder, how very wise of you. It is such a trouble, once begun; I frequently wish that I had never adopted it. In France, you know, they say that a million pounds in weight of powder is used every year by the populace. Quite outrageous when you think about it, is it not? I may call you Cassia? It is so much easier when one is on first-name terms.' As she finished speaking, three hounds appeared from behind her skirts and began to scrutinize Cassia.

Now that Joanna Peacock was close to her, Cassia could smell her perfume; she loved the scent of roses, and attar of roses itself was still one of her favourite perfumes, but she would never be able to smell it without thinking of the Sultan and his strange mechanical lovemaking, for he had always been liberally doused in it. She was determined, however, that the scent of roses billowing from out of the folds of Joanna Peacock's beautiful gown would not deter her from making a friend of the woman. She must think of The Children of Liberty who were in desperate need of sponsors such as Joanna and her brothers.

'They are here.' The speaker was a dark, pleasant-faced man, slightly taller than his sister and with a ruddier complexion, and dark twinkling eyes. He wore a jacket of fine mulberry satin, heavily encrusted with silver embroidery, and his waistcoat was of silver brocade embroidered with mulberry marguerites. His knee breeches were mulberry brocade, and his stockings of ivory silk. He, too, wore a wig, tied behind in the highly popular pigtail style, with a mulberry and silver silk bow.

A fop, Cassia thought, amused. Vincent did not tell me that.

Paul Peacock bowed low over her hand in a most elegant fashion. 'Paul Joseph Peacock at your service, ma'am, and delighted to meet with you. And how thrilling it is to know, ma'am, that I have something in common with such a rare beauty as yourself.'

Nor did Vincent tell me that he was a flatterer, Cassia smiled to herself, greeting Paul Peacock with a delicate curtsey, which brought a look of delighted admiration to his kindly face.

'Enough of this!' exclaimed Joanna Peacock, as if bored by such courtly proceedings. 'Lunch awaits us within. Come everyone, to the dining hall.'

'Is Andrew not at home?' Vincent wanted to know, at which Joanna gave a mysterious smile.

'Ah, he will be here anon. He comes and goes much as he pleases, no clock has ever managed to control Andrew. We told him what time we would be starting lunch, and if he is late – well, that is just unfortunate for him, but we shall not be going hungry awaiting his arrival.' Her tone sounded somewhat tart, but the expression on her face belied her acerbity. Cassia guessed that Andrew might well be Joanna's favourite brother, but that she fought hard to conceal this.

Accompanied by the bounding dogs, they entered the house. The main hallway of Peacock Hall was spacious and elegant, with a central winding staircase of gleaming Italian marble. Joanna led them through a small side room furnished with carved benches and into the dining room, where a table was set in readiness for five.

Immediately the first course was under way, Paul Peacock began talking of the slave trade and his hopes for The Children of Liberty.

'A fine name you have chosen, Vincent. Children suggests rebirth and a new beginning, I like that very much indeed. It has a better ring to it, I think, than The Sons and Daughters of Liberty, which is our sister society in America. We are all God's children, black and white. Yes, a fine ring to it.'

Cassia nodded vigorously. 'Yes indeed, sir. We devised the name of the society ourselves, between us.' She flung an adoring glance at Vincent.

'How rare,' twinkled Paul Peacock. 'A wife who is in accord with her husband! Lackaday, but that is not often seen, and even less frequent, alas, is a sister in accord with her brother.' He cast a half-wry, half-amused glance at Joanna, who tut-tutted quietly beneath her breath.

'Take no notice of my brother; he should not bring private squabbles to a public table.'

'Now did I say we squabbled, dear sister? Indeed, I did not. It is just that I would wish on occasion to have a sister's support when I feel it vital.'

'And have I not always supported you, brother? When we did not want Andrew to become engaged to Ulla Bertington, did we not present a united front?'

'Alas, I have forgotten that one great occasion,' Paul twinkled. 'How remiss of me! To think that I lied. Why, yes indeed, my sister has supported me once.' He patted his chest lightly with his fingertips, as if relieved to have set matters straight.

'Andrew is the youngest in the family, I gather,' Cassia said.

'Yes, and a headstrong boy,' answered Joanna. 'I fear we spoiled him. You see, we lost our parents when we were small, and in our efforts to fill their place Paul and I protected Andrew too much, I fear. We felt that it would be cruel to discipline him, to force him to do things, when he had no mother or father to turn to. Alas, what a mistake we made.'

'The boy is now ungovernable?' Cassia wanted to know.

'In many ways, yes, but we cannot really call him a boy any more. He is four and twenty years of age, but I fear he has mingled with unsuitable folk in the past. Ulla Bertington was totally wrong for him in every way, a flighty flibbertigibbet with absolutely no fortune.'

Cassia wondered how much Vincent had told them about their own lost fortune, and whether the Peacocks knew that the man and woman they had so generously invited to lunch and to stay at their house were virtually destitute.

She was saved from any further conjecture by the opening of the dining room door, which slammed back on its hinges as a large untidy hound crashed through it, pink tongue hanging out. Panting excitedly, he snuffled at the feet of the guests and then went to Joanna and sat serenely at her feet, eyeing her plate with hopeful glances.

'This is Raven, Andrew's dog. That means he cannot be far away,' Joanna said.

At that moment Andrew stepped into the dining room, and Cassia saw the boy about whom there had been so much discussion. He had his brother's kindly smile, but there the similarity ended. He was far taller than Paul, and he had windswept reddish-gold hair. His eyes were a hazel-flecked green, and they looked pleasant and free from guile. He had a straight, squarish nose, a strong-boned face, and immaculate, healthy teeth like his sister's. He wore a rather crumpled black coat, dark brown knee breeches and brown woollen stockings.

He looked like a country squire, not a city man.

Cassia liked the look of him immensely. She liked his ready smile, his frank greeting, and the way he took his place at table without any fuss, Raven slinking to his feet and lying down silently beside him. The introductions over, a first course was brought for Andrew, who ate with gusto, his manners leaving just a little to be desired. But it was good to see someone enjoying his food so much. The others slowed down a little, so that by the time the second course was due they had synchronized their eating.

Talk centred on the slave trade and The Children of Liberty, and Cassia mentioned her experience at the Custom House that day.

'How terrible, terrible,' murmured Andrew sympathetically.

Although Andrew looked young and carefree, he was every bit as eager to participate in the society and to work for the liberation of slaves as were his brother and sister. He seemed extremely well informed on the subject and told Cassia and Vincent that he had already partially persuaded some of his friends to join the society.

'One of my friends in particular is anxious to join us,' he said. 'He has for some time been deeply in love with a black girl called India. His father is a politician,' Andrew told them, 'and India is one of the servants in his household. My friend, Charles, has loved India for some two years now and all in secret, for it is of course a forbidden love. I do believe that he is courageous enough to make her his wife, if only the abolition of slavery can be brought about very soon. As things stand, such a marriage would be totally impossible.'

'Charles sounds as if he will be an excellent ally, and work energetically for our cause,' Vincent said. 'Shall we have the opportunity to meet him in the near future?'

'Indeed yes. If Joanna does not mind, I had planned to invite all my interested friends here to meet you.'

'Of course I do not mind, Andrew. That is what we plan to

134

do, get all our friends together, and *their* friends – and their friends, until we have a whole network of people all working for Abolition,' Joanna said. 'Tales are given out about how happy the slaves are, how their lot is being improved when they are taken captive, how they sing and give thanks.'

Her voice took on a passionate note. 'Imagine what it must be like after a lifetime in the sunshine and the open air to be confined below deck for days, weeks, with the hatches covered, water in short supply, frequently running out, the blacks huddled together, wailing and sobbing. Every morning when one of the crew goes down below decks to inspect them, there might be thirty or forty newly-dead bodies, which will be immediately hoisted overboard without any proper burial. The sailors say "More grub for the sharks!" as they fling the corpses into the sea. Often, down in the hold, there is an outbreak of fever, and more are near death. Those who are not broken by the fever are broken by homesickness, and the stifling conditions. When the ship puts in at, say, Kingston, in Jamaica, it will spend some two or three weeks selling off those slaves who are still capable of being sold, and then the ship will be loaded up with sugar and rum in readiness to depart for Liverpool. This is what they call the Triangular Trade.'

'Yes, Vincent has told me something of that,' Cassia said. 'I believe extremely high profits are made in this fashion.'

'That is why they do it,' said Paul. 'This way they have three ports where they can sell the contents of their hold, and all at a great profit.'

Joanna pushed her plate away and gripped her hands together. 'The journey of those poor black prisoners must be like a descent into hell. But the ones I feel really sorry for are the ones who are never going to live in a decent household, and those are the ones who haunt my dreams at night.'

'Who are the ones who will never live in decent homes?' Cassia wanted to know.

'When you saw what you did on the Custom House steps, were there men only present?'

'Why, I think so. I certainly did not see any other women. No, I do not think there were any women at all except myself.'

'On some days you will see a woman there. Oh, to look at her you would never think she was evil: she dresses fashionably with panniers and a powdered wig, she apes the ladies. But she is not a lady. She is a . . . a woman of ill-repute; her reputation in the city is of the lowest.' It was obvious that Joanna was searching for words which would not offend the delicacy of her lady guest. If only she knew, thought Cassia.

'She is the Madame of a string of notorious brothels in the city. Perhaps the worst thing about these places is the children involved.'

'Children?' gasped Cassia. 'You mean they are child brothels?'

'Alas, yes,' Joanna said grimly. 'There are one or two white girls who have joined of their own accord, but in the main the girls are black or half-caste, for it is the colour of their skins which entices their gentlemen customers to visit. The novelty of – of –' Joanna's voice died away. She seemed overcome with emotion.

'You mean the novelty of bedding with a woman whose skin is other than white?' Cassia finished for her, showing that she was not ashamed to bring the matter out into the open.

'Why, that is it exactly!' Joanna gasped. 'Dare I hope that you feel as I do about these poor children?'

'I do, most deeply. Their plight must be appalling. Snatched from the freedom of their homeland, carried in a noisome hold, half-starved and ill-treated, their companions thrown to the sharks if they become sick, and then stood in chains, naked, to be mauled by those who want to buy them, not even being given the chance of a decent Christian life, but being forced into prostitution at so tender an age. Poor innocents.' Cassia was thinking of her own baby, who would be born white-skinned to a life of freedom, who would never be forced into a life of immorality.

Having found an ally, Joanna looked much more cheerful.

She took Cassia out into the garden while the men drank Madeira in the library. The two women were halfway across the rose garden when they heard a shout from the house. It was Andrew, telling them that he was taking Vincent on a ride round their estates, and that they would not be long.

The two women waved, and then proceeded to walk amongst the roses. Cassia was pleased to be out in the fresh air, for she had found the room stuffy after a time, despite its size. She suspected that she was still not over the terrible shock she had had that morning, of seeing the slaves being so cruelly treated, the boy being wrenched from his mother, the man who had died. It had upset her deeply, as enforced separations always did now. She did not have a headache, it was true, but there was a low throbbing ache at the base of her spine and a taut feeling there, so that when they came to a rustic bench she was relieved to sit down.

Joanna, noticing her guest pressing the base of her spine with her fingers as if to relieve a pain, looked at her with astonishment.

'You are with child?' she asked. 'Oh, why did you not tell me, I would not have made you walk so far.'

'Oh, I am quite healthy, I do assure you, Joanna. It is only a few days since we travelled from Cornwall up here to Liverpool. I have always had plenty of stamina. But this morning, seeing those slaves, it upset me dreadfully, I fear.'

'We will sit here for a little while until you are rested and then I will take you back into the house and you must lie down on a *chaise-longue* and put your feet up, my dear. And when is the baby expected?'

'Oh, not until the autumn. There is plenty of time yet. I hope to be back in Cornwall by then with my aunt, for she will of course want to see the new baby when he or she is born.'

'That is your mother's sister?'

'No – my father's; his only sister. There were just the two of them. My mother left home when I was a baby. I fear she did not take to domesticity.'

'Oh, you poor lamb!' Joanna's kindly face wore an expression of consternation. 'What a terrible thing! So you were brought up by your father, then? Which means, I suppose, that you are very close to him?'

'Alas, no, Joanna. There is no love lost between my father and me. He never forgave my mother for turning out as she did, and I'm afraid that I was put in the same category as was she: namely, womankind who is unreliable and fickle.'

'Well, you have your handsome husband now, which I suppose makes up for everything.' Joanna patted Cassia's hand.

'Yes, it does. We have been very fortunate, Vincent and I. The manner of our meeting was extraordinary, quite extraordinary.'

'He has told us very little about your background, but I believe that he rescued you from pirate-slavers. Is that correct? Seeing you sitting there before me, looking so pretty and lady-like, I find it hard to think that you have been in such an incredible situation, my dear.'

'It is *because* I have that I want to help other people who have been abducted in a similar way,' Cassia said. 'You see, it is from my own experience that I want to help these poor slaves. I am not just a do-gooder,' she smiled. 'Yes, it is true, I was kidnapped by pirate-slavers off the coast of Cornwall one day while I was innocently walking on the beach. Much later, after many and varied adventures, I was rescued by Vincent. It is not a time that I particularly like to talk about,' she added, as she saw Joanna's mouth opening to ask questions. She did not want to enlarge on her story to this so-respectable lady. Could she tell her that she had been a prisoner of the Sultan in his harem for many months, that she had become his favourite? To admit this would be to admit that she had lived a life of immorality and been little better than one of the prostitutes about whom they had been speaking only moments before. Perhaps when she knew Joanna better she would be able to tell her the whole story, but for the moment she would stay silent.

Joanna seemed to understand, for she changed the subject,

talking about the roses which she said her mother had planted in the garden many years ago.

It was a pleasant, tranquil scene as they discussed the glorious blooms, gently pulling down one blossom and then another to inhale the smell from the scented, satiny petals. But the weather had decided to undergo one of its typically English changes: a gust of wind buffeted across the rose gardens, swirling at the women's skirts, loosening dead rose petals and flinging them in a wild cavorting dance through the air.

'My goodness, there's a storm brewing,' Joanna exclaimed. 'We'd better go into the house quickly before the rain comes. Look at the change in that sky, the blue has quite vanished, it's as black as old pewter now.' In answer, fat wet droplets of rain were splashing down on them, heavy and drenching.

Joanna took Cassia's hand to lead her carefully across the crazy paving of the rose garden. All would have gone well but for a piece of the paving, which at some earlier date had been loosened by a clumsy heel and which was projecting upwards. When Cassia caught her toe on the crooked stone slab, Joanna tried to support her, but Cassia fell awkwardly, tumbling to the ground in a flurry of rain-spotted skirts.

Joanna struggled to help Cassia to her feet so that she could get her into the house, but she struggled in vain.

'My ankle – I think I've wrenched my ankle,' Cassia said. 'See if the men are back. Fetch Vincent, he will carry me into the house. I dare not put any weight on my foot.'

'Oh dear, but I do not like to leave you here on your own in this rain. Oh, you poor girl! What are we going to do?' Joanna was biting on her lips and wringing her hands, showing nothing of the phlegmatic temperament which hitherto had seemed to be hers.

'I shall be quite all right,' Cassia said, as soothingly as she could manage, although she was suffering some pain with her wrenched foot. 'Go to the house now, don't wait a moment longer. Get Vincent to carry me into the house.'

Casting one last tortured glance at her guest lying supine on the ground in the drenching rain, Joanna Peacock scuttled towards the house.

At any other time, under any other circumstances, it would have been almost amusing, if she had not been in so much pain, Cassia thought, as she lay there getting wetter and wetter. She wondered if she had broken her foot; it felt worse than a sprain. Had the pain from that not been so bad she might have noticed the other pain earlier, but when she did she bit on her lips in rising panic. No, no, it could not be! she thought. Why, all I have done is fall over a loose piece of paving in the ground. I hardly hurt myself when I fell — not the rest of me, that is, only my foot. She gasped out loud in pain. No, no please, dear God, don't let it be that, she prayed.

She tried to calm herself, saying it could not possibly be happening already. Had she not travelled miles and miles in all those different coaches, right across England, with no mishap, in such good health? And now for this to happen here, when they had barely been in Liverpool two days . . . Her thoughts trailed off, for pain was increasing, a deep cutting pain which seemed to tighten round the lower part of her stomach. Tentatively, she placed her hands on the area. Her muscles had constricted to form a band of tightness, and then just as quickly they were loosening themselves. Moments later they had tightened again. Contractions.

Tears filled her eyes. 'Vincent, Vincent, where are you?' she cried out loud. She wanted to scream his name, but feared she would damage the baby more. If she lay very still and very quiet and did not move, surely the baby would be all right? Surely it would not be born now? She had heard that if a mother lay quietly and still, she could sometimes save her baby even if the birth had begun, so she tried doing that now, though with all her heart — more than anything else in the world — she wanted to scream Vincent's name and call to him to come to her.

Instead, she heard Joanna's voice and the footsteps of two valets whom she had brought with her to assist Cassia into the house. She took one look at the white-faced girl and suppressed a shriek.

'It is not − ? Oh, heaven help us, do not tell me that . . . ?'

'Yes, Joanna. I am most awfully sorry, but I fear the baby has begun. Vincent, where is Vincent?' She looked over Joanna's shoulder when he did not appear.

'He is not back yet, they must have taken shelter somewhere on the estate when the storm began. Oh, dear, what am I going to do?' Joanna wrung her hands together again.

'I don't want to move. That is, I don't want to have to walk,' Cassia gasped, as another pain gripped her. 'If there is some way the men could get me into the house . . . But I think it would be better if I did not try to walk.'

'Walk? Oh, my dear, of course you must not walk!' Joanna turned round, issuing orders to the two men who were standing behind her, gaping. 'Fetch my sedan chair to get Mistress Sauvage into the house,' she ordered. 'At once, do you hear me, at once! And bring blankets and pillows! Quickly!'

When the men had rushed off to do her bidding, Joanna knelt down in the rain by Cassia, stroking back her forehead to clear the wet tendrils of hair out of her eyes.

'Oh, my poor dear child, this is terrible, this is disastrous. I shall never forgive myself. It is all my fault, if I had not brought you out into the garden −'

'Oh, Vincent, I wish Vincent were here!' Cassia gasped. She began to sob, but tried to control her weeping for fear that this too would disturb the baby and speed its birth. 'Oh, where is Vincent, where is he? I want him, I need him!' she moaned. 'He should be here with me, he told me he would never leave me, he said he would never go away when I needed him. He promised to be with me when the baby was born!' Fresh tears burst out of Cassia's eyes, and now Joanna too was crying with her, holding her hands and chafing them, trying to keep her warm, for she feared that the soaking would chill Cassia and bring on a fever.

When the two valets returned with the sedan chair they slowly and very gently lifted Cassia up into it, swathing her in blankets and padding her with pillows so that she would not be jolted during the journey. Then, ignoring the lashing rain, they made their way to the house. Rather than bear Cassia up the stairs in what would surely be an uncomfortable journey, Joanna ordered them to take her into the morning room where there was a wide *chaise-longue* on which she might be placed. This the men did, carefully and tenderly lifting her out of the sedan chair and placing her on the couch. Other servants were on hand now to assist: a plump and efficient-looking house-keeper, two maids, who had brought hot water to wash Mistress Sauvage and dry clothes to wrap her in, and the same for their mistress.

Joanna did not want to take the trouble to wash or change while Cassia was suffering, she wanted to sit by her and comfort her, but since the housekeeper's husband had been sent for the doctor some time ago, they could do nothing now except wait, so she divested herself of her soaking gown and pulled on a warm wool dressing-gown, while the housekeeper and the maids undressed Mistress Sauvage and patted her dry. They placed a spotless white chemise over her head and a gossamer wool cape over her shoulders, with warm rugs to cover the lower half of her body. The soaked and muddy clothes had been taken away to be dealt with by the laundresses.

'Raspberry-leaf tea to ease the pains,' the housekeeper said, ordering one of the girls to fetch a brew of the same. But when the girl came back with the herbal concoction Cassia was in too much pain to stay still long enough to sip at it. She flung her head from side to side and bit on her lips to try and quell her screams, and all the time, in between her gasps, she moaned Vincent's name and begged him to return to her.

It was quite pitiful to hear, and Joanna more often than not had tears in her eyes, as did the motherly housekeeper. In case Vincent, Paul and Andrew were not too far away, Joanna had sent one of the valets off in search of them. The man had not yet returned. She was thinking of sending off a second man, for the least she could do when this poor child was in such agony was to make sure her husband was by her side.

And where was the doctor? Why had he not come by now? Joanna paced up and down the room, chewing on her lips. If he could only get here in time to save the baby! But things did not look at all good; the poor girl had begun to lose blood, and that was an ominous sign. She was going to miscarry her first infant and it would be a tragedy; to get so far with the pregnancy so that the baby had begun to seem like a living, warm and human being, and then to lose it. It would have been better had she lost it much earlier, if she had had to lose it at all. All these thoughts spun through Joanna's mind as she waited for the doctor, every now and again going over to the windows and looking out to see if she could see him riding up the driveway. Cassia seemed to be sleeping fitfully, exhausted, and Joanna prayed that she would stay like that until the doctor arrived. But it was not to be, for another pain woke her with a scream. At once Joanna was at her side, clasping her hands.

'The doctor should not be long now, my dear. We have sent messengers for your husband and he should be here too any moment,' she said, displaying a confidence she did not feel. The storm was raging wildly outside: from the window she could see the trees bowing and dipping as the wind gouged at them. Only a man who knew that his wife was dangerously ill would ride through such a storm. She wrung out a cloth in cool water and placed it over Cassia's forehead, and when the pain had eased she helped her to sip at some of the raspberry-leaf tea. She remembered a tincture which the doctor had given her some time ago to kill pain when she had one of her bad megrims, but she dared not give any to a woman in labour for fear that it damaged the baby. If only the doctor would come! Where in God's name could he be?

It was after four in the afternoon when the doctor finally

arrived. He was drenched through, and he had lost his hat in the wind. He had nearly lost his bag, too, but had managed to retrieve it. He had been administering to a woman giving birth to twins, and there had been complications. He could not have left her, he said, and he made his apologies. The twins had both died, he whispered in an aside to Joanna, and as he glanced across at the deathly white face of the woman lying on the *chaise-longue*, he thought to himself that he had come on another tragic errand. Rapidly he tore off his soaking jacket and towelled himself dry, rubbing his hands together to warm them before he began to examine the stricken girl. As he replaced the coverlet over Cassia, Joanna came back into the room, lips tightly pursed and eyes wide in expectation. Seeing the doctor's expression she felt her heart sink.

'We shall need more hot water, Mistress Peacock, and clean linen.'

'Oh, yes, Doctor Vaughan, at once.' Then she hurried out of the room to give her orders to the servants, and when she had done so she concealed herself behind one of the heavy curtains at the bottom of the corridor, took out her kerchief and cried heartily, but as silently as she could manage.

It was dusk when Vincent and the Peacock brothers returned to the Hall. They had been out in the open when the storm had broken and so they had taken refuge in a derelict farm building. Later when they had emerged they had continued their ride round the estate, and then Andrew's horse had gone lame, and they had had to look for a replacement. It was all quite innocent and ordinary, and it would have meant nothing if Cassia had not lost her baby while they were out.

When Joanna greeted them at the door, her face ashen, her hands trembling, Vincent knew instantly that something was terribly wrong. When she told him, his face went even paler than hers, and he headed straight for the morning-room and the *chaise-longue* where his wife lay. Her skin was so pale that it was waxy, there were dark smudges beneath her eyes, her cheeks looked pinched. She was lying staring into space as Vincent approached her and sank to his knees at her side, reaching out to take her hands in his, her name on his lips. He could not believe what happened next. Her hands were rigid, they would not unbend to curl into his.

'Where were you when I needed you?' she said in a low, strained voice, and then she simply turned her head away from him and closed her eyes.

Chapter Nine

Vincent could not have been more heartbroken or more mystified about his wife's reaction. Again and again he tried to tell her that he would have been with her had he known, that it was all a sad misfortune, that all he wanted to do was take care of her now and get her health back so that she would be strong again. She would not meet his eyes, nor would she speak freely to him. She made the barest of responses, and sometimes would say nothing at all.

'Her spirits are very low. She has received a tragic shock,' Joanna tried to explain. 'Give her time to recover, she will be herself again soon.'

'I would have been with her if I had known. She feels betrayed. I told her I would always be with her when she needed me and I wasn't.'

'You must not blame yourself, Vincent. Be gentle with her, she has lost a baby, her first, and that is not easy for a woman to accept. Sometimes they are apt to blame their husbands for the pain and the suffering, I have seen that happen before. I do not often speak of this these days, Vincent, and I am only telling you so that you will know I understand. I was married once — oh, some ten years ago. My husband was a friend of Paul's, he was also a captain on one of the trading routes. His ship was lost with all hands in a tropical storm. I was carrying his child, and when I heard of his death I lost the baby, just as Cassia has lost hers, so I know what she is going through, and I know that it will take time for her wounds to heal. Be patient with her, Vincent, I beg of you. Do not take her behaviour to heart.'

'Forgive my self-pity, Joanna. I had no idea. It is very good of you to tell me this, to ease my suffering. Does my wife know?'

'We have spoken of it. I told her to make her feel that I

understood what she was going through. I panicked at first, and behaved in the most witless fashion when she fell and I knew that the baby was going to be born too early. You should have seen me, I was like an old maid, but I gathered my wits in time, I hope, and now I enjoy looking after your wife. She is a good patient, a sweet-natured girl, and that is what makes me say that she will get over her tragic loss and be herself again eventually.'

'It obviously pains her so much to see me that I have been thinking it would be better if I did not go into her room.'

'That is a decision only you can make, Vincent. I would not attempt to influence your decisions. No doubt, even if she behaves in an unfriendly fashion, she will be secretly glad that you have troubled to go and see her, so I think that I would be tempted to go on visiting, even if she gives you short shrift.'

'Yes, I feel sure you are right.'

And so Vincent did continue to visit his wife frequently. As he and Cassia had been invited to stay at Peacock Hall anyway, he brought over their belongings and baggage to the Hall. He would sit in the bedroom alone, gazing into space, bemused, unable to believe that, downstairs in the morning-room, lay his wife, whom he loved more than life itself, and who only a few days ago had been his doting wife. Now she was like a stranger, cool and distant. She blamed him for not having been there when she had lost her baby. Did she not know that he felt guilty enough without her silent accusations? If only she had stayed behind at Penwellyn with Julitta this would never have happened, but he knew that Cassia would never have allowed that; she had insisted on coming despite his efforts to dissuade her.

And now she would barely speak to him. He must cling to hope, to what Joanna had said, that she would get over it. He must remind himself that not only her body but her mind had suffered a severe shock with the loss of the baby. He went over his last visit to her, how he had knelt down by the side of the bed and reached out to take her hands, and how unresisting her hands had been, as they had in the times before. Stiff and un-yielding, they had remained in his grasp, only on sufferance. She had looked at him once, her gaze dark and fathomless, full of suffering and accusation, and then she had turned her head away and her lower lip had trembled slightly, as if she was sup-pressing great emotion.

'Cassia, *doucette*,' he had begged, 'please, let us be like we were before. Please let us heal this rift.'

Slowly her head had turned back in his direction and she had looked at him almost angrily. 'You were not there when I needed you, Vincent. You were not there, and you promised me that you would never leave me alone again. I cannot forget.' Her voice had trailed off, she had closed her eyes, and she had looked so pale and tired that he had blamed himself for exhausting her. But all he had wanted to do was be friends with her again, for them to be close, lovers, as they had been only a few days before.

Cassia could not help it, even if she silently remonstrated with herself, saying over and over that Vincent had not really deserted her, that it could not be helped, that the storm had interfered with his return. Logic has no place in emotion, and Cassia was doubly upset because not only had she been betrayed, as she saw it, by the man who loved her and had promised never to leave her alone in her hour of need, but she had lost her baby, too, in the most painful circumstances.

She only knew that she felt the deepest of deep depressions, a morbidness of spirit, an exhaustion where before she had sparkled. She had never known the loss of a child could make her like this; indeed she had never contemplated losing her baby, but, now that she had, she was facing what other women had had to cope with in similar circumstances. Even though the baby had not been fully formed, even though she had been only halfway through her pregnancy, nonetheless to her it had been a baby, a beloved child, and she was grieving. Her heart ached for the little mite she would never hold in her arms, the little face which would never smile up into hers, the chubby pink arms she longed to kiss. She wanted to weep when she thought about them; frequently she did when she was alone. Her dreams were jumbled and nightmarish. In them she was pursuing brigands who had stolen her baby, and she knew that if she could just reach them, just run those last few feet, she would be able to snatch back her baby from their arms. She would wake exhausted and aching, her eyes wet with tears.

Joanna was a rock and refused to take any gratitude for her devoted care. When Cassia began to feel more like visitors, Paul and Andrew came, too, bringing her gifts, Andrew a kid pouch full of lace kerchiefs scented with lavender and Paul a pomander, which she could gently press with her fingers to release the scent of oranges and cloves to freshen the air. She was delighted with the gifts, and she wished that she could have thanked them properly, but she felt so listless. Nothing had prepared her for this bone-crushing tiredness. She slept a great deal in the daytime, which was fortunate, for her nights were disturbed, the wild dreams seeming to get worse instead of better.

Andrew's hound, Raven, took to slinking into her room in the afternoons and lying at her feet to sleep. Sometimes Andrew joined him. At first they seemed awkward together, for Andrew, as he quite frankly said, had had little to do with invalids, and begged her pardon if his behaviour might appear somewhat brash. But the silences became companionable and, in time, they found quite a great deal to discuss.

It seemed the most natural thing in the world for each member of the Peacock family to have his or her most hated aspect of the slave trade. With Joanna it was the child prostitutes in the seedier area of the city. With Paul, who had been a slave-captain himself and who had seen the worst that was to be seen, it was the voyages of the slaves which he wished to reform most of all. And with Andrew it was the habit of branding each slave.

'Each slave is branded with a trader's initials before he or she leaves Africa,' he told Cassia. 'Most brands are made of silver, because the weals from that heal faster than those made with iron. Some slaves are branded more than once, some repeatedly, on their foreheads, their chests, buttocks. If a slave runs off and he or she is marked with a certain set of initials, or a name, then the advertisement can be put out for a slave with that brand so that he can soon be found. There are plenty of arguments on that score, men saying that without the brand the traders would not be able to keep track of their property. But if we look at the situation fairly and justly we will see that these blacks cannot be any man's property, branded or unbranded.'

'I did not see any Christian slaves marked by the Turks in this way,' Cassia said thoughtfully. 'Oh, they were ill-treated, beaten, and so on, and left to languish in appalling conditions, but I do not think that they actually were given brand marks.' She had told Andrew something of her adventures, on the same lines that she had told Joanna, nothing more. He had shown great interest and his alert features had softened. If he had thought her nothing more serious than a lady of fashion, intent on do-goodery, he must have been startled at her confession.

They seemed to have a common bond, and Andrew's pleasant nature alleviated Cassia's depression as nothing else seemed capable of doing. She would hear Raven barking in the distance and know that he was on his way and that most probably his master would be a few yards behind him. Instantly she would feel brighter, looking forward to the moment when the door would open and Andrew would step inside, with his ready smile and his cheerful hazel eyes flecked with green. Sometimes she would look at the green lights in his eyes and think of Vincent and try to shut out the thought.

One day, she was sitting by the French windows looking out over at the garden, with Raven supporting himself on his front paws on the edge of her chair, she stroking his ears and talking to him. Andrew had been sitting nearby in an armchair in a sprawling position, one leg across the other. They had looked very comfortable in one another's presence, like old friends, which indeed by then they felt as if they were. It had been at that moment that Vincent had stepped into the room. Thinking it was Joanna come to join them, Cassia had looked up with a smile. Her smile had frozen. Vincent stood there, framed in the doorway, his face inscrutable. He had stood there for a few moments, looking from one to the other of them, saying nothing, before turning his back on them and going out of the room again.

She had called out his name, but only in a low voice, and he had not heard her. Andrew had glanced at her as if to say, 'Oh, do we have to be tolerant of his moods, then?' and they had exchanged a rueful smile. Raven had begun to bark, for he was impatient for a game, and Andrew had gone out onto the terrace in search of a stick to throw him. It had all been very pleasant, very peaceful. If only she could forget the knot of guilt she felt – and with good reason – for spending so much time with Andrew instead of with her husband.

Had she not been feeling so heartbroken over her loss, she might have been able to understand her feelings, to understand that she was partly suffering from the cumulative affect of all her adventures over the past two years. Being abducted, kidnapped by Nathan Dash, being sold in the slave market, forced into a life of imprisonment in the Sultan's harem, all those things had accumulated inside her to bring on the depression she was now feeling, and which had made a barrier between herself and Vincent, who had caused much of her distress at the time. Consciously she had long ago forgiven him for it all, but subconsciously, if she had but been able to guess it, she did blame him.

Joanna came into the morning-room with purposeful tread. Having given the barest of smiles to Cassia, she said, 'You cannot go on like this, you know, my dear. 'Tis not right. 'Tis four or five weeks or more since you lost the poor little infant and though I know you've grieved over it, life must go on.

There will be more babes, you know, you're a healthy young girl. Yes, there *will* be more. But there won't ever be another life for *you*, at least not one that you'll know of.'

Cassia looked down, with a tinge of pink in her cheeks. She had been sitting reading by the window, watching two ring-necked doves billing and cooing at each other. She had suddenly thought of Andrew with his light, easy movements, and she had been wishing that he was sitting with her, with Raven's head resting on her knee, his limpid eyes gazing up at her. She did not want to disturb her tranquillity of thought with any more difficult considerations, she did not want to have to shake herself out of her lethargy, or to return to the world. That would be too much effort in her present drained condition. It was true that she had begun to feel a little more cheerful, but usually only in Andrew's presence, for he was such an uncomplicated young man; he never made demands on her of any sorts. She did not have to be witty or sophisticated or bring forth sparkling conversation in his company; she could just be herself, sometimes tired, sometimes quiet, very often uncommunicative. Tall, strong Andrew, with his red-gilt hair and green-flecked eyes, seemed to understand her every nuance of mood.

She knew that Andrew was Joanna's favourite brother but that, nonetheless, he had given her a great deal of trouble during his youthful years. He had never taken to studying, but much preferred outdoor pursuits, riding and hunting, walking with his dog. He had never shown any interest in the sea, and so Paul had never been able to teach him anything in that sphere, to his regret. Had Joanna not had such very high hopes of Andrew it would have been better for him. Cassia felt that so very much had been expected of him that he had feared that he would be unable to satisfy all the demands. Rather than exert himself and perhaps fail, he had decided not to try at all. Cassia was not slow to see that his friendship with her might well do him good. There was nothing like a consuming interest to bring out the best in a man or woman. Andrew turned up regularly to sit with her, which, she gathered from Joanna, was most unlike him. Hitherto he had been unfathomable, unreliable and at times petulant when any attempt was made to restrain him. Now here he was like a lamb, visiting Cassia daily, discussing all things under the sun, displaying an interest in her health and her spirits, and not showing any resentment when Raven frequently seemed to prefer her company to his.

Cassia saw them as two wounded soldiers affected by life's cares, both with scars which needed careful nurturing and healing, both with a common bond: their inability to be understood by those around them.

It was a fine fanciful notion, and greatly inaccurate, but it was, for the moment, to serve her well.

'You *cannot* go on like this, you know, Cassia my dear,' Joanna repeated. 'There's a whole wide world out there waiting for you. You have travelled a long way in the past two years. You came all the way here from Cornwall to help the slaves, and although your husband is doing just that and becoming a very busy man, my dear, with his meetings and lectures, you seem to be showing little desire to join him.'

'He is getting along very well without me, Joanna. As you say, he has so much to do these days that I see little of him.'

'I believe that he has asked you to join him and that you have said no. My dear, do you really want a schism? Such an awkward thing, so damaging and so difficult to heal again.' Joanna sounded stern.

Cassia looked at her hands, feeling uncomfortable. A schism, that was exactly what she and Vincent had A great big ugly split between them. And it was all her fault. She felt, in her present fragile state, as if she could never rely on a loved one again. There was pain inside her, sharp and prickly, which hurt whenever she was reminded of its presence — which was often. It was the pain of grief, of feeling so unsure of depending on anyone ever again – even Vincent. Losing her baby had made her feel like this and she was quite helpless to know why, or what she could do about it.

'But my dear,' Joanna's voice was anxious now, 'my dear, you can do so much together as a couple. You are a beautiful young lady, a *real* lady. That will have a great effect on altering men's opinions, and wives who see another wife coming along will give more credence to what Vincent says at his lectures. It is time we women made our presence felt.'

'I'm not stopping you doing what you feel must be done, Joanna.'

'But I would like to do it with you, Cassia. The united front is so important. You and your husband make such a splendid couple, you capture all eyes and that is so vitally important, for when the eye is won the heart is not far behind. Oh, Cassia, my dear, I have such high hopes of us helping those poor children in the brothels. If you only knew how much sleep I lose over them, the playthings of those foul sailors who come on shore with their pockets filled with money and lust in their hearts. Those poor young girls do not stand a chance.'

'I know – I think of them too.' Cassia's face shadowed. 'I do want to help them, Joanna, more than any, I think.'

'You do? Oh, my dear, I am so pleased to hear that.' Joanna's face lit up. 'We can start our work as soon as you like, you know. All we have to do is pack a basket with the sort of things we think the girls might need – toilet water, lace, ribbons, pomanders, perhaps a home-made pie to share out amongst them. We can ask them if they want anything else. So far I have little idea of what their basic needs are. We know, of course, what their spirits are lacking. It is most important, first of all, to win over their confidence and trust. They will learn to bring their problems to us, I hope, and look to us for help and comfort. You know, Cassia, if my daughter had lived she would have been eleven years old now, just the same age as many of those poor girls, but she, being born with a white skin, would have had the world as her toy. Those girls, with their

154

black and coffee-coloured skins, are the toys of the entire world.'

'Yes I know, Joanna, you don't have to lecture me. I feel just as you do about these girls. Their lives must be sordid and degrading.'

'They're only wanted while they are young and pretty. When their health is ruined and their looks have gone they are thrown out into the streets. They do not last very long after that. Disease and malnutrition all take their toll. As I see it, we could do all sorts of things to help, besides supporting our menfolk in every way we can to actually halt the slave trade so that these poor children will no longer be brought here to be sold into the brothel. But we can care for those who are already in that situation, watch over them and guard their health, let them know that they are not alone, and then I do not see why we should not also start a home for them, where they can retire when their health is too bad to continue. Ideally, of course, we would want to protect them so well that their health does not become damaged, but on that score I would have to get advice from a physician. Perhaps we could insist that the girls are regularly examined by a doctor.

'If our past experience is anything to go by, we will find reactions from womenfolk of two kinds: there will be those who refuse even so much as to acknowledge the existence of the brothels; and there will be those who, having had them brought to their notice, will insist that they are immediately removed from the face of the earth.'

'They won't want us to take care of the poor children?'

'Not if those children are immoral or have been immoral in the past, for they will see them as a danger to their menfolk. I remember some trouble a few years ago about a notorious bordello down by the waterfront. I believe it was nicknamed the Captain's Cabin. Once word had got round amongst respectable women that such a place existed and was notorious even amongst the notorious, these was a public outcry for its demolition. There was talk of burning it to the ground, even of bringing it down by Act of Parliament. There were riots in the streets; some prisoners broke out from Liverpool Gaol and joined in the riots. There was total confusion.'

'And what happened?'

'Oh, the Captain's Cabin is still there. Now and again there is a furore about it and it is denounced, people say it can no longer go on as it is, but it does. Now, are you game, my dear? I plan to visit the first of the bawdy houses on Monday next. I shall be leaving about ten of the clock in the morning. Will you be coming with me?'

Cassia hesitated only a moment before agreeing. They planned to take one of the coachmen with them and his assistant, for they did not want to take any risks in what might prove to be a dangerous area of the city. They would take a hamper of food and gifts for the girls and, as a precaution, they would wear their plainest, darkest gowns and take no money with them.

'You will take care, Cassia?' Andrew said, his face concerned. 'I cannot think of a safer time for you both to go than ten o'clock in the morning, but all the same you cannot judge those people by our standards.'

'We are only going to see the young girls, to find out how they live, and if we can help them in any way.'

'Have you anticipated the possibility of not being allowed in?'

'No.'

'Do you always expect victory?'

'Yes.' Cassia gave a little smile. 'I do not see what they will have against us, and indeed they should welcome us, as we shall be taking gifts.'

'All the same, you can meet with some very unpleasant types, men who would think nothing of ill-treating a lady.'

'We are not the only ladies who do this sort of charity work, you know, Andrew. Women from time immemorial have been doing just this, under all sorts of conditions. In war, in peace, in famine. I would not want you to be worried on my account.'

'I know that Joanna has been anxious to do this work for a long time. You have been the catalyst, for until you came she had not summoned the courage to go out alone to help these girls. Oh, she has tried to find a partner to assist her, but so far without success.'

'We are not planning to do anything shocking, you know, Andrew. All we are doing is going down into the first brothel we have decided on, a short walk from the Old Dock, and we are going inside with our basket of gifts to get to know the children there. We shall not be doing anything officious, or which might put the brothel-keepers on the alert, for we do not want them to know what we are doing, we want them to think us just do-gooders. Secretly, of course, we shall be taking note of everything, ready for a report which we intend to make when the time is right.'

'Yes, we shall be preparing our reports, too: on the slave trade in general, and how it affects the city. We shall be in contact with the London and Bristol Abolitionists, and we all hope to make representations together to Parliament when we have our reports ready.'

'I'm getting quite excited now,' Cassia said. 'To think that *I* shall be instrumental in something so vitally important, saving all those slaves from a life of hell − !'

'And freeing them, we hope, eventually,' said Joanna, coming into the room. 'That is what Abolition is all about, and we have a much better chance of success with all of us working together. We must put personal losses aside for the sake of those poor souls who have lost everything, their homes, their families, their freedom.'

'You put me to shame, Joanna. Yes, I know you are right, and that is truly what I want to do. That is partly the reason why I came to Liverpool with Vincent. After our own unfortunate experiences we had both vowed to spend our time freeing those who have been forced into servitude, and I have not changed my vow, believe me. It is just that, well, losing my baby − it has been a terrible shock, so unexpected.'

'I do understand, dear, you know I do, but I think now that you are over the worst, you are ready to take your place in the world again. So you will come with me on Monday at ten of the clock?'

'Yes.'

The building was shabby and decrepit. At one time it had been a warehouse, a store-place for bales of cotton from the West Indies. Tiny pieces of lint still clung to the wire mesh which was affixed to the lower windows. There was nothing to proclaim it as being a brothel, except for the dusty red-shaded oil lamp which stood at the front door, and which was lit as soon as dusk gathered each night.

The two women, who were standing in front of the building surveying its gloomy facade, now looked at each other. They both wore dark brown, plain dresses, and simple hats with one feather, and they each carried a basket.

'Do we knock or just walk in?' Cassia said, looking at the solid door with misgiving.

'Both,' said Joanna decisively. So they rapped smartly at the door and when it was not opened for them within a few moments, Cassia stepped forward, tried the handle, found the door to be unlocked, and pushed it open. The one-time wide open and spacious storehouse had been carefully partitioned off into corridors and various rooms, and they stepped straight into a dark, narrow passage, from which many doors led off. It looked dirty and dingy, totally uninviting. Cassia tried to imagine customers rushing here to see their girls and found the image not coming easily. They had walked halfway down the passage when suddenly a door burst open and a tall, forbidding-looking woman appeared. She seemed even taller in the narrow confines of the passage, and Cassia and Joanna instinctively drew back.

'I do not believe that I know your names,' the woman said, her voice gritty. It was obvious that she was attempting to control a coarser accent. This was the woman Boderley, the woman responsible for the string of child brothels in this area, the woman who went to slave markets, like the toughest of men, to purchase children for her bordelloes. She had a heavy, coarse face, a large spade chin, and her brows were thick and met over her nose. Deep creases ran from the corners of her eyes down to the corners of her mouth, splitting each cheek almost in two. Cassia had never seen anything like them before, they gave the woman an eerie forbidding expression. Her eyes were small and hooded, very dark, almost black; there was no feeling in them, which did not surprise Cassia. What did surprise her was the elaborate array of fashionable clothes which the woman was wearing. Her panniers were so wide that they almost scraped the sides of the narrow passage; her hair was thickly powdered, gathered in a thicket of ringlets, and decorated with two artificial silk roses and a number of feathers. Her gown was a hectic shade of cerise pink, and it was decorated with frills and gathers, tucks and twists and folds, and all manner of ornaments. She might have been dressed in readiness for a ball; certainly she looked startlingly out of place in this shabby, run-down building.

Joanna spoke first, knowing exactly what to say, knowing, as she did, something of this woman.

'Ah, Mistress Boderley, how pleasant to see you. We did knock at the door but no one replied. We are from Saint Xavier's Mission. For some time we have been going through the city helping poor unfortunate girls, cheering them, you understand, and bringing them gifts. We have no wish to interfere with the running of your business, of course. We merely wish to make the girls' lives more pleasant.'

'I never could understand you charity workers,' Mistress Boderley sneered. 'What possible good can it do you, taking gifts to prostitutes? They're no better than the dirt on the floor. Would you care for that, too? I cannot see why you have come here, my girls are well looked after – I see to that personally.'

'Oh, we have heard the very same, Mistress Boderley,' Joanna cooed. 'But you see, we are given so much money to

159

spread amongst those in need in the city, and we seem to have visited everywhere possible and yet we still have quite a large proportion of money left over, for benefactors have been generous this year, you see. If we began distributing our gifts and money amongst those people who had already received the same there would be talk of unfairness, and outcry, you see, so we thought we would come here. That is, if we have your permission — ?'

The corners of Mistress Boderley's mouth went down, making the strange creases in her cheeks appear even deeper and darker, so that it looked as if two lines had been painted upon her face.

'They are children, they enjoy surprises. If you must, then give them some, but do not involve me in this work, I want nothing to do with it. I do not want to see or hear you, or know that you are in the building.'

'Thank you, Mistress Boderley,' Joanna said sanctimoniously, and when the woman had retreated into her office, firmly closing the door behind her, Joanna whispered to Cassia, 'The old witch. She has a heart of steel and the morals of a slave-master.'

They were alone now in the corridor, with nothing to tell them that anyone else had been present except the sickly scent of cheap violets, which the woman Boderley had been wearing. They had no idea which doors to try or where to knock or where to look for the girls, and Cassia, on coming into this place, was reminded of her own entry into the harem in Constantinople, when she had been led by the other concubines, ordered to bathe, to strip off the tattered clothes that she had worn for the long weeks of incarceration in the hold of Nathan Dash's pirate-ship, and that were replaced by floating silk caftans embroidered with silver and gold. But there was no such glorious beauty here. What had made Cassia think of the harem was the knowledge that here in this drab building were incarcerated young girls, kept here for men's pleasures, girls who had been bought into slavery by Mistress Boderley and who would probably only be released from this place by death.

The two women glanced at one another, drew in their breath as if gathering their courage, then Cassia knocked on the first door. There was silence for a few moments and then a faint voice called out, 'Who is there? Is that Mistress Boderley?'

'No, it is Joanna Peacock. I and a friend have come from the city to visit you and the other girls here, to bring you presents, to talk to you.'

'Go away!' the voice hissed. 'Go away, I don't want to see you.'

'But we mean you no harm, my dear,' Joanna said. 'We have some nice things in our baskets. We've brought you presents, you can take your pick of all the things we have. Fruit, sweets, lace or ribbons, a shell brooch perhaps?'

'Go away!' hissed the voice again, ending in a strangled note as if drowned by tears or misery.

'We can try here again later,' Joanna murmured to Cassia, and so they stepped to the next door, and this time they had a better response. The door opened immediately and a bright little face peered out at them.

'Charity workers? Me like charity workers, come in, do,' the girl said, ushering them into the room. It contained a strange hotch-potch of furniture, some cheap metal, some even cheaper wood. Curtains which clashed horribly in colour hung over the windows, the bed was covered in multicoloured blankets which hit the eye far too boldly, and brightly coloured handmade rugs were on the floor. It was a jumbled room, filled with far too many objects: too much furniture, too many curtains and covers and rugs, too many pots and pans and dishes and ornaments, ornaments everywhere. Over some ribbons hanging in the corner was suspended washing to dry. Black stockings, four pairs, and two rather shabby petticoats. It was obvious that the girl lived and slept in this room and, from the look of it, rarely went out.

Joanna asked the girl her name. She said that she was called Doombi, and that she thought she was eleven years old, but she could not be sure. She had a bright face, expressive, with large eyes, the whites healthy and glowing, the pupils limpid and dark. Her nose was snubby and pert, her mouth curvaceous and full. Her hair was gathered all over her head in tight little plaits, each plait tied with a pretty coloured ribbon. She wore a plain calico dress, and a check shawl across her shoulders; her feet were bare.

'Present for me?' she asked, her eyes eager, and Cassia lifted back the lid of the basket and told Doombi to take her pick of what she wanted. She chose one of the shell brooches, pinning it to her dress with a broad smile. 'Pretty brooch,' she said, 'Doombi lucky.'

'Tell me, Doombi, is there anything wrong with the girl who is in the next room to you on that side?' Joanna pointed.

'She near death, very ill,' Doombi said simply, as if it were a common fact of life that a girl should be dying in the next room to her. 'She have burning, much sick, no save her.'

'We must go now,' Joanna said, trying to hide her stricken expression, 'but we will come again and we will bring you more gifts.' What was most important this first time was to befriend the girls, to win their trust; the questions could come later.

In the next room a girl was asleep in bed, but she woke at their knock. She too seemed uncomplicated, straightforward and friendly like Doombi, and she told them that her name was Geli. She too chose a shell brooch for her gift. She smiled a great deal but said very little, although she remembered to thank them and to ask them to come back to see her again. Her room was very like Doombi's; perhaps not as crammed with objects, but colourful.

Sulamee was the fifth girl they saw, and the moment Cassia set eyes on the child she lost her heart. Sulamee was ten years old, and she had that particularly delicate shade of fawn skin which Cassia's friend Xenobe had had. Xenobe had been her constant true friend while she was a prisoner in the Sultan's harem, a prophetess given to strange, unfathomable prophecies which always seemed to come true in the end; a girl of great beauty who had been called Black Pearl in the harem because of her beautiful eyes. She had not fought against her destiny as had Cassia. Now, here was a miniature Xenobe: little Sulamee, only ten years old, already a prostitute, with velvet, fawn skin and dewy dark eyes which shone in her delicate face. Her lips were like plums, soft and rounded, and her nose was small for a half-caste girl and pretty. She was shy at first, but warmed to Cassia's interest. She chose a length of lace for her gift, and held it up against her cheek with a smile of delight. Then she asked Joanna and Cassia to sit on her bed, and she brewed them tea on the little spirit stove in the corner of her room. She did not have as much furniture as the other girls, merely a bed and a chair, for she had not been in the brothel very long. Cassia wanted to hear her life story, but she was very shy and spoke only slowly, hesitantly.

She said that she had lived with her mother, who was black, in Bristol until she was seven years old. Her father had been a white man, she said, somewhat derisively. He had loved her mother very much but he had deserted her when she became pregnant. It was the old story, as common amongst white people as amongst black. Sulamee had been seven when her mother had died of a fever, and it was then that Mistress Boderley had bought her.

'I too small then. Body too small for men,' Sulamee said, in the most matter of fact way, making Joanna and Cassia shudder that such a little mite should know things like this at the age of ten. 'I wait on Mistress Boderley, take care of her, till six months ago when I brought here to this room where I stay now.'

'Are you ever allowed out?' Cassia asked.

'I no wish go out. Nothing to see, nowhere to go,' Sulamee said, shrugging her shoulders. 'All life is here, in this room.'

'But that is terrible, Sulamee. Don't you ever want to go out, to see the trees, the fields, the birds, to see the sea and the ships?' Cassia wanted to know.

'I see all that in Bristol. Bad memories,' Sulamee said, lifting up the lace and holding it to her cheek again with a sigh.

'We could always ask Mistress Boderley to let us take you out.'

'She not let you, not ever. I know this. She guard her girls, not let any go out, only favoured few. Ella, Tina, Rose maybe, but not Sulamee.'

Cassia was experiencing the strangest sensation. She was captivated by Sulamee, she was reminded not only of Xenobe, her long-lost dear, close friend, but of her own lost child. In these few moments of talking to Sulamee, of absorbing her sweet air, the innocence she managed to give off despite the fact that she was, after all, a prostitute, all had entranced Cassia. She wanted to stay talking to the girl, but Joanna said that they had better hurry up, they still had many more girls to visit and there were some new members of the society calling at Peacock Hall this afternoon, so they would have to be back in time for that. Regretfully, Cassia left Sulamee, glancing back as she stepped out of her room to see the little girl, so petite and ethereally pretty, watching her go with a look of longing in her big dark eyes.

All sorts of thoughts and notions were thronging through Cassia's head as they visited the rest of the girls. She could not wait to go back and see Sulamee, to find out more about the girl, to befriend her and show her that she could be trusted.

The two women were very quiet as they returned to Peacock Hall. They were thinking of the girls they had seen; the sick ones, the healthy ones, one only nine years old, the rest aged between ten and twelve. They were thinking especially of the ones who were dying of venereal disease – what the girls called 'the burning' – and of the girls who were drug addicts, who smoked pipes filled with opium. To see them, so young, girls who should have been running about playing happily in the fields and parks, smoking opium pipes in a drugged stupor, barely able to speak, drowning all their pains and sorrows, miseries and homesickness with drugs.

'Do you think we will be able to go on with this work?' Joanna asked.

'How can we stop?' Cassia replied. 'It is worse than we thought, is it not?' Joanna nodded. 'So if we persist in our work, if we go on and let nothing stop us and refuse to be dismayed or stopped by whatever happens, we may eventually be able to hold our heads up again. How can we rest knowing what we know now? How can we walk through rose gardens or sit in one of the beautiful rooms of Peacock Hall without thinking of those poor girls in their terrible conditions, without thinking of the ones who are dying, the ones who are drug addicts already at the tender age of ten or eleven? We must free them, Joanna. We must not rest until we have changed the law.' Cassia caught her friend's hands and looked earnestly into her eyes.

'Oh, I feel the same, Cassia, do not doubt it for a moment. And as soon as we can we must find some better way of helping those girls. To take them gifts is not enough. Their health, oh what can we do about their health? Stuck in those damp rooms all the time, barely going out unless they happen to be Boderley's favourites, living on cheap food, gruel and cereal and potatoes. If we could persuade Boderley to make sure they all got milk each day that would be something.'

'I think we would sooner get blood out of a stone.'

'But if we paid for the milk ourselves she might be more easily persuaded.'

'Yes, 'tis a thought. We could pay for the milk. Surely she could not refuse then?'

They were coming in sight of Peacock Hall now and they could see the carriages of their guests drawn up in the driveway. They hastened inside quickly to change their dresses before they were seen, stripping off their dark clothes and hastily washing. When Joanna's maid had finished helping her to dress in a pale green brocade gown with panniers, and dark green lace frills at the shoulders, she went to Cassia's room to help her dress.

Joanna's dressmaker had made some new gowns for Cassia, and it was one of these which she now put on. A buttercup-yellow gown with an underskirt of china-blue and rose-pink silk flowers which had the appearance of real blossoms in full bloom. She had tried on one or two of Joanna's wigs, and she had even had another attempt at powdering her hair, but still she did not like this artifice, and so she wore her hair loose and plain in ringlets on her shoulders as usual, its glorious blaze of Titian colour a perfect foil for the yellow gown.

On a gold chain round her neck she wore a single topaz, a parting gift from Julitta. She thought of her aunt as she fastened the gem at her neck. Julitta wrote regularly, long and interesting letters about Penwellyn and Satan and his foal, and how the Briscoes were managing the estate for her. She had bought a new peacock and a new peahen, naming them after the two who had been killed, George and Charlotte, for the King and Queen. She said that it was good to be roused by their raucous screeching in the mornings again.

Cassia wrote equally frequently to Julitta, answering her every letter and sending her some extra ones whenever there was a snippet of news to relay to her. She had told her all about Liverpool, the city, the ships, the slaves, and all about *her* Peacocks – Andrew, Joanna and Paul. She had wept as she told her aunt about the lost baby, but, since then, many warm and loving letters had passed between the two women, and Julitta seemed to be getting over her deep disappointment. She frequently said she hoped that it would not be long before she had another chance to become a great-aunt, an expectation which Cassia took with mixed feelings, for things were no better between herself and Vincent. Nothing had prepared her for the change in emotions which had been the result of her losing her baby. She had had no one with whom she could freely discuss motherhood, no older, wiser woman to tell her how feelings could be drastically altered by pregnancy, by childbirth, most especially by the death of a beloved infant; no one to tell her that even the closest couples could be wrenched apart by grief and guilt and misery. So she felt embarrassed and uncomfortable, blaming herself for her coldness, and yet also blaming Vincent – though subconsciously, knowing she was being illogical, she hated herself for it.

The memory of herself as an ardent, responsive lover was becoming nothing more than that, a ghostly memory. And with each day that passed she was bottling up more and yet more of her feelings and emotions.

Soon there would be an outlet of a kind for them, but not yet.

Dressed in her finery, Cassia glanced at herself briefly in the mirror. The door opened and Vincent entered the room. Joanna's maid, taking one look at his face, bobbed a curtsey and left them alone together.

'*Doucette*,' his voice reached her across the mists of time and yet it could not penetrate the barrier of cold and grief encasing her, 'our guests have all arrived, and they are waiting to meet you.'

Cassia did not reply. She rearranged a curl at her ear and straightened one of the ruched silk flowers on her bodice.

'Will you not speak to me, *doucette*? Tell me how I have offended you?' Vincent pleaded, hurt by her silence.

She turned to look at him bitterly. 'You were not here when I needed you. If you had been here things might have been different. You could have carried me into the house, I would not have been left lying out in the storm.'

'I know you blame me, *doucette*, but I did not make the storm, it was beyond my control. I thought you were safe and happy with Joanna, enjoying women's talk.' He paused, looking at his wife's closed, cold face. 'Is there no way I can make you see the truth?' He stepped towards her, arms outstretched. She turned, a shiver coursing over her skin. In her mind's eye she saw herself lying lashed by the storm in the gardens of Peacock Hall, her baby being born too soon. If Vincent had been beside her how different it would all have been, she *knew* it. 'Why do you turn from me, *ma mignonne*?' Vincent asked, a spasm of pain crossing his face.

'I cannot forget, oh, how can you expect me to forget?' She turned to him exasperated. 'I am in mourning for our lost child, Vincent. Why aren't *you*?'

At her words he turned away, deeply wounded. Did she think just because he put on a brave face and behaved as a man was expected to behave that he did not mourn too? How could she misunderstand him?

He tried again. '*Doucette*, you have forgiven me so much in the past . . .'

'Perhaps I forgave you too much. Perhaps that is just it. I forgave you too much too soon. But this I cannot forgive you, Vincent.'

They would have gone on, but Joanna's light tap at the door interrupted them. 'Are you ready, you two? Our guests are waiting. They are anxious to meet you. Oh, you look beautiful in that gown, Cassia! You make me green with envy. I swear that if I chose such colours they would look horrendous on me.' Joanna was wearing a dress of wine brocade with a trimming of ivory ruched silk. She wore her hair powdered, as usual, one ringlet carefully arranged on her left shoulder. Garnets blazed in her ears and on her breast.

'We are coming now, Joanna,' Cassia said, not looking at Vincent as she swept to the door, carefully stepping through it sideways to allow room for the wide panniers of her gown.

Their guests were awaiting them in the conservatory: some half dozen men and two women. The taller of the two women was somewhat mannish looking, dressed in plain countrified clothes, her hair unpowdered and tied back in a black ribbon.

But it was the second woman who was dominating the room. The men were clustered round her, hanging on her every word, and she was smiling and making arabesques with her fan as she spoke. She was like a flower, dressed entirely in the most fragile and delicate shell-pink satin with a tiny ruche of exquisite lace at her breasts. Round her neck and at her ears were fat pink pearls, and diamonds glittered on her fingers. She wore one of the new low wigs, festooned with pale pink rosebuds and pearls. Yet she did not look over-dressed, only eminently beautiful. She had dainty bones, a slender waist, small neat breasts, a pretty sculpted face with lips which matched the decorations in her hair, a tiny neat nose, very slightly retroussé, two rapturous dimples in her cheeks, and silver-fair winged eyebrows over cool grey eyes. The lady was introduced to Cassia as the Comtesse Blanche de Renate, who was a widow recently arrived in England from Paris. She was an old friend of Joanna's, for they had gone to finishing school together in France. Everything about the Comtesse was exquisite: her tiny, flower-like hands, her perfect teeth, her pretty turn of phrase with the attractive French accent.

Besides her, Cassia felt drastically under-dressed and lacking in artifice, yet she had been so pleased with her new gown until she had seen the Comtesse's outfit. She noticed how the men present lapped up every word the Comtesse spoke, staring at her with round eyes as if they could barely believe what they saw.

When Vincent was introduced to the Comtesse he bowed low over her hand in his most elegant fashion. 'A country-woman!' he exclaimed. *'Je suis plus enchanté, Madame la Comtesse!'*

The moment she heard them talking in French, Cassia knew the strangest sensation, a feeling of bald dejection. She tried to reason with herself. Was it not natural for her husband, a Frenchman, to respond warmly to his countrywoman? Surely he would have done the same had she been as mannish and un-attractive as the other lady present, the Honourable Margaret Channing? But whatever she was thinking about Vincent's response, she could not help but see how taken the Comtesse was with him. She abandoned her flirtatious discourse with the other gentlemen present, and became, apparently, enthralled by Vincent.

Cassia watched with a sense of unreality as her husband responded blatantly to the Comtesse's charm. Joanna had told her something of the Comtesse before she met her. She was a very wealthy widow who was prepared to spend her money on the Abolitionist cause; her funds would be invaluable to help the growth of The Children of Liberty, but did Vincent have to make it so patently obvious that he found the woman physically attractive?

Seeing a shroud of gloom passing over Cassia, Joanna stepped in at once, introducing her to the men who were present. They were mostly stolid Lancashire businessmen, all of whom wished to assist in the cause of freeing the slaves. They were warm and they were responsive to Cassia's beauty, but she could not prevent her glance from hastening back to Vincent and the Comtesse every now and again. They were getting on famously, laughing and flirting with one another.

Cassia was beginning to feel her facade of social cheeriness slipping. She felt her smile faltering and knew that she was losing control of the situation. That woman was flirting outrageously with Vincent, and he, loving every moment of it, was responding wholeheartedly. She would have languished, lost the desire to speak or smile, had it not been for Andrew, who had arrived at that moment, late as usual, taken in the situation at a glance and presented himself at Cassia's elbow with an admiring bow.

The two sturdy Lancashire men who had been trying to win Cassia's sole attention were somewhat disgruntled at Andrew's polished social graces. Within moments of his arrival he had totally won the attentions of the beautiful red-haired lady they had so wanted to captivate themselves, and he was handing her a glass of wine and a wafer, which they should have thought of doing. Soon the lovely Cassia Sauvage seemed not to notice anyone else in the room except Andrew Peacock. She even found time to pat his dog, Raven, who was sitting at his feet, on his very best behaviour.

The afternoon wound down pleasantly after that; warm new friendships had been forged, which was what had been intended by the gathering; this, by its very informality, could leap barriers.

Later, when the guests had gone, Cassia did not follow Vincent up to their room to change. She sat in the library with Andrew, feeling that she had every right to do so after Vincent's outrageous behaviour with the Comtesse. She told Andrew about their first visit to the brothel by the Old Dock, and he listened intently to every word she spoke.

When she had finished he said, 'What we need is expert representation in Parliament. It is no good our working away here and worrying over all the injustices we find if we do not expect one day to change the law. As it stands, the slave traders have all the power and make all the profit in every way they wish, and no one says nay to them. So far we do not have a local Member of Parliament who will speak up for us in London. We shall do our best to coerce the members we know, but it may have to end with one of us becoming an Independent member, the success of our seat resting on the cause of Abolition. We are inclined to feel that, as a reformed slave captain, Paul is the one who would most likely be listened to.'

For an insane moment Cassia wondered what Andrew would say if she blurted out that Vincent, also, was a reformed slave captain, that he had not only dealt in black flesh but in white, too – that he had captured Christian slaves, herself included, from off the shores of England itself, carrying them back to Constantinople to sell into the Sultan's harem. Her moment of madness was over instantly: she could never commit such a terrible betrayal. It would be better all round for Paul to be their representative, their spokesman at Westminster, knowing all the intimate facts of the black slave traffic at first hand as he did, and being English by birth.

Raven nuzzled against her hand, thrusting his nose into her palm, eagerly seeking a favourable reaction. He was an adorable dog and she would have given anything for him to be hers. She needed something to fill the gap left by her lost baby, someone or something she could mother and shower with tenderness, all the tenderness that was bottled up inside her waiting to spill over. When Andrew announced that it was time to take Raven for his late afternoon walk Cassia declined to join them. She needed time to think; she wanted to mull over the day's happenings. It had been a satisfying but a disquieting day also. She knew that she wanted to visit the girls in the brothel again, that she would not be happy until she had made her utmost efforts for them.

She fell to thinking about Sulamee – so like her lost friend Xenobe. It was as if Xenobe had been given back to her, and yet Sulamee was a slave; she legally belonged to Mistress Boderley. She was as much a slave as Xenobe had been in the Sultan's harem. But if she, Cassia, could work to free the child, now that would be a blessing indeed. Her spirits rose at the prospect. She wanted to free all the girls, of course, all the slaves, everywhere throughout the world, but these matters were like acorns, only in time would they grow into oaks. To free Sulamee – it was a blissful notion. To take the child from that immoral and degrading existence and take her back to Penwellyn, a kind of replacement for the child she had lost . . .

In her mind's eye she saw Sulamee romping on the moors around Penwellyn, flinging back her face to absorb the sun's healing rays, learning to ride a pony, picking bluebells and all the other wild flowers which grew in such profusion around Julitta's home. Sulamee, free, and being raised as one of her own family. She wrapped her arms round her body, hugging herself at the thought. Someone on whom to lavish all the stored-up maternal love and affection.

She wondered what Vincent would think of her idea.

Chapter Ten

There had been another brutal murder. The whole city was horrified, gathering into itself and discussing the crime in hushed whispers. Parents ordered their children to be safely inside their homes even earlier than usual; respectable women stayed off the streets; men who loved their families ensured that they were all safely protected wherever they went. This was not the first such murder, and there was only one consolation: yet again it had taken place in the seamier areas of Liverpool where decent people would never dream of setting foot. This time one of the young prostitutes in the brothel they called the Captain's Cabin had been horribly battered to death, and her dismembered body flung crazily around the room so that the walls were besplattered with blood.

'It is a risk all prostitutes take,' Joanna said, after hearing of the shocking details. 'Each girl knows that there is a chance a customer will turn nasty at some time or other. Of course, the slave girls have even less choice than the prostitutes who have taken to that life out of preference. There is that much more coercion to be used on the black girls. They can be brutally beaten, ill-treated, tortured even, by their owners in their efforts to make them submit, and this applies to customers too, alas.'

'What will happen now? Will the law forces set about finding the murderer?' Cassia wanted to know.

'No doubt they will make some half-hearted enquiries, but do not forget, the girl was a mere prostitute, and they are considered lower than the lowest, not worthy of protection. That poor girl is not the first victim, nor, sadly, will she be the last. The city has known for some time that there is a maniac abroad, but while he confines his monstrous crimes to women of ill-repute little will be done about it. Now, if a respectable lady were so much as approached there would be public uproar: you would hear the furore from here to Chester.'

'The double standard is very depressing,' Cassia said, looking down at her hands.

'But they are slaves, my dear, do not forget that. Think what the average opinion is of a slave. A serf to be crushed beneath one's heel, one who has no voice nor is allowed any opinion. He has no standing, no legal rights. If he dares to try and escape he can be horribly, brutally tortured to death as a deterrent to other slaves, or he can have his ears or his nose lopped off, a hand or a foot, to prevent his straying again. So if some crazed murderer decides to come along and destroy yet another of these wretched creatures, who is to complain? Remember what that woman said to you in the shop in Dove Street – they have no souls. What officer of the law is going to risk his life taking on some crazed killer to protect soulless slaves?'

'You are right, Joanna. But it is so crushingly depressing. Sometimes I think about the task we have ahead of us and I see it as an enormous mountain which is absolutely insurmountable. Shall we ever succeed, Joanna?'

'It is no good becoming melancholy, my dear. If every man who set out upon some enormous task pondered upon whether he would be successful or not, then I vow that many men would never get past the first thoughts on the subject.'

'Again you are right, Joanna. It is not like me to be melancholy, nor to look on the black side of things. You must bear with me.'

'You are ready to visit the slave girls again? You have not changed your mind about doing that work with me?'

'Indeed no, anything but that. I have been thinking deeply about those children and wondering how we can help them. Is there any way we could prevent Mistress Boderley from buying more girls? Could we perhaps blockade her attempts to purchase slaves?'

'For that we would need bold men, inestimable wealth, and

a great deal of courage. The freedom to purchase at the slave markets is one of the most jealously guarded freedoms. If we began to interfere before we had proper support for our cause we might damage our prospects. I do not want to sound faint-hearted, my dear, but those who make their fortunes out of a certain merchandise will not willingly let that merchandise go. We must appeal to their better instincts, to the Christian and more noble side of their natures, but it will take time. Yes, I would most heartily wish to go down to the slave markets and buy girls before Mistress Boderley could do so, but do you think that she would allow such interference without recipro-cating in some way? She is a powerful woman; I suspect that she would be vicious if provoked. She has the support of all the slave captains, indeed of all those who have slaves to sell at some time or other, for she pays well for healthy, attractive girls.'

'She is prepared to pay more than the average price for her girls?'

'Indeed yes. For the right girls, ones who are in good condi-tion and above average attractiveness, she will pay princely sums, so Paul told me. He also said that there are some captains who procure girls particularly for her requirements and that those girls are carefully looked after on the voyage here from the West Indies. So, in a way, her demands are improving the lot of at least a few of the slaves.'

'But the life they lead after they have been bought by the Boderley woman is surely all too degrading and humiliating.' Cassia said nothing of her own past experiences to Joanna, but she was remembering how she had felt being sold into a harem, being used by the Sultan, being forced to exist solely for a man's pleasure, having no will of her own. To her, it had been the most abject misery and abasement and she had been forced to respond to one man and one man only: these poor young girls, who were still children, were forced to submit to the desires and whims, and probably also the perversions, of any number of men. And would not those men by their very predilection for those children declare themselves as perverts? She tried to imagine what manner of man would seek a child to satisfy his unnatural lusts. She found such a man difficult to construct in her mind's eye. Would he be a brute, a savage, bestial, animal? Would he be a man who associated children with lust and vice versa? And in that case what would happen with his own children, with the children of his friends and family? Would he be able to control his animal passions in their presence, or would his desires overcome him? Again, possibly the men, or some of them, were quite normal on the face of it, keeping their perversions for their visits to Mistress Boderley's brothel. She shuddered at the thought of it.

Then a thought occurred to her. 'Joanna, we have agreed that it is unlikely the Justices will exert themselves to discover the murderer of that poor prostitute the other day. But had you thought that we, in our capacity as charity workers, will have ample opportunity for learning various facts about the girls and their visitors? In our everyday conversation with the girls we will have a chance to find out more about their customers, the men who visit them, what they are like, their names, and so on. Do you not think we might come across a clue as to the killer's identity if we persevere with our enquiries, whilst all the time appearing to be engaging in light conversation only?'

'So you would have us as lady Justices, is that it?' Joanna smiled. 'I must say the idea does appeal to me, killing two birds with one stone. I see no harm in it, but we must be very careful of course. We are not dealing with any normal man — this murderer is, I have no doubt, quite insane. Probably he will be prepared to murder again and again in order to hide his tracks. Who knows who he is? If he is some titled gentleman, some important personage in the city, think how desperate he will be to conceal his identity.'

'How often have these murders occurred, Joanna? Had you considered the possibility that he might be a sailor, a man who goes off on this Triangular Trade and travels round the world with his ship, and then returns to Liverpool to commit a murder each time?'

'I had not thought of that. I shall ask Paul to check up on the length of time between each murder. There have, I think, been three so far, but I cannot be too sure of that. Of course, we don't know that they were all by the same man.'

'There must be certain similarities if the murder is by the same man, surely? Paul will be able to find out, will he not? He knows the sailors, he knows the men down on the quay. He can make enquiries. Have the other murders that you remember been of young girls in the bawdy houses?'

'Yes, as far as I remember. All young girls, too, in the region of nine or ten.'

'So we are already narrowing down our clues.'

'Yes, but unless we know details of all the men who have this appalling predilection, we can hardly fit the clues to the murderer, can we?'

'But if we question the girls as I suggested before, yet with care, merely as if we are showing a friendly interest in their activities, we shall build up details of their clients and, who knows, one day we may realize that we have a clue as to the murderer.' Cassia gripped her hands together, excited at the thought of saving more helpless children from this savage brute. To be a slave, to be a prostitute, and to know that one was also the prey of a crazed murderer! Those poor girls must be living in purgatory. Cassia was determined she would help them.

After one or two visits to Mistress Boderley's brothel, it became obvious that not all the girls were equally in need of their aid. Mistress Boderley's favourite girls, Ella for example, were haughty creatures who had special freedoms allowed them which the other girls were never given. For a time Cassia wondered why such a strange woman as Mistress Boderley would have favourite girls, and she pondered over this. Was it because the girls were particularly popular with the customers and brought in more money? That seemed the most likely idea. And then one day, as she was about to tap on Ella's door to announce her arrival to the girl, her arm was jabbed by one of the other children.

'You not go in today,' the girl said, her eyes large and frightened looking. 'You stay 'way today. Ella not want.'

Cassia was always ready to oblige such wishes, knowing how easily they could be forbidden entry into the brothel if they offended Mistress Boderley. Leaving Ella's door, she tapped at Sulamee's door a little farther down the corridor. Sulamee opened it instantly, a broad smile upon her exquisite face. Just as Cassia was about to step into the room, she heard a door farther back along the corridor creaking open slowly. She glanced back: it was Ella's door. Mistress Boderley was leaving Ella's room, clumsily fastening up the bodice of her gown.

There had been women like that in the harem, and Cassia had always stayed well away from them. To realize that Mistress Boderley was like that, too, filled her with a sick despair. These girls were being preyed on from every side, corrupted and depraved, before they had a chance to grow straight and strong. No wonder Ella behaved as if she were queen here, giving out orders to the other girls, and looking haughtily at Cassia and Joanna when they visited. Hastily Cassia averted her head, stepping into Sulamee's room as quickly as she could manage, hoping that Mistress Boderley had not caught her watching. She wanted no trouble from the woman, nor did she wish her to think that she was prying.

Her thoughts were soon taken from Mistress Boderley and her favourites, as Sulamee's beaming face shone happily at her presence. The child was eager to see what she had brought her today, and so Cassia lifted the lid of her basket and brought out a selection of fripperies: blue satin ribbons with embroidered rosettes at the ends; a set of gaudy glass buttons, for she had soon found out that the negresses adored bright colours; a packet of toffee, and one of marchpane; some detachable red frilly cuffs to wear on a gown; a pink satin rosette to wear in the hair. As always she gave Sulamee her choice, and this time the child chose the frilly red cuffs, immediately fitting them onto her rather shabby gown and looking at them with ecstatic joy.

'Pretty, so pretty,' she said, stroking the frills and holding them against her cheek, which was one of her favourite mannerisms. Everything she liked at some time or other was held against her cheek.

'And how have you been since I last visited you, Sulamee? Have you been well, has your cough cleared up?'

The girl nodded, her eyes wide. 'Cough all gone. Medicine you give me soon cure it, like magic.' Sulamee patted her chest expressively. Then she ran to the corner of the room, fetching one of her other gowns to show Cassia, a look of delight on her features. 'See, see!' she said, pointing to the emerald green lace which Cassia had brought on her last visit and which Sulamee had now sewn onto her second-best gown, a blaze of green at the neck.

'Oh, you have done that beautifully, Sulamee. How pretty it looks! I think at the bottom of the basket somewhere I've got a green ribbon which will go with that lace to perfection.' Cassia delved into her basket and came out with a ribbon which did, indeed, match the lace. Sulamee immediately took up the ribbon, half-closed her eyes and held it against her cheek, crooning a little song to herself. Then she reached out one of her tiny, delicate, fawn hands to take Cassia's and to kiss it, once, twice.

Cassia felt sharp tears pricking behind her lids. She was deeply moved by the child's gesture of innocent gratitude. How sweet, how natural Sulamee was, as were so many of the other girls. How could that appalling woman, Boderley, corrupt them? Or let others corrupt them? It was nauseating.

A spasm of impotence swept through her. She wanted to be able to change the world instantly. To accept the realization that she could not was more than difficult, it was painful.

'I not have lace for many years,' Sulamee said. 'My mamma

have many pretty dresses, with lace and flowers, pretty beads. She give me pretty dresses also, many colours.' The child sighed, memories an ache within her. 'My mamma love me, she care for me. I have many gifts, toys, all the time. Mamma's friends bring me gifts, too. Many gentlemen bring fine presents for Sulamee.'

'Your mother must have been very beautiful, Sulamee,' Cassia said. 'Tell me about her.'

'She have pretty cream skin, rich like sun browned.'

'She was not black?'

'No, her mother black, her father white, like my father. That why my skin so white, Mistress Boderley say.'

So Sulamee's mother had been a mulatto, the child of black and white parents. And that made Sulamee a quadroon. Cassia was beginning to learn about the different degrees of blackness which comprised the negro race: quadroons were highly prized, for they were virtually white, some being indistinguishable from white folk. She believed that there were Quadroon Balls in New Orleans in the Americas where beautiful, nearly white, women gathered to display their talents to all the gentlemen who were interested enough to attend, which was usually a great many. If Sulamee should have a child by a white man that child would be called an octoroon, and would probably be indistinguishable from a white person. Of course, there were throwbacks. Paul had told her about those: unexpectedly, a black baby could be born to apparently white parents. She was wondering about Sulamee's future, how the child would adapt to life in Cornwall with white people, the possibility of her marrying and having babies of her own one day, for it was unthinkable that she should not lead a normal life. Of course, if all the slaves were freed there would be a quadroon or an octoroon man to marry off to Sulamee, which would be ideal, but, if not, then some tender, loving, understanding man might be found for her one day.

A man like Vincent. The thought came unbidden into her mind, but she repressed it hastily. She was not ready to accept such thoughts of her husband yet. Indeed, where was his tender understanding these days? Of late he had had nothing but criticisms and reproaches for her.

She would have liked to stay with Sulamee all day. Next time she came she planned to bring the child some books and begin to teach her how to read, but for now there were more pressing visits she must make. There was a young girl, just a few doors away, who was an opium addict. She just lay on her bed hour after hour, smoking an opium pipe; she barely troubled to eat, and it was difficult to communicate with her. She lived her life in a blurry haze. Her frame was skeletal, and there were hollow pits where her flesh had sunken in between her bones.

Cassia had tried on a number of occasions to talk to the child, trying to elicit some sort of response from her, but in vain. She did not want to give up, however. She entertained a thought that if the child were made to respond to the outer world once more, she might possibly find the will to give up her addiction.

Nola seemed a little brighter. Her glinting dark eyes shone as she saw Cassia step into her room, and she lifted her head a little to see what she was carrying in her basket.

'Have you eaten today, Nola?' Cassia asked. 'I have brought you a pie, and some Cheshire cheese. Did Sulamee bring you the milk?' Cassia had instructed Sulamee to make sure that Nola got at least one cup of milk a day.

Nola nodded. 'Yes, I had my milk,' she said in her slow, slurred speech. Her fingers came over the bed-covers like questing spiders. 'What you brought me today?' she asked.

Cassia put the basket on the bed where Nola could see it and lifted up the lid. 'I have brought you a special treat, but before you see it I would like you to do something for me. I would like you to eat at least one piece of this pie I have brought.'

'Not hungry,' Nola said, turning her face away.

'You have to eat, Nola. It is no good saying you are not hungry every time I bring you food. You are growing thin, you know. This is a delicious pie, it has chicken and vegetables inside it, and look at the lovely crusty pastry.' Nola did look, but without visible pleasure. 'Don't you want to see what I've brought you, Nola?'

Now the deep-set dark eyes did light up. Plainly Nola did want to see her gift. One of the spidery hands came towards the pie, and hastily Cassia broke off a slice and put it into the thin palm. Then she supported Nola's head with her hand while the girl took a bite of the pastry. It was slow going. She bit into it carefully and chewed slowly, as if in some pain; her swallows were gulps. As Cassia watched her, she felt a surge of pity. This poor child, allowed to have drugs, allowed to smoke one of those evil pipes, instead of eating her proper food. Mistress Boderley could not possibly gain anything by letting her girls become opium addicts, why did she let them do it? Surely it was in her interests to keep them healthy as long as possible? Unless . . . Cassia thought of the ever-changing occupants of the harem in Constantinople. Apart from the few top favourites, the chief wives and the chief concubines, the other members of the harem were being added to or changed constantly. Some Sultans, acutely bored with their concubines, had ordered the entire harem to be drowned in the Bosphorus. Probably that was what was beneath the woman Boderley's careless regard for her girls. If they had not become chief favourites in the brothel, girls who had won her esteem or engaged her perverted desires, or who were in regular demand with major customers, then they were dispensable. New faces would bring in new customers and ensure that old customers returned again and again. Cassia found the whole prospect crushingly depressing, even more so than she had in the harem in Turkey, for these girls were mere children.

Nola had eaten three mouthfuls of the pie, and was lying back on her pillow, exhausted. 'Nice,' she said, 'nice pie. More tomorrow.'

'Are you sure you cannot eat more now, Nola? Please, do try,' Cassia coaxed.

'No, cannot,' Nola said with a sigh. 'Tired now.'

'Don't you want to see your gift, then?'

'Yes.' The word was very faint.

Cassia took out the litle carved box, painted in blues and reds and greens with a design of rosebuds and leaves, and slipped it into Nola's hand. The child looked at it through half-closed eyes, her lips curving into a smile, then her eyes closed completely, her breathing coming evenly.

Gently Cassia pulled the covers up around her neck, ensuring that she was completely warm, and then she picked up her basket, put the remains of the pie in it, and tiptoed out of the room.

Chapter Eleven

The same crusading Liverpool zeal which had built the Bluecoat School and Infirmary, founded and supported by public subscription, the Work and Poor House in Hanover Street, the Sailors' Sixpenny Hospital and the Sick and Lame Hospital in Shaw Street, and the Alms Houses in Dale and Hanover Street and on the Heath, along with the free school, was also to finance the work of The Children of Liberty.

Subscriptions were flooding in. There were enquiries from citizens who wished to become members of the society, and offers of help. The Peacocks' friends and associates were doing their work well, passing word throughout the city and surrounds, letting everyone know the facts regarding the Triangular Trade, branding, and child brothels. Vincent spoke regularly to crowded halls, as did Paul Peacock. They had mixed receptions for their lectures, but none so violent as the reaction to Vincent's lecture at Toxteth Hall one Saturday evening. He was accustomed to men in the audience who were vociferous in their condemnation of the Abolition movement, men who said that Liverpool had become great only because of the slave trade, and that it could not survive without it, but the men who were heckling in the audience at Toxteth Hall were raucous-voiced and refused to be silenced.

'Liverpool cannot survive without its slaves!' one of the hecklers bellowed, a second roaring his agreement. 'We shall all be without work, penniless, begging in the streets like after the wars with France! No one must interfere with slavery!'

Vincent replied immediately, standing up and speaking strongly and firmly. He had barely managed to say two sentences before three men clambered onto the dais where he sat and began to attack him. Security men rushed to assist, but before they could get on the dais, Vincent had dealt summarily with the three ruffians, who were lying shocked and bleeding on the boards, not knowing what had happened to them. However, there were more who tried to reach Vincent, six or seven, all with snarling faces, all determined to put him out of action so that they could, as they saw it, save their jobs.

Vincent dealt with them all in the same cool, accomplished fashion, and they were dragged away by the security men. The evening progressed without further incident until Vincent stepped outside the Hall to climb into the carriage waiting for him.

A throng of enraged men burst round the corner of the Hall and set upon him with clubs and fists. Had they been a moment sooner, they would have caught him on foot but, as it was, he had reached his carriage and from this vantage point thrust away the first attackers with his booted feet, his fists fending off others who attempted to seize him. They fell back, and would have been joined by more had not Vincent whipped up the horses and set off at a terrific pace. Beside him, the coachman sat stunned, unable to assist for he had been paralysed with fear on seeing the rioters.

It had been a narrow escape, and it was a warning not to lecture alone. In future, they must accompany one another everywhere – it was only sense.

This was not the only occasion on which Vincent returned home exhausted, but he said nothing to Cassia about his ordeal, not wanting to frighten her. He had become completely involved in the formation of the society and the work arising from this, which had kept him occupied for some weeks now. His naturally active temperament needed total absorption to be subjugated, or he would have become intolerably restless.

Cassia was putting the finishing touches to her *toilette* in readiness for dinner when Vincent returned from another lecture. He looked white and drained, and there was little sparkle in his rich emerald eyes.

Seeing him look so tired, Cassia felt a momentary spasm of

pity, but it was only momentary. After all, he was doing the work he had vowed to do. So was she . . . She returned her gaze to the mirror, tying a blue satin ribbon amongst her curls. She made every effort to keep her eyes on her reflection and not on the reflection of Vincent as he sank onto the bed behind her, a sigh of total weariness escaping his lips.

'How did things go at Boderley's today?' he asked her.

'Fair,' she said, still keeping her eyes firmly on her reflection.

'How is Nola?'

'She seemed a little better today. She ate some of the pie I took. I have asked Sulamee to make sure she gets milk every day.'

'Good.' Vincent began stripping off his jacket and breeches, his soiled shirt. He ran a hand through his hair and sat for a moment with his elbows on his knees, looking down at the floor, in a pose of dejection.

Cassia knew that this should have been the moment when she went over to him, sat down beside him on the bed and put her arms gently round him to kiss away his tiredness, to revive him with her love. She saw, in her imagination, the scene as she went over to Vincent and took him in her arms and kissed away his cares, spoke to him of her love, and of how they would win through together. She saw, but she could not move.

The familiar coldness had her in its grip: an emotional paralysis which seemed to clamp down on her movements so that when she wanted to behave as she once had done towards Vincent, in a warm and loving and spontaneous fashion, she could not do so. Something had happened to her when she had lost her baby. It had frozen her emotions, transformed her from the loving and ardent wife she had been to a frigid, un-communicative nun, and there was nothing she could do about it.

Pretending that all was as it should be, she continued with stiff fingers to fasten the ribbon into a bow, to arrange the bow carefully amongst her curls. With a wooden arm she picked up her comb, arranged her hair as she wanted it, then with wooden hands she straightened the lace on her bodice. She looked down to see that the pendant on her bosom was straight, and then she looked up into the mirror — and into Vincent's eyes.

She felt a shock as if cold water had been dashed against her. He was looking at her so hungrily, with such need in his gaze. If only she could run to him . . . But her legs were wooden, too, as was her heart, and she had lost the key to her love for Vincent. There was something else, too: the memory of pain and fear and loss forever now to be associated with sexuality. Lovemaking, which before had been impulsive, beautiful, ecstatic, had become something to be shied away from, for it had brought her the painful miscarriage, her baby's death. Now, lovemaking could no longer be eagerly sought, for it had been proved to have a very unpleasant consequence. It would take time for the bad memories to fade.

'*Doucette*.' He was beside her, his hands on her shoulders, his brilliant jewel eyes boring into hers. She felt herself shrinking inside. He sensed her withdrawal. '*Doucette*, why are things different between us now? What has changed us, why do we shy away from each other? Do you not love me any more?'

'I —' She paused, wanting to cry out that of course she loved him, that she always would, that nothing had changed between them, but knowing it would have been a lie. She was so confused; her thoughts, her emotions, her fears, were all jumbled up inside her; she could not tell one from the other. She felt panic rising. He was so close, his hard body pressed against hers. His mouth came down, soft and warm and velvet firm. She wanted to drink up his love, but that way lay pain and suffering, and she had already borne too much of that.

'Why do you not answer me, *doucette*? What have I done to offend you?'

'Nothing,' she whispered.

'Then tell me what is wrong. Oh, my love, do you not realize how you are hurting me by being so cool?'

'I am sorry.' Her words sounded clipped, insincere. She almost wished them unsaid. His lips brushed against her cheek, her forehead. She wanted to coil her arms round him and draw him close, dissolve in his embrace, belong to him heart, body and soul, as she had done before. But things had changed, oh, how they had changed, and she was helpless to mend them. She wanted to plead, to beg his forgiveness, but her pride would not let her, nor would the coldness invading her bones, forcing up the barrier between them. As he came closer she moved farther away emotionally, and it was as if she had also moved physically, for he was a man of sensitivity, and he could sense her inner rebuttal of him.

'I would not wish to hurt you,' he said in a low voice. 'I remember what the physician said.'

Her head flew up. 'What did he say?'

'That you must be protected and not risk another baby for the moment.'

'Oh, that.' There was a wealth of emotion in her voice. He could not tell whether she was being derisive, speaking from a fund of bitterness. He remembered how she had thought with joy of the birth of their child, how she had planned and dreamed, telling Julitta that she was going to be a great-aunt, talking of their child learning to ride on the moors around Penwellyn, of the happiness they would have together as a family. A woman's dreams could be profound, far more profound than ever a man's could be, and he acknowledged that. He had a wife whom he loved obsessively, whom he had once believed lost to him forever. All too vividly he remembered the pangs of that loss, and he had no desire to suffer them again. He would die if she died. How could he tolerate a world devoid of his Cassia? The answer was that he could not, and he knew it, but he had always been a man of powerful desires. Before he had fallen in love with Cassia he had kept a harem; only a small one, but none of its occupants had ever had undue reason to complain about being neglected. It was true that he had much to occupy him of late, but his passions could only be partially submerged even so.

He had no recourse but to take his hands from her shoulders, a feeling of sadness engulfing him. He was bone-weary, almost too tired to eat. There would be time later to improve relations between them.

The dinner gong sounded throughout the house, a low, brassy cacophony. Cassia had dressed with extra care, for there were guests tonight: the Comtesse de Renate and Andrew's friend, Charles, the young man who had the misfortune to be deeply in love with India, a negress who was his father's slave.

'Our guests are waiting, Vincent, we must go down.' There was a strange expression in Cassia's eyes as she looked at her husband. He tried to analyse the expression, and he felt a chill of foreboding. It was a coolness, putting a great distance between them. It made her a stranger to him, in a way she had never been, not even in those first few hours after he had kidnapped her from the Cornish cove. He thought longingly of those weeks when she had tried to convince him that he loved her, when she had spoken only of their feelings for one another, dismissing his cynicism regarding love as ignorance and unenlightenment. What he would give to have those times back again!

The dining-room glittered with silver and porcelain. Joanna, resplendent in a dress of sky-blue satin trimmed with black, ordered drinks to be brought for Cassia and Vincent as they took their places in the room.

The Comtesse was, as usual, a vision. Wreaths of cerise rosebuds entwined her white-powdered hair, and her gown was cerise and ivory striped silk. Moonstones encircled her slender, swan-like neck and glowed like the moon itself on her fingers. She looked like an exquisite doll sitting at the table, almost too ethereal and beautiful to be real. Vincent's eyes flew straight to her, as did Cassia's as she took her seat.

Joanna spoke first. 'The Comtesse tells me that she has been collecting amongst her titled friends with the aim of opening a home for those girls who have been unfortunate enough to become destitute and have no recourse but the streets.'

'Not necessarily negresses, you understand,' the Comtesse put in, with an angelic smile, 'but any poor girls in difficulties. Your husband,' she turned to Cassia, 'has told me all about the Bluecoat Hospital and the other Alms Houses which abound in Liverpool, and I immediately saw that there was a great need for a home especially for these poor girls, many of whom are pregnant and have nowhere to go to give birth to their babies.'

'I hope you will be extremely successful in your collection, *Madame la Comtesse*,' Cassia said, smiling back serenely. 'I cannot think of a cause dearer to my heart. Many of the girls are but children and have never had an opportunity to play as children should. They need somewhere to go where they can enjoy a haven from a world which has proven to be callous to them and, as you say, they need some place where they can have their babies in peace and tranquillity.'

'I see we are agreed on that, then,' said the Comtesse, altogether as if there had been a long string of disagreements between herself and Cassia.

The meal began, starting with delicious turbot from Liverpool Bay itself. The wine was French, light and delicious, but even its heady influence apparently could not encourage the diners to talk. After the first flush of conversation, dialogue died away, Joanna trying her best to elicit some response from her guests. She raised many subjects but little was said on any of them. Vincent was too exhausted to engage in social chit-chat. Cassia was somewhat preoccupied, thinking of Nola and Sulamee and wondering how Nola would be the next day when she visited her. The Comtesse glittered, but needed a response to continue glowing and tonight she was short of that. Andrew seemed thoughtful, and Paul also looked tired, for he had been with Vincent throughout that day.

Finally, the wine and the good food did its work, mellowing their moods and relieving their weariness. Vincent began to speak of the day, of the difficulties they had had with hecklers, how exhausting it had been.

'Yes,' said Paul, 'we had one man who insisted that an honest living could be made out of slavery, that it had brought prosperity to Liverpool, as it had to Bristol and London before it, and that to cut off such a source of prosperity would be insanity.'

'We tried every argument against him,' said Vincent, shrugging his shoulders slightly. 'We told him of the dejection, misery, anguish and pain suffered by the negroes, how they are branded and collared and manacled, how they are thrown alive to the sharks when they prove to have some disease. The man rejoindered by telling us that he had made five hundred pounds this year from slavery, and that if he had not had that income available to him he would have been destitute.'

'By now Vincent was furious,' Paul put in. 'I could see that he would have liked to strangle the man. He was handsomely dressed in showy bright green and there were velvet trimmings on his jacket, a preponderance of silver and gold embroidery on his waistcoat. I could see Vincent looking at him and thinking of all the slaves, the hundreds and thousands of negroes who are kept naked. He said as much and the man with the bright green jacket went purple in the face.

'"Would they not be just as naked in their home territory, in the wilds and jungles where they live?" the man shouted back. "It is only when they come to this country that they learn how to wear clothes. Negroes would not have been put here in abundance if God had not meant them to be used in this way! To ignore them would be a crime against God, a rebuttal of His good works and what He has provided for us!"

'"What would you have done if the tables had been turned?" Vincent demanded. "Would you have accepted your lot as calmly as the negroes are expected to accept theirs? Would you have endured the horrors of sea voyages, being flung overboard to the sharks if you happened to catch some illness? Would you be prepared to be sold naked in the marketplace and kicked if you disobeyed, to be branded on your chest or forehead, to wear a heavy metal collar and manacles so that you could not get far if you had the wit to escape?"

"'But that's not how it was made, sir,' the man raged at Vincent. "God did not pattern it that way, and we should accept God's pattern without question."

"'If God had wanted men to be enslaved there would still be serfs in England," Vincent said, looking the man straight between the eyes. "But that was a heinous crime which was put right by enlightened men, as slavery will be put right, and soon.'" Paul looked round the table. 'The response to Vincent winning that argument was uproar, but of the best possible kind. He was loudly applauded, and long.'

'Bravo, Captain Sauvage!' The Comtesse lightly clapped her hands together. 'Will you come and talk to my friends, for I still have some foolish acquaintances who need to have their ideas reformed about slavery? They are rich, and look only for some object on which to shower their gold, some charity or other, it does not matter to them which one, so it might as well be slavery, might it not? For that, to my mind, merits the greatest need.'

'I would be honoured, *Madame*,' Vincent said, slightly bowing his head.

When the meal was over, the ladies retired to the drawing-room and the men went into the library to smoke. Joanna herself poured out coffee for her guests and handed round a plate of pretty sweetmeats in different colours, green, pink and yellow.

Cassia found it difficult to relax, even leaning back in a comfortable chair with a cup of coffee in her hands. She kept wondering what was happening to Nola and Sulamee, for it was evening now, the time when their clients visited them. She could not help but worry about the maniac who had murdered the prostitute at the Captain's Cabin and who had not yet been caught. Over and over she had warned the girls to take care with their clients, to ensure that they were regular customers whom they knew well. But it was not easy for them; they were slaves, they could be severely chastised, even tortured, for refusing a customer, and some men were aroused by reluctance on a girl's part . . .

'You have no children, Madame Sauvage?' The Comtesse's question came out of the blue, causing Cassia to gather her thoughts together quickly.

'No, unfortunately I recently lost a baby.' It was the first time she had spoken of it to a stranger.

'Alas, how sad, I am so sorry.' The Comtesse's words sounded totally insincere. 'I myself have two sons, both very healthy boys. They are with their nursemaid.'

'How delightful for you,' said Cassia, wondering if the Comtesse was being deliberately cruel. She felt a spasm of pain course through her but did her best to conceal it.

The Comtesse refused one of the sweetmeats which Joanna handed to her, saying that she had no wish to over-fill her stomach. Joanna raised her brows slightly, then helped herself to two of the marzipan confections. Cassia also refused: she had found it difficult to eat a little of the dinner put before them. What she truly wanted was to be alone in her room, with the curtains drawn and a cold wet cloth on her forehead. Arduous charity work did not go with prolonged social entertainment in the evenings. She stifled a yawn, and it seemed that instantly the Comtesse's piercing eyes were upon her, as if critical. The Frenchwoman never seemed tired or strained or out of control of any situation. She was a few years older than Cassia, and it was those years which had added to her maturity and sophistication. Few can make a young woman feel as ill at ease as an older woman of experience.

To Cassia's intense relief it was at that moment that the gentlemen came in to join them. The Comtesse's eagle eyes were becoming all too much for her; she was feeling more drained with each passing moment.

Vincent took one look at his wife's face and immediately went to her side. She looked very white, drawn, and he feared that she had been overdoing things, working too hard, too soon after the miscarriage. He put his arm round her shoulder. She tried not to flinch, conscious of the Comtesse watching them.

'My love, you look exhausted, you should be in bed,' Vincent said. She did not demur, but allowed him to lead her gently through the door of the room, where she turned to say her goodnights before going up the stairs.

When she had gone Joanna sighed. 'Poor Cassia, she worries so much about those girls down by the Old Dock. Especially that little Sulamee and Nola. I do not know what will become of them.'

'They are in good hands with Cassia to take care of them.' The words were from Andrew, who had said very little through the evening. After he had spoken he bent almost self-consciously to pat Raven, who, as ever, was at his feet. He hoped he had not shown his feelings in his voice, for the Comtesse was a very perceptive woman; it would not do for her to guess what he was beginning to feel towards one of his sister's guests . . .

Cassia was so tired she did not hear when Vincent came to bed, treading softly so as not to disturb her. Her dreams were distorted, jumbled, bordering on the fearful. She moaned in her sleep, and turned over in bed, then began to throw her head from side to side, her eyelids flickering and her hands tugging at the bedcovers. Suddenly she awoke with a start, panting, her face bejewelled with sweat.

'No!' she cried out. '*No!*'

Vincent sat up, reaching out to light the candle by the bed. 'You've had a bad dream, *doucette*. It is all over now, you are awake.'

Cassia thrust the back of her hand into her mouth as if stifling gasps. 'It was horrible, *horrible*!' she said.

'It helps to talk about dreams, it disperses their power. Tell me about it, Cassia.'

'I dreamt that I went to speak to Nola and I found that she

was dead. But more than that, she was just a bundle of bones on her blanket. Then – then Mistress Boderley appeared, looking horrific, all in black, and she had great sharp teeth and – and she – oh, I cannot speak of it, it is too nauseous.'

Vincent gently put his arms round Cassia. She leaned against him, in her need forgetting her rejection of him.

'She – she picked up one of the bones and put it in her teeth and began to chew on it like – like a cannibal.' Cassia thrust her face into Vincent's chest and began to sob. 'Those poor girls, what sort of life do they have ahead of them, what hope is there of saving them, Vincent? They're all doomed,' she wept. 'They will all die like – like –'

'Like our baby?' Vincent finished for her. 'But does the fact of death not prove that life goes on? Is there not a constant rebirth everywhere, amongst humans, amongst nature? Those girls have *you* now, and a future which they did not have before you came to Liverpool. They must realize that the quality of their life has been altered for the better, and now that they have seen a new and brighter way for them they will want to stay with it.'

'I want to give them more than hope, that is such an empty quality. That is what you give when you have nothing else to offer.'

'But without hope there is no future, there is no life, so if you give hope you give both those things, and surely happiness follows them? You demand too much of yourself, *doucette*.'

'But I give so little, and I want to give so much. I don't want anyone else to die because of me, because of my failings.'

'We will all have to die some time, *doucette*, and I do not think it is in our hands to decide when or where that will be. If you can prolong those children's lives just a little longer, show them a different side to existence, make their span a little easier, you will have done more than most, my love. I am so proud of you, *doucette*. You are so brave.'

'It is nothing, I do nothing, Vincent.' Fresh tears bubbled in her eyes. She was thinking of the grief of loss – would it ever leave her? She, too, needed a rebirth.

They lay together in one another's arms comfortingly for some time until Cassia's tears had dried, until sleep overcame them both. It was one of the greatest advantages of the marriage bed.

Next morning Vincent was leaving early with Paul to visit the St Sebastian Society on the outskirts of Toxteth. It was a society which had been formed to execute charitable deeds, and it was hoped that it would one day merge with The Children of Liberty, thus forming one single society. The fact that Vincent had planned to leave early with Paul meant that he had gone before Cassia woke. She stirred and sat up. A golden river of sunlight was flooding the room. She yawned and looked around. Where was Vincent? Then she remembered that he had been leaving early. Perhaps it was just as well. Memory of her nightmare returned to her, and the manner in which Vincent had comforted her as she wept. Looking back into the dark recesses of the night, it seemed unreal, as if that too had been part of the dream. She shivered, clasping her arms round her waist. How near she had been to danger! Yet he had not taken advantage of her, he had not tried to make love to her when he so easily might. For that she must thank God. A moment of helplessness gripped her. What were they going to do, what could they do? The physician had said no more children for the time being, he had warned that it took time to recover from a miscarriage, that another baby conceived too soon could result in another loss. Vincent had been patient with her so far, but how much longer would he go on allowing her to remain at arm's length? She knew that he was a man of ardent desires; that, as a rule, he was an indefatigable and virtually insatiable lover. How she had revelled in that once . . .

Recovering from her spasm of panic, she got out of bed and slipped on a peignoir in preparation to dress. When she reached the dining-room everyone had eaten except Andrew.

He and Raven were dining alone. When Cassia entered they both looked up and it seemed to Cassia that there was a smile of greeting on Raven's face, too, as well as on Andrew's.

It was altogether a warm and welcoming scene, one which she needed very much after the harrowing events of the night before.

Andrew jumped up immediately. 'What can I get you? Coffee or tea?' he said.

'Tea, please,' Cassia said, patting Raven on the head before taking her seat at the table.

'What will you have to eat?'

'I don't feel very hungry, actually.'

'Are you sure you will not have some of these delicious scrambled eggs? And the toast is only just made, it is still hot.'

'Some toast then, thank you.'

'And not a little of the scrambled eggs, too?'

'All right then, thank you.' She did not think she would be able to eat anything, but Andrew was only being kind, after all. She appreciated it.

'Where is your sister?'

'She breakfasted early. It is her day to help at the Bluecoat Hospital.'

'Oh, yes, I had forgotten. She promised that I could go with her one day to give my help, when I feel stronger.'

'You cannot expect to be feeling like new just yet. When the same happened to my sister she slept a great deal and was always making her excuses to go to bed. The body knows what it needs and you must give it what it demands, otherwise the recovery period will take all the longer.'

'I am sure you are right, Andrew, but there is so much I want to do. I wish I had enough energy to help at the Hospital and the Alms House, as well as to help all of Mistress Boderley's girls. But as it is, visiting each girl takes up so much time if I want to do the job properly, and some days I only manage to see half a dozen of them.'

'You always make sure that you have left there well before

dark, do you not, Cassia? You do not want to get involved with the clientèle.'

'Oh, yes, I am always well away from there while it is daylight. The last thing I want to do is to meet their customers. I have been even more careful since the murder; indeed many of the girls seem quite edgy. Security has been tightened up in the brothels. The murderer may well find it too difficult to carry out his evil deeds, so he may turn to those girls who have even less protection, the ones on the streets.'

'Let us hope that he is driven completely into hiding, that he does not dare strike again, but it seems unlikely. I do not suppose that you have read a book called *The Criminal Mind* by Edgar Storrington? He has made quite a study of murderers, and he says that although some murders do run in cycles and murderers can actually lie low for years, it is far more likely in the case of a violent murderer that the pressure of his desire to commit the crime will override all the murderer's more normal feelings. There is only one consolation, apparently: although the man might be able to be careful in the beginning, to cover his tracks, eventually he will become so desperate to murder that he will become careless. One day our vicious Liverpool killer is going to put a foot wrong. He is going to be seen in the process of committing the crime. And it is more than likely that he has a family. If they have not already suspected something, eventually they will, and then it will only be a matter of time before he is caught.'

'I hope that you are right, Andrew. I fear terribly for those poor girls; they are like lambs in a pen, being circled by a ravenous wolf. They have no protection. If they are attacked and they scream who will come to their rescue? And, besides, this man works quietly, albeit violently. Nobody knew that other girl had been murdered until her body was found the next morning by her colleagues. The room was wrecked, covered in blood, she was horribly mutilated, and yet nobody had heard a single noise.' Cassia shuddered.

'I have not been entirely inactive regarding the murder,

Cassia. I have spoken to the Magistrates about it on more than one occasion, but their attitude has always been the same: those girls want to live a life of decadence and corruption, so they must pay the price.'

'But that is so unfair, Andrew! Admittedly, many of those girls *have* chosen that life themselves, but the ones who are brought here in slave ships have had no choice at all.'

'I know, I know, my dear, you do not have to tell me that. We are doing our best to support the Abolition Bill that we hope will be going through Parliament as soon as possible. It is just these early stages which are so difficult, persuading people that there is a need for such a Bill. It is not easy. We have as many violent antagonists as we have fervent supporters.'

'If there is anything else I can do to help, Andrew, you have only to ask me. I can speak of what I have seen, the sort of life these poor girls lead, if it will influence any of these antagonists . . .'

'The report that you and Joanna are preparing from your experiences in the bordello will be superb ammunition for our cause. And yes, certainly, if I hear of any occasion when you can talk about what you have seen, or speak to any Member of Parliament or Abolitionist whose word will carry weight, then I shall let you know. There is a man on whom we may well pin our hopes. His name is Granville Sharpe. He has let it be known that he may well be prepared to fight for our cause, but he will need support, details, facts; he must be amply prepared: there will be a terrific amount of opposition. He cannot go into the situation half informed or he will be summarily dealt with by those whose fortunes are invested in the slave trade.

'Remember what I said – take care of yourself,' Andrew smiled, his eyes filled with an expression almost as soft and pleading as Raven's. It gave Cassia a jolt. As he walked out, his faithful hound at his heels, she realized that Andrew was very fond of her, that he was holding in check a deeper emotion than mere friendship. Disturbed, she sat thinking while the maidservant cleared the table, oblivious of the clatter of plates and cups, seeing in her mind's eye Andrew's green-flecked eyes filled with warm, caring feeling, hearing his words of caution over and over in her head.

Cassia had agreed to accompany Andrew and Paul to one of their meetings, but, as soon as they arrived at Liverpool Hall, they saw a group of men at the entrance, shouting and waving their fists.

'We must slip in the back way,' Paul said. 'Keep your heads down – and Cassia, pull your hood over your face. The men on the door will have kept out the ruffians.'

But when they got inside the hall they found a very riotous company indeed. Shouts and yells echoed through the air and two or three men were on the ground slamming their fists into one another. The security men were doing their best to separate them and to quieten the audience.

Cassia, Andrew and Paul took their seats on the dais and waited for the hubbub to die down. After some moments, when it was obvious that the security men were failing to control the hecklers, Paul stood up and begged for silence from his audience. Immediately, a handful of men stood up at the rear of the hall and began bellowing insults at the trio, their society, and their aims. The men who had been fighting managed to involve a fourth and then a fifth man in their affray, and then others were joining in, all equally determined to land a fist as hard as possible against somebody's jaw. Shortly, the hall was a riot; no voices could be heard above the racket.

'This has been arranged by the slavemasters I've no doubt,' Paul gritted furiously. 'Come, there is nothing for it but for us to leave. We shall try again as soon as possible of course. We must not let them think we are beaten.'

As Cassia followed the two brothers off the dais, a missile flew through the air and slapped against Andrew's head. It was a rotten tomato, and others followed in rapid succession. Before they had hurried down the rear steps of the dais, their clothes were stained with red juice and seeds.

When they arrived home, the brothers made Cassia rest and brought her a brandy which they insisted she drank to restore her nerves.

'It was quite exhilarating really,' she said. 'But what a noise they made! I am sorry of course that we did not manage to speak to them. I was quite looking forward to it. How often does that sort of thing happen, Paul?'

'Less than you would think. That was obviously all well organized and paid for beforehand by our enemies, but we shall carry on as if nothing has happened. How could we do anything else?'

'How indeed!' Andrew agreed, brushing the last few tomato seeds from his sleeves.

Raven had his ragged head on Cassia's knee and was looking up at her with pleading eyes. Smiling, she fed him two pieces of cake, which he chomped heartily before resuming his look of doleful hunger.

'Oh, Raven, you cannot be as hungry as all that,' Cassia chuckled. 'I know that your master does not keep you short of food. I expect that you have had a generous dinner already.'

'It is true, he has,' said Andrew, 'but it is also true that however much he eats he never gains an ounce of weight. Where he puts it all I do not know.'

Cassia stroked the dog's untidy head. His coat always looked as if it had been ruffled by a strong gust of wind.

A maidservant appeared with a tray, in readiness to clear the table.

Chapter Twelve

'And how did you spend your day, *doucette*?' Vincent asked Cassia. Was it her imagination, or was there a barb behind his words? He had come home exhausted again. She, too, was tired after another day with Sulamee and the other girls at Boderley's. Tension vibrated in the air between them.

'I slept late then breakfasted with Andrew,' Cassia began.

'You see a lot of Andrew, do you not, *doucette*?'

'He does live here in the house with us.'

'I live here in the house with you, too, *doucette*, but I see very little of you these days.'

'That is by your choice, Vincent. You go out all the time to your lectures and your public meetings and making collections for the society.'

'And I suppose you do not go out, also? Are you saying that if I returned home during the day I would find you here?'

She looked at him, surprised at the acerbity of his tone. 'On some days maybe.'

'Only some? What of all the others when I might need my wife?'

'But, Vincent, we are both working together for The Children of Liberty, we decided that long ago. This is partly why we came to Liverpool.'

'Did we not decide that we would work together?'

'Yes,' she said doubtfully, 'but as things have turned out we have found our ways going in opposite directions – not that they cannot be brought together again.'

'So you will come with me to one of my meetings?'

'If you insist, but naturally after my experience at Liverpool Hall I am somewhat reluctant . . .'

'Do I have to insist, then? Will you not come of your own free will?'

'Now you are twisting my words, Vincent. You know I did not mean that.'

'Then why did you say it, *doucette*?' His emerald green eyes glittered with cruelty, or could it just have been a trick of the light? She hung her head.

'You are right to look ashamed.'

'Ashamed – ? Why should I look ashamed?'

'Because you have not been a proper wife to me for some time now,' Vincent retorted, his words cutting through the air between them, seeming almost to slice against her flesh, so that she winced.

'You know full well why that has been. The baby –'

'It is over two months now since the baby was lost,' he interrupted cruelly. 'Are we to go on like this forever, with this distance between us growing ever wider, hardly daring to express our feelings to each other for fear of what will result?' He crossed the room and took her by the shoulders, his palms searing into her skin through the silk of her gown. 'I want you, I need you. You are my wife,' he said simply. 'I did not marry you to gain an ornament, a pretty doll who will speak now and then, wear beautiful clothes and look fragile. I need a warm, loving, breathing human being to share my bed; a woman I can crush in my arms and kiss and caress without fear of her breaking.'

'I – I will not break, Vincent. I do not know what you mean.'

'So everything is all right now?' he said. 'If I took you in my arms like this, and kissed you soundly like this, you would not object?'

She writhed in his arms as if being suffocated, taken unawares, behaving as if she were shocked by his kisses. Oh, why did he not understand that things were different now? *She* was different. Everything had changed with the death of her baby. A mind image of her baby, the tiny little corpse, flittered into her thoughts. If Vincent had been there he could have saved her, he could have carried her into the house, and she would have recovered from her fall.

'So I was right,' he said huskily, pain darkening his features. 'You do not want me any more.' He clenched his teeth. 'Is it because you have found another whom you prefer to me?'

'*Another?*' she gasped. 'I do not know what you mean!'

'Oh, surely you do, *ma mignonne*, surely you do. How many times have I returned here to find you alone with Andrew Peacock in the library, on the terrace, in the dining-room, but always alone with him?'

'That is sheer coincidence,' she said, outraged. 'We talk about the society, about our work, the reports we are both drawing up. He is pleasant, undemanding company.'

'And *I* make demands on you, is that it? *I* am such an inhuman, avaricious monster that you must turn to another for comfort?'

'No, no, it is not that at all . . .'

'Then what is it, Cassia?' The sound of her name on his lips startled her; he used it so rarely. Always, before, he had employed tender endearments, but now he was calling her by her name, as if he were very angry with her.

'As I said, it is sheer coincidence, nothing more.'

'But you prefer him to me?' Vincent's jewel-green eyes were as cold as glass.

'Certainly not, that is nonsense.'

'Cassia, I have waited many weeks now for you to recover. I think that I have given you enough time. I have been patient when many times I have felt far from patient. I do need you, you are my wife. It seems hardly a moment since we were married, and now you no longer want to know me. What am I supposed to think? What am I supposed to do? I am a man, with a man's healthy appetites. Are you telling me that I must look elsewhere to satisfy them?'

His words were like a slap in the face. She almost reeled from them. Her Vincent, making love to another woman! It seemed a century since she had found out about his harem, now long since disbanded, of course. She had been as outraged and shocked then as she was now, to think of him dallying with another woman. She clenched her fists, half turning from him, not knowing what to say.

'Well, must I? Is that what you really want me to do, Cassia? Because the opportunity is there for the taking if I want to take it.'

'It is?' Her voice was husky, her throat dry. This conversation was a nightmare, she could hardly believe that it was happening.

'Yes, it is there. Up until now I have not felt tempted, for my first loyalty, naturally, is to you, my wife – but if you no longer wish to be my wife, Cassia, then I shall have to think again. I am not accustomed to a celibate life. I find it very difficult, it interferes with my logical train of thought, it interferes with my work, with what I want to do in the society. How can I progress with our lectures when my body hungers for satisfaction, when everywhere I look I see you, when my thoughts are filled with you, and more than anything I want to make love to you?'

'Can you not wait?'

'Wait? Until when? Have I not waited long enough now? It seems to me that years have passed since I last made love to you, since you last came willingly to my arms. I am forgetting what it was like to bed you, Cassia, and that is a very dangerous state of affairs.'

'You frighten me with your warnings, your threats.'

'I do not mean to threaten you, but I suppose in a way I am warning you. For your own good, for my good, for *our* good. We have a relationship to sustain, a marriage to nurture. It takes two to make a marriage, to uphold it. Two people working together, through thick and thin, through better and worse. You taught me that.'

'That is just it, Vincent. This is the worst now. If we cannot get through this then we have no marriage, so you should be beside me.'

'And you beside *me*, Cassia. Will you be beside me? At the moment you are far away, there is a great distance between us.

Sometimes I feel that we shall never be as one again. I am as frightened by that thought as you are frightened by what you call my threats. They are not threats, they are pleas. We have come through so much together, Cassia – do not let us be divided now.'

She felt cold, as if somehow a freezing wind had intruded into the house and was wrapping itself round her. She looked at her husband as if he were a stranger, feeling that he had, by this very conversation, made the barrier between them all the greater. Before, she had been able to deny its existence. Now, she saw it as clearly as did he. But what was most unnerving of all was that it did not terrify her.

During the next few days Cassia and Vincent did not speak to each other, a heavy, chilly silence hanging between them. Joanna was the first to notice and, hesitantly, she questioned Cassia.

'Have you two quarrelled, my dear? Vincent positively glowers these days, that is, when I see him; he is hardly ever in the house, any more.'

'No, we have not quarrelled, Joanna. We have had a, well, I suppose you could call it a disagreement.'

'Oh well, I suppose all lovers have their little tiffs.' Joanna smiled, but was worried by Cassia's pallid face, the shadows beneath her eyes. She remembered the glowing and radiant girl to whom she had first been introduced, and she would have liked to see her return again. It was so sad to see a schism between two young people so obviously made for each other. The spirit which fired the young could also hinder their happiness and interfere with the everyday smooth running of their lives. Being older and wiser, she felt it her bounden duty to assist Cassia and Vincent in every possible way, but she knew that she must tread carefully or she would make the situation worse.

'Yes, call it a tiff if you like,' Cassia shrugged. She did not want to answer Joanna's probing questions about her relationship with Vincent. She wanted to be left in peace to get on with her work for the society, seeing Sulamee daily and building up a good strong relationship with the child in preparation for the day when, she hoped, she would be able to adopt her. She clung to that hope fiercely, but because of the awkward situation with Vincent she had not yet spoken of it to him. She dreaded what he would say when she did. What if he flew into a rage? It seemed quite likely these days that he would; he was becoming quite snappish. Her palms felt clammy as she thought of his rage, his refusal to foster Sulamee. She would need to pluck up all her courage to ask him and she would dread the occasion, for, if he said no, she believed that her world would end.

She had lost far too many people in her short lifetime, each new loss seeming doubly intolerable, a wounding imprint on her mind and heart. But while she considered the heartbreak that would ensue if she had to forfeit her plans for Sulamee, she was forgetting that if she went on as she was she might well lose Vincent . . .

Andrew had been on a trip to London to meet Granville Sharpe and to inform the scholar and philanthropist that there would be reports on the slave situation coming from Liverpool as soon as they were prepared. He had brought gifts for all of them: honey water for Joanna and Cassia, a mixture of vanilla, cloves, orange flower water and musk, which delighted them, and Eau de Cologne for Paul and Vincent. Paul was delighted with his Sweet Water, liberally splashing himself with it, inhaling deeply, and preening. Vincent looked a little more undecided about his gift. He had never used cologne or any other variety of scented water, even though they were highly popular now with both men and women. He thanked Andrew and put the bottle to one side.

Tea was served, and, as it was a scorching July afternoon, they sat on the terrace to enjoy it. Joanna's dogs were romping through the rose gardens in their accustomed undisciplined fashion, ears flopping, tongues lolling, and tails bouncing. She glanced fondly at them now and again, happy to know that they were happy, even if they were causing something close to chaos amongst the flower beds. Raven, considering himself more mature, reclined in kingly fashion at Cassia's feet, occasionally looking up at her with a devoted expression.

'Raven has really taken to you, Cassia,' Paul commented. 'I do not think that I have ever known him to take to anyone else in such a fashion – apart from Andrew, of course. Raven lost his mother when he was only five weeks old, you know; she was knocked down by a carriage, and Andrew proceeded to raise the pups by hand himself. Raven's two sisters went to friends' homes: Charles took one and an old school friend took another. It always seemed to me that Raven fully understood he was an orphan, and knew just how to use that knowledge to get what he wanted. That ragged, slightly forlorn expression he practises so frequently, which pulls at the heart-strings, and the way he appears to be half starved even when he has just had a large meal.'

'I have noticed,' Cassia grinned. 'I wish that he were mine.'

Vincent glanced up at her words and they exchanged penetrating glances for a few seconds.

The sun beat down determinedly, and soon Joanna's dogs were lying panting on the cool stones of the terrace, servants bringing out bowls of water for them. Seeing that no bowl had been brought especially for him, Raven assumed his hang-dog air and shortly he, too, was given a drink.

'You see, he has his act off to a fine art,' Paul said. 'He would do well on the stage of the Theatre Royal.'

The scent of rich blossoms eddied through the air towards them, energetically rivalled by Paul's liberal application of Eau de Cologne and Joanna's honey water. There was only one thing to mar that peaceful afternoon. It was found that after she had sat in the sun for some fifteen or twenty minutes Joanna's honey water – for it must be that – was attracting wasps and bees, much to her discomfort and anxiety. Very soon she had to go into the house and splash herself with cool water to remove the scent.

Joanna gave the honey water to Cassia, telling her to use it as a gift for one of her girls at Boderley's, so Cassia decanted off what remained of the liquid into a smaller flask to take to Sulamee, who greeted it with thrilled appreciation.

'Honey water,' she said, over and over, 'honey water is good, smell good.' She could not hold the liquid against her cheek, but she did the next best thing – she dipped her finger into it and tasted it, tipping her head to one side as she assessed the flavour.

'I do not really think you are supposed to drink it, Sulamee,' Cassia laughed. 'It is to be splashed on the skin, on the wrists and the neck, behind the ears. And you can dab it on your kerchief, too, like this, look.' She took out her own lace kerchief and acted out the sprinkling of some of the honey water onto the soft material, Sulamee watching with grave eyes.

'Wet ker-chief with honey water,' she said thoughtfully, as if such a thing had never occurred to her before.

'Now tell me how things have been with you since I last saw you, Sulamee.'

For a moment a shadow flittered across the exquisite *café au lait* face. 'Visit from big master. Not good,' she said.

'Big master? Who do you mean, Sulamee?'

'Big master, great big man. Power, much power, he have.'

'Oh, you mean somebody very important in the city?'

'He own this place.'

Cassia looked at her, puzzled. As far as she knew, the owner of the place was Mistress Boderley.

'Who do you mean? I do not understand, Sulamee.'

'Big man who own all this place and other place, too. You know, Captain's Cabin, and those place. He great, true close friend of Mistress Boderley. He come visit girls here every now and 'gain.'

So there was someone else behind these brothels, Cassia mused. That did surprise her, for Mistress Boderley had the air of one in authority, one who had complete and total power in this place. She wondered who he might be.

'When does he visit you, Sulamee?'

'Late at night, when it dark. Only then, never early evening or daytime. Always in dark, in much secret. He swear us to secret, also, 'bout his visits. We not to say anything, but I know it all right to say things to you, dear Mistress.'

Cassia looked at the child with fond eyes, whilst considering what she had said. A man who visited Boderley's in secret late at night. He must be somebody very important in the city indeed, somebody famous, whose face was so well known that he had to hide it or there would be a scandal. A man who not only financed these brothels and was the power behind them, but who also made use of the girls. Her thoughts flittered across those men whom she had met in her months in Liverpool, all the important personages she had been introduced to at Society meetings, at afternoon tea, at dinner, at the Peacocks' house and at other people's homes. Could she possibly have met the man, the evil, corrupt man, who was behind these brothels? She pondered for a moment on what it would mean if such an important personage was responsible for the plight of these girls. To denounce a woman like Mistress Boderley would take nothing more than anger, but to denounce someone who played a prominent part in city life might prove to be a different matter. She imagined how he would fight to keep his identity hidden. They would have to step very carefully indeed if they wished to bring this man down. But first of all, of course, they would have to find out who he was . . .

Which made Sulamee's words all the more astonishing.

'Mar-shall Atch-er-ley,' Sulamee said. 'That name of man who visit in secret.'

'So he has told you his name?' Cassia could not keep the surprise from her voice.

'Oh, yes, he not hide his name. Always he tell it to all of us.'

Cassia racked her brains to think of a Marshall Atcherley whom she might have met in the previous weeks. Was there a politician, a councillor, a merchant, of that name? No, she could not think of one, but then she had not met everyone as yet. She would ask Paul and Andrew if they knew anyone of that name.

But they had not heard of a Marshall Atcherley, nor had Joanna.

'Strange that we who have lived here all our lives should not have come across that name,' Joanna said, mystified.

'Could he be a foreigner who does not live in Liverpool but only visits here, by ship, say, from abroad?'

'I do not think so, Paul, for Sulamee said that he visits them regularly. Perhaps he does not live in Liverpool, though.'

Paul frowned. 'From what you have told us, Cassia, this man, this Marshall Atcherley, seems to appear out of the mists of the night, visit these girls, and then slip away. A very mysterious life, do you not think? An evil, nocturnal creature who does not want his face to be seen by anyone, and yet who freely broadcasts his name. Now I find that intriguing, it gives me food for thought.'

'You will tell us when you have prepared your meal?' Joanna grinned fondly at her brother.

'Indeed I will. I shall be busy preparing it over the next few days.'

'Yes, it does seem conflicting that he skulks about at night, hiding his face, and yet not his name. But then, if no one knows who he is, he cannot harm himself by using it and, indeed, what has the man to hide which Mistress Boderley does not also have to hide?' The speaker was Vincent, who had been listening to the conversation with interest. 'They have the law on their side. They are in favour with the slave captains and the merchants, they pay good prices for their slaves. If this Marshall Atcherley, the man behind these brothels, is creeping about at night and keeping his face hidden, why is not

Mistress Boderley doing the very same? I think the truth is that this Marshall Atcherley has something unpleasant to hide, something other than his involvement with the brothels and the slave girls.'

'It is highly likely that such a man will have been deeply involved in crime and corruption, so yes, you could be right, Vincent. And talking of crime and corruption, have you come across any trace of that Nathan Dash you were searching for?'

'Not yet, Andrew, but I will, I will, never fear. I have colleagues here on the lookout for him, and throughout Lancashire and Cheshire and beyond, and all the members of our society who are travelling about have been told to watch out for Nathan Dash or anyone answering to his description.

'Indeed, I thought I had the man some two weeks back when I got a report from Charles that there was a retired sea captain living in a decaying cottage down by the waterfront. He had heard that the man's name was Nathan Daniel, and he immediately thought that it was a distortion of the name Nathan Dash affected to conceal the man's true identity. We went down to the cottage together to call on the man.'

'You did not tell me, Vincent!' Cassia said.

Vincent looked at her quizzically. He did not want to say out loud in front of the Peacocks that their relationship had been so poor of late that he no longer confided in her, but she understood the meaning of his look.

'I did not tell you in case it was a false alarm, which indeed it was,' he said. 'The man was not Nathan Dash, most definitely not. He has white grizzled hair, he is much older, and he has retired because he is dying of consumption which is in the advanced stages, poor man. We gave him some money and left him in peace. I am afraid that is the nearest we have been to Nathan Dash since . . .'

'Since he sold me into slavery in Constantinople,' Cassia finished for him, holding her head high as she surveyed the startled faces of the Peacocks.

'So it was he who abducted you?' Joanna said.

'Yes, it was he.' Let them think no one else was involved in her abduction, for it would serve no purpose to tell them that Vincent himself had been the first one to carry her off.

'The swine!' This from Andrew, who gritted his teeth, a frown on his red-gold brows.

'Oh, he was that and more,' said Cassia. 'There is no punishment severe enough for him. Even to speak of him makes me shudder.' She wrapped her arms round her waist, half closing her eyes.

'Then do not speak of him, Cassia, my dear. Let us change the subject at once,' Joanna said firmly, and they did.

Cassia curled up into a tight ball, pretending to be asleep, while Vincent slipped off his clothes before getting into his side of the bed. He blew out the candle and then lay still in the darkness for a long time. When he stirred restlessly she held herself as motionless as she could manage, her eyelids tightly closed.

'Are you asleep, *doucette*?' His voice was warm and coaxing. She did not answer. He spoke again.

'*Doucette*, are you asleep?'

She gave a little sigh, as if in her sleep, and he must have taken it for response, for he curled towards her, sliding his arms round her waist, his breath fanning warmly against her cheek. '*Ma mignonne*, can you forgive me for my harsh words?'

She did not answer, but froze in his arms.

'So you have not forgiven me, we are still at war? I would not wish it this way, *doucette*, you know that I would not.'

'It can be no other way,' she said through gritted teeth. 'If you love me give me time, Vincent.'

'But we are wasting half our lives waiting, *doucette*, and did we not vow after our long wait before that we would never do so again?' He began to kiss her face, his lips dropping like velvet on her forehead and cheeks, her chin, and then her lips. She wanted to respond, to melt against him, to sigh and breathe his name voluptuously. She wanted to stroke his hard stomach and his broad strong shoulders, to slip her hands down to that most manly part of him and bring him to the peak of ecstasy. But she could not. She was as powerless to react to him as if she were in the topmost tower of a crystal palace and he were down on the ground below, with no method of their meeting. The warmer he became, the cooler she grew.

He tried again, curving his arms round her body, touching her breasts gently, tenderly. A shudder rippled across her body. He persevered, for he needed her desperately.

'Oh, *doucette, doucette,*' he whispered. 'How I love you, how I need you! Please do not let this barrier come between us.'

She felt his hands caressing her breasts, stroking her stomach and thighs, probing between her legs, and as his breath grew hotter against her cheek and she felt his desire, she knew that her heart had frozen into a tight hard ball of crystal. Cold as ice, white as snow. She could feel its glittering crystalline surface stabbing within her like a knife's sharp blade. She wanted to weep hot tears to dissolve the ice, but she was impotent. She wanted to fling her arms round Vincent and kiss him and beg his forgiveness and say that she loved him, too, and that nothing must ever, ever come between them, whatever happened. But the ice was spreading rapidly throughout her whole body, freezing not only her limbs but her emotions. The man breathing hotly by her side, his leg flung over hers, his lips like flame, was a stranger, a total, absolute stranger.

'Cassia,' her name was strangled in his throat, 'in God's name say something, do something! I cannot bear this silence!'

'There is nothing to say, nothing to do,' she whispered.

When he turned from her he cursed beneath his breath, words which he had never spoken in front of her before. She felt somehow befouled by them, made unclean.

Starved of her loving confidant, Cassia turned to Andrew Peacock for solace. There was nothing physical in their relationship, certainly nothing of which she was aware, and it was exactly this relaxed and easy kind of friendship which Cassia wanted at this moment. She needed to talk about Sulamee and what she planned for the child, yet she knew that she could not broach the subject with Vincent, not as things stood between them.

'You want to adopt one of the girls at Boderley's? But do you realize what is involved, Cassia? The way of life those girls have been forced to lead, their experiences . . .'

'Someone has to take care of them, Andrew. When they are all freed, as we hope they will be one day soon, they will all need foster-mothers, homes to go to.'

'A home, yes. An orphanage where they can all go as one family and be raised by people who have their best interests at heart, like the Quakers, for example. But as to taking one of the children into your own home as your daughter . . .'

'So you do not approve of my idea? And I was so sure that you would.'

'I didn't say that I would disapprove. I was simply trying to get you to see both sides of the situation.'

'I think I already do, Andrew. Sulamee is a delightful child, so pretty, and her skin is so pale that it could be mistaken for white. Her mother was a half-caste and her father was white. It is particularly poignant to think that if she had been born in a Roman Catholic country she would have been granted manumission at birth, and perhaps her mother also, but instead, because she was born in Bristol, in these unenlightened islands, she takes her mother's status.'

'Have you thought of buying her freedom?'

'Buying her from the Boderley woman, you mean? Yes, I have thought of that, more than once. That is why I am raising the subject with you now, Andrew. Truth to tell, I am somewhat wary of broaching the matter with my husband.'

'You think that he would be against adoption?'

'I will be frank with you, Andrew. At the moment he seems very much against everything I say or do. I hope that I'm not embarrassing you by telling you this, but I feel that you are a friend and that you will understand.' Cassia lowered her hydrangea-blue eyes, feeling a slight flush of heat creep up her cheeks.

Andrew's face lit up. 'I am that indeed, Cassia, my dear. You cannot know how I have wanted to speak of my feelings for you, of our good friendship. I have been waiting only for the right moment, and this seems to be it.'

'Oh, Andrew —' Cassia sounded perplexed. 'Friends, yes we are *friends*,' she stressed the word.

'Cassia, my dear, I have not distressed you, I trust?' Andrew leaned forward, taking her slender ivory hand in his warm brown one and pressing it. To her total amazement, she felt a warm thread of response beginning deep inside her. There was none of the rejection, the chill, she felt at Vincent's proximity. Andrew was so open, so cheerful and uncomplicated; she had thought so from her first meeting with him. True, maybe he had been spoiled as a boy, but then he had been an orphan and his brother and sister had only been doing their best to protect him. He had changed now, he had settled down, and, although he was still a poor time-keeper, often not turning up at all when he had promised he would do so, he had an endearing temperament. Cassia found him a consolation. Yes, that was the word exactly, a consolation. And since the tragedy of losing her baby that was exactly what she needed.

Now Andrew's hands were clasping both of hers, and she was thrilling to his touch, finding its very innocence sensual. Andrew was no threat to her self-imposed retreat from sexuality. He had no rights to her body. Therefore, she could keep him at bay without feeling a tremendous guilt as she did with Vincent. With sacred vows she had tied herself to her husband, swearing to love him, to honour and obey him, through the good and the bad. To have made a sacred promise which she had found she was unable to keep, had been like a dash of cold water in her face. She had tried to pretend that it did not matter, but it did, and very much so, for she was a creature of high principles: if she gave her word she believed in keeping it. But on her wedding day she had not envisaged such a time as this. Then, she had never imagined a day when she might not love and adore Vincent and long for his touch. That such a moment had come had caught her by surprise. It made her uneasy, confused inside, and the knowledge that Vincent did not understand her state of mind brought a sharp painful edge to the matter.

'Cassia, I believe that we are two of a kind.' She heard Andrew's voice as if from a great distance. His eyes looked green as jasper, with the emotion flooding behind them. If eyes truly were the mirror of the soul, she thought, then Andrew's soul must be overflowing with love for her – and longing. She realized that with a little start of surprise. Longing. He wanted her . . .

'Cassia.' He spoke again, his voice rich with emotion. 'Do you deny it? Do you deny that we could be more than just good friends?'

She did not answer for a moment, her tongue running lightly over her lips, for they had gone dry. The unexpectedness of this situation had completely eradicated Sulamee from her mind. She had wanted to ask Andrew's advice on solving a problem and instead she was finding herself faced with a fresh one. She considered her answer carefully.

'Andrew, I think we are very good friends. I think we have been very good friends right from the first moment we met. It is true that in many ways we are similar, but perhaps not in good ways. We are both headstrong and determined to go our own way at times; we are inclined to put ourselves before other people on occasion.'

'You think that I am selfish?' He looked forlorn, and immediately she felt sorry for the sternness of her words. He had been looking to her for warmth and instead she had given him coldness.

'Not selfish, merely young.'

'So you think that I will grow out of it?' he grinned, more

cheerful now. 'And in your list of faults and virtues which you appear to have catalogued about me, do you include the ability to love?'

She tried to joke. 'Even the young and selfish and immature are allowed to love.'

'Oh, Cassia, you are evading my meaning. You are trying to slip away from me like a will o' the wisp, and I had hoped to bring us closer, much closer.' She realized that her hands were still tightly gripped in his, that there was no way she could release them without directly and firmly withdrawing them. She tried, but he had no intention of releasing his hold.

'Andrew, please,' she said.

'Cassia, you will break my heart,' he whispered. 'Insult me if you will, call me all the names you can think of, say that I am immature, a callow youth. I will take it all with a good grace if only I can feel there is some hope for me. To be excluded from your warmth, your company, your affection, would destroy me.'

'Oh, Andrew, I beg you not to be so emotional. You make things very difficult for me. You seem to forget that I am a married woman.'

'It has not escaped me that you and your husband do not get on. He is barely here, he hardly sees you. You never seem to exchange one word, and of late things have grown much worse. We have all noticed it. In the beginning I know my sister for one hoped that things would improve between you two, that it was only a momentary disaffection, but time has proved that there is little chance of your making up. If your husband can indulge in dalliance, then why not you, too? We all need love, Cassia.'

Shock brought two spots of crimson colour to her cheeks. 'My husband indulging in dalliance? What do you mean?' Her voice trembled.

'Surely you knew, Cassia? Surely it could not have escaped you?'

'What escaped me?'

'Why, his —' Andrew's voice faltered, 'his — that is, your husband's involvement with the Comtesse de Renate. Is it really true, you really did not know?'

'No!' Cassia tore her hands out of Andrew's fingers, leaping to her feet. Immediately, a swirling dizziness assailed her, so that she gave a little moan and sank back into the chair from which she had just risen. Instantly, Andrew was bending over her solicitously.

'Cassia, Cassia, are you ill? Oh, my God, what have I done?'

'I shall be all right.' Her voice was low and tortured. She felt as if a hand were encasing her throat in a throttling grip. Whether Andrew had told her in all innocence, or whether he had been carefully preparing to impart this information to throw her into his arms, she could not say. Whatever had been his intention she had certainly been affected by the news, deeply affected. She was feeling shock and anger and nausea.

Andrew had brought her a goblet of water and she was sipping at it, hardly noticing what she was doing. Her lips felt like paper, her limbs like lead. She knew that if she had tried to stand she would have collapsed. Vincent and that French bitch, with her powdered wigs, her overpowering scents, her elaborate gowns and dazzling jewels. She had not been wrong when she had seen covetousness in the Comtesse's eyes all those weeks ago when she had been introduced to Vincent. And the way they had chattered to one another in French, so freely and excitedly, like children who had found one another after a long separation . . . The goblet slipped out of Cassia's nerveless hand. She did not notice the splash of water against her breasts and stomach.

Andrew, thinking she was fainting again, hastily snatched up the goblet and, taking her hands, began to chafe them.

'Oh, forgive me, Cassia! What have I done? I thought you knew, I really thought you knew. I thought that was why you and Vincent were not speaking, because of his — because of the Comtesse.'

Ashen-faced, Cassia whispered that no, she had had no idea.

'God forgive me for what I have done,' Andrew said. He was almost as white as Cassia.

She took pity on him, even in the midst of her misery. 'You were not to know, Andrew. It was a perfectly reasonable conjecture on your part. They are both French, and naturally fellow countrymen in a foreign city will gravitate towards one another. I had noticed how she makes eyes at him, but then so do many women. He is a spell-binding man. But – but I had thought him faithful to me.'

'Cassia, my dear, I do not know what has gone wrong between you, and in truth it is none of my business, but I wish with all my heart that I had not spoken of this.' He took her hands again, looking pleadingly at her.

'There is definite proof?'

'They have been seen together in the city. At the Drury Lane theatre once, sitting in the same box, and walking in Toxteth Park.'

'Hand in hand?' Cassia whispered.

'I do not think they would make so bold in public. They may be French, and it is true that a certain wilder standard of behaviour is expected of Continentals, but Liverpool society does tend towards the prudish. She may be a widow but he is a married man. I think that they have been careful about their meetings.'

'Sitting together in the same box at the theatre, that is being careful?' The colour was back in Cassia's cheeks.

'Friends, even strangers, share the same box at the theatre, Cassia. Only those who knew them both, seeing them together, would understand what was meant by it.'

'And I thought he was at meetings . . . But instead he goes to the theatre, and without me. Oh, how could he!'

'I imagine that the Comtesse is a very persuasive woman, accustomed to getting all that she wants. She is known to have had lovers. No doubt more than one of them has been after her money.'

'You are not saying that Vincent ... ?' Cassia looked horrified.

'No, I did not mean to suggest that at all. Forgive me.'

Cassia thought of her own estate. For the moment she was virtually penniless, but one day she would inherit Penwellyn and her aunt's fortune – though of course she hoped most strongly that it would not be for many years yet. Could it be true that Vincent had wearied of the long wait and was now courting this rich and amorous widow? After all, Nathan Dash had failed to turn up, and she, Cassia, had lost the baby who would have received a large sum of money in gift from Julitta. Vincent was a man accustomed to great fortune. He had spent years pillaging and looting, rifling Spanish and other ships, filling his own hold with treasure-chests and booty. He had never wanted for wealth, not until Nathan Dash had stolen his gold. Was he consoling himself in the arms of that rich bitch, seeing in her the hope of regaining a fortune? Cassia clenched her fists, causing Andrew to withdraw his hands.

'It is good that you are angry now,' he said. 'That is a far more constructive emotion than shock or tears. All the same, I wish that I had said nothing. Tact has never been my strong point.'

'I am glad that you told me.' Cassia's whisper belied her words. 'I had to know sooner or later and it is better that I know sooner, otherwise I would have been floundering in a sea of ignorance.' A tiny crystalline tear squeezed out of her eye. Furiously she brushed it away. There was much of the old Cassia in her expression as she went on. 'I shall find out the truth of this, all the truth. To think that I have been duped all of these weeks while those two have been cavorting together in secret!'

'If I can help you in any way, Cassia, my dearest ...' Andrew kneeled down by her chair, slipping his hands round her waist, craving to lay his head upon her soft, rounded breast, but not as yet having the courage.

'Thank you, Andrew, I will let you know.' Gently she drew Andrew's arms away from her. She had enough complications at the moment without an ardent young lover paying court to her. But if she would discover that he was right, that Vincent and the Comtesse *were* lovers, well, that would be very different. Very different indeed.

Chapter Thirteen

Inside the comfortable drawing-room of the half-timbered house in Pinfold Lane, Captain Vincent Sauvage reclined on a settle, his arm around the beautiful shoulders of the Comtesse de Renate. He was dressed in his outdoor clothes: a waistcoat of beige corded silk embroidered with royal blue and apple-green irises; breeches of matching beige corded silk; a shirt of ivory lawn; glossy blacktop boots; and a jacket embroidered at the hem with dark blue velvet. The Comtesse wore only a fragile, semi-translucent peignoir of eau-de-nil lace. She wore no wig tonight, and her silvery hair, soft and fine, curled around her shoulders, draping across Vincent's arm. She was arching her brows at him in a tempting fashion, smiling sweetly so that her dimples showed deeply. Her silver-grey eyes were alight with passion.

Behind them, on a Queen Anne table stood a beautiful engraved silver candelabra, its three candles the only illumination in the room.

They looked like two lovers, two ardent, enamoured lovers, flirting with one another as a prelude to going to bed.

The woman standing outside on tiptoe, gazing at them through the window, felt dizzy at the sight. She felt like sinking to the ground in a faint, but she knew that she could not, for she was in a strange part of the city and alone. It was dark, and as she turned away from the warm glow of the window she could not help but think of the maniac who was at large in the city. Oh, why had she come, why had she followed Vincent to this place, this house which was rented by the Comtesse de Renate? Her experience had only brought home to her that what Andrew had said was true, truer even than he knew, that Vincent and the Comtesse were lovers, that many of those times when she had thought her husband was at lectures and meetings associated with The Children of Liberty, he had, in fact, been in the company of the Comtesse. She felt shaken to the core. Her palms were slippery with sweat, sweat dewed her forehead. She flamed with heat, then became icy cold in turn.

Carefully making her way across the soft soil of the flower beds she reached the lawn, her heels sinking into the grass. She wore a voluminous cloak with a hood. No one would have recognized her if they had seen her. At the bottom of the lane her horse awaited her. She would have enjoyed her ride earlier through the balmy night air if only her destination had not been one that she dreaded. Now, she must return home knowing that what Andrew had said was correct, knowing that, in the greater part, she was responsible for it. It had been her coldness, her argumentativeness, the change in her temperament since she had lost her baby, which had caused the barrier between herself and Vincent. She was to blame.

Having come to the edge of the lawn, she narrowly missed a rockery in the darkness, scraping her ankles against the stones, causing tears to spring into her eyes. Tears which were not entirely due to her grazed skin. In God's name, what was she going to do? She was filled with panic. She had lost her beloved Vincent to another woman, a woman whose wiles were far superior to hers. She had never tried by false or affected means to inveigle any man into her arms. She reached her horse, putting up her hands to clasp the reins, then glancing round in the darkness. It would serve her right if the crazy murderer leapt out at her from the shadows and bludgeoned her to death. She would be better off dead now; there was no reason to live without Vincent. She had known what manner of man she was marrying: he was no milksop monk to be kept waiting on her pleasure. He had received her message loud and clear: she no longer wanted him in her bed, and he had acted accordingly. What fools they had been to think that their love could survive every twist of Fate. Were they so special that they thought themselves immune to the effects of life's tragedies, its ups and downs? She had kept her husband at arm's length for months now while that French bitch was flaunting herself at him temptingly. He would not have been a man if he had resisted.

Having mounted her horse, she looked back once down the lane to the mock-timbered house, her eyes on the lighted window. And as she looked the light was suddenly extinguished, the window became black.

You have got what you deserve, she thought. You have been a fool and fools must pay the price. Then she spurred her horse back to Peacock Hall through the black-pitch night, with only the occasional hoot of a hunting owl to keep her company.

The next days passed in a blur. Cassia did not see Vincent during the daytime, she was only half aware of him sliding into bed beside her late each night and leaving before dawn. She heard of his activities from Paul or Andrew. The three of them had been travelling through Lancashire and the Wirral giving talks on Abolition to interested parties. They intended to have covered as much of the Wirral as they could manage before winter set in and the roads became a quagmire.

If Cassia thought seriously about the lonely weeks ahead she became very despondent. It was natural that she throw herself even more energetically into her charity work — and that, to quell her feeling of loss and isolation, she turned to the nearest person who offered warmth and comfort. That person was Andrew. His uncritical acceptance of her was heartening. He would give his advice when asked, and he did not always agree with her, but he never found fault with her unduly, seeming to be quite content with her as she was. In his company Cassia could be herself, even if that self was sometimes moody and withdrawn. And there was no physical threat from him. He might touch her hand or drop a kiss lightly on her forehead or cheek, encircle her waist with his arm in an affectionate fashion, but he made no demands on her.

How different was his bright, alive and boyish face from

Vincent's stony expression, his gritted jaw, and scowling brows. Vicent's temper was ill-managed these days and, although she did not like to admit it, there were times when she was almost frightened of him. Not that she would flinch from standing up to him, but what she needed at this time was a malleable, mellow relationship within the bounds of which she could relax, feel protected but, most of all, be loved.

She was growing to love Sulamee very deeply indeed, and she believed the child was beginning to feel the same about her. They were like mother and daughter, or sisters, when they talked and played together, and it was good and satisfying. Cassia had given the child so many gifts that she needed somewhere to put them all, and so Andrew had sent along a small chest which was engraved with a design of roses and leaves. Sulamee clapped her hands in delight when she saw it, opening the drawers and cupboards busily and peering inside. Then she and Cassia transferred all the ornaments and gewgaws into the chest. It looked very handsome standing in one corner of the room, but it made everything else look extremely shabby. Sulamee did not seem to notice, however. She stood in front of the chest looking at it with her head to one side, her hands clasped together at her breast.

'Beau-tiful, beau-tiful,' she said over and over.

'One day you will have many more beautiful things, Sulamee, I promise you,' Cassia said. 'This is only the beginning.'

Sulamee turned to Cassia and flung her arms round her in her first abandoned gesture of affection. 'You beautiful, too, Mistress,' she said, 'much beautiful. I sad when you go.'

'And I'm sad when I go, too, Sulamee.' Cassia had been plucking up courage for two days now to speak to Mistress Boderley about Sulamee. She felt nauseated at the thought of buying a slave, but she intended to purchase Sulamee only so that she could immediately set her free. She said nothing to the child, of course, for she did not want to raise her hopes. Today, after her visit, she intended to speak to the Boderley woman.

She had no idea what kind of reception she would get, but, as Joanna had often said, too much thought precluded action. So she had tried not to think of the coming interview.

As she watched Sulamee marvelling over her carved cabinet she armoured herself with thoughts of Xenobe, far away in the Sultan's harem in Constantinople. Poor Xenobe, who would never be free again. Alas, there was nothing she could do to help her old friend, but she could help Sulamee.

'Sulamee, have you ever ridden on a horse?' Cassia asked, seeing in her mind's eye the child riding on one of Julitta's more sedate mares.

Sulamee opened her lambent dark eyes wide. 'Horse? Me? No, never,' she said. 'I ride in carriage once, twice, that is all. You not bring me horse as gift, not here? I have no room for horse.'

Cassia laughed. 'Oh no, Sulamee, I was not going to bring you a horse here, do not worry. One day it would be nice for us to ride together, would it not?'

'Oh yes, but Mistress Boderley not allow, not ever. She not let her girls out, I tell you this before. Only favourites go out. She frightened of secrets being spilled.'

'Secrets? What secrets?'

'I not supposed to tell. Some things I have said to you before 'bout that man,' Sulamee lowered her voice to a whisper, 'Marshall Atcherley. We not allowed to speak of him or else bad punishment.'

'But why? I do not understand,' Cassia said, frowning. 'Is he in some sort of trouble with the Justices?'

'I not know. Know nothing, only his name and what he look like.'

'And what does he look like?'

'White hair, thick and wild. Heavy, ugly face, not pleasing. He have rough, coarse skin. I not like. But – but,' the child shuddered, 'I must pretend to like when he come here.'

'Oh, poor Sulamee! I do understand what you must have to go through.' Cassia gave the child a hug and a kiss. 'I will try and do my best for you, I promise.'

Later, when she had said goodbye to Sulamee, Cassia tapped at the door of Mistress Boderley's office. At first she thought the woman was not going to answer, and then the door opened slowly and Mistress Boderley stood there resplendent in a bright apple-green gown embellished with black and silver embroidery. She was heavily rouged, and on one cheek she had a black patch in the shape of a star and on the other cheek a patch in the shape of a moon. She wore a tall, thickly powdered wig, decorated with two green roses, and peridots flashed at her neck and in her ears. Close to, Cassia could see the coarse, uneven texture of the woman's unhealthy skin, which was thickly daubed with white lead; the cheeks carmined; the lashes stiff with lamp-black. Against the stark, white coating, the rims of Mistress Boderley's eyes stood out like two red rings, and the deeply indented lines from her upper cheeks to the corners of her mouth were like two crescents. No amount of powdering and painting could disguise them. Beneath the cheap violet scent Cassia could smell something else: an unpleasant smell of decay and putrefaction, and she knew from whence it came when Mistress Boderley opened her mouth to ask her what she wanted. The woman had not one undecayed tooth in her mouth: they were all black and rotting.

Trying not to reel from the smell, Cassia smiled politely. 'There is something I would like to discuss with you, Mistress Boderley, it you have a moment.'

'Discuss with me? More of your charity nonsense? Did I not tell you not to involve me in it? I have enough to do.'

'No, this is something else, Mistress Boderley. I wonder if we might go where it is more private?'

Reluctantly, Mistress Boderley ushered Cassia into her cramped little office. It was sparsely furnished, but what furniture it contained was impressive. A George I walnut bureau, a carved settee with delicately embroidered upholstery, a satinwood drop-side table, a satinwood desk, and a carved corner candleholder.

Mistress Boderley did not ask Cassia to sit down, so the two women remained standing, facing one another somewhat awkwardly in the confined space, made all the more cramped by the excessive width of Mistress Boderley's panniers.

'It is Sulamee I wish to discuss,' Cassia began. 'I – that is, my husband and I, would like to adopt the child . . .'

'Adopt her? But she is a slave, a *whore*!' Mistress Boderley exclaimed.

'I am fully aware of that, Mistress Boderley.' Cassia fought for control, not wanting to speak her thoughts and alienate the woman. 'But despite that she is only ten years old, and I have grown very fond of her in the three or four months that I have been visiting here.'

'She is a slave and *my* property,' Mistress Boderley said grimly.

'Yes, I know, but I wondered if we could not come to some arrangement. I would double what you paid for the child.'

'Double! I bought the child off the streets, she was destitute. I paid two pounds for her. Are you suggesting that I now relinquish her for four pounds! I have kept her, fed her, housed her, for over three years; am I not to have some recompense for all that outlay?' The woman drew herself up to her full height, looking outraged.

'Surely you have had her earnings?' Cassia said. 'Her income from – from –'

'From prostitution, you mean? Yes, and so I have, but these girls have hearty appetites, they eat and eat and eat. They need clothes; they must be kept warm in the winter; they are always begging for new additions to their rooms, some fanciful notion or other. It is I who have to supply all their needs.'

'I am fully aware of this, Mistress Boderley. So you are telling me that you will be asking a higher price for Sulamee?'

'Indeed I am doing no such thing, Mistress. Have I intimated in any way that she is for sale?'

'No, but –'

'Well then, who are you to assume that she is?'

'Oh, but I had thought — that is —'

'You come here doing your charity work, spreading your gifts around and winning favours from my girls,' Mistress Boderley's face grew even grimmer, 'and then you call on me unannounced and tell me that you wish to buy one of my most popular girls and you expect me to agree to this purchase. It would cost me a great deal more than twice the price I paid for her three years ago. There will be the trouble of filling her place, having to go to the Custom House again to look out a girl who will be as popular as Sulamee has been. And how shall I know whether this new girl will be as popular until I have tried her out? What if she proves to be less popular?'

'Surely you are an expert at picking out the most suitable girls, Mistress Boderley?' Cassia said archly.

'That may be so, but one can be wrong even when one is experienced.'

'Then will you take enough money to buy two girls, surely one of whom will prove as popular as Sulamee?'

'Have you any idea how much two girls will cost?' Mistress Boderley drew her lips together, making a thin line of them.

'No, but if you will tell me?'

'Yes, I will tell you, Mistress Do-gooder. One hundred guineas.'

'One hundred guineas!' Cassia gasped. 'But that is an incredible amount, far more than even two slaves are worth!'

'Take your choice, Mistress. That is the price for Sulamee.' Mistress Boderley half-turned, rifling some papers on her desk in an impatient fashion.

'But I have not the money.' Cassia felt desperation rising inside her. How dared this woman ask so much? It was robbery.

'Then if you cannot afford to buy Sulamee, you cannot have her. It is as simple as that,' Mistress Boderley said coldly. 'Now if you will be so kind as to leave me, I have business to attend to.'

Cassia stumbled out of the bordello with tears biting behind her lids. That evil, wicked woman, who dared to ask a hundred guineas, knowing full that two new girls would cost little more than ten pounds. And there was the moral side of the matter. Could Cassia in all charity buy a slave and know that Mistress Boderley would replace the girl by two more? Two girls enslaved for the rest of their lives in place of Sulamee.

She got into her carriage and instructed Jeffers to drive her straight back to Peacock Hall. As the carriage bowled along she noticed little of the passing scenery, nor the fresh invigorating sea air blowing in from Liverpool Bay. There was a sick, uneasy conflict deep inside her. She wanted Sulamee as much as she had wanted her own child, yet she and Vincent simply did not have one hundred guineas. And, indeed, she doubted if he would pay such a large sum even if he was in possession of it. It seemed an impossible situation and she could not think of a solution. She knew that the Society had, on various occasions, made collections so that they could purchase slaves in order to free them. But the sums involved had been reasonable. She could remember three pounds for an old slave, two pounds for one who was very sick, seven pounds for a healthy young boy who had a club foot, twelve pounds for a strong worker, that last price being the highest the society would consider paying. Besides, they were contributing every spare penny they could get towards the home for the female slaves who would be granted manumission at a future date. One hundred guineas would free ten, possibly twenty, slaves. Mistress Boderley must have taken her for a very wealthy woman, and she could not blame her for that: it was a perfectly reasonable assumption. Of course, if they had found Nathan Dash it would have been true. Cassia clenched her fist, slamming it down against her knee. That man! How he had altered their lives, like some monstrous genie who had the power to pop up wherever and whenever he chose and commit any crimes against them that pleased him. Was he never going to be found? It looked very much as if he was not in Liverpool, after all. Possibly that informer in Algiers had lied, or been genuinely mistaken. But they could hardly leave the city now that they were so totally involved in the Abolition work, nor could they go elsewhere in search of Dash if they had no lead to follow. He could be anywhere in the world by now. She should have guessed that he would be too cunning to allow himself to be caught.

Her thoughts soon left Nathan Dash to return to Sulamee. If only she had the money to buy her. She ached with longing to make the child her own. She wanted to weep when she thought of her incarcerated in that dreadful place, with the Boderley woman hovering over her like some sort of loathsome witch. Perhaps the woman was involved in the occult. Just to think of her black, stony eyes made Cassia shudder, and those deep crescent-shaped grooves at either side of her nose, just like a man's.

That thought made the hairs at the nape of Cassia's neck stand on end. Was all that heavy paint and powder employed to hide something more sinister than an ugly countenance? It was true that the Boderley woman was very tall: could *she* possibly be a *he*? But what feasible reason could she have for dressing up as a member of the opposite sex? No, it was too fanciful an idea. Cassia dismissed it.

Peacock Hall came into sight and she felt grateful to be nearly home. Andrew would be waiting and she would be able to relax and discuss the day's events.

'Did she say yes?' Andrew's face was alight with expectation as he hurried to welcome Cassia into the house. Then he saw the expression on her face and his shoulders slumped. 'I take it she refused? But what possible reason could she have to say no?'

'Oh, she has her own good reasons, Andrew. Spiteful and malicious ones. I doubt she knows any other. We discussed my buying Sulamee and do you know what price she put forward? One hundred guineas! She spoke of Sulamee being particularly popular and of how difficult it would be to replace her.'

'One hundred guineas! In heaven's name, the woman is insane! Who would pay that sort of price for a ten-year-old child?'

'I would, Andrew, if I had the money.' Cassia gripped her hands together, shaking her head sadly. 'The Boderley woman has taken me for a rich woman – very rich – and so she is charging me accordingly. She is a cunning creature.'

'And avaricious! So Sulamee has suddenly become extremely popular and irreplaceable, has she?'

'Oh, that part is not true, Andrew. There are others more popular. Ella and Rose and others. Their rooms are more splendid and their clothes, too.' Cassia had not told Andrew of how she had seen Mistress Boderley sneaking out of Ella's room that day; she did not think it a subject that she could safely discuss with him even now.

'So what are we going to do, Cassia? Things look black, do they not?'

'I shall ask her again, of course, and I shall keep on asking her. With good fortune she will become so infuriated by my constant questioning that she will relent and let me buy Sulamee for a much smaller sum.'

'I do not suppose there is any way that you and Vincent could raise such a figure?'

'Not at the moment, Andrew.'

'I wish that I could offer it to you. If only I had it, it would be yours, Cassia my dear, you know that.'

'You are a dear, Andrew. I do appreciate your offer. But even if you did have the money I do not think that I could bring myself to accept it. It would be taking advantage of you.'

'There is nothing you could do, my dear, which would take advantage of me. Everything I have is yours, all that I am is yours.' Taking her hand, Andrew planted a fervent kiss on the soft white skin, making her cheeks flush with colour.

'I do hope that I am not disturbing anything.'

Vincent's caustic tones made them leap apart, Andrew dropping Cassia's hand as if it had been a burning coal. Cassia's husband stood straddled in the doorway, hands on hips, his face black with fury.

'Would it be convenient, sir, if I had my wife to myself for a short time? Only a short time, you understand. I would not wish to keep you waiting.' Vincent advanced on Cassia, taking her by the arm and drawing her into the hallway and out through the front door into the gardens.

'Vincent, you are hurting me!' she gasped, but he did not loosen his grip on her arm. Plucking up courage to look at his face, she saw that it was thunderous, that his mouth was a thin slash. They reached the privacy of a hedge and for a moment she thought that he was going to strike her, for he half raised his arm, then, seeming to think better of it, he lowered it.

'Yes – what did you want, Vincent?' she said, trying to keep the quaver out of her voice.

'What else would I want but my own wife?' he said cuttingly. 'Do I have to have a reason for her company?'

'Her company? That you have not wanted of late!' she cried.

'How would you know when you are never there when it is wanted?'

'That is a lie! I have waited around for you for weeks now and you have not cared to come home.'

'But why should I come home when I know that you will not be there?'

'That cuts both ways, Vincent.'

'That is a weak excuse. A wife's place is waiting for her husband, not gallivanting around and flirting with other men.'

'So now you want me in what you think is my place, do you? Waiting at home for you in the vain hope that you will return one day? That is not how you used to think of me. Once you wanted us to work for the society together.'

'If you remember, I did not want you to come to Liverpool with me. I wanted you to stay behind in Cornwall, to wait for me.'

'That was only for safety, not because you truly believed a wife's place is in the home waiting for her husband.'

'Perhaps it was. Perhaps even I did not guess it then, but I do now.' He gritted his teeth, looking down at her as if he loathed her, while fury boiled inside her as she thought of his dalliance with the French Comtesse. How dare he criticize her for doing what he himself was doing!

'So you believe that there is one rule for the man and one for the woman, is that it?' she blazed.

'I do not know what you mean.'

'So you pretend innocence? How clever. But I know better, *and* I have proof.'

'Proof? Proof of what?' He looked genuinely mystified.

'Why, proof of your infidelity, of course.'

To her utter astonishment, he put his hands on his hips, threw back his head and laughed out loud. 'You will never have proof of that, *ma mignonne*. Never, if you searched for a million years.'

'And will I not? But what if I tell you that I have got that proof?' Cassia put her own hands on her hips, facing him boldly, chin jutting, eyes flashing.

'And I say that you cannot have proof of something that does not exist,' he stormed back.

Who knows what would have happened next if Joanna had not come rushing across the lawns towards them, flinging her hands in the air and crying out their names in an anguished fashion.

'Vincent, Cassia, come quickly! There has been an accident! Paul has been attacked in the city!'

The three returned hurriedly to the house to find Paul lying on a make-shift stretcher in the hallway with the two servants who had borne him home. There seemed to be blood everywhere, and for one awful moment Cassia thought that he was dreadfully mutilated about the face. But then, after water had been brought and she and Joanna had bathed him, they found that the blood had come mostly from surface cuts. He had bruising on his cheek and round both eyes, a badly cut lip, two lumps as large as eggs on his head, a broken arm and two broken ribs.

'They jumped me. They were waiting for me in an alley just

235

outside the Meeting Hall where I had given my lecture,' Paul explained later when he had been cleaned up and bandaged and was lying on his bed, the doctor having left. 'I had sent Jeffers for the carriage and so there was only Eric to defend me. He put up a good fight, but they felled him with a blow.' Fortunately Eric had recovered without any after effects and was stricken with guilt at having let his master down, as he saw it.

'Have you any idea who they were, Paul?' Vincent wanted to know. He too was feeling guilty, for this was one of the few times when he had not accompanied Paul to one of their meetings.

'They looked like ruffians to me. They were none too clean and their clothes were tattered. I would not think that they had any particular thoughts on Abolition. Probably they were paid by somebody who has a fortune invested in the slave trade.'

'And that could be any merchant or slave captain in Liverpool,' Vincent finished for him.

'We've been lucky not to have had this happen before. I know that we usually stick together, but a bunch of ruffians could soon finish us off if they had a mind to. Indeed, those ruffians this afternoon could have finished me off, but I think that they had been ordered to give me a nasty beating and that was all. Something to frighten us off, to stop us doing our Abolition work.' Paul groaned as a stabbing pain from one of his head wounds shot through his skull.

Immediately Joanna was by his side, taking his hand. 'Paul, you must rest now. We will leave you in quiet. Close your eyes and try not to think about this horrible experience. Jeffers will stand guard outside your door.'

Paul looked up at his sister quizzically. 'The ruffians are not in the house, Joanna dear.'

'I know, Paul. Oh, this has been so upsetting. I have dreaded something like this happening. You men take so many risks and there are so many people who are against Abolition. People whose livings depend on the slave trade.'

'We have always known the risks, Joanna,' Vincent said

soothingly. 'In future we will just have to stay together at all times and take more servants with us.'

Joanna looked unconvinced. She was very pale and she kept twisting her hands together. To give herself something to do she straightened the sheets on Paul's bed, which were already immaculate, and then again instructed him to rest, before she and the others quietly left the room.

Eric had declared that he felt well enough to continue his normal day's work, but Joanna had shooed him to bed as well and ordered him to remain there until the morning.

They took up their seats in the library, where Cassia poured a glass of brandy for Joanna as she still looked pale.

'Sip this, Joanna, you will feel better.'

'Brandy! I have never liked the stuff,' Joanna said, but she did as she was told all the same.

Andrew and Vincent had taken up seats at opposite ends of the room and were avoiding each other's eyes. After a few moments of restless sitting, Vincent got up and began to pace up and down at his end of the library. He knew that he would continue to feel guilty for many a long day for what had happened to Paul in his absence. It could have been much worse: Paul could have been murdered. He supposed that he must thank God for that. But he wished that he had had a better reason for being at Peacock Hall when he should have been with Paul. For many weeks he had suspected that there was something going on between his wife and Andrew, and today he had decided to arrive home unexpectedly to catch them in a compromising situation. That he had succeeded did not make him feel pleased with himself: he felt bitter about the whole situation. If he could have trusted his wife he need not have left Paul alone today with such dire results. He glanced at his wife. How beautiful she was! He would never cease to marvel at her ivory skin. So many other women with fair skin looked pallid or sickly, or were covered in unsightly freckles, but not she. Her white flesh was fresh and wholesome as milk, her hydrangea-blue eyes shone out of it like flowers blooming on a sunny day. And that crown of luxuriant auburn hair which tumbled about her shoulders, a sea of flame. A tremor of desire coursed through him. Hastily he suppressed it. *Bon Dieu*, but she was desirable! That sensual, richly curved mouth, the swan neck curving down to the heavy, full, white breasts and tiny waist, the swelling hips. He could have taken her in his arms now before the other two if there had not been so much trouble between them.

It galled him to think that she could prefer the callow attentions of a younger, less experienced man than he, a man who had nothing to engage his attentions except the care of his dog and the meagre assistance he gave his brother in the Abolition cause. Andrew Peacock held little responsibility: he came and went when he pleased and he seemed to do as he liked about most things. He had been thoroughly spoiled by his brother and sister. It would serve Cassia right if she did turn to him, for she would soon discover that her idol had feet of clay, that she could not lean on him nor expect his stolid support through all weather. He felt angry and disgruntled. It was hard to remember the happy days before their marriage and during their journey from Cornwall to Liverpool. How sunny their relationship had been then, and uncomplicated. Now, it was shadowed and strange, full of shifting darkness and changing currents. Something had gone terribly wrong with it and he could not say what, nor even why, unless all this upset and alteration could stem from the loss of their child. Being a man he found this difficult to countenance. She had come through so much without breaking, without even showing the slightest signs of cracking, that he expected her to take her loss in the same way. He had thought her sturdy and iron-willed; to find her otherwise was a shock to him. It was like discovering another person in place of the Cassia he loved; another person whom he did not know: a stranger.

He remembered, with feelings of irony, how energetically she had worked to convince him that they were in love. Two years ago, but it seemed a continent away: another world, a different universe. Now, she was cold, she rebuffed him, she would no longer meet his eyes. Once he had lived for her glances, drinking in her gaze, feeding off it rapturously. Now, he was angry and grieved at the loss of this delicious sustenance.

'I shall take my turn in nursing Paul,' Cassia said. 'No, Joanna, I insist. We owe you so much, it is a very small price to pay for all the weeks we have lived in your home and eaten at your table.'

Joanna blew her nose loudly and then sniffed a little as if tears still threatened. 'You are a sweet girl, Cassia, and you have been the perfect guest; Vincent, too. You have helped us so much with our work.'

'And you with ours,' Cassia said.

A servant tapped at the library door and entered, making a half bow.

'Madam, sir, the Comtesse de Renate is without.'

Andrew leapt to his feet but Vincent was nearer the door and it was he who went out to greet the Comtesse and to invite her into the house, much to Cassia's chagrin. Soon the Comtesse was ensconced in the library, hearing about Paul's misadventures and expressing her sympathies.

'I may be allowed to visit Captain Peacock?' she asked, looking first at Joanna and then at Andrew, her silvery-fair brows raised questioningly, mouth rosebudded.

'When he is a little better, Madame la Comtesse,' said Joanna. 'He is very shocked – badly bruised and shaken. He is resting now. Perhaps you would care to return tomorrow or the day after to see him.'

'So I have the long wait, that is sad. I had hoped to see the Captain today. He has done so much work for the society, I wanted him to know that we are all deeply concerned for his well-being, and that our members wish to know how he is.'

'I think I can tell you that, Madame.' Joanna folded her hands across her stomach. 'He is, as I said, badly shocked; he has two lumps on his head; lacerations to the face; a deeply cut

239

lip; a broken arm and two broken ribs.'

'So his injuries are quite serious?' The Comtesse gave a little gasp and fluttered her fan in an agitated fashion as if desperate for air. 'Oh, *Sacré Vierge*, this is a most terrible thing! When we embarked on this work we did not envisage violence.'

'We have always felt that the threat was a possibility, Madame,' Vincent put in. 'There are many unscrupulous men in Liverpool who depend upon the slave trade for their existence. We always felt that at any time they could strike at us and now they have done – literally. I only wish that it could have been myself they attacked.'

'You are too brave, Captain Sauvage,' the Comtesse said, with an admiring glance at Vincent – a glance which made Cassia curl her her fingers into her palms with fury. How dare the French bitch flirt openly with her husband here before them all and while Paul lay upstairs so ill! She doubted that the woman had come here to see Paul at all: she had probably used his injuries as an excuse to see Vincent again. What audacity! Cassia would have liked to dig her nails into the Comtesse's ornate, powder-blue satin gown and rip it to shreds, tearing off the rosettes and frills and flounces, until she stood in only a tattered chemise. The woman was decked as if for a court appearance; she had obviously taken extreme pains with her dressing, and all so that she could rush here and pretend to be upset about Paul. In reality, the silver-grey eyes were devoid of any true emotion, but displayed their habitual look of covetousness laced with sensuality.

'You will take tea with us, Madame?' Joanna asked, but the Comtesse said that no, she would decline but that she would be delighted to visit the next day or the next to see how Paul fared, and in the meantime she would be pleased if they would send a messenger, a servant perhaps, to keep her informed of the Captain's progress.

Vincent she means, thought Cassia, outraged. She wants Vincent to go hurrying over to her house to tell her how Paul is and then she will seduce him with her wiles – the scheming hussy!

240

Cassia turned her back on the Comtesse and appeared to be paying particular interest to a large book which projected from one of the shelves. She did not turn round till the Comtesse had gone, the door closing behind her. She threw Vincent a shrivelling glance and exited from the room as coolly and gracefully as she could manage.

Cassia dearly wished that she was in her own bedroom with her own belongings around her so that she could smash and rend them all to smithereens. But there was something she could do. Going to the massive oaken wardrobe where Vincent kept his clothes, she flung open its door to survey the jackets and waistcoats hanging inside. Carefully, she picked out his favourite, a cream velvet suit printed with a small flower pattern in green and blue, the edges of which were lined with dark blue satin, with a waistcoat of cream silk, the borders and pockets of which were embroidered with flowers in blue chenille thread. Then, reaching for her nail scissors, Cassia proceeded to cut the suit and waistcoat into shreds. As she worked, she grew more and more angry, thinking of Vincent in the Comtesse's bed, kissing her and touching her naked body. She imagined how swiftly he would tear off his clothes to leap between the sheets with the French woman and how eagerly he would remove her flimsy peignoir. Piercing acid tears thrust behind her lids and her cheeks scorched with angry heat. If those two were here now she would have lunged at them with the scissors. She would cut off the Comtesse's silver fair curls and mark her beautiful face forever, just as Paul's had been slashed today, then she would turn to her husband and stab him right through his lying, deceitful heart!

Chapter Fourteen

Cassia was sitting in the drawing-room of the Oates's mansion on the edge of Toxteth Park listening to Charles Oates speak about the black girl whom he loved. Charles was a personable young man aged about twenty-six. He had brown hair fastened back in the popular pigtail, frank brown eyes, and a squarish face with a somewhat heavy chin. His nose was blunt and turned up, his mouth full and wide, his brows straight and rather untidy. He wore a grey watered-silk suit, lined with cream silk, and a pale blue brocade waistcoat embroidered with floral sprays of violet, the particular shade of which Cassia rather fancied for a gown.

'My father brought India home as a gift for my sister, to wait upon her, and I confess that the moment I set eyes on her I fell wildly in love. She has the sweetest temperament: she is so gentle and loving and kind. What I want more than anything is legislation so that all slaves can be freed and she and I can marry without any repercussions. As things stand, my father will not hear of my having any relationship whatsoever with India. He would have dismissed her instantly but for my sister's pleas that she remain. To keep my father happy I have not spoken again of my feelings for India. I think he assumes that I have got over what he sees as an infatuation for her. It is not so superficial an emotion, however, for I have loved her now, and deeply, for over two years. When I heard of your husband and The Children of Liberty I was overjoyed, and since I joined no one has worked harder or more diligently for the Society's aims than I. When Abolition comes, and I say when, not if, my first step will be to marry India.'

Cassia was moved by the tale of fidelity and love, thinking wryly of her own situation. 'It is a touching tale, Charles. There is nothing quite so marvellous as the story of true love, and you deserve to have your dreams made possible.'

'It has not been easy for me, being my father's heir. If I should anger him there is no doubt that he would cut me off, for he has a quick and fierce temper. Other members of the family have also suffered from it. My two younger brothers are in the Colonies, where they went to escape his wrath. My sister is his favourite, so it is easier for her, and I do not envy her that position, for she is extremely useful as a mediator.' He grinned disarmingly. 'But you see, if I were cut off I should have no money to keep India in comfort, and I could not possibly consider making her my wife if I were a poor man. She deserves better than that. She was a chief's daughter in her homeland, you see.'

'Shall I be able to meet her? I am looking forward to it,' Cassia said.

'We shall have to arrange that carefully, Mistress Sauvage, not to arouse my father's suspicions. It will be quite in order for India to put in an appearance with my sister when she arrives.'

'I fancy that you and your sister are frequently in one another's company, then?' Cassia grinned, at which Charles Oates blushed and gave a lop-sided smile.

'That is so – you have uncloaked me, Mistress Sauvage.'

'And you are fortunate that your sister is on your side. Does she support the idea of your marrying India?'

Charles nodded. 'Oh yes, indeed she does. She is a very free-minded young woman.'

'It seems that most of your family are free thinkers.'

'That may very well be because our father is so hidebound and narrow-minded. In rebelling against him, we have no choice but to entertain free thought and all the most modern, up-to-date notions.'

'My father, too, was dictatorial,' Cassia said. 'He had a very violent temper. He had only to twitch his thick black brows and I shuddered with dread. I, too, could not wait to get away from my home.'

'I believe you had little choice, as it happens.' Charles pulled a comic face.

Cassia laughed. 'That is one way of putting it. Has Joanna told you something of my background?'

'A little. I think that she thought it would be more suitable if you told me yourself.'

'I tend to agree. These things can sound rather strange if not explained as they actually happened.' Cassia proceeded to tell Charles something of her abduction from the cove in Cornwall, skirting very briefly over the next two years until she was, as she put it, rescued by her husband and taken back to Cornwall.

'A thrilling tale. To be compared, in many ways, to the story of some black slaves.'

'We were not shackled in our pirate ship,' Cassia explained, 'but nonetheless it was a harrowing voyage. We were sorely neglected, given no water to wash, and barely any food. One woman died in childbirth and I could do nothing to save her.'

'How dreadful! How you must have suffered.'

'It is all in the past now,' Cassia said airily, knowing full well that she was still undergoing the results of those terrible months.

At that moment Charles's sister Victoria entered the room, smiling widely. She was petite but on the heavy side. She wore a high wig dressed with orange ribbon, and her gown was of rust-coloured tubed silk brocade embroidered with chocolate-brown pansies. She stepped into the room sideways as her panniers were so wide, and Cassia noticed that she had surprisingly dainty feet, encased in brown velvet backless mules with orange silk rosettes at the toes.

'Mistress Sauvage, how delightful to meet you,' said Victoria. 'I have heard a great deal about you from Charles, and from your husband, too, whom I met at one of the Society's meetings which was held at our house a few weeks ago.'

'I hope they were good things you heard,' Cassia smiled.

'Indeed they were.' Charles's sister gave a trilling laugh,

slapping one pannier with her closed fan before taking a seat on a chair built specially to accommodate the awkward shape of wired gowns.

It was then that Cassia noticed the slender dark girl standing behind her. India wore a plain but attractive gown of ivory watered silk, cut low at the bodice to display her slender shoulders and neck. She had a very small bust, a long slender waist, and her gown had small panniers. Froths of snowy white lace edged her sleeves, hanging down almost to her knees. But it was her skin which captivated Cassia. She wore a white wig dotted with white silk daisies and ribbons, and against this her skin had the sheen of much polished light oak. Her bone structure was superb, her teeth regular and white, her eyes a rich dark mahogany. She held herself gracefully, as if raised as a Lady, and there was immense pride in the straightness of her shoulders and back.

Cassia smiled at her and she smiled back a little shyly.

'I believe that you are a princess, India?' Cassia said.

'That is so, Mistress Sauvage. My father is a great king in what you call West Africa. His name is Abanata. But, alas, he has a fickle nature, and he tired of his chief wives and daughters, and when a slave-master came near our kingdom he exchanged his wives and all his daughters for a shipload of brandy, silk brocade cloth, muskets and gunpowder, plus a few trinkets thrown in for good measure.' India's face showed no trace of bitterness as she spoke. In fact, the way she delivered her words was even more shocking for her lack of anger.

'I have heard of these things before, India. Do you miss your homeland very much?'

'I did at first. I felt sick and ill. The voyage was horrifying, we were shackled all the way. We were supposed to be allowed up on deck twice a day to be fed beans, but we were not. Weeks went by and we had nothing to eat except ship's biscuit and water. Many died around me. My mother did not survive two weeks.' Now sorrow did come into the girl's eyes. She brushed away tears. 'We were not the first to whom this happened and we shall not be the last.'

'India too has had her unhappy adventures, as you can see,' Charles said, 'but I think we have served to make her happier now.'

'You speak beautiful English, India. I am very impressed,' Cassia smiled.

'Thank you, Mistress Sauvage, you are very kind. Charles taught me all that I know. I could speak no English when I came here. I have learned to read and write, also, thanks to Charles.'

'Do not forget me, India,' Victoria put in, 'I have had my share in teaching you, too.'

'Yes, that is true, Mistress Victoria, I had not forgotten.'

'Oh, call me Vicky, father's not in hearing,' Victoria said impatiently. 'I think it is ridiculous that my brother's future wife has to call me by such a formal title.' She patted India's hand affectionately.

A servant arrived with tea and cinnamon cakes. The cakes were delicious, light and of a melting texture and with just the right amount of spice.

It was altogether a very pleasant afternoon, and if only things had been better between Cassia and Vincent, she would have felt happy indeed. As it was, she left the Oates household reluctantly, not wishing to return to whatever might await her at Peacock Hall. When she got there she went straight upstairs to see how Paul was. Two weeks had passed since his attack and he was much improved. Fortunately, he was healing rapidly and the physician who attended him said that it looked as if the lacerations on his face would heal with only minor scars, something which relieved them all immensely, for they had feared that Paul would be disfigured for life.

'Cassia,' he said, pleased, as she entered the room. 'You're looking very well, my dear.'

Cassia sat on a chair by Paul's bed. 'Thank you, Paul, and so are you. Have you read the book I brought you?'

'Yes, it was very interesting, most informative.'

'Charles Oates has sent you two more to read. One is a novel and one is about Abolition, by an associate of Granville Sharpe.'

'That should be good.' Paul glanced at the books, opening their covers and looking at the first few pages of each. 'How is Charles?'

'Glowing I think is the word,' Cassia smiled.

'And how is India?'

'I think the same adjective would apply to her, too. And to Victoria.'

'Tell me, what do you think of Victoria?'

'What exactly is it that you want to know that you do not already know?' Cassia narrowed her eyes at Paul, who was lying back on his pillows trying to look disinterested despite his question.

'Well, can you see her as the mistress of Peacock Hall?'

'I see, so that is how the wind blows. Her deportment is excellent, her dress sense seems reasonable enough. But haven't you forgotten something?'

'Forgotten? Forgotten what?' Paul sat up anxiously, wincing at the pain from his healing ribs.

'Well, if, as I assume, you are thinking of marrying Victoria, she will come to live at Peacock Hall and naturally she will bring her maid with her. There is no other daughter resident at the Oates mansion, so there will be no reason for India to stay behind, and so —'

'And so Charles will be deprived of his future wife's company. Good heavens, I had not thought of that.'

'Are you desperately eager to marry Victoria?'

'Truth to tell, I had been pondering over it for a year.'

'A year? And you are still only pondering? Then I would say you are not as keen as I had imagined.'

'Oh, I am keen, be assured of that. But there are other things to consider. Joanna would have her nose put out of joint if Victoria came here as mistress.'

'Do they not get on?'

'There is a little – what can I say – frisson between them of a somewhat acid nature. I have never been able to envisage them living under the same roof and being amenable to each other.'

'Oh dear, so you do have a problem, Paul.'

'Yes. Even if I won Joanna round to my way of thinking and she agreed to accept Victoria here, just imagine the ensuing years of coolness, perhaps even open hostility and bickering between the two women vying for supremacy in the household. My life would be unmitigated hell.'

'Oh, poor Paul!' Cassia patted his hand. 'But do you not have a weapon at the moment?'

'A weapon? How do you mean?'

'Joanna has been seriously troubled by your injuries. She has talked constantly of the possibility of your being scarred.'

'Yes, she has told me how very distressed this would make her. What is it that you are suggesting, Cassia?'

'Would this not be an ideal time to put to her your feelings about Victoria?'

'Play on her gentle heart while it is even gentler than usual, you say? Hmm, that is an excellent idea. Now why did I not think of that!' Paul clenched his fist, banging it lightly on his knee, then wincing again. 'You are a genius, Cassia.'

'I should proceed as quickly as possible, Paul, while you are still an invalid. Strike while the iron is hot, as the saying goes. Broach the subject when Joanna comes to bring you your dinner. Do not say it outright, but suggest that you would feel a lot more hopeful and happier, and inclined to get well all the speedier if you had something really marvellous to look forward to, such as your marriage to Victoria.' Cassia gave a conspiratorial wink.

'Brilliant, brilliant! I shall do exactly as you suggest.'

'I shall wait eagerly to hear the results.'

At dinner that evening Joanna seemed particularly pensive. She ate slowly, as if she had a weight on her mind, and Cassia

248

glanced at her occasionally wondering if she would raise the subject of what Paul had just put to her, but she did not.

It was a restful evening. Restful in the wrong way. After dinner, Andrew sat reading one of the latest tracts on Abolition; Joanna did some needlework. She was embroidering a waistcoat for Paul as a surprise for when he was well enough to leave his bed.

Cassia sat at the window looking out across the lawns and flower-beds to the trees beyond, until dusk drew in and she could no longer see out. Once or twice she looked at the empty chair by the hearth where Vincent usually sat when he was at home. How she wished that he was there now, sitting in it, looking across at her with his vibrant jewel-green eyes, his mouth tenderly curving with love for her. How she wished that everything was as it had been five months ago, before they had come to Liverpool. But of what use were regrets? Once, what seemed like a full lifetime ago, she had vowed never to indulge in regret; it was aging and embittering, it caused hollowed cheeks and shadowed eyes. So she had lost her husband. Well, she knew that she would pay the price for it for the rest of her life. Even now, loneliness was seeping into her very bones, obliterating the buoyant happiness which had been her nature before. Vincent had the power to make her ecstatic or broken-hearted. No one else would ever have a similar power over her; she knew that instinctively. Vincent was her fate, her Kismet. She would live and die loving him and him alone. But she, too, was a woman of eloquent passions. She needed tenderness and empathy and affection. And if Vincent was otherwise engaged . . .

Cassia looked across at Andrew's red-gilt head bent over his book, and suddenly a wave of hungry longing swept through her as she imagined Andrew's arms encircling her waist, his feather-like kisses on her face. She would not have been human if she did not need warmth and attention.

As if sensing her gaze, Andrew looked up, his green-flecked

eyes bright. Caught unawares, Cassia looked away, trying to pretend she had not been looking in his direction. But Raven, too, seemed to sense her interest, for he got up, stretched, and came over to her chair, looking up at her quizzically.

'Are you ready for a walk, Raven?' She patted the ragged silky head. His answer was a bark of excitement.

'I shall be taking him in a moment,' Andrew said. 'Will you accompany me, Cassia?'

'Yes, of course.' She had a brilliant mind-image of the two of them walking through the scented dusk, hand in hand, with Raven romping along beside them. Now and again they would stop to kiss, to exchange sweet words of love. It was a beautiful thought which brought tears to her eyes, for it was not really Andrew with whom she wished to hold hands and kiss. It was Vincent – but that was her tragedy.

The night air was mild, even though the month was October, and Raven romped like a puppy, lolloping towards Cassia and jumping up in front of her and then lolloping across to his master and jumping up in front of him. In the distance, on the rise at the bottom of the gardens, they saw a servant exercising Joanna's three dogs. Raven saw them, too, and barked by way of greeting, the three dogs returning his call.

'Those are three of the handsomest hounds I've ever known,' Cassia said.

'Do not let Raven hear you saying that, he is somewhat jealous of them. He already thinks they get preferential treatment.'

'Well, they do belong to the mistress of the house,' Cassia smiled, watching Raven's ears pricking as she and Andrew spoke. It really did appear as if he knew what they were talking about.

'Raven had designs on one of them some time ago. He behaved every bit as if he had fallen in love with her. Hophra, the one with the reddish coat. But I'm afraid Joanna would not allow it, she said she did not want a house full of ragged puppies.'

'Oh, poor Raven, what a disappointment.' Cassia smoothed the hound's great, catkin-like ears.

Both Andrew and Cassia knew that they were talking to delay the advent of the mood which had begun to come upon them in the house. Perhaps they would be embarrassed by voicing deeper feelings, so, for a time, they exchanged light chit-chat. But eventually their conversation wound down and they found that they were walking closer together than before.

'Cassia,' Andrew began.

'Yes, Andrew?'

'Cassia, we have all noticed that things are even worse between you and Vincent.'

Cassia felt the heat flame into her cheeks and was grateful for the dusk. 'That is so,' she said in a low voice.

'I do not mean to intrude upon your privacy, nor to distress you, but I would like to help you, Cassia. I've told you so before, but I'm repeating my offer. I feel it my duty to do so.'

'Duty is such a cold companion,' Cassia said.

'But it is duty born out of –' Andrew paused, then added, 'very deep affection.'

'Oh, Andrew, you know that I am married.'

'Yes, I know that, Cassia my dear, but what sort of marriage is it? It seems to me that it barely exists any longer. Your husband has his soulmate, why not you?'

Suddenly Andrew was only inches away from Cassia and his strong arms were slipping round her back, pulling her close to him. Uneasily she looked round, but the dusk had now descended completely and she could not see the servant in the distance walking the dogs, for which she was grateful as it meant that he could not see her. She relaxed a little. Andrew felt the tension ease from her body and took it for response.

'Oh, Cassia, my dearest,' he whispered against her ear, 'you cannot know how I have longed to hold you in my arms. I dream of you all the time, I long to make you my own.'

'Andrew, please do not speak this way. What you propose

251

can never be. I have made my vows to Vincent and I must keep them.'

'Oh, Cassia, you break my heart when you speak that way. Life is meant for happiness, for love, not for coldness and loneliness. You are young and beautiful, you need a lover, not a man who is foolish enough to neglect you for another who is not worth a tenth of you.'

Cassia would have replied, but Andrew's hard questing lips were on hers as he crushed her to him. She felt the blood pounding in his body and the stirring of his passion, and it reminded her poignantly of the times when Vincent had taken her in his arms in just this way. Strangely, she was filled with a hungry longing, and she closed her eyes as Andrew kissed her again and again until her mouth throbbed. Then his lips lowered to her neck and shoulders and his hard fingers pushed aside the neckline of her gown to plant kisses on the rise of her breasts.

She did try to push him away then, but in vain; he was ardent and strong and he had waited a very long time for this moment. She murmured his name but it only seemed to fire him, and then she felt his probing fingers inside the bodice of her gown, his hot palm cradling her breast. To her astonishment, a sparkling tingle coursed through her body, bringing in its wake a craving for further intimacy.

She opened her eyes to see Andrew looking around for a place where they could lie in privacy and shelter. Seeing a large shrub, he led her behind it, and began again to kiss her furiously. Her breathing increased in intensity, coming so rapidly that she felt dizzy. A delicious rapture was spreading through her limbs. She was safe with this man: he had not let her down, nor would he. She felt that most strongly. Oh, how she needed a lover she could trust and depend on!

The velvet darkness of night descended upon them like a coverlet. Not even Raven disturbed them, for he had gone off in pursuit of a rabbit. With the velvet green turf soft against Cassia's back they could have been in bed. It will be all right, she said to herself. Vincent had his woman and now she had her man. This was obviously the plan; how it was meant to be, each having their own lovers. And what better lover for her than Andrew, devoted and attentive?

'Cassia,' he plunged his fingers gently into her hair, coiling its silky texture against his hands, 'your hair is like living fire. I do not think that I have ever seen such a glorious auburn colour. And I suspect that your passions are as fiery, my darling. Tell me, tell me that I am right.' He nuzzled her neck, dotting kisses along her jaw and to her lips, then slipping his tongue in between her teeth in a way that made little shivers trickle across her body. 'Oh, you are beautiful, my fire-haired angel, and I adore you. I have never loved anyone in this way before, nor shall I ever. I want no one but you, Cassia, my angel.'

His hands went down to her bodice, tugging away the embroidered silk from her breasts so that she felt the night air rushing like silk against her flesh. And then Andrew's tongue was against her nipples, caressing them sensuously, and she curved against him, her arms sliding round his neck.

If she closed her eyes and kept them closed, she could imagine that it was Vincent who was making love to her, that everything was all right between them, that there had never been any division. She could imagine that it was she and Vincent lying on a Greek sward all those months ago when they had fled from Turkey. Because, if it were her husband making love to her now, it would not be wrong. And, more than anything, she wanted what she was doing to be right.

Andrew was breathing heavily as he rained kisses on her breasts, and then his hand slid down towards the hem of her skirt, and seconds later his strong young hands were caressing her thighs and moving towards the auburn silk triangle between her legs. When he touched her there it was like being shocked, but in the most pleasurable way, and she gave a little cry, pulling him closer to her. In response he stroked her lightly, until she thought that she would scream with desire.

Then he bent over her, and when she felt his tongue against her she felt faint with ecstasy. He worked expertly, seeming to know exactly what would rouse her most, and her head was swimming with longing. She could feel him iron-hard against her and she wondered how a man so passionate could wait so long before entering her.

'You do not need anyone else, my angel,' he whispered. 'You do not need Vincent, you need only me. I can satisfy you, I can make you happy. Forget Vincent!'

Vincent's name, coming unexpectedly in the middle of her passion, was like a dash of iced water, seeming to bring her to her senses. How could she be here, lying on the grass with a man who was not her husband, a man who was plainly intending to make love to her as only her husband should?

'No, Andrew!' she cried. 'No, stop, *please* stop!'

But Andrew was virtually at the point of no return, and during the next few minutes there was a most ungainly struggle, while Cassia cried out repeatedly that he was to stop, that he must not do what he intended to do, that it was a mistake, a great mistake, and she should not be there.

'You are jesting, Cassia! You know that we were meant for one another,' Andrew said thickly. 'How can you want me to stop now?'

'You *must* stop, Andrew. This is wrong, very wrong. If we go any farther we shall both bitterly regret it.'

'*Never!* I shall never regret making you my own, Cassia, my angel.'

'Yes! We shall both regret it, both of us. You must stop, Andrew, you must stop now or I shall never forgive you, I shall never speak to you again.'

This did seem to bring him to his senses. He drew away from her, looking at her with pained eyes. 'You are serious, my angel, but how can this be? We were meant to be lovers, I feel it more strongly than I have ever felt anything in my life before. My only regret is that I did not meet you before you married Vincent; but why should we let that stand in our way? He has not let marriage interfere with his desires.'

'That does not mean that I have to be the same,' Cassia said in a whisper. She was hastily covering her breasts and pulling down her skirts. 'Andrew, we must never be alone in this way again, it is too dangerous.'

'Cassia, you break my heart!' Andrew tried to take her hands, but she snatched them away.

'It is better if you do not touch me, it can only lead to more trouble. Andrew, if anything happened between us it would wreck more lives than ours.'

'Do you not think that enough lives have been wrecked as it is, without adding our own to them?' Andrew said, sounding bitter and choked. 'Your husband did not think of how he would destroy your life by taking a mistress, did he? He expects you to wait around for his return when it pleases him. When has he put your well-being before his?'

'Andrew, please do not speak like that.' Cassia felt wretched. She should never have come out here alone in the dusk with Andrew. Now she had hurt him, too. She suddenly felt sick with guilt. Having tidied her hair and pushed it into its ribbon, she turned to go back to the house.

'Cassia, is that all you have to say?' Andrew's voice sounded strangled. He reached out a hand to catch her arm but she shook it away.

'There can be no more, Andrew, do you not see that? You speak of lives having been destroyed, but how many do you think would be destroyed if we became lovers? Joanna, for one, would be broken-hearted. It would be a betrayal of her trust.'

'If Paul can have his Victoria, why can I not have you?'

'But consider Paul and Victoria, Andrew. Has Paul not put his sister first for a year or more, considering her wishes before his own? That is always the more honourable state. See what misery is caused by a man putting his desires before his duty. It leaves a trail of shattered hearts, crumbled dreams.'

She turned again and walked purposefully towards Peacock Hall, ignoring Raven who bounded up, wagging his tail at her.

She felt bruised and shaken at how near she had come to betraying her marriage vows. Infidelity was not her, not her at all. For better or for worse was the promise she had made and she would keep it, however much effort and anguish it took. Let others more fickle and foolish betray their vows; she would not. Her head was beginning to throb and she knew that she was going to suffer an almighty megrim. She felt soiled somehow, unclean. Tears were beading her lids, sharp and fiery as acid. She was a prisoner of her vows. Tonight, she could have broken them. She could have been in Andrew's arms at this very moment, revelling in his lovemaking, but her conscience would not allow it. Suddenly her conscience was like a great, mountainous weight within her, bearing her down, dragging at her heels, so that she felt every bit as if she were manacled like a slave.

Chapter Fifteen

It was a beautiful October day, an Indian summer, when Nola died in Cassia's arms. Sulamee was with them, and, as Nola's eyes closed and her head tilted lifelessly to one side, the quadroon girl burst into tears.

'But I gave her the milk, I gave her the milk!' Sulamee wept.

Cassia, who herself had been about to dissolve into tears, pulled Sulamee into her arms. 'Yes, you did, Sulamee, dear. You helped her a great deal. She would have died long ago if you had not brought her her milk every day.'

'But it not save her, it not save her,' Sulamee sobbed.

'We all did our best. If I had come earlier perhaps we might have saved her, but we were too late.'

'Too late,' Sulamee echoed, burying her face in Cassia's shoulder.

'Remember, Sulamee, if anyone, even Mistress Boderley, brings you opium to smoke, you must say no. Promise me that, Sulamee. You must say no.'

'I promise,' Sulamee whispered.

Nola's face looked peaceful now but very pale, and the skin round her eyes was pearly grey. It was a tragedy that she had had to die, but at least she had died without pain, knowing nothing but the increasing lethargy which had finally overcome her. Death seemed to haunt these children in one form or another: if drugs or disease did not get them, then the murderous killer would. Cassia stroked Sulamee's silky black hair and kissed her smooth *café au lait* forehead.

'Nola is with the angels now, Sulamee. She will never have any more suffering again. All her pains have gone and she is with Jesus.'

'With Jesus,' Sulamee echoed, seeming to find some comfort in those words.

Mistress Boderley was not to be found that day, so Cassia told Ella what had happened. Ella shrugged, as if a child's death meant nothing to her. Then she flushed and looked away as Cassia's eyes bored into hers.

'A child has died, does no one care?' she said.

Ella shrugged again. 'Mistress Boderley not here. She would deal with it if she were.'

'So she is not here, then who *will* deal with it? Nola's body cannot be left there in her bed.'

'Oh, it will not be left there; the room will be needed for another girl. Mistress Boderley is at the market at this very moment.'

'She knew Nola was going to die?' Cassia was astonished, and the hairs at the back of her neck stood on end.

'That was not difficult to see.' Ella tossed her head, hooking a thumb into the belt of her gown and thrusting out one hip in a jaunty pose.

'Right to the very end I hoped and prayed that she would live,' Cassia said.

'You do what you wish, Mistress. Here, we thought differently.'

Cassia turned away, heavy-hearted. The callous way in which life was treated in this place was unbelievable. Children died and shoulders were shrugged; fresh children brought in immediately to take their places. No one mourned, no one grieved. She doubted that there would be a proper funeral for Nola, but she was not going to have the child buried in a pauper's grave. She thrust back her shoulders and looked Ella squarely in the eye.

'Ella, I want you to arrange a proper funeral for Nola.'

'That is impossible,' Ella said coldly.

'Why is it impossible?'

'Who would pay?'

'I will.' Cassia had no money on her, for she had always come on her charity work without her reticule to lessen the risk of being attacked and robbed. 'As soon as I get home I will send a coachman with the money, if you will promise, Ella, that you will see to the funeral yourself. I do not want Nola buried in a pauper's grave, nor do I want her to have a pauper's funeral. She must have a proper, decent funeral, and I will send enough money for that. Do I have your promise that you will see to it?'

Ella's mouth twisted, as if the thought of doing a charitable deed was beneath her. But finally she agreed. 'Yes, I will do it. But it will not be easy. Who can I get to come here to fetch the child's body?'

'If you think that will be difficult I will send two coachmen and they can take the child's body away.'

'What vicar would bury a harlot?' Ella said disparagingly.

'I'm sure that I can find one if you do not think that you can. In fact, from the look of it, I might as well arrange the entire funeral myself.'

'Why not?' Ella sniffed in a bored fashion.

'Why not indeed,' Cassia snapped.

And that was what she did. When it was over, when she had arranged for the little body to be prepared for burial, and when she had found a vicar willing to commit the child to a grave in his churchyard, she returned home, exhausted. All she wanted to do was to crawl into bed. She kept seeing Nola's face, the eyelids closing, the head tilting to one side, the breath issuing from the little body for the last time. It was like her own baby dying all over again, reviving the half-healed wounds.

'My goodness, Cassia, what has happened?' Joanna greeted her at the door. 'You look terrible.'

'Nola,' was all Cassia said before she sank onto the carved bench in the hall, her head in her hands.

'She is dead?'

'Yes.' The word was a sigh.

Joanna sat down beside Cassia, putting her arms round her friend. 'It had to come, we all knew that. But how terrible, all the same. Oh, how very upset you must be, my dear. Do you want to go straight up to your room? We shall not expect you for dinner tonight, we shall quite understand. I shall have some food sent up for you.'

'I could not eat anything, Joanna. Thank you, all the same.'

'I shall send something up in any case. We shall see if we can tempt you.'

The tray when it arrived was crammed with delicious and tasty food. Stewed carp to begin, then succulent roast chicken, followed by flummery, an almond jelly enriched with cream and laced with chocolate. There were six vegetables to choose from, with Cheshire cheese and fragrant wine to finish. Cassia sat and looked at the food and wanted to cry all over again. She was thinking of the struggle she had had to make Nola eat one or two mouthfuls of food each day, and how the child had wasted away before her eyes in spite of all her efforts. She wanted to pick up the tray of food and fling it across the room, and a surge of anger raged through her body so strongly that she almost did just that.

It was cruel, too cruel to bear. She was stricken by a feeling of approaching disaster, her thoughts centring on Sulamee. One child was dead; she must get the other out of that place before she, too, died. However unpleasant the task, she must confront the Boderley woman again. And somehow, somewhere, even if it made her enemies, she must get the one hundred guineas to buy Sulamee's freedom.

Mistress Boderley threw back her head and screeched with laughter when Cassia raised the subject of buying Sulamee. Her cheeks flaming, Cassia waited for the peals of raucous hilarity to end. When they did she put her question again.

'Is the price for Sulamee still one hundred guineas?'

'Do you think that I am likely to reduce it?' Mistress Boderley sneered. 'If you do then you are a fool. You have made it plain that you want the child. Well, you can have her – for two hundred guineas.'

'*Two* hundred?' Cassia gasped. 'But –'

'But what? You want her; well, she is yours for two hundred

guineas. If I were you, I would hurry up and pay the price, because it will be going up again very soon.'

'How can you!' Cassia raged, her eyes flashing. 'I want to release a child from a life of hell, and you would charge me two hundred guineas to do it.'

'To me, she is nothing more than a slave and I have many of those. I am hardly likely to start having qualms of conscience now, after all this time. I leave that sort of feeling to the likes of you.'

'But I no more have two hundred guineas than I had one hundred. Oh, this is quite ridiculous!' Cassia clenched her fists.

'The offer has been made, take it or leave it,' Mistress Boderley shrugged.

'I must leave it, as well you know.' Bitterness grated in Cassia's throat.

Mistress Boderley folded her hands across her stomach. Cassia noted that they were large and red and ugly, more like a man's hands than a woman's.

'If I were you, Mistress, I would hasten to find the two hundred guineas for Sulamee, before she goes the same way as Nola. Children do not last long here in this place, you know. They soon die. Sulamee is coughing again, did you know?' The woman gave an ugly grin, which was more like a leer. 'The other girls complain that she keeps them awake at night with it.'

'I shall bring her the same medicine which cured her before and give it to her myself,' Cassia said firmly, head held high.

'I should hurry and do that, Mistress. And it had better be good medicine, one that can work miracles.'

'What do you mean?'

'Go and see the child for yourself, then you will know what I mean.' Mistress Boderley smirked.

Cassia obeyed immediately, her heart pounding. What if Sulamee were really ill, what if her cough really was much worse? She rushed into the child's room, panting for breath, and stood in the doorway with waves of relief consuming her.

Sulamee sat on a stool, sewing. She looked up delightedly as Cassia came into the room, putting down her sewing and scampering across to kiss her good friend.

'Why, Mistress, you tremble?' Sulamee said, as she put her arms round Cassia and felt the tremors going through her body.

'Oh, it is nothing, Sulamee. I came down the passageway too fast, that is all.' That vile woman had lied to her to give her a fright. What a vixen she was! Sulamee was not ill at all. 'How is your cough, Sulamee?' Cassia asked tentatively.

'My cough went away. You forget? Medicine cure it, Sulamee better now.'

'Oh yes, of course, Sulamee. How foolish of me to forget.' Cassia sank onto the bed, pulling Sulamee down beside her and giving the child a hug. 'How is everything?'

'Sulamee miss Nola. No one to take milk to.' Sulamee leaned her head on Cassia's breast, relaxing against its soft warmth.

'Poor Sulamee. Yes, I miss Nola, too.'

'She with angels now.'

'Yes, that is right, Sulamee. She is with the angels now.'

'She happy there?' It was a question more than a statement.

'Yes, I am sure she will be happy there, Sulamee. The angels love little children.'

'Sulamee play with angels soon.'

Cassia's body went rigid. 'No, Sulamee will not be playing with the angels soon; certainly not! Sulamee is going to live to be a very, very old lady.'

'Girls at Boderley's not live long.'

'I know, Sulamee, but I am going to do something about that as soon as possible.' Cassia held the child again, revelling in the feel of the dainty little body in her arms.

Sulamee looked up at Cassia, her mahogany eyes questioning. But Cassia was determined to say no more. She had endeavoured all along not to reveal her plans in any way, for she did not want the child to live on tenterhooks of excitement as week after week went by without the plans being brought to fruition. There was always the possibility, although it was one which she refused to accept, that she might fail, and then Sulamee's disappointment would be even greater.

Seeing that her dear friend was not going to say any more, Sulamee went on. 'Last night *he* came visit Sulamee.'

'He? Who is *he*?'

'Mar-shall Atch-erley. He wicked, cruel man. Hurt Sulamee.'

'He hurt you?' Cassia cried. 'What did he do, tell me?' She held the child at arm's length, looking closely at her face and hands for marks or bruises, but could see none.

'Sulamee show you.' Sulamee pulled down the bodice of her dress to reveal six lacerations, deep weals which had fetched blood. 'Ella give Sulamee some cream to rub on and pain go a little.'

'My God!' Cassia breathed. The child had not even winced when she had hugged her! What a little stoic she was. But how terrible that she should have had to suffer what must have been a very painful beating. The man was insane, a maniac, to come here and prey on these little girls in such a way. Tears rolled down Cassia's cheeks, Sulamee putting up a finger to touch them gently.

'Mistress, not cry, no need cry. Sulamee brave.'

'Oh, I know you are, my darling. But why should you *have* to be brave?' Cassia tilted the exquisite little face towards her, looking deep into the rich mahogany eyes. 'Why should you have to suffer such terrible things, Sulamee? God meant children to play, to run about and be happy, not to be cruelly beaten by maniacs.'

'*He* owns this place. Sulamee have no choice, must do as *he* say. If not, Boderley will beat Sulamee also.'

Cassia gritted her teeth. She knew what she would do to Marshall Atcherley if she got her hands on him. And as for that Boderley woman, she should be strung up and beaten. She was a witch! There was nothing for it, she would have to get that two hundred guineas as soon as possible, before the price went up. Somehow, some way, she must find the money. She would have to write to her aunt immediately and tell her the whole story. She was sure that Julitta would send the money immediately, especially when she found out that she was going to have a great-niece after all.

Cassia returned to Peacock Hall to find Victoria visiting. It was Paul's first day out of bed, and he was sitting in state in the drawing-room, with Joanna fussing round him affectionately and Victoria fluttering her eyelashes at him.

Cassia was still feeling tense and dispirited, but Joanna ushered her into the drawing-room and offered her tea and cinnamon cakes, which she accepted.

When she had taken her seat and was sipping her tea, Joanna said with a pleased smile, 'Paul and Victoria have something to tell us.'

'They do? And what is that?' said Cassia innocently, as Paul winked at her behind Joanna's back.

'Well, I think they had better tell it to you themselves. They have already told me.'

Cassia sat expectantly while Paul tried to stop the broad grin which was threatening to break out on his face. Victoria sat looking very bashful, hands demurely clasped in her lap, eyelids lowered, the skirts of her apple-green brocade gown spread out around her like flower petals.

'Cassia, you are one of the first to know,' Paul began. 'Victoria has agreed to become my bride.'

'Why, that is marvellous, Paul. Oh, Victoria, I am so glad for you both. My congratulations, may you have every happiness and joy.'

'Why, thank you, Cassia, that is very kind of you,' Victoria said shyly.

Joanna offered round more cake. 'The poor dears, they have been trying to keep it secret from me, you know, thinking that

I would not be in favour of their match. I have told them how foolish they have been. Nothing will please me more than to see Paul settled down.' She beamed first at Paul and then at Victoria. 'A man of thirty should have a wife and be thinking about having children, too. I confess that I shall be delighted to become an aunt.'

'Children are more demanding than dogs, Joanna,' Paul grinned.

'No doubt I shall find that out in the best possible way,' Joanna said, with a little nod of her head. 'Look, we are embarrassing Victoria; she has gone quite pink.'

'Perhaps we should leave talk of children until after Victoria and I are married, eh, Joanna?'

After a while Cassia excused herself, saying that she had a letter to write. She went up to her room and took out pen and paper. How did one write a begging letter to a beloved aunt, telling her that one wanted to adopt a half-caste girl, but first that the girl must be purchased for the sum of two hundred guineas? Cassia sat for a time, pondering on how to phrase her sentences and then, as inspiration did not come, she stood and began to pace up and down the room. She thought of her dear aunt at Penwellyn, of the moors displaying their autumn tints. For some time, she had longed to see her aunt again, to go riding on the moors, with seagulls wheeling overhead and the waves crashing in the distance.

She thought of the loyal Cornish folk who had rallied round when Julitta was so ill. She thought of the Briscoes, she always adorned like a bird of paradise, lavish with lace, scents and jewels, he in his dun clothes, drab and plain as a peahen. And she wanted so much to see the new peacock and peahen which Julitta had acquired.

If only she were at Penwellyn now with Sulamee, walking hand in hand on the Downs, looking up at the swirling white clouds travelling breezily through the sapphire blue of the sky, and looking out from the cliff edges to the crystalline sea, so many vibrant colours mixed as one: periwinkle, peacock-blue, jade green, and glittering silver. She knew that the child beside her would be as filled with wonder as she always was to see these things, and she imagined Sulamee growing straight and tall and strong in the healthy Cornish air.

It was this thought which took Cassia back to her writing desk and which made her take up her pen again. She began the letter slowly but soon the pen was dancing across the pages as she spoke of her love for Sulamee, of the child's unhappy life, and all that she hoped to do for her.

'Aunt Julitta, if only you could see Her! She is so Beautiful, dainty and fragile and pretty, like a little Doll. She has the softest, waviest, black silk Hair and deep, deep brown Eyes, a very similar colour to yours. Her skin is very pale for a half-caste, and has a pearly Radiance. Her teeth are small and perfectly shaped and, fortunately, have not suffered from her poor diet, for they are unmarked. (I have told her to drink as much milk as she can lay her Hands on.) She has the tiniest hands and feet you could imagine, and such a slender Body, yet she in no way looks thin. I have taken her many gifts, ornaments and sweetmeats, food, jewellery, books (I am teaching her to read), lace, and frills to add to her two gowns. She has sewn these on very prettily. I cannot wait to see her in the new dresses I plan for her, with her hair dressed in ringlets.

'She has the sweetest of Temperaments; she smiles and is somewhat shy. She rejoices when I am Happy and she is quiet when I am sad. In the past months we have seen each other a great deal and grown very Close. She has, in many ways, replaced my lost Baby. But this is only one reason why I want to adopt her. Remember that friend of mine of whom I spoke to you, Xenobe? Well, Sulamee reminds me very much of Her. It is quite unnerving, the physical likeness between them. I imagine that Xenobe looked very much as Sulamee does when she was ten years old. I had to leave Xenobe behind whether I liked it or not, which brought me much Unhappiness, but I am determined that this will not happen with Sulamee. I am determined to adopt Her, to make

her my own, to raise her as my own Daughter.' Cassia underlined the last seven words heavily.

'But there is a problem, Aunt Julitta. A very large Sum of Money is needed to buy Sulamee from the harridan who now owns her. The woman is a witch, a monster, but unfortunately she is Sulamee's legal owner. She and I have discussed my buying Sulamee, and the sum put forward was two hundred Guineas.' Cassia paused, imagining her aunt's stunned reaction to this knowledge. Then she went on. *'I see no alternative, dearest Aunt; I must buy the Child before a dreadful fate befalls her, as it did Nola, whom I told you about a few days ago. I do not think that I could ever have another peaceful Day if something happened to Sulamee when I could have prevented it. I feel totally responsible for Her, I feel as if I were put on this earth to love and care for Her.'* Cassia paused, gazing unseeingly ahead, elbows resting on the writing desk, trying to analyse exactly what it was about Sulamee which attracted her so much to the girl, made her want to care for her so much. Then she went on writing. *'In many ways she reminds me of myself at ten, dear Aunt. She is motherless, there is no one to hug her and Kiss her excepting myself. Yes, that is it: she is like me at ten. And how I wish that I had known You then so that you could have behaved towards me as I now wish to behave towards Sulamee. I feel wretched asking you for the Money, dearest Aunt, and you know it is alien to my Nature to beg or plead, but I am doing both now. I want this child brought to safety before something terrible befalls her. Be assured that as soon as Vincent recoups his Gold you will be fully repaid. And if it were possible for me to Love you more because of the Loan, then I would do it, Aunt.'*

Cassia bowed her head in her hands, sighing with weariness. There was so much she had to do that evening, but she was so tired. She folded the letter and sealed it, and gave it to a servant to post, then she took out her report book and added that day's report to it. The book was very nearly full now, soon she would need a fresh one. When she had first been given it by Paul she had thought she would never fill all its blank pages, but how rapidly she had done so. Everything had gone in, right from her first impressions on the Boderley bordello to her vain attempts to purchase Sulamee.

She began to write down what had happened over the past few days, and was startled to hear the dinner gong, for she had not realized it was so late. Hastily, she tore off her day gown to reveal her white frilled lace bodice, petticoats, and the bulky wire frame of her panniers. Going to the wardrobe, she chose a gown of pale blue-green, trimmed with black velvet bows. As she reached up to take it down she saw the suit of Vincent's which she had cut to shreds, and she put a hand to her mouth. She had forgotten all about it, and he had said nothing, absolutely nothing, about its condition. She felt a pang of conscience at her lack of control on that occasion, yet she knew that if she ever felt that way again she would probably behave in a similar fashion. Being a realist, she knew that even genuine remorse was not necessarily enough to purify.

Dinner passed without incident, Vincent not appearing. Cassia retired early and shortly was tucked up in bed, asleep.

Vincent was again at the Comtesse's house in Pinfold Lane, telling her of his latest reform work. She sat beside him on the settle, stroking his forehead with gentle hands, listening to his every word as if entranced, though in fact she was becoming increasingly bored with all this talk of slaves and reform. Her early enthusiasm had all but vanished.

She lay back enticingly on the settle, displaying her beautiful pale shoulders and the upper halves of her breasts to great advantage. Surely he would stop talking about his boring obsession now, she thought. She was wearing a cherry silk gown fluted in silver lace. It had an exceedingly low neckline, which was why she had chosen it for Vincent's visit. A ruby suspended on a gold chain hung between her breasts and rubies flashed in her ears. Cherry silk ribbons fluttered in her silver-fair hair.

'*Pauvre chéri*, you work too hard. How I wish that I could comfort you more often. Why do I not see more of you,

Vincent? How happy we have been in the past.' She moved a little closer to him, for she had been careful to wear her adjustable panniers, and these could be lifted up or down to make sitting and intimacy more comfortable. She stroked Vincent's hand with delicate fingers, leaning forward a little so that he could not help but look down the bodice of her gown. She took his other hand, brushing her knuckles against his thigh as she did so. She knew what a passionate man he was, how quickly he was aroused. It should not take her long, she thought. Soon he would have forgotten that stupid work of his.

'Oh, *mon ange*, tell me what I can do to make you happy now! I will do anything, anything . . .'

Vincent could not help but notice the swelling of the beautiful white breasts only a few inches away from him, nor the intoxicating musk scent which emanated from the Comtesse. Despite himself, he was beginning to remember their passionate nights of love and it seemed an age since he had last been in bed with a woman.

The Comtesse was skilled at arousing men by the most subtle means as well as by the most obvious. She knew that Vincent was in a particularly sensitive and delicate mood, because of his wife's coolness. One step wrong and she would ruin her chances.

Kissing him gently on the cheek, she leaned her head against his shoulder, slipping her hand inside his jacket to feel his heart beating strongly beneath the thin silk of his shirt. How masculine he was; how vigorous. Built like rock, with not an ounce of spare flesh on him. There was nothing flabby or slack about Vincent Sauvage; he was a man of steel. She was so impatient to make him love her, but knew that she must tread carefully. And, of course, she must not appear to take anything for granted. She did not care if he was a pauper, if he told a crazy story about his money having been stolen from him by an evil pirate captain. She had more than enough money for both of them. He was the first penniless man with whom she had been willing to consider anything more than a temporary relationship . . .

They made a brilliantly handsome couple, she knew that. She wanted the delight of Vincent at her side for the rest of her life, his virile, tanned skin and jet black hair the perfect foil for her own fairness. His darkness made her appearance twice as radiant. But he had this ridiculous love for his wife, even after all these weeks of sharing her, the Comtesse's, bed. She could not recall ever having met a man who had loved his wife in this way before. Oh, many men had pretended to, but their love was soon revealed for what it was: a thin veneer which soon cracked and vanished. Once, long ago, she had loved two men at the same time, so she knew that this was a possibility. So she was quite prepared to believe that Vincent could love Cassia and her at the same time. She had been carefully, but implacably, building up her relationship with Vincent, determined to make him love her more, so that one day he could, without a qualm of conscience, leave his wife. When a relationship was strong it could survive the ups and downs; a man would return and keep on returning despite quarrels or disputes or arguments. She did not yet know how strong her relationship with Vincent was, nor did she dare to test it at this moment. She could only continue in the same vein as before; being the tempting seductress, willing, warm and pliable.

They kissed lightly for some moments, the Comtesse believing that she was distracting Vincent completely. She understood enough of him to know how his passions flared up and she wanted them to do that now, so that he would bend her backwards on the settle, push down the bodice of her gown, and caress her breasts, then murmur that it was time for them to go to bed.

The force of Vincent's breathing was increasing, his cheeks were slightly flushed. She was winning, she was winning! Delight filtered through her body. When her hand went lower than his chest it seemed to brush against him as if by accident. She felt the instant pulse of his reaction.

Murmuring, 'Oh, Vincent, *mon ange*,' the Comtesse put her hand inside Vincent's breeches, caressing him lightly. He gave a low moan, leaning towards her, scooping her into his arms and crushing her lips with his. She was exultant: everything was going to be all right. Their relationship had not altered at all, she need not have feared.

'Blanche,' he whispered against her throat, 'Blanche, you are *plus belle, plus enchantée*.' He stroked her narrow pale neck, feeling the pulse in her throat beneath his palm. It was beating very fast, as if she were excited. Her eyes were sparkling, her cheeks stained with more than rouge. The musky odour of her expensive *parfum* intoxicated him, as it was meant to do. He needed a woman; he needed comfort. Without Cassia's lovemaking his life was empty and banal. To nestle here warmly, in this seductive woman's arms, was surely one way of lightening his loneliness?

Why should he feel guilty? He kissed the pink cheeks and lips, the soft lids covering the silver-grey eyes. He gently pushed back the tendrils of pale blonde hair so that he could see the *petite* face more clearly and marvel at its exquisite perfection. He could have believed that her face was carefully painted upon porcelain like that of a doll, painted by a master whose work fully emulated reality. He lowered his head, brushing kisses against her shoulders and breasts, pushing down the bodice of her gown to reveal her pale nipples, which hardened as his mouth brushed against them. She was whispering his name and curving her arms round his back, digging her nails into his strong muscles, urging him on. She wanted this moment to last forever and yet she could not wait for the next stage of their lovemaking. Impatience flared through her, making her tug at his shirt so that a button flew off. He did not heed it, nor did she. He paused only to tear off his jacket and embroidered waistcoat. Then he began to massage her breasts expertly, so that it was her turn to moan and sigh.

She moved slightly to one side so that she could lift her legs up onto the settle. He followed suit, lying down beside her, caging her with his arms and finding renewed interest in her lips. Time passed, but still he did not lower his hand to her thighs, for which she was yearning. She believed that she would expire if he did not touch her there soon. Normally, he was as impatient as she, paying little attention to the preliminaries of lovemaking. Today, he seemed thoughtful, preoccupied, even as he displayed his accustomed lustiness. She was dubious about provoking him into taking the next step. He was the masterful one, always very much in control.

Suddenly the Comtesse found herself scooped up into muscular arms and borne upstairs to her bed as lightly as if she were indeed a doll. There, Vincent stripped off his clothes and helped her to undress before slipping into bed with her and pulling the sheets over them.

The feel of his hard masculinity was divine and the Comtesse revelled in it, clinging to him and sighing his name. He responded ardently, but as infuriatingly slowly as before. There were kisses in plenty, caresses too, but he did not fling himself on top of her as he had always done on other occasions. She fondled and embraced him, gently pulling him on top of her coaxingly. Some time elapsed and the Comtesse was silently screaming for union with him. Finally she moaned, 'Take me, take me now, *mon ange*. Oh, take me! Is something wrong, *chéri*?' she asked plaintively.

'What could be wrong?' Vincent murmured between kisses.

'I thought – I only thought that –'

'What did you think?'

'Well, we – we have been here some time now and you have not –'

'What have I not done?' Vincent said, but the room was dark and she did not see the warning.

'*Mon ange*, I did not mean to criticize, but –'

Already he was drawing away from her. She could feel his coldness like a shroud between them and her heart plummeted.

'You would criticize me?' he said hoarsely.

'No, no, *mon ange*. Do not mistake my meaning.'

'You do not like the way I make love to you?'

She began to panic. 'Oh, it is marvellous, *plus formidable*! Never, never have I been so thrilled by any man. I —'

Vincent sat up, lighting the candle at the bedside. It was nothing that the Comtesse had said or done which had cooled him. All along he had been regretting his visit here. However beautiful and charming the Comtesse was, she was not his Cassia. Nothing could change her delicate structure into Cassia's voluptuous curves, nor her silver hair into brilliant Titian. Her eyes were grey, not hydrangea-blue, and she was altogether too obsequious. He ached for Cassia's spirited response. He had been wrong to come here. He had thought that the mere satiation of his animal passions would be enough, but it was not; his soul was as barren as before. Only Cassia's presence, Cassia's arms, could heal the hollow wound inside him.

The Comtesse was now sitting up, staring at Vincent in puzzlement, her mouth pouting. 'You do not like me anymore, Vincent, *chéri*? Oh, what have I done wrong? How have I angered you?'

'You have not angered me, Blanche.'

'But I have. You are enraged, I can feel it,' she protested, trying to keep her voice even and sweet when really she wanted to clench her fists and beat them against his back for leaving her in mid-air as he had done.

'I am not angry with you, Blanche.'

'You are not telling me the truth, *chéri*.'

'If you think that I am lying, then I am lying.'

She wanted to storm and hiss at him. How infuriating and stubborn he could be when he chose! Sometimes she had a little insight into the difficulties Cassia must have encountered: but only a little, for she was not a shrewd woman, only greedy and acquisitive and sufficiently clever to disguise these motivations.

Vincent flung back the covers and got out of bed in one easy, fluid movement. Turning his back on the Comtesse, he began to dress. Not sure what to do next, she leaned back on the pillows, staring at him. He was a superb figure of a man; she did not think that she had ever seen a finer. If only he was hers, tied to her by marriage, how happy she would be. What a fine step-father he would make for her children. Perhaps she could appeal to him on their behalf? But not at this moment, of course; now was not the time. She was sure that she knew what to say to him, to ensure that he came back again, but she just could not think of the words. For once her *élan* was failing her.

Vincent continued to dress, saying nothing. He flung on his clothes, not caring how untidy he looked. He wanted to be out of this place. Suddenly, his affair with the Comtesse had soured. How could he have imagined that she could ever fill Cassia's place? No one could do that. He must get away from here, go back to Cassia . . .

Having flung on his jacket, Vincent turned on his heel and strode from the room. The Comtesse lay back, too stunned to call after him, listening to him clatter down the stairs and out through the hall, hearing the front door slam behind him, hearing his horse's hooves beating their way across the pathway and onto the turf. Why had she not spoken before he left? A paralysis had seemed to grip her tongue. This had never happened to her before. No man had ever roused her then left her; it had always been she who had done the deserting, whatever the circumstances. She sat in the bed, staring ahead, seeing nothing, oblivious to the cold which was creeping round her naked shoulders and breasts. She must devise her plan of campaign, win him back, have him at her feet again. Her vanity would allow for nothing else. If only she could collect her thoughts . . .

It was the creak of the bed which awoke Cassia, and the over-powering smell of brandy fumes.

Vincent had come home drunk! She had never known such a thing before.

Vincent was speaking in his native tongue, the rapidity of his words and his slurred speech making it impossible for her to decipher what he was saying. She began to feel fearful, for he had flung back the covers and climbed into bed beside her, his powerful hands gripping her shoulders so she could not move. She struggled, balling her hands into fists and beating against his chest, but all to no avail.

'Vincent, no, *no!*' she cried, but he seemed not to hear her, his arms crushing her tightly against his naked body, his lips devouring hers. She was a prisoner, unable to move or cry out.

'I warned you,' she heard him saying, this time in English, 'I warned you, *doucette*, that I could not wait. I am only a man, not a saint. Do you think me a monk, that I can live with you, sleep with you, be in your company, and not want to bed you? All these long weeks I have yearned to make love to you and you have kept me at arm's length.'

'No, Vincent, no,' she managed to gasp between his kisses, 'you must not do this! Please, please, you are drunk, you do not know what you are doing.'

'Oh yes I do. I am making love to you, *doucette*, and nothing is going to stop me.'

'*No!*'

'*Yes!*'

Cassia grasped a hank of his silky black hair, tugging at it with all her might, but he only laughed. She tried to scratch at his face, but he caught her wrists tightly and she was paralysed.

'So you would mark me, you vixen. Do you want all the world to know that you are a wildcat in bed?'

'If I am a vixen then it is only in self defence,' she cried, sickened by the smell of the brandy fumes and the brutal way he was behaving. This was a side of him she had never seen before; savage, callous, caring only for his own desires. It was a side which repelled her. She wanted none of it; she wanted the old Vincent back again more than anything on earth.

When his hard, lustful body crushed down on hers, she gave a sob of anguish. This could not really be happening. Surely it was a nightmare and soon she would wake? The weight of his body was like a great stone suffocating her, so that she could barely breathe. Silver stars darted out of the corner of her vision, her lungs were desperate for air. Surely he would see that she was suffocating . . .

The long months of pent-up passion had full control of Vincent. Nothing short of threats at gunpoint could have stopped him now. Cassia had no gun, nor a knife, but she had her nails and she did her best to use them. She thought of screaming, but knew that she could not possibly bring Joanna and her brothers running to the privacy of her bedroom to see her own husband raping her. She would never live down the shame and the discomfiture. She fought, bringing up her knees, pummelling with her hands, clawing with her nails. She could feel him iron-hard against her, pressing into her stomach and then lower, forcing entry between her thighs. In one smooth, confident movement, he was inside her. She started to scream but he clamped a hand over her mouth.

'A wife does not scream when her husband makes love to her,' he said. 'Would you wake the household?'

She choked the screams in her throat, her breath rasping as she struggled to control her reactions. He scythed in and out of her body, vibrant and forceful, while pinning her shoulders to the bed with his stony grip. When she tried to wriggle away he put his knee on her thighs, which caused her such an intense pain that she immediately ceased to move. She felt sick and bitter and sad all together, and something else: a sense of consuming tragedy, for here was her husband forcibly making love to her and even as he drove fiercely in and out of her body and scorched her lips with his kisses, she could not respond. Every move of his made her withdraw all the more, growing colder and more isolated.

276

Tears rolled out of the corners of her eyes, trickling into her hair. She was aching from head to foot. Her thigh, where he had bruised her with his knee, was throbbing. She wanted nothing more than for him to finish so that she could curl up in a ball and cry herself to sleep.

He went on to the bitter end, and then collapsed on top of her, panting. She lay still beneath him, hands clenched, eyes tightly shut on the tears which hammered behind her lids for release. When he rolled off her, stood up and began to dress, she hardly dared to breathe. He was going, leaving her. She did not care! Oh, how she cared! She loved him to distraction, but she also hated him, and the two emotions were confused into a tight twisting pain in her breast. When the bedroom door slammed shut behind him she drew her knees up to her chin, pulling the blankets up over her head and sobbing into the pillow.

Cassia did not see her husband again for a week. When the Peacocks spoke of his lecture tour of Manchester and the surrounding area she pretended to know all about it. At least he was not with that French hussy.

Each day seemed like an insurmountable peak which she must struggle to conquer alone. There was a flat, empty feeling inside her which she found almost intolerable, and she struggled to come to terms with it in vain. She knew that Vincent would be exerting himself in speaking to societies and churches, committees and congregations, every afternoon and each evening. She knew that he would be facing hecklers and hostility, perhaps even violence, and although he had taken four of the Peacocks' servants with him, all sturdy men, she felt uneasy. What if something should happen to him while things stood as they did between them? She would die of remorse.

Joanna fussed round her constantly, putting tempting meals before her and insisting that she rest frequently.

'I am not an invalid, Joanna dear,' Cassia said with a wry smile.

'No, but you will be if you go on like this, neglecting yourself, dear. How are you sleeping? I passed your room the night before last and saw a light under your door.'

'Oh, I often get up when I cannot sleep and write some more of the report.' Cassia leaned her elbows on the arm of the chair and stretched out her feet on the footstool which Joanna had provided for her.

'Writing away in the middle of the night? Well, I do not call that healthy at all. You will bring some sickness upon yourself, my dear, and I feel so responsible for you with Vincent away. What if he should come back to find you ill? I will get the blame.'

'Perhaps he would not care, Joanna.'

'Not care? But he is your husband, my dear.'

'I fear that he will not wish to be my husband for much longer, Joanna. I — I do not believe he loves me any more, not after the way he has behaved towards me.'

'The sharp words and that French widow, you mean?' Joanna narrowed her eyes, thinking of the painted doll who seemed to think that Liverpool was her Garden of Eden and she its Eve.

'And other things, Joanna,' Cassia said, her face grim.

'Oh dear, so there is worse than that, is there?' Joanna patted Cassia's hand. 'My dear, I do feel guilty, you know.'

'Guilty? Why on earth should you feel guilty?' Cassia's head flew up.

'Well, if you had not come here to stay, we would never have had that get-together and Vincent would never have met the Comtesse. So you see, it is my fault.'

'Oh, you must not feel that way about it, Joanna. Make no mistake, it is his fault for falling into her trap. He did not have to, you know.' She ran a hand through her silky Titian hair. 'He has behaved like a bachelor all through these past months, just as if he had no one to consider but himself. I fear that he married too late and could not mend his ways.'

'He was a philanderer before, then? Oh dear.' Joanna's face fell.

'I would not say that, Joanna. He certainly liked women . . .' Cassia paused.. How could she tell Joanna of Vincent's harem, all the women he had kept for himself and himself alone, in Algiers? No, she could never speak of that, even though Joanna was broad-minded. 'He – he was used to having women at his beck and call. His first wife died tragically of a fever in Spain. Many years ago, that was.'

'So he has been married before? Well, I would have thought that marriage and all his travelling would have given him plenty of time to see the world and sow all his wild oats. I would have thought he could settle down now, especially with such a fair, sweet wife such as you, Cassia. Perhaps he is just having a little rebellion against the thought of marriage itself. Perhaps in a few months he will have come to his senses.'

'I have hoped that we can patch things up, because I want to tell him of my plans for Sulamee. As yet I have not dared mention adopting her – and it seems a foolhardy step when her prospective foster father is behaving like a bachelor, with a French mistress, and cannot even come to terms with having a wife, let alone a child.'

'Yes, I suppose you are right there, my dear.' Joanna frowned thoughtfully.

'I have written to my aunt asking if I might loan the money to buy Sulamee.'

'So you are actually going ahead with it? Well, I can understand how you feel, loving the child as you do, my dear. But I think the price that Boderley woman is asking is outrageous.'

'But I have no choice, do you not see? Each day that passes I fear for Sulamee. I see her dying in my arms like Nola did, dying of some disease: consumption, or the smallpox. That place is terribly unhealthy, you know, and their diet leaves much to be desired. Only Boderley's favourites are allowed out in the sunshine, and at night when their customers are gone they are locked in like felons. That is one of the reasons I get up in the night and write my report. It is all I am able to do at the moment towards freeing Sulamee and all the others. When Granville Sharpe gets these reports from us, and the case histories we have recorded, I do not see how we can fail to change the law. Unless people's hearts are made of stone, they are bound to listen and be moved.'

'Did Vincent tell you of his ideas, to publish our reports and the case histories and distribute them throughout Liverpool and Lancashire?'

'No, he did not. He – he went in such a hurry that we hardly even said goodbye.'

'Well, I think it is an excellent idea. The society will pay for the printing, of course, and the leaflets will be distributed to as many areas as we can afford. People need awakening about the true facts of slavery; they need to know what it means to be manacled, to be branded, to lose one's freedom.'

'Do you realize, Joanna, that I am the only one in the society who has actually been a slave? So when I write I can write from my own experiences. I know what it means to be imprisoned, to be treated like a serf, to have no rights, no wishes, to be less than a puppet in the hands of one's owner. So when I write my report and the case histories of the other girls and Sulamee, in a way I am writing about myself, too, although the conditions where I was a slave were splendid and luxurious compared to the Boderley place.'

'Yes, you are very valuable to us for that reason, Cassia, as well as others, of course,' Joanna smiled. 'I do not think anyone has suggested it so far, but perhaps it would be a good idea if you went to London and spoke to Granville Sharpe yourself.'

'I? But will the reports and the case histories not be enough?'

'Oh, they will provide plenty of ammunition for us but, as you say, you are the only member of the society who has actually been a slave, albeit in luxurious surroundings. You can tell Granville Sharpe exactly what it means, and you can tell him from your heart. He has many colleagues who at the moment are somewhat half-hearted in the cause, but I am sure that if you spoke to them you could inspire them to free the slaves now.'

Cassia stared into space for a few moments, considering this thought. She to meet Granville Sharpe and his colleagues in London? She wondered if she would have the courage to face them, to tell them that she had been a Sultan's favourite, incarcerated in a harem in Constantinople for many months. Would she falter and become tongue-tied with the shame of her confession?

'I will think about that, Joanna.'

'You will need a lot of courage, but remember they are humanitarians. They will not be there to condemn you, nor to judge.'

'I should not be hesitating, Joanna. Indeed, I do not know how I can. Of course I shall do it. My faint-heartedness these days is beginning to appal me, I really must do something about it before it takes me over.'

'It is a natural result, my dear. You had a great shock, losing your baby, and you have worked so hard since you came here.'

'All the same, I cannot go on forever making excuses for myself. It is winter now, I lost my baby many months ago. I should have thought of meeting Granville Sharpe myself long ago, before the colder weather came, and the roads became impassable. Truth to tell, the thought of leaving Sulamee even for one or two weeks fills me with dismay.' She bit on her lower lip. 'If I go to London, you will promise me that you will keep a close eye on her, visit her every day and take her food?'

'Indeed, I will, Cassia, it will be my pleasure,' Joanna smiled.

That night a violent storm howled up the Mersey and into Liverpool Bay, striking directly at the city. Shacks were blown down by the waterfront, trees hurled into the air. Even dogs were blown into the river by the great gusts of scouring wind.

Cassia lay in her bed listening to the cacophony outside and worrying about Sulamee in her makeshift room. How would the child keep warm? What if the roof leaked, or the wind blew down one of the prefabricated walls? Tomorrow she would take Sulamee extra blankets and some form of heating. It would have to be safe, of course, for children were apt to be careless, and the room was crammed with ornaments and knick-knacks, fire hazards all. She thought of travelling through the winter winds and mire to London to meet Granville Sharpe. She knew that she would miss Sulamee dreadfully, and that the child would probably fret for her. Even with Joanna keeping an eye on the girl, could she still go away, even for a short time, and enjoy peace of mind? She doubted it. Even before Nola's death she had had recurrent forebodings of disaster, and with good reason. There was the maniacal killer still at large; there was the Boderley woman with her sneering, jeering manner and callous nature; and, of course, there were the clients at the Boderley place, those brutal, loathsome men who visited the child brothel without any resultant qualms of conscience. Savage murder. Disease. Squalid conditions. The threat of violence. Any or all of these could befall Sulamee while she was away in London.

Cassia tossed and turned in the bed, listening to the storm and feeling an answering storm in her breast.

Chapter Sixteen

It was Joanna's day to help out at the charity hospital, and so she dropped Cassia off at the Boderley place, waving goodbye to her and saying that she would see her that night. Cassia turned, adjusting the two heavy baskets on her arms, and went inside the converted warehouse. She had brought extra presents for Sulamee and for two of the other girls who were showing signs of sickness. Today she was steeling herself to tell Sulamee that she had to go away, but only for a short time, and that she would soon be back. As a sort of consolation, she had brought the child some extra sweetmeats, knick-knacks, and a pair of satin slippers with gilded pom-poms on the toes.

Cassia was a few paces down the narrow corridor towards Sulamee's room when she realized that something was different today. She knew she had arrived earlier than usual, for she had come in Joanna's carriage, but how silent the whole building was. Usually there was the sound of girls bickering or arguing, sometimes crying, or loud laughter. Today there was a total lack of noise. Perhaps they were all still asleep; she knew that they did sleep late in the mornings, especially if they had had a busy night.

Coming to Sulamee's door, Cassia paused to adjust the heavy baskets again before reaching out to the door handle to turn it. The door swung in slowly and she turned sideways so that she could get through the door with her two baskets.

The first thing she noticed was the sickening reek of tobacco. Then she saw that Sulamee was not alone. A man was sitting on the child's bed with Sulamee on his knee, and he was fondling her.

Cassia felt a surge of furious rage course through her. Oh, she knew what the customers did with the children — was that not why she wanted to save them? But to come here like this

283

and to actually see it happening: it was too much! Had she not been burdened by the heavy, bulky baskets she would have rushed across the room and struck at the man, snatching the child out of his arms. As it was, she positively glared, not caring if she were upsetting the natural order of things in this most unnatural place.

The man was heavily built. He had shaggy white hair, bushy white brows, and a vast untidy white beard. Two stony eyes peered out from folds of flesh, wrinkled and creased; the mouth, which was concealed by the straggling beard, was thin and lascivious and cruel.

'*How dare you!*' Cassia raged, putting down the baskets and stepping towards the man. '*How dare you do that!* Leave that child alone, you monster!'

Sulamee had gone white. She was trembling. She managed to stutter out: 'M-mistress, it — it Mar-shall Atch-erley!'

Cassia paused for only a moment, for this was the infamous owner of the bordello. The fiend responsible for so much misery; the brute who on his last visit had lashed poor little Sulamee with a whip, leaving permanent scars on her chest.

'You brute, you savage! Put that child down,' Cassia cried, fists clenched.

The man looked at her with bulging eyes. He seemed to be terrified of her, shrinking back. For a moment she was puzzled. She knew she had spoken fiercely, but was she not, after all, only a woman? The man had a broad sash round his stomach and two daggers were stuck in it; another dagger peeped out from one of his baggy, brown leather boots. The bulging coal-black eyes continued to stare at her, the thin mouth gaping open.

Sulamee took advantage of the man's paralysis and slipped off his knee, running behind Cassia and clinging to her skirts, her little face ashen.

Cassia stared at the man, waiting for him either to speak or to leave. What a weird looking man he was, with his stony black eyes, straggly brows, and the stark white bushy hair and shaggy beard. A great hooked nose jutted out from the leathery brown cheeks, and he was now quivering with what she thought to be fear. Why on earth was he so terrified of her? There he sat, so huge, healthy and muscular, loaded with daggers, and here she stood, a mere helpless woman, unarmed. Did he have a fear of adults? Was that why he skulked around at night? But if so, what had brought him to Sulamee's room this early in the day?

For the first time she noticed, with disgust, his state of undress and what was revealed projecting from his gaping breeches. But his manhood had apparently suffered a mighty blow by her appearance and was rapidly dimishing.

Had she not been so furious she would have noticed sooner that there was something familiar about the coal black eyes and the hooked, hawk-like nose. He had done his best to disguise himself. He had changed his name and he had bleached his hair and beard. He had also gone through the tortures of a mercury treatment for his loathsome skin disease, of which he was now cured, so the skin which had been seething with pustules, oozing and suppurating in some places, dry and scaly in others, was now a uniform leathery brown all over. He was momentarily paralysed by the sudden appearance of a woman he had thought never to see again; a woman whom he had tried to rape and who, instead, had snatched his dagger and stabbed him fiercely. By way of revenge he had taken her to Constantinople in the hold of his ship in the most squalid conditions, to sell her to the Kislar Agha who was responsible for purchasing new concubines for the Sultan's harem.

As far as Nathan Dash knew, no one ever escaped the harem of the Grand Turk once they had been taken into it. Death was then the only means of freedom. Yet here was this woman, whom he had stolen from his worst enemy, Vincent Sauvage, after turfing his dead body overboard. How had the woman got out of the harem? How had she got here, of all places? Here, in Liverpool, where he had thought himself safe from retribution by any of Vincent Sauvage's or Captain Dash's colleagues, not to mention all those others who wished him dead for the evil deeds he had perpetrated against them.

Cassia stared in dawning recognition at the man who had left Vincent for dead and sold her into slavery. Now she knew the identity of the notorious Marshall Atcherley, of whom Sulamee had spoken with such trepidation. Dropping her baskets, she put her arms round Sulamee to shield her, her eyes darting to the door. Could they escape? *They must!*

But Nathan Dash had seen her glance at the door and knew what she planned to do. Here was a woman who knew the full extent of his crimes, one word from whom could send him to the gallows.

She must die.

The last noise Cassia heard was Sulamee's scream ringing in her ears, and then the little metal spirit stove struck her hard on the temple and she crumpled to a heap on the floor.

The jerking movement woke her. She had been flung unceremoniously over the back of Dash's horse and a rough blanket then thrown over her for concealment. Her hands and ankles were tightly bound, and her mouth was gagged. Her head throbbed with agonizing pain, and when she first opened her eyes she could not focus them properly. Something wet was trickling down the side of her face and she realized that it must be blood.

Memory returned to her in all its stultifying horror. She was – again – a prisoner of Nathan Dash. Vincent's worst enemy – her worst enemy. Dust from the blanket clogged her eyes and nose and filled her throat. It was like a return of all the previous horrors she had experienced as Dash's prisoner, then, after having displeased the Sultan, being tied in a sack and flung into the Bosphorus to drown. And Sulamee, what of Sulamee? That poor child, who would have seen her dear friend struck on the head brutally. She would have been terrified. Oh, God, if Nathan Dash had harmed Sulamee . . . Oh, God, let nothing have happened to the child. If only

Sulamee were safe, it did not matter what happened to her.

Where was he taking her? The horse seemed to be travelling over rough and uneven ground. She could smell rain-soaked gorse and heather permeating through the blanket's density. She could hear sea-birds calling high above, but that gave no indication of where they were going, for sea-birds flew all over Liverpool. The effort of trying to gather her wits had made her head throb more painfully, and her limbs were becoming numb. For a few moments her thoughts were muddled, so that she believed she was again really in the sack, being flung over the balcony from the Sultan's palace. She seemed to be sinking down into darkness, as she had then, falling, falling, until she hit the icy waters, plunging beneath them, choking for breath, nearly suffocating as dust and fragments from the sack filled her mouth and nostrils. She was again bobbing up and down in the cold water, being played with by the currents, dipping and whirling, her air supply growing less and less with every second so her breathing was becoming laboured, her lungs screaming for air.

Mercifully, she blacked out again, knowing nothing until she felt herself being lifted and flung over a shoulder. Then she was thrown down onto a rough wooden floor, her knees and elbows cracking against the planks in the most excruciating fashion. She yelped with pain and heard the cruel, leering laugh which turned her blood to ice. Nathan Dash, the most inhuman, brutal and evil man she had ever had the misfortune to meet. He was standing over her, laughing sadistically, thoroughly enjoying her discomforture, her helplessness.

The blanket was still over her head, so she could not see him, but she could imagine his ugly, gloating face and black shark-like eyes. What was he going to do with her? Her heart began to pound as she contemplated her fate. Then, to her surprise and relief, she heard footsteps leading away from her, the door banging shut, and then silence. He had gone, or perhaps he was only fetching something else from his horse or tethering the animal? She waited, hardly daring to breathe, her head a fiery agony, the hard wooden boards biting into her back and heels. The waiting was intolerable. If she heard that door open and his footsteps coming towards her, she would faint with dread, she knew it. But time elapsed and he did not return. The room was still and silent. She remembered the gorse and the heather and thought that they must be somewhere out on the moors.

She began to move her head from side to side to try and shift the blanket so she could see where she was. Finally, she did move the blanket so that her eyes were freed. She was in a little wooden shack, she thought, of two, possibly three, rooms. The room she was in was simply furnished: a bed, a bench, a chair. A small table was littered with the debris of many meals, congealed dirt, paper, unwashed knives and forks and spoons, plates with congealed food from days, weeks, ago, a lump of cheese, bright green with mould, part of it eaten away by mice, or could it be rats which had made those teeth marks? She shuddered. Rats, and she was so helpless. She had heard of rats eating babies and invalids who could not beat them off, and she imagined them advancing upon her and tearing at her flesh. The thought brought her out in a cold sweat. Please, let it be mice and not rats!

The whole place reeked of disorder and decay. Cobwebs festooned the corners of the room, the furniture too, even the congealed food. That was something else to fill her with revulsion; the thought of fat, black, hairy spiders scuttling over her body, running across her face, her mouth. But at least the blanket kept her reasonably warm, although the floor was cold and mightily uncomfortable.

Even though her limbs were numb and she longed for a bed, she prayed that he would not return. Somehow, knowing him as she did, she would not see him feeling any empathy for her condition, nor ministering to her needs in any but the most lascivious way. Her heart gave a painful leap. Could that be what he planned? Oh no, oh surely no! But she was so much at his mercy. How could she beat him off? He was huge and strong and totally vindictive. Why had he brought her to this squalid, isolated place? Perhaps he was going to ransom her. Yes, maybe that was it. He would demand money from the Peacocks and Vincent for her return. Then a thought occurred to her. Vincent. Of course, Dash would not know that Vincent was still alive; he thought that he had left him very much for dead in the sea not far from Algiers. That was why he had thought it safe to return to the Barbary Coast, to murder his own half-brother, the Captain, then to steal his fortune and Vincent's inheritance. But it was obvious from the way he had been skulking around at night, and the way in which he had tried to disguise his appearance, that he lived in dread of someone discovering his identity. There would surely be many who loathed him, for his existence had only been barely tolerated in Algiers because of his brother the Captain, who was loved and respected. He was the type of man who, wherever he went, would make enemies. She thought of the beating he had given Sulamee and, for a moment, her anger made her forget her bruised and aching limbs and back. He had always had a predilection for very young girls. She remembered him watching her and the other girls being sold to the Kislar Agha. He had had a young girl with him then, and he had been fondling her openly.

She wondered how far she was from the city; how soon it would be before Vincent discovered she was missing. With a pang of remorse and guilt she thought of the barrier which had arisen between them, the coolness of their relationship, how she had rejected him so coldly. Oh, if only he were here now how she would make it up to him! If only the door would crash open and he would step through in all his dazzling vigour and strength to rescue her . . . If she tried very hard she could almost reconstruct his face in her mind, the smooth, tanned planes of it, the stunning emerald green eyes, the sleek straight nose with its cleanly sculpted nostrils, the sensual curved mouth, the frame of luxuriant black hair caught back with a bow.

Sadly, the squalid surroundings intruded upon her mind image, the scent of decaying food reaching her nose in a sickening waft. It meant that a wind was getting up outside and blowing through the cracks in the cabin. The light was going; she must have been here for hours. If only she had some way of telling the time.

She had travelled to Boderley's in Joanna's carriage this morning, and it would be calling there to pick her up at around four of the clock, before dusk began to set in. They would wait outside for perhaps five or ten minutes; then, growing restive, Joanna would send the coachman inside to collect Mistress Sauvage. He would return to say that Mistress Sauvage could not be found, that she had called in briefly early in the day but had gone. Would Joanna's face register alarm immediately, or would she think that the independent Cassia had gone about some other business? Perhaps another two or three hours would elapse before Joanna began to panic and send out her servants in a search party. As the evening drew in, dark descending in its full regalia, the Peacocks would realize that something was very wrong. But before they sent a rider to bring Vincent back from Manchester they would want to leave no stone unturned. Perhaps Mistress Sauvage was lying injured somewhere, some natural accident having befallen her? Linkmen would be hired, lighting the streets with their smoking pitch lights. Every street and alley would be scoured.

What would they do when they found out she had vanished without trace?

Beads of rain began to patter against the cabin's roof, and soon the pattering had turned to a venomous lashing, rain driving through the cracks and crannies where the wind had whistled before, pools of water forming here and there on the cabin floor, one very near Cassia's head, so that the ends of her outflung hair became drenched. She was numb now with cold as well as with pain, thinking longingly of a warm, comfortable bed, the cosy cocoon of a mattress and blankets. The blanket flung over her smelt of dirt and earth; there was no way she could get away from the unpleasant odours. If she turned her head one way she could smell the nauseating stench of the blanket, if she turned it the other way she could smell the equally noxious smells from the table.

The storm was growing in intensity, driving against the cabin with a deafening resonance, like the sound of a dozen hoof-beats. She wanted it to stop, for there to be a peaceful stillness, comfort and warmth. Chills began to trickle up and down her limbs, across her back; her hands and feet were icy. The bruise on her temple, the ache from which had receded, now began to pain her again, and in the darkness she saw flashing silver sparks dancing across her vision.

Would she die here, neglected and alone, starved to death? Had he put her here so that she would die where no one would find her? He was a man who was skilled at extermination, such activities being second nature to him. She did not think that he would feel the slightest prick of conscience at her death; a man like that would not know the meaning of the word conscience.

Oh, Vincent, Vincent, if only you were here, she thought, unable to speak the words of longing because of the gag cutting into her lips and cheeks.

It was after midnight when the hoofbeats were heard pounding along the turf towards the cabin. Dash did not trouble to rub down his wet horse or to house it in the lean-to shack at the back of the cabin; he just left it out to graze in the storm. As he crashed up the ricketty steps and through the cabin door, Cassia's heart leapt and bounced agonizingly in her breast. He could not see the terror in her eyes because of the darkness, but soon he had lit two candles on the table and he was standing gloating down at her, hands on hips, feet straddled wide apart.

'Well, my fine pretty, did you think I had left you? Did you think you were going to die here, and that I would not be back? Nathan Dash is not such a fool as to pass over a golden opportunity, not where you are concerned, my pretty. I have a score to settle with you. Yes, a score. I thought that you had had your punishment being sold into the Sultan's harem, but I see that you have escaped. The Devil knows how you managed it, and only he knows why you are here in Liverpool of all places.'

As Cassia tried to say something through the gag he waved his arms from side to side.

'No, I do not want to know your story, or what happened to you. All that really interests me now is that you are here, at my mercy.' He gave a spine-chilling chuckle, then muttered as if to himself. 'Now I have his woman as well as his booty.'

Cassia's eyes flew open wide at his words, his open acknowledgement that he had stolen Vincent's treasure. She struggled to free her hands, but knew from past efforts that it was hopeless.

'There is no use struggling, my pretty. You are not going to get away from me, you are my prisoner now, my slave.' He laughed again, throwing back his head, opening his mouth wide, revealing decayed and green-slimed teeth. She shuddered with apprehension, trying to look away from him but finding her vision drawn back as if by magnetism. Sweat beaded her brow and the palms of her hands, her gown felt clammy against her skin. She would have given almost anything for a drink. If only he would free her hands and ankles and take the painful gag out of her mouth, so that she could chafe her bruised and aching limbs and try and recover some semblance of life in them. But it was obvious that if he ever intended doing that he was going to take his time about it.

He went out into the denseness of the night, crashing the door shut behind him, returning in a few moments with a sack, which he flung down upon the table in the midst of all the filth, dust and rotting food. He took out some half a dozen objects, a pie and a cake, a flask of wine, a hunk of white Cheshire cheese, crumbly and fresh.

Cassia watched him, the scent of the food reaching her nostrils, making her realize how ravenous she was. It must have been around fifteen or sixteen hours since she had had her breakfast. But most of all she wanted a drink. Her throat felt inflamed. It rasped when she swallowed, as if she were trying to down broken glass. The taste of the dirty, ragged gag was nauseating; the more she tried to push it away from her lips the more the threads and filaments seemed to invade her mouth chokingly. Food. Water. Her mind was filled with longing.

Dash sat down at the table, the ricketty chair groaning beneath his weight. He began to shovel the pie into his mouth, smacking his lips and chewing noisily in the most repugnant manner. In between mouthfuls he gulped down the flask of wine. When he had finished, he took a second flask out of the sack and drank that one also, as he devoured the cheese and the cake.

Cassia's stomach grumbled as she watched him eat, but at least while he was doing that he was not doing anything worse. She knew that he was capable of the utmost bestiality. Even if she had not known of his involvement with the child prostitutes in Liverpool, she knew of the manner in which he had behaved before. How he had tried to rape her; his reputation for lechery and depravity. In Algiers and the Barbary Coast there had been many similar men, pirates and freebooters, who had lived debauched and self-indulgent lives. All had owned their own harems and used women without conscience. Only Vincent had cared for his concubines, the girls in his care, but he had been very special indeed.

She must have either fainted or drifted into exhausted sleep for some moments, for she woke with a start of shock as chilling laughter sounded close to her. Her eyes flew open, to see Nathan Dash leaning over her. He prodded one of his black-nailed fingers hard into her breast once, twice, until the pain overrode her other discomforts. Then his filthy paw slid down her waist and stomach to clamp itself between her legs, through the silk of her gown. Nausea rose in her throat. She thought that she would be sick. He was very intent upon what he was doing, his breath rasping noisily in his throat. She waited, paralysed with dread, for what his next move would be.

Slowly he lifted her skirts, inch by inch, his noisy breathing increasing as her ankles, her calves, and shapely thighs were gradually revealed. He slid his hands up and down her legs. Then he lifted her skirt a little higher to reveal the auburn triangle between her legs. He panted when that came in view, resting back on his haunches and staring hard and lasciviously. Oh God, what would he do next? She was quite helpless. Even if he had loosened her hands and ankles from their ropes she would not have had the strength to fight him off, for her limbs seemed quite dead, as if the blood had ceased to circulate in them. Tears of exasperation jutted behind her lids and squeezed out of the corners of her eyes. She was totally helpless, totally at his mercy, just as she had been before, that time in Algiers. She wanted to sob Vincent's name, to scream out loud for him to come and rescue her. Silent screams rang in her head, almost as powerfully as if she had uttered them, but they would not bring her Vincent, of course. How would he ever find her in this place, with this depraved and odious pirate?

To her astonishment, Dash pulled down her skirts as if having had second thoughts about assaulting her. He stood up, grunting to himself. Then he put his huge, thick hands under her armpits and dragged her across the room to the bed. She thought she knew what he was going to do: he was taking her to a more comfortable place to rape her. Her heart gave a painful jerk. She began to pray, positive that she would not outlive being raped by Nathan Dash. But, to her surprise, he picked her up and flung her onto the hard, uncomfortable mattress. Then he took a dagger from out of his baggy topped boot, and bent over her. She shrank away, more silent screams ringing in her head. But all he was going to do was to cut the ropes round her wrists. He then proceeded to tie one wrist to the left side of the bedhead and the other wrist to the other side, after which he proceeded to do the same with her ankles, so that she was spreadeagled on the bed. He did not remove the gag. She prayed silently, begging for a storm to blow away the cabin, for an attack of some kind to strike Dash dead, for anything to save her from the appalling fate which was to come.

'The punishment first,' he rasped, the blood-curdling chuckle beginning deep in his throat. 'The punishment first.' He pushed back his filthy sleeve to show Cassia a long, deep scar on his forearm. '*You* did that to me. You did that in Algiers, remember? I have not forgotten what you did. No one has ever dared lay a finger on Nathan Dash and survived the experience, nor will you. When I have finished with you, my pretty, you are going to die, just like all the others. But first, the punishment. And then, well, we shall see. Perhaps there will be something else to please you before you die.' He rubbed his hands together gleefully, his sharp black eyes glinting.

Oh God, he was going to punish her in some way. What would he do? Her mind ranged over possible tortures and she shrank down into the mattress, terrified. How much longer could she survive this experience, which was in itself the most terrible torture? Oh, Vincent, Vincent, come for me, she sobbed silently.

Dash went to the far side of the room. She heard the noise of running water and realized what he was doing, to her total disgust. He had not even the decency to go outside the cabin to void himself. Pray God he would do no more than that! He returned, his breeches fastened untidily, and she saw that he had a long, thin cane in his hand. She cowered, yearning to scream out, and the fact that she could not made her suffering all the worse.

'The punishment. I told you there was going to be a punishment, did I not? Don't you wish that your fine, handsome Captain was here now to save you, my pretty? But he is dead, so I can do with you as I wish, entirely as I wish, and do not doubt that I shall. For tonight a good thrashing for a vicious vixen who dared to lay a finger on Nathan Dash, who dared to scar his flesh for life.' Dash raised the thin cane, bringing it down with a tremendous thwack across Cassia's thighs. Sweat sprang out on her brow and tears gushed. The pain was intolerable, cutting and fiery. Again the cane came down across her legs, twice, three times, four times, five times. Tears poured from her eyes. She must have passed out, for when she came round Dash was gutting the candles in preparation for sleep. He unrolled a thick blanket from one corner of the cabin, spread it out on the floor at the far side, away from the bed, and coiled himself up in it. Soon, his raucous snores were filling the little shack.

It was hard to sleep with the racking pain spearing her legs and the gripping hunger and thirst, but she was totally exhausted and drained from her suffering. The cacophony of snores made it difficult to sleep also, but soon she did.

When she awoke Dash had gone. Blood had congealed along the stripes on her legs, and she was still tied to the bed, unable to massage them, to try and bring back feeling. She wondered if she would be scarred for life, but then, she thought wryly, if her life had only a few more hours or days to go it would not matter if she was deformed. Who would see the lacerations on her legs? No one, except Dash.

She wondered what would be happening at Peacock Hall. There would be out-and-out furore by now. Joanna would be panicking, rushing up and down, wringing her hands. Andrew and Paul would be doing their utmost to stir the servants into searching for her, and they themselves would be riding here and there trying to find some clue as to her whereabouts. A messenger would by now have gone to Vincent, she was sure, and he would perhaps already be on his way back from his tour of Manchester. She had no idea how long the ride would take him, but she knew that he was a consummate horseman and that he could travel great distances in a very short time when he chose to do so. Possibly he would be in Liverpool that morning, adding his efforts to the search. They would question Sulamee, of course. Would she be too terrified to reveal who had abducted her great friend? Would she tell them the name of Marshall Atcherley and, if she did, would they be any the wiser? The girls at Boderley's knew nothing about

Marshall Atcherley except his name; that was how he had planned it. Even if all the girls were questioned, nothing more than his name would be revealed. It was unlikely any of them knew of his hideaway shack on the moors. It looked such a decrepit, ramshackle building from inside that she was sure it could not look any better from outside, and, therefore, should anyone ride within sighting distance of it they would dismiss it as abandoned and unoccupied, which was probably exactly how Dash intended it. Yes, he must have planned his life down to the last careful detail, not relaxing the vigil on concealing his identity even though he had come so many, many miles away from the Barbary Coast.

Would her rescuers arrive in time, she wondered. Or would they find her dead, tortured and then murdered, just like those poor girls in the brothels in Liverpool, like that last brutally slaughtered victim at the Captain's Cabin? For a moment her mind seemed eager to grasp a certain fact, but she was so hungry and in such pain that the fact slipped away. She thought of Vincent finding her dead body here on the bed. She thought of his guilt and remorse at the way he had neglected her when they lived at Peacock Hall, how sorry he would be to find that it was too late for them to make up. She began to sob at the thought that it was too late for them, that nothing could bring them together again now. This time there was no way that Fate could rescue her. Miracles rarely happened once, let alone twice; she could not hope for another one like that which had reunited them after each had thought the other lost. There was no way out of this, no escape for her. Dash had got her where he wanted her and he was hardly likely to let her go. It was too soon for resignation to overcome her, too soon for anything except hunger and thirst and pain and the intolerable ache to have Vincent walk through the door of the cabin and rescue her.

Chapter Seventeen

On the day that Cassia was abducted by Nathan Dash, Andrew had set off to collect some funds which had been collected by an associate Quaker Society in Warrington. They were to be put towards the home for young slave girls when they were freed. It was a crisp November day and the journey was smooth and straightforward. Andrew collected the pouch of money and set out on his homeward journey.

It was at a bend in the road by Upcross Wood that he was ambushed by three brigands lying in wait for passers-by carrying money or other articles of value. Andrew was felled to the ground with a blow, the pouch of money snatched up, and the brigands rode off.

It was a particularly brutal blow, and, by the time Andrew came round, it was dark. Cold and shocked, he was bleeding profusely from his head wound. He did not have the strength even to crawl to the shelter of a rock. He lay there, sometimes losing consciousness, sometimes awake, in great pain, throughout the night, the effects of the shock increasing as he grew colder. Occasionally he had the wit to chide himself for having ridden alone, knowing that it had been a foolish thing to do; but Paul was busy elsewhere and Vincent was away and the servants had all been occupied about their daily tasks when he had wanted to leave. He knew that he should have learned from Paul's experience, and taken along at least one man to accompany him.

A storm began, the rain lashing against his unprotected body. He grew wet and frozen. His wound stung as the rain bit into it, washing away the blood only for fresh blood to bubble up. All he could hope for was that some passer-by would see him in the morning and that he would be rescued. Soon, his brain became too numbed to think.

*

When Joanna called for Cassia at the Boderley place late that afternoon, she was told that Cassia had left almost immediately after arriving, as far as anyone knew. Perhaps she had been so shocked at what she had seen that she had run out in terror, for, some time later, Sulamee's body had been found. It was another particularly loathsome and brutal murder, just like the ones which had taken place at the Captain's Cabin and the other brothels in the area. The child's body had been horribly mutilated; she had been decapitated, her arms and legs hacked off and flung round the room. There was blood drenching the walls, the furniture and the floor.

No one at Boderley's could understand who had done it, for, as far as they knew, all their clients had gone home by that time. But they thought that possibly a client had stayed longer during the night with Sulamee and then had attacked her. Many of the girls were sobbing over the tragedy, for everyone had loved the sweet and gentle little Sulamee.

Joanna was deeply shocked. She sat in her carriage with her hands gripped together as the coachman drove the horses towards Peacock Hall. Had Cassia gone into the brothel that morning and found Sulamee's body horribly decapitated, then rushed out somewhere, overcome by horror? Possibly she had gone back to Peacock Hall and Joanna would find her there. Poor girl, what a terrible shock it must have been for her to discover that the child whom she loved had died the victim of the crazed murderer! Tears for Sulamee and for Cassia sped down Joanna's cheeks as the carriage rolled along.

Some moments later, when she found that Cassia had not been back to Peacock Hall all that day, Joanna knew the first twinges of unease. Had Cassia been so deeply disturbed that she had gone walking and met with some mishap? Knowing how Cassia doted on Sulamee, Joanna thought that the best thing possible would be to get in touch with Vincent immediately and bring him back. Cassia was going to need all the comforting she could get in the next few days.

Joanna sent Eric riding to Manchester to track down

Vincent and bring him back post-haste. He was carrying a message written by Joanna, in which she told him of what had happened at the Boderley place and that she thought it would be wise if he returned immediately, as Cassia could not be found. Then she instructed her other servants to go out in search of Cassia, which they did. It was ten of the clock before they returned, saying that they could find no trace of her anywhere in the city, that they had searched high and low.

Joanna paced up and down, biting on her lips and wringing her hands, just as Cassia had imagined she would, and then she sent her servants out again, telling them they must not return until they had found Mistress Sauvage. They went out armed with flares and torches, but eventually they had no recourse but to return unsuccessful. By this time Joanna was also growing exceedingly anxious over Andrew, who had not come home. He intended to collect some money from a Quaker Society, he had said, and he would be back by mid-afternoon. Now it was nearly midnight and there was no sign of him.

It was then that the first suspicion jabbed at Joanna's mind. Cassia had disappeared; so had Andrew. What if they had planned to go away together, to elope? What if Cassia knew nothing about Sulamee's death? Oh, this was terrible, terrible! Joanna increased her frenzied pacing, chewing her lips until they were red and raw. She did not know whether to be tearful or furiously angry. An elopement, and her own foolish young brother involved. It was all his fault, of course; he must have talked Cassia into running off with him – she was far too sensible to think of it alone. Oh dear, this was all her, Joanna's, fault! She had spoiled Andrew when he was a child. He was so accustomed to having his own way, to having everything he wanted, and, when he had discovered that he wanted Cassia, he had taken her, just like that. Joanna had not failed to notice that there was a rapport between Cassia and Andrew, for they had spent so much time in each other's company and their faces lit up on seeing one another. She had thought of speaking sternly to Andrew, of telling him that Cassia was a married woman and that he must behave himself. But she had delayed this, thinking that she might give extra credence to the seriousness of the attention if she told Andrew that she had noticed it. It was a very delicate path for her to tread, seeing the brother she adored with a friend she had grown to love, they being drawn to one another. Yet she had known that their close friendship must never be consummated. She could not possibly allow such a thing beneath her own roof – or so her thoughts had run. Now, it seemed that her worst fears had come to pass.

She clutched her hands together, drawing them up to her mouth and biting on her thumbs, her thoughts distracted. Then a little sanity returned. Of course, if they had run off together surely they would have left a note somewhere in the house? For her, if not for Vincent. Joanna spent the next minutes scouring the house: the drawing-room, the library, the morning-room, the sitting-rooms; she even went into every bedroom, looking on mantelpieces and cabinets, sideboards, chiffoniers, the side table with mermaid legs, the console tables, bureaux, bookcases. She searched the drawers of Cassia's kneehole dressing-table, her dressing-room and Vincent's dressing-room, in case a note had been left in there for him. Then she searched Andrew's rooms, twice over. When she had finished, and found no note whatsoever, she sank down onto a ladderback chair and wept out of sheer helplessness. The sooner Vincent arrived, the better; he would know what to do.

She went to bed and tried to relax, but found it impossible. Each time she drifted into a tortured slumber she would wake with a jolt, thinking for a moment she had had a nightmare in which something dreadful had happened and then remembering that the nightmare was true. One time when she dozed off, she dreamed that the Liverpool murderer was loose in her bedroom, about to throttle her, and she woke screaming, sitting up in the darkness, petrified. Within seconds Paul was sitting on the side of her bed, his hands on her shoulders.

'Sister, sister,' he pacified, 'you have had a bad dream, that's all it was. It is over now. You are here, in your own bedroom at Peacock Hall. And here I am, sitting beside you – Paul, your own brother.' Joanna looked at him with dazed eyes, the miasma of the dream still hanging over her. She told Paul about it and he held her close, dropping a light kiss on her forehead. 'As you can see, dear sister, your bedroom is empty but for us. No one is going to harm you.'

Paul had been out searching with the servants until late that night, so she had had little time to speak to him, and he had come in after she had gone to bed. Now they were alone together, she unburdened her fears to him. In answer, he looked at her in astonishment.

'You think that Andrew and Cassia have run off together? Can you honestly think that they would do such a thing? I know that Andrew has been wild in the past, and is intent upon achieving his own aims, but would he really run off with another man's wife, and that man a guest in his house, that wife, also? Do you not think that even for our hotheaded brother that is incredibly foolhardy?'

'What else am I to think?' Joanna whispered, leaning her head against his shoulder. 'You must have seen how they looked at one another, their eyes were always catching. They spent so much time together, they had similar interests, they agreed on so many points. They went walking together alone out in the garden on many occasions; they could have been planning anything. For all we know, this has been brewing for months.'

'But what would they do about money?' Paul spoke without thinking, then dashed his hand against his forehead. 'Of course, the collection from the Quaker Society! Yes, you are right, sister, this must have been how they planned it. Andrew would ride off to collect the money and then he would meet up with Cassia at some point previously arranged, and with the collection money they could elope.'

302

'Elopement means marriage,' Joanna said, her mouth twisted bitterly. 'They can hardly marry while Vincent is still alive, nor would I want them to. Oh, Paul, this entire affair is so very unsavoury. How could our brother do this to us? It is so cruel, so thoughtless and unkind. How shall we live down the shame? What shall we tell the Quaker Society, our colleagues in The Children of Liberty? Gossip will be rife throughout the city; we shall never live it down. Oh, how I wish Andrew were sleeping in his bed now, and Cassia also, with her husband, where she should be. I have sent for Vincent, you know. I did it straight away. I thought that, whatever had happened, he would want to be here.'

'You did right there, sister. God's arms, what shall we tell him?'

'Oh, I did tell him in the letter I sent what had happened, or all that we knew at that time, of course. Not what I later realized, just that Cassia had disappeared and we had no idea where she was, but that we were searching. I imagined her having had some accident, perhaps being knocked down by a carriage, or having been jumped on by some ruffians. I was so worried for her safety.'

'She must have gone off before Sulamee's death was discovered. I cannot see her running off with any man once that had been found out. She would be too shocked and ill, she would want to mourn, not carry on with such a hare-brained, impassioned scheme.'

'I feel sure that you are right, Paul. Oh, this is so upsetting. I feel so sorry for her, for how she will feel when she finds out about Sulamee. And that poor little child, so brutally murdered: it makes one wonder if God is in His heaven. But I am angry, too, Paul. Angry that those two have been so selfish, running off together.'

'We are still not sure that they have, dear sister. It is still only conjecture at the moment. You say that you did not find a note or any message left by them?'

'No, that is true, I did not. But, all the same, do you not

303

think that it points to an elopement? They have both disappeared without trace at one and the same time, and there is that collection money involved. It all seems to hang together so well.'

Paul could not deny that. He held his sister tenderly in his arms and stroked her hair, and they pondered upon the wilfulness of youth and the capriciousness of lovers.

Vincent was with the amorous French Comtesse when the message arrived from Joanna. Having read it, he leapt to his feet, stunned. Cassia had disappeared? How could that be? What could have happened to her, where could she have gone? He paced up and down the room in an agitated manner, forgetful of the Comtesse reclining on the bed in a transparent powder-blue peignoir, her silver hair soft and curling against the lace pillows, her breasts rising and falling gracefully beneath the silk material. She became petulant after a few moments of being ignored.

'What is it, Vincent beloved; what is amiss? 'Tis cold here in bed without you. Come back to me, *chéri*.'

Vincent did not even seem to notice that she had spoken. He clenched his jaw and thought of all the possibilities surrounding Cassia's disappearance. Had she been set upon by brigands or footpads? Had she fallen ill somewhere, alone in some lonely alley or park? Had she simply forgotten to tell Joanna that she had gone on some distant journey and would be back late? The computations were endless, yet he could not take the risk of there being a simple explanation, not where his Cassia was concerned. Although he felt fierce physical desire for the Comtesse, it was Cassia whom he loved, and that love soared in his veins now as he was reminded of the last time they had been separated, when she had been abducted by Nathan Dash. Such an agonizing experience could never be forgotten, and the slightest reminder could bring it back in full force. It was back now, and he was filled with a sick, hungry, uneasy sensation.

'Vincent, *chéri*!' The Comtesse's petulant voice intruded upon his thoughts. She slipped out of the bed and came to his side, allowing the powder-blue peignoir to fall open as she did so. Her every movement was artful, planned for the greatest effect, and as her snowdrop-white breasts were revealed, and the silvery triangle between her legs, the rounded hips, she was sure that Vincent would be distracted from whatever message had arrived in the letter. 'Vincent, *mon ange*, come to bed; it is so cold without you. I am eager for your loving, *chéri*, so eager. Can you not see it?' She caressed his cheek with a soft white hand.

'We have to go back to Liverpool,' Vincent said tersely.

'Back to Liverpool!' the Comtesse gasped, clutching at her peignoir. 'Now, at this time of night? Oh, surely not!'

'I am afraid so. An urgent message has arrived from Mistress Peacock.'

'Surely it is not so urgent that it cannot wait until the morrow?' the Comtesse pouted. She slipped her dainty hands inside Vincent's shirt, caressing his broad, muscular back and hard, flat stomach. He pulled her hands away almost roughly, causing her to give a little gasp of astonishment.

'Vincent, *chéri*,' she said, reproachfully. Were their meetings always doomed to end abruptly?

'I have to leave now, Blanche. I must dress. You can stay here if you wish.'

'But, *chéri*, I am only here because you are here. That was our plan, to travel together. I should be so lonely and afraid without you.' She pouted again, mindful of the other time he had suddenly deserted her.

'Then you must dress also, but make haste for I do not wish to be delayed.'

The Comtesse wanted to cry out, to admonish him for speaking to her so brusquely, but she dared not. The expression on his face was forbidding. He had turned in readiness to dress, and she sank down onto the bed, looking around her in a somewhat perplexed fashion as she considered which clothes she could don hastily. She had never dressed rapidly in her life. Her toilette usually took two hours, three hours when she was going anywhere special. Was he actually expecting her to attire herself in a few minutes? *Sacrée Vierge*, but it could not possibly be; she did not even have one of her maids here with her, for she had come in the greatest secrecy . . .

Vincent noticed her sitting on the edge of the bed, and he snapped: 'If you wish to come you had better make haste, Blanche. I am all but dressed.' Having put on his winter topcoat, Vincent began to fling the rest of his clothes into his bag. Seeing that he was serious, the Comtesse leapt up with a squeak.

'Do not leave me, Vincent. I shall dress, I shall dress!' she cried.

'Then do as I say, make haste about it. I am going down to see that the carriage is made ready. I shall be back for you.'

'*Oui, oui*, I shall be ready, *chéri*.'

The Comtesse nearly wept with frustration as she struggled to dress herself unaided. Ribbons snapped off in her hands and she could not make fastenings meet. She stubbed her toe on the bedpost and her hands were shaking so much with suppressed anger that she smeared her rouge and smudged the lamp-black which she wished to apply to her fair eyelashes. Stamping her foot in a rage, she attempted to remove the blotches and only succeeded in making them worse. She dragged on her hat, and faced him with cheeks red with frustration rather than with rouge.

He barely glanced at her, so that she wanted to strike him across the face for his arrogance, but she controlled herself. She wanted him, she had wanted him from the first moment she saw him. Never had she desired a man more than Vincent Sauvage, and never before had he infuriated her so much which, to her, meant that she loved him incredibly. If it had been any other man she would have told him to go to perdition and returned to her warm, comfortable bed.

The carriage was icy cold, the leather seats chilling to the touch. Vincent remembered himself enough to wrap the Comtesse round with warm blankets, a fur rug over her knees and cushions at her back, before they set off, their coachman whipping up the horses and heading directly into the night.

They arrived at Peacock Hall at eleven of the clock the next morning, having stopped on the way only to assist a lady whose carriage had gone into a ditch. Joanna greeted them at the door, her face a picture, her three dogs at her heels but looking somewhat subdued as if they knew that there was trouble in the air. Vincent went straight into Peacock Hall, leaving the Comtesse sulking outside in the carriage. She did not wish to be seen, for reasons of discretion – and because of her unkempt appearance. She must be thankful that Vincent had barely noticed her during the journey. What had brought him back here in such haste she could not imagine. There was only his pig-headed wife to keep him at Peacock Hall, and he had made it plain from the vigorous way he made love to her, Blanche, that he no longer loved Cassia.

The Comtesse tapped her fingers impatiently on the carriage window-ledge, glancing out cautiously now and again to see if Vincent would return. She did not wish to instruct the coachman to drive off, to take her home, for Vincent might prove to be so angry that there would be a rift between them. She had no wish to emulate his wife by behaving high-handedly; he had had enough of females of such kidney, that was why he had turned to her for consolation, a fact on which she prided herself.

Finally Vincent did return, his face thunderous.

Grimly he muttered that he would visit her shortly but for now it would be better if she returned to her home. He apologized, though somewhat tersely, for the way in which he had rushed her back to Liverpool.

'Do not blame yourself, Vincent, *chéri*. I am sure it could not be helped. I will see you later, then, *mon ange*.' She reached out a star-like hand and caressed him lightly under the chin, attempting a smile and praying that he did not notice her untidy state of dress and paint.

Vincent went back into the Hall, to Joanna and Paul, his face white and frozen with fury. But there was unease behind the rage. He knew, of course, how much time Cassia and Andrew had spent together in the past months, but he could not forget that last scene between himself and Cassia, how he had forcibly made love to her then stormed out of the bedroom without any explanation, not even telling her that he was going away. If she had eloped with Andrew, then he was as much to blame as they. Looking back, he knew that he had been impatient and intolerant. He had put his own desires first, like any selfish bachelor; but he was not a bachelor any more, he was a married man, and he had a wife who had lost a baby and who had looked elsewhere for the gentle consolation he had failed to give her.

'Vincent?' Joanna's troubled voice broke through his thoughts, 'Vincent, oh Vincent, what are we going to do?'

'As they have both disappeared together and at much the same time, we must assume that what you have conjectured is the truth, Joanna, and that they have run off together.' His voice sounded choked. 'But, nonetheless, we must not rule out all other possibilities.'

'Our servants spent all the last eve, late into the night, searching for Cassia, Vincent. They scoured the city in case she had been in an accident, or been set upon by footpads, not that she ever carried any money when she went to Boderley's. Oh, it is so distressing.' Joanna wrung her hands together. 'And that poor child, Sulamee −'

'What of Sulamee?' Vincent knew enough to know that his wife doted on the child.

'Oh, I have not told you yet, have I? She has been brutally, horribly murdered by − by − well, it must be by the same man who murdered that last poor child at the Captain's Cabin some weeks ago. The − the poor little body was horribly

308

savaged. I believe that her head had — had been cut off.' Joanna clamped a hand across her mouth, shuddering as she thought about it.

'My God — do you think Cassia found out and was so shocked that she ran away and was perhaps in some accident while her mind was disturbed?'

'That was the first thing I thought of, Vincent,' Joanna assured him. 'For some hours I was convinced that that was exactly the case; that she had gone to Boderley's, opened Sulamee's door, seen the — the poor little child in that terrible state, and rushed off. People have been known to lose their memories when deeply shocked. I — I did think of that at first, Vincent, yes. But then, when Andrew did not return by mid-afternoon as he had promised, and the hours passed, I came to a different conclusion, as you know. Oh Vincent, I am so sorry. I blame myself, I truly do. They were left together so much, those two. We have all been so busy, I fear that we neglected Cassia when she needed us.'

Vincent's jewel-green eyes were dark with regret as well as with anger, yet how could he, in all justice, reproach Cassia when he had been doing exactly the same in Manchester with the Comtesse? He slammed a hand into his fist. There was a cold, parched feeling in his stomach. This was a tragedy and he was as much to blame as anyone — more so if anything, for he should have known better; he was the oldest of them all by some years. His maturity should have overcome all problems, yet it had not.

He looked directly into Joanna's face. 'We shall search the city again, and the outskirts. Every street, every highway, every alley and passage, however small and mean. We shall go down to the docks and we shall question everyone we meet, the men and the sailors.'

'Sweet Angels, do you think they could have gone away by ship? Oh, I had not thought of that! Together, to some far-off land. I shall never see my brother again.' Joanna collapsed onto a settle, ashen-faced, shoulders bowed.

'It is a possibility.' The words sounded torn from Vincent. He began to pace up and down the drawing-room, his unleashed vitality preventing him from standing still. His beloved Cassia, perhaps on her way to the New World, with Andrew Peacock. If that were so, if that was where they had gone, he would be on the next ship after them. He would bring her back, he would heal their relationship, tell her how sorry he was, beg her forgiveness. If only she was safe . . .

The next few hours were fraught with activity as servants, Vincent, Joanna and Paul, crossed and criss-crossed Liverpool and its outskirts, questioning people wherever they went, asking them if they had seen a beautiful young woman with red hair and a young man with reddish-blond hair. Vincent scoured the docks asking sailors the same questions. He went aboard ships, enquiring of captains; he asked about ships which had left the previous day and where they were bound and if they had carried any passengers. Drawing a blank wherever he went, he did not know whether to be relieved or anxious. At least if they had set sail for the New World or elsewhere he could have followed them immediately. As it was, he still did not know where they had gone. Dusk was drawing in when he returned to Peacock Hall to snatch a brief rest and some food. Then he was off again on his horse, alone, riding beyond the city out onto the moors. He rode until it was too dark to see anything, returning, deeply dispirited, to the Hall around midnight. To have no result to his questions and searches was crushing in the extreme. He was a man accustomed to results; he always anticipated success in his every endeavour.

He could not sleep. He strode up and down his room, sick at heart. He tried to settle down to write something of his report for Granville Sharpe, but found the words congealed in his head.

Cassia, Cassia, Cassia. Her name rang in his mind. He had been worse than a fool, he deserved a good thrashing. He seemed to have lost his wits on arriving in Liverpool.

'Oh God,' he groaned aloud, his head in his hands, 'let Cassia be safe, let her only be safe, and I shall find her and bring her back where she belongs, with me.'

'Dear heart, look away.' The voice was querulous, the speaker a pot-bellied, middle-aged man dressed in clerical grey. He was speaking to his wife, a prim and fastidious-looking woman of about the same age, much overweight, as was he, and wearing a severe dark brown dress trimmed with white lace. They were driving along the road to Warrington in their open carriage when the man, Thomas Stubbs, had seen what looked like a dead body at the side of the road. There was caked blood on the head and the face was so deathly white that he did not believe the man could still be alive. Nonetheless, warning his wife yet again to avert her gaze, he drew the carriage to a halt and jumped down.

It was fortunate that he was a doctor's son, for during his upbringing he had picked up snippets of information which were of vital importance now. He knew about feeling the pulse for signs of life, about placing a hand on the man's chest to feel if his heart was still beating. He asked for his wife Henrietta's vanity mirror so that he could see if any breath was escaping the cold blue lips.

'Dear heart, you may look now,' he called up to his wife. 'This is not a dead body; there is still some life in the man. I fear he has been set upon by footpads, for he has received a very nasty blow to the head. He must have lain here all night, for he is quite soaked through.'

'Oh, Thomas, what are we to do? Oh, we must take him home and care for him. His clothes are well cut, he is no pauper.'

'They must have taken his horse and any money he was carrying, his watch and other valuables. The fiends, to leave him here in this state. They must have thought they had left him for dead, so he could not identify them.'

Henrietta climbed down and they slowly, with some effort,

managed to half drag, half carry, Andrew's body into the carriage, placing him full length on one of the padded leather seats and covering him with travelling rugs.

'Yes, he looks a gentleman, dear heart,' Thomas said. 'His features are quite refined, the material of his clothes is of the best quality broadcloth.'

'I know a gentleman when I see one, Thomas.' Henrietta pursed her lips. 'Now, we must get this young gentleman home at once and care for him, and let us pray that he will soon recover and tell us where he comes from, for I vow that there will be some very anxious young wife somewhere, perhaps young children asking for their papa.'

The carriage bowled off, taking a turning to the left some yards farther on and stopping beside a neat little house backing onto the moors. Shortly, Andrew was divested of his saturated garments and tucked up in a warm bed, with his head wound bathed and bandaged and a few sips of strengthening wine down his throat. But it was to be some hours before he regained consciousness, the next day in fact, and by then Master and Mistress Stubbs believed that he had received such a severe head wound that he was permanently damaged and would perhaps never speak or move again. Thomas had seen that happen to more than one of his father's patients. It meant death in life, and for such a very personable young man as their patient it would surely be a terrible tragedy.

Henrietta had shed one or two tears at this thought, but in case there should be a better prospect she set about making a large array of invalid foods. She brought eggs from the larder, ready to be coddled; she boiled a chicken for chicken broth; she despatched a servant to purchase all the ingredients for making calves' foot jelly. She mulled red wine and curdled it with fresh milk and kept this simmering gently in case the patient should wake.

When Andrew did open his eyes, he stared unseeingly round the room for quite some time, trying to focus his gaze. The room and its two occupants were a blur, but he could hear their voices.

'Oh Thomas, dear Thomas, he has come round! He will be all right now.'

'Patience, dear heart. We must see if he can speak before we raise our hopes.'

'Sir, sir, can you hear me?' A dark blue figure bent over Andrew's bed. 'Sir, sir, can you speak to us?'

Andrew tried to move his lips, but they felt as if there was a heavy weight pressing against them and the effort made his head whirl. He tried to move his hands, his feet, but he was too weak. He could not even manage one word.

'Rest then, sir, you must not fatigue yourself. Sleep, and we shall return later. But do not fear, my wife and I are keeping a good watch over you.'

When they had gone Andrew lay in the semi-darkness, trying to gather his thoughts, his memories. He could remember falling off something, landing with a terrible crash. He could remember, but only faintly, being struck on the head. Money . . . Had he not been carrying a large amount of money? The thought of that having been stolen made him try to sit up, but he could not manage it. For some time he could not remember anything having happened before the fall. There was just a great white blank. A name floated through it: Cassia . . . Then another name – Joanna. Then a third name – Raven. But he could not put the names together, nor make anything sensible out of them. He wanted to clench his fists with impatience but could not manage even that. Finally, exhausted from his efforts, he sank into a deep sleep.

It was midnight when he awoke and he felt much stronger. So much so, in fact, that he tried to sit up, flinging out an arm to gain a purchase from the bedside cabinet and in doing so he knocked off a vase which was standing there. Within seconds, Thomas and Henrietta Stubbs were by his bed.

'Sir, sir, pray do not try to get out of bed; you are too weak.'

Andrew's lips moved for some seconds before the first word came out. 'What – ?' he said, then he paused, tried to swallow, and mumbled, 'Drink, drink, please.'

'Of course,' Henrietta beamed, and soon she had returned with the tray laden with invalid foods and drinks, a wide selection of each. Andrew was too feeble to do anything more than sip at the curdled wine, but he managed to empty the whole goblet. Then he sank back against the pillows, his head hammering with pain.

'Sir, can you remember your name? Can you tell us who you are?' Thomas asked. 'We fear that your family will be much distressed by your disappearance.'

'My – name? Paul. I am – no! I am – not Paul – Andrew – I am Andrew . . .'

'Can you remember your surname, sir? We must know it; we must inform your family. They will be distraught.'

'Andrew – I am Andrew . . . Bird. No, no – not Bird. Pheasant?' Suddenly light dawned. 'Peacock – I am Andrew Peacock.'

'Heaven be praised,' Henrietta said.

'Sir, we shall inform your family immediately. Do you live at Peacock Hall?'

'Yes, that is it – Peacock Hall. My sister will be out of her mind with worry. Please, you must send a servant to her at once.'

'We shall do that, sir, even though it is past midnight,' Thomas grinned.

It was one of the clock when the Stubbs's coach-driver drew up outside Peacock Hall and hammered on its door. Within minutes Paul, Vincent and Joanna had heard the news, and that Andrew was quite safe and being carefully nursed. If they wished to visit him immediately they might do so, but it would be better if he slept as it was so late at night, and they must feel free to visit him the next morning.

When the coachman had gone, Joanna flung herself into her brother's arms. 'All this time we were thinking evil of Andrew and we were wrong. For all we knew he could have been dead, lying on that lonely road, badly wounded,' she sobbed. 'What fools we have been to think that they would run off together. We should have known better.'

Paul comforted his sister as best he could, while Vincent stared blankly into space, summing up the meaning of this new turn of events. So they had not eloped. Andrew had a perfectly genuine reason for not having returned when he had said he would. Meanwhile, Cassia had disappeared into thin air, leaving no trace, not a word, not a message, and no indication of where she might have gone or what might have happened to her: just as if she had been kidnapped. For a few moments, uncharacteristically, he did not know what to do next. Joanna's sobbing was decreasing and she had turned her face to look at Vincent, realization flooding her eyes.

'Holy Angels, where then can Cassia be?' she gasped, her voice cracking. 'Two days she has been gone, two whole days!' Joanna's voice rose hysterically. 'She might be –'

'Hush, Joanna,' Paul said sternly. 'We shall not speak in that fashion. How could anything bad have happened to Cassia in Liverpool? She was carrying no money, there was no reason for anyone to attack her. It must be as we first thought, that she went to Boderley's and stepped into that room of carnage. Remember, she is a beautiful, striking woman; she would not be able to wander about unnoticed. We have left word with dozens and dozens of people throughout the city and her description is with them. Someone will see her sooner or later. That is, if she does not return of her own accord. Perhaps she felt the need to be alone, to think, to gather her thoughts after such an appalling shock. For there is no doubt, she must have been stricken by what she saw. She loved Sulamee as her own. Andrew told me how she wanted to adopt her, to take her back to Cornwall. Then to find her dead, brutally murdered, must have been more than her mind could take.'

'She wanted to adopt Sulamee? But she never told me that,' Vincent interrupted.

'I am sure that she would have done in time, Vincent. I think she was a little afraid of your reaction.'

Vincent swallowed, a knifing pain in his throat. It was as painful as a physical blow to learn that there was something Cassia was too afraid to tell him.

Where was his wife, where in God's name was she? They had looked in her bedroom and her dressing-room, to see if she had taken any clothes with her and had found that she had only the outfit in which she had been dressed for that visit to Sulamee. One gown, one shift and petticoat, her cloak and shoes. Nothing else. And she had no money with her, no means of subsistence. They knew that she was not staying with any of the friends they had made during the past months, for they had been to all their houses and questioned them. And those friends, in their turn, had made enquiries of their friends and colleagues. It was just as if Cassia had vanished, become invisible, like the victim in a disappearing act. The impotence was crippling. It crusted in his throat like poison.

Feeling a gentle hand on his arm, he looked down to see Joanna, the tears drying on her cheeks, staring up at him compassionately.

'Poor Vincent. What can I say or do, what can any of us do at this moment? We know Andrew is safe but that is all. I pray you, Vincent dear, to return to your bed now. It is late and it is dark outside; there is little we could gain by going out into the night searching. Go to your bed and try hard to sleep, for you will need your rest on the morrow. As soon as daylight is here we shall begin to look for Cassia and meanwhile I shall be praying that God is keeping her safe where she is.'

'Thank you, Joanna,' Vincent replied hoarsely, being too stunned by the turn of events to do other than obey Joanna's gentle command.

*

Vincent returned again and again to Boderley's to question all the girls, one after the other, and Mistress Boderley herself. She was rude and deliberately uncommunicative, glaring at him furiously, her black shark's eyes fierce with animosity.

'As I told your friends on previous occasions, I have no idea whatsoever where your precious wife has gone. She has treated my establishment as her home for some time, whether I liked it or no. She pampered my girls, so that they became discontented with their lot, and when it became known that she wished to buy Sulamee from me, it made the other girls restive, envious. Your wife caused no end of trouble here, sir, but I always treated her with patience and, I think, gentility.' The woman crossed her big, red, raw hands on her stomach, the creases on her cheeks deepening.

'My wife wished to *purchase* Sulamee?'

'Did you not know, sir? She was prepared to pay a great deal of money for the child.' A shadow of regret passed across the woman's ugly, painted face. She was thinking of her lost two hundred guineas, now that Sulamee was dead.

'Can you tell me what that sum of money was?'

'I am surprised that your wife did not tell you these details herself, sir.' Mistress Boderley was being deliberately perverse.

'Nonetheless, Mistress Boderley, she did not.'

'As I said, it was an enormous sum. I must say that I wondered at the amount. I have never heard of a slave being sold before for a figure such as that.'

'Such as what?' rasped Vincent, becoming impatient.

'Why, two hundred guineas, sir.' The black eyes narrowed. She was watching Vincent's reactions maliciously.

'Two hundred guineas!' Vincent said, astounded, beginning to realize something of the feeling Cassia must have had for Sulamee.

'That is what I said, sir, two hundred guineas. I was expecting a payment any day.'

Vincent did not reply, knowing that his wife had little

money of her own and certainly not enough to pay out two hundred guineas for any reason. Nor could he. But it dawned on him that somehow Cassia must have obtained the money, begged or borrowed it, perhaps, and that was why she might have disappeared. If it had been known that she was carrying money, if she had been seen with a pouch clinking with coins, she might well have been set upon as she left Boderley's the day she disappeared. Or perhaps even inside the brothel . . .

'So you have not been paid, Mistress Boderley?'

'Indeed I have not, sir,' she said snappishly.

'You do not think it was likely my wife was bringing the money to you on the day she disappeared?'

Mistress Boderley shrugged. 'That may well have been the case, but how can I say? I never saw her that day.' The big red hands were stiff and wooden, the nails square and blunt, the knuckles coarse and wrinkled. Vincent noticed them with a curious feeling of disorientation. They were suggestive of violence; no gentle, pious woman would have such hands, he thought. What if they had circled round Cassia's neck and choked the life out of her? What if the two hundred guineas was now in the Boderley woman's possession and she had had, all along, no intention of parting with Sulamee, but only of taking the money and then disposing of Cassia? His blood chilled. The woman needed a fright, he decided.

'I have, of course, no intention of letting this matter lie unsolved. I shall not rest until my wife is found, and meanwhile I think it only proper the Justices' men should come here and question your girls and yourself, Mistress Boderley, and search this place.'

The woman's face paled considerably. The hands shook slightly, the creases in the cheeks becoming black slashes. 'But there is no need, sir, I do assure you. Your wife must have gone from here or we would have found her. Every room here is occupied by a girl or myself, yet no one has seen your wife. No one even saw her come in here the day she disappeared.'

'But we only have your word for that, Mistress Boderley.'

Vincent stood up, squaring his shoulders. This woman made his flesh creep. He could have believed that she was a man in female dress, the cheap, sickening scent of violets which eddied from her being insufficient evidence to convince him of her femininity.

It was much later when he had finished interrogating the girls, but gently, for he was shocked to see how young some of them were. He discovered that Mistress Boderley was not the sole owner, perhaps not even the owner at all, of the brothel, but that she appeared to be the manageress. Strangely, it had been Ella who had divulged this information in her efforts to protect her lover.

'You should not be hounding Mistress Boderley in this way,' she had said, her small head held high. 'She has done you no harm, nor would she do anybody any harm. Besides, you cannot punish her, nor blame her for anything which happens here.'

'And why is that?' Vincent had asked.

'Because she is only the caretaker here, put here to oversee us, that is all. She is not the owner.'

Vincent's head had jutted forward. 'Then who *is* the owner?' he had rasped.

'Marshall Atcherley owns this place and others in the city. If you want to blame anyone you must blame him. Take your complaints to him, but do not come here picking on Mistress Boderley. She has enough on her hands as it is.'

'And where can I find this Marshall Atcherley?'

Ella shrugged, parting her rouged lips. 'How should I know that? We see him only when he chooses to visit us. He comes and goes as he pleases, as befits the owner of this place.'

'But Mistress Boderley would know?'

'How can I say? You must ask her that.'

Vincent could see that he would not get anywhere with this girl, for she was hostile and high-tempered. He took his leave and returned to Mistress Boderley's office.

He caught the superintendent smoking a clay pipe, her office clouded with smoke. He sniffed, half expecting opium, but it was ordinary tobacco. He did not see her as an opium smoker: she did not have the glazed eyes and listless manner of the drug addicts whom he had seen on his sojourns in the East. The woman glared at him, furious at being disturbed yet again. She spread out her big red hands on the desk as if preparing to leap from her seat to attack him. Undeterred, he asked her the questions to which he must have the answers.

When he came to Marshall Atcherley's name, he asked her about the man and if his wife could in some way be connected with him – could she possibly have visited him to ask him about purchasing Sulamee? Mistress Boderley's black eyes nearly bulged from their sockets, her face flushing a startling crimson colour.

'Who told you? Who told you who owns this place? They had no right to tell you. He is a very private man, he would be angry if he knew –'

'If he knew what, Mistress Boderley?' Vincent asked her coolly. 'I merely want to speak to the man. Can you please tell me where I may find Marshall Atcherley?' He raised his voice on the last two words.

'He does no one any harm,' blustered the woman.

'No one is accusing him of anything, Mistress Boderley. I merely wish to know where I can contact this man. One or two of the girls have mentioned his name and they say that he is a regular visitor here. It is possible that he knows where my wife is, only a possibility, you understand. But as my wife has now been missing for some days I must investigate every road.'

'I can assure you that he will not be able to tell you anything, sir. I have not seen him here of late. No, not at all. I do not see that he can have any connection with your wife or with her disappearance. As far as I know, they never even met.'

'But my wife did know of this man, she has mentioned his name before.'

'She had no right –'

'Surely she has every right to mention any name she wishes, to discuss anyone who interests her?'

'Why should he interest her?'

'You know that my wife has taken an interest in this place and the girls who are here. Would it not be strange if she were not also interested in its owner?'

'*I* am the owner, sir.' Mistress Boderley drew herself up to her full height, which was considerable for a woman.

'I believe otherwise, Mistress Boderley.'

'You can believe what you like, sir, but you cannot alter the truth.'

'That is correct, I cannot. And the truth is that Marshall Atcherley is the owner of this place and of other brothels in the city, the Captain's Cabin, for example. I have it on the best authority.'

'I regret to inform you that your "best authority" is wrong. *I* am the owner; no one else is involved at all.'

'Are you going to tell me where I can contact this man?' Vincent reiterated.

'*No!*'

'I shall report you to the authorities, Mistress Boderley.'

'You may do that, sir. You may come here any night and you will find more than half of them here with my girls.' It was the woman's trump card and she knew it. She faced Vincent triumphantly, beefy red hands folded across her stomach.

Realizing that he was wasting his time, Vincent turned on his heels and strode out of the brothel.

Two more agonizing days passed and Vincent was experiencing the beginnings of total desperation. He would have given anything to have his Cassia back safe with him. He would not have minded if she had been repeatedly unfaithful to him, as long as she was back here at Peacock Hall and things were as they had been months ago when they had been so joyfully happy together. Behind his desperation was a vigorous hunger to be in Cassia's arms again, to be able to hold her and kiss her and stroke back her Titian curls. He felt as if he had lost his soul, as if he were devoid of life, of spirit.

As the third and fourth days passed and all their continuing efforts to trace Cassia failed, the blackest depression began. He was back in the days when he had been the prisoner of the dominant Princess Jasmina, when he had not known whether Cassia was alive or dead, when he had believed that he would never see her again. But he had not stopped loving her, nor did he do so now. He wanted her more fiercely than ever before, and her continuing disappearance was making life unliveable for him.

As for the Comtesse, she attempted to re-engage his interests, thinking that her moment of triumph had come, but to her dismay she was treated with the utmost coldness and contempt. She had to withdraw, defeated, and as broken-hearted as her steely heart would allow.

Chapter Eighteen

The days seemed to have blurred into one. She had lost count of them. Was it four, five, seven days she had been here in this appalling place? Dash kept her reasonably well fed at first, untying one of her hands so that she could eat bread or the unpalatable soup he gave her once a day. Sometimes there was water too, but never enough. Her throat seemed to have shrunk and she found it difficult to swallow. But the worst thing of all was the waiting. Frequently he stood over her, gloating, looking her up and down, a lascivious sneer on his ugly face. Frequently, too, he fingered her body, probing at her breasts and between her thighs, telling her that he was only keeping her alive for his pleasure and that when he had wearied of her, as he would do soon, she was to die.

'I will just ride away and leave you. No one knows you are here; no one knows about my little hideout. You will starve to death. You can scream and shout all you like; no one will hear you, no one will come to rescue you.'

She would look at him with eyes full of loathing. He did not seem to notice. He would be breathing stertorously, humped over her, touching her with one hand while his other hand touched himself. She wanted to vomit, wanted to scream out to him to get off her, to go away, to leave her alone, the filthy rag in her mouth coarse and rasping against her tongue. All she managed was a whimper, which seemed to excite him all the more. He would become puce-faced, his lower jaw hanging open, saliva dribbling on his lower lip and down his chin. She watched in utter revulsion. He was the lowest of swine, bestial and foul. Oh God, when would Vincent come for her?

At least once a day, sometimes twice, Nathan Dash would perform his obscene rites. But in all that time, he never entered her body. Not until the day when he suddenly appeared from one of his mad rides across the moors and advanced towards her, a malevolent leer on his face. Reaching out a hand in which lay a knife, he brought it to her face. Her heart nearly stopped beating. He's going to disfigure me, she thought, or else he's going to cut my throat. She did not know which would be worse. At least if her throat was cut she would die instantly – she hoped. Instead, he cut away the gag and her joy at its removal was rapidly destroyed as she saw what he intended to do next. It was not the first time that she had felt like vomiting, nor would it be the last. The bile rose in her throat as he approached her, kneeling across her body and opening his breeches. She wished that she could faint. Anything to relieve the unmitigated horror of this moment. He was laughing deep in his throat, steadying her head with his hand, gripping her hair so tightly that it seemed her scalp was on fire. Then her mouth was being prised open. She fought with all her strength, which was not very great as she was weak from enforced inactivity. She compressed her lips and gritted her teeth together tightly. But he tore at her hair, then, taking grip on more hair, he dealt her a stunning blow to her temple. Even then, she did not open her mouth as he kept commanding her to do. Finally, he lifted the knife above her face.

'Do as you are bid, my pretty, or this knife will gouge out your eyes. How would you like that, eh? To have your eyes gouged out. You would still be alive, you know. You would feel them being cut out of your sockets. You would be blind, in terrible agony, and you would be able to do nothing about it. You would die a slow, lingering death.'

She felt the knife's blade piercing her eyelid before she did as he ordered. She gagged immediately, causing him to curse furiously.

'Damn you, you bitch! Do as you are told.' He stabbed the knife down into her shoulder so that she screamed, which was what he had intended her to do. He took full advantage of the moment.

Waves of nausea and dizziness took control of Cassia. Her shoulder was a fiery mass, so was her scalp. Blood poured from the cut in her eyelid, trickling down her face, hot and sticky. And still the onslaught continued, on to the very bitter end. He moaned, slumping across her, but fortunately, she lost consciousness at that moment.

It could have been that same day or the next day when she recovered consciousness. She had no way of knowing. She was alone. He had left her right hand untied and, on the table by the bed, a hunk of bread and a cracked mug containing water. She could not untie her other hand or her ankles with her free hand, for he had brought manacles – the same as those worn by slaves – which he had fitted to her other limbs, locking them and riding away with the key.

Memory returned to her and she gagged again, biting on her free hand, trying to quell the shame and distress which arose. He was a fiend, there was no doubt of that, and the thought that he would return again and commit further unspeakable acts against her was terrifying. Tenderly, she felt her wounded shoulder. The blood had congealed around the wound. Fortunately it was in the fleshy part and she did not think that she was seriously damaged. All the same, the pain was bad. Threads of her hair lay on the pillow where he had torn them out of her scalp.

After she had felt her wound and gently massaged her scalp, she drank the water and ate as much of the bread as she could manage, even though her stomach felt queasy. Then she managed to sleep.

She thought she was dreaming at first. The low maniacal laughter, the heavy tread across the wooden boards, the pressure on her body. It was surely a bad nightmare – or was it? She woke with a start, sweat breaking out on her forehead. The room was dark but she knew that she was not alone. She heard the noise of a tinderbox and then a candle's flame flared in the gloom. He was back. First he squeezed her breast until the pain threatened to engulf her, and then he seemed to lose interest in her. Tramping across the floor, he kneeled down in the far corner and began to prise up the floorboards. What was he doing? She heard him laugh again. Then he began to speak.

'You do not know what I have here, my pretty, do you? You cannot guess. I am a clever fellow, very clever. No one is going to get the better of Nathan Dash.'

She heard the clunk of metal and saw him lift up a small chest, then another, and another.

He looked up, seeing her staring at the chests. 'I have more than three here, my pretty; these are just the smaller ones. Underneath this floor is all my treasure. Who would guess, looking at this little shack, what it housed?' He flung back the three lids. She heard the clink of coins.

'Gold. Hundreds of gold pieces, my pretty – all mine, all *mine*. If your fine husband knew he would be crazy with fury. This is his gold. *Was* his gold.' Dash threw back his head and bellowed with laughter. 'And there are emeralds here, and rubies and diamonds. Rare white opals, black pearls, jade, gold collars, and crowns set with diamonds. All mine, mine, all mine!' He roared with laughter again, plunging his hands into the gold coins and pressing handfuls to his face ecstatically.

'My half-brother was a fool. An ignorant and witless fool. Like so many of you fine folk who think you are better than Nathan Dash. He welcomed me as a friend, you know, brought me into his bedroom and offered me wine and food. We were alone: I took advantage of it. Did they tell you how he died? I cut out his heart, you know; that faithless, lying heart. And then his entrails, and I spread them out over his bed as a warning to others who had dared to cross Nathan Dash. He thought he could leave his fortune and his empire to your husband, but he thought wrong. I am his half-brother and *I* am his rightful heir. He could not change that fact.'

He stood up. She saw the flash and glitter of gems. He came towards her, holding out a magnificent emerald collar. She recognized it immediately. Once, what seemed like centuries ago, she had worn the emeralds on Vincent's ship, *The Poseidon*, glorying in their brilliant colour against her skin. Now, Dash placed them round her neck, sniggering to himself.

'You would like to be wearing your fine clothes, would you not, my pretty? With this necklace round your neck, going to a ball with your husband and your friends? If they could see you now in your rags, manacled like any slave, wearing that emerald collar. A fine jest. Yes, a fine jest. If your husband came in here now I wonder what he would look at first – the emeralds or you, my pretty. I vow it would be the emeralds. You might as well enjoy them, my pretty. Wear them round your neck until you die. They might as well be there as under the floorboards.' He ran a hand up one of her legs, pinching at her thigh. 'Jewels and gold rouse me, my pretty. Did you know that? Just seeing you lying there with those emeralds round your neck makes me want to take you, here and now. But I am saving that pleasure for later. There are other things I can do to you now.' He tore away the shreds of what remained of her bodice, clamping his mouth on her breasts and biting at the soft flesh. Simultaneously, he pressed his huge, hard fist across her mouth to quieten her screams.

'If you make a noise, my pretty, I will put another gag on you. Is that what you want, to be gagged? I will make it even tighter next time.'

'No, please no,' she whimpered.

'Then behave, do as you are told, my pretty.'

Cassia closed her eyes, trying to imagine that she was anywhere but here, that this was just a terrible dream from which she would soon wake, that everything was going to be all right soon. Soon.

Chapter Nineteen

The parties of searchers who scoured the moors did not come anywhere near the ramshackle cabin completely concealed in a niche in the hills. If anyone had ever known that the cabin was there, they had long ago forgotten. It had once been the home of a shepherd, but he had died more than thirty years before, and his successor lived nearer the city on a farm. Every day the searchers went out, beating back bushes and shrubs for an injured or dead woman, exploring the beds of dried-up streams in case Cassia had fallen into them and been unable to get out. They even looked down into the chasm between the two mountains called the Sisters of Doom, so named for strangers to the area had been known to fall to their deaths in that place. All the results were as before: completely negative.

Two weeks had passed now since Cassia had disappeared. Vincent had lost weight. He was even leaner and hungrier looking; his cheeks had hollowed, his jewel-green eyes were heavy with repressed misery. Joanna wept frequently and devoted her every spare moment to caring for Andrew. Paul, when not out with the search parties, paced up and down at Peacock Hall or walked through the gardens, deep in thought. Even Raven was subdued; he seemed to know that something dreadful had happened. He was very quiet, very obedient. He even took care not to beg for scraps at the table, as if he might incur someone's wrath.

So the days passed, and the gloom deepened. Nothing could be said or done to alleviate the pall of dark depression which hung over the Peacocks and Vincent, radiating to everyone who was involved in the search.

Letters arrived from Granville Sharpe thanking the Peacocks and Vincent and Cassia Sauvage for their reports, which had delighted him and which, he said, would be invaluable in the coming Court case which, if its results were as he hoped, would grant manumission to all the slaves in Britain. The date was set for the hearing and he was now fully prepared, thanks to them, he wrote.

Knowing how Cassia would have delighted at the news, Vincent felt like weeping as he read the letters. Together they had worked for the best part of a year for just such this moment and he knew that, without their reports, it would have been many, many more months before Granville Sharpe would have been ready to move. As he did not yet know that Cassia had disappeared Sharpe had written to her, asking if she would consider giving evidence at the hearing. He wanted her to put into words what she had written to him in her letters. Her feelings on having been a slave, what it meant, the sufferings and anguish. She was a particularly valuable witness, he said, for few white people had been enslaved.

With deep sadness, Vincent wrote back to Granville Sharpe, telling him what had happened to Cassia; or rather, that they did not know what had happened to her, that she had simply vanished without trace. He wrote that had his wife still been with him he was sure that she would have been all too glad to give evidence, to help in any way she could, but as things stood it would be impossible. When he had finished writing he stared blankly at the papers, seeing not the large black writing but his wife's sweet face. The burden of guilt was heavy; even if he could be cleared of it, it would always lie on him. Had he not been cold, unfeeling and unsympathetic to Cassia's needs she would have come to him, been his confidante before. They would have discussed everything together; he would have known that she wanted to buy Sulamee and adopt her, instead of Cassia being too frightened to speak to him about her plan. She would have told him if only he had been approachable. The child might have been theirs weeks ago, living at Peacock Hall until they returned to Cornwall. She would still have been alive now, and Cassia would never have gone into that room at the Boderley place and seen that most terrible sight – the child she loved brutally murdered and hacked to pieces.

For, as the days passed, he became more and more certain that that was what had happened. He could see no other reason for Cassia's vanishing. The fact that it had happened more or less simultaneously with Sulamee's murder could only point to that.

He rested his head in his hands, thinking of his wife wandering somewhere. Perhaps the shock of seeing Sulamee dead had unhinged her mind, made her lose her memory. Perhaps at this very moment she was walking aimlessly through the streets or on the moors, wondering who she was and where she lived. He knew now that Cassia had not handed over any money to Mistress Boderley for Sulamee, because two days previously a letter had arrived from Julitta with the two hundred guineas which Cassia had begged her to send. At least in that, the Boderley woman had been telling the truth. So he knew that Cassia had not been set upon because she was carrying a large sum of money.

But there were other reasons why Cassia could have been attacked or abducted. She was a vibrantly beautiful young woman, voluptuous and unwittingly tempting. At the thought of some repulsive sailor laying his hands on Cassia, Vincent knew a spasm of white-hot fury. He clenched his fists, crashing them down on the desk where he had been writing. His Cassia – his wife and his alone.

Would it have helped if, that day, she had gone to the brothel on her own in the carriage with Eric or Jeffers as she usually did, they waiting outside for her to take her home? If she had come out bemused, stunned, in a state of shock, Eric or Jeffers would have seen her immediately and helped her into the carriage, to escort her home safely. Unless, of course, she had gone out of one of the back doors of the brothel. There were some, for he had seen them when he had been interrogating the girls. But whichever coachman had been waiting for her would have realized that something was wrong when she did not put in an appearance, if that had been the case, and the alarm would have been given that much sooner.

So many regrets; so many 'if onlys'. Whatever he said, or

thought, or did, he could not remove the blame from where it rightfully rested: squarely on his shoulders. He was her husband. He had brought her to Liverpool. He had neglected her, refusing her the tenderness and understanding she needed. He had let the chasm grow between them. There was nowhere for him to soothe his throbbing head, nor to pacify his unhappy heart. There was no solace, no comfort, no surcease with anyone but his Cassia.

He wanted her – oh God, how he wanted her! He rubbed his hands roughly across his eyes to push away the heaviness, the burning sensation. If she did not return soon, if he did not find her soon, his life would be over. He would be as good as dead. He would contemplate joining her if it should be found that she was no longer alive. But how could he contemplate her death? Would that not be to relinquish all the power he had, to admit defeat, failure? He must not do that, he might be signing her death warrant. He must nourish faith, hope, optimism, keep her alive in his mind's eye, alive and vibrant. All else was madness.

A servant brought in a tray of mulled wine which Joanna had sent him. Hardly noticing what he was doing, he picked up the flask and drank down the warm, spiced wine as if it were water. It had no taste. No food, no drink, had had any taste since the day Cassia disappeared. All were ashes. He only ate and drank because Joanna kept insisting that he must keep his strength up. But how could he enjoy an appetite when Cassia might be lying dead or injured somewhere, or be in the hands of some odious criminal?

He was exhausted, his mind deadened with worry and lack of sleep, otherwise, he might have pondered on what he had just thought, enlarging upon it and, perhaps, even approaching the truth some little way. As it was, he bade the servant goodnight, his voice low and grim, then flung himself onto the bed, fully dressed, and stared up at the hangings of the half-tester bed until his lids collapsed across his eyes.

*

Cassia had counted seventeen nights. Although she was icily cold and left in total darkness, at least she was always alone at night. She had no idea where Nathan Dash went when darkness fell, but he always disappeared about that time. Visiting the poor little prostitutes she supposed, or the girls who roamed the city streets looking for customers.

The assaults on her body continued. She believed that if it were possible for her to do so, she was becoming almost hardened to them. Certainly the first appalling shock had diminished somewhat. But nothing could reduce the revulsion, the nausea, the repulsion, she felt at his proximity. He had only to come and stand by the bed for her skin to crawl painfully, the hairs on her neck to stand up. He had let her off the bed two or three times, but each time he had kept a thin cord lashed round her neck, he holding on to the other end of it lashed round his wrist, so that she could not run off even if she had had the strength to do so, which she doubted. To walk after her enforced inactivity was the most peculiar sensation. Her legs felt like crumpled paper, without any power or muscle. They shook and trembled and the blood pounded in them painfully. There were deep weals round her wrists and ankles where she had been tied with either cords or manacles; and her skin had been grazed raw, blood congealing only to be rubbed away again and a fresh wound made.

When she was back lying on the bed and securely lashed down, Nathan Dash would go to his treasure hoard and take out a gold and ruby collar or ropes of pearls, the emeralds with earrings to match, or whatever gems he laid his hands on, and place them on Cassia's body, decorating her as if she were to attend a ball or feast. He seemed to get a particular delight out of this, which was unfathomable to her. She would have given away any of those jewels in exchange for a bath. Oh, to sink into steaming hot water, scented with herbs and rose oils, to soak in the luxuriant silky waters!

Sometimes Cassia would allow her mind to wander, to escape from her unhappy plight. She would picture Vincent's loving face and his strong, lean body; she would recall happy moments they had shared together. Once, she remembered, she had been relaxing in the bath and he had entered the room. He had scooped up the soap and lathered her back, massaging the scented foam into her skin until she was glowing. Then he had taken off his clothes and slipped into the bath with her. They had reached out to caress each other's body, sighing, kissing. Then, pulling her close, caging her in his arms, he had entered her in one fluid movement. She remembered the little slap of water as they came together, the sight of foamy bubbles bursting before she closed her eyes with bliss, and she leaned her head against his shoulder. Too vigorous a movement flung water over the sides of the bath, so they had to move gently, voluptuously, occasionally opening their eyes to smile at one another, as if sharing some wicked secret.

Oh yes, she would give any amount of jewels, rubies, emeralds, pearls, diamonds, to be back with Vincent in that time, that place, or indeed in any place with him . . . She knew that she would never see him again now. Nearly three weeks had passed, and Dash was not feeding her nearly so frequently. Much of her strength had waned. When he allowed her to walk round the cabin and sometimes even outside for a moment in the dusk, her strength did not last for more than a few steps and then she felt a decimating weariness and was almost glad to be lying back on the bed. No, Vincent would never find her now; how could she expect him to? He would have given up his search by now. He would have assumed that she had left him of her own free will. And if he thought otherwise, how would he connect her with Marshall Atcherley/Nathan Dash? Even if he managed to find out the Atcherley name, how would he connect it with Dash, or think that Atcherley had any reason to kidnap her? It was all too flimsy, too unlikely. She would be a fool to hope for rescue. Instead, she had her dreams. They were her comfort and her armour. As she came closer and closer to facing Death, he had Vincent's face and Vincent's arms to hold her.

Chapter Twenty

India did not like the new coachman at all. Although she spent much of her time with her mistress, Victoria, there were occasions when she came across the coachman; perhaps when running an errand for her mistress or when they went out in the coach together for an airing. The man had been taken on some three or four weeks earlier and India consoled herself with the thought that he must have passed the rigid conditions imposed upon would-be servants by Victoria's father or he would not have been hired.

The man's name was Todd Bastley and he had a surly, scowling face. His hair was a black thicket, his eyes small and narrow, his nose wide and rough-cut, the mouth beneath crooked and misshapen. His teeth were good, which was one credit in his favour, but even in his full, resplendent coachman's uniform he had a squalid, seedy, rundown look. India could not help but notice his hands, which were carpeted with long, thick, black hair which made her shudder, and the same long black hair grew out of his nostrils and ears. He never looked clean-shaven, for the thick black growth of hair which thrust out from his chin always left a shadow on his face even when he had just spent some time with a razor.

India spoke of her misgivings to Victoria, who confessed that she, too, disliked the man. It was as much his sly, sidelong glances as his beast-like physical appearance which perturbed her, and she fully intended to speak to her father about it if his manner did not improve. Meanwhile, she told India to keep a close eye on the man, to watch his activities. One never knew how honest servants were, and this man, she thought, behaved in a shifty manner – as if he had something evil on his mind.

India did as instructed, and within three or four days she saw the man behaving in a very suspicious manner indeed. He had

334

taken herself and Victoria to Toxteth Park in the coach, where Victoria ordered him to wait for them while they strolled round the gardens in the frosty air. Victoria was doing a series of seasonal nature sketches and wanted to find some good samples of evergreen foliage.

India had thought that Todd Bastley appeared somewhat restless and uneasy as he drove them to Toxteth Park. She glanced through the window to view him sitting on his coachman's seat and noticed how his right foot was tapping and how his fingers twitched on the reins. Also his head turned from side to side frequently, as if he were searching the horizon for someone or something. Once at the Park, the girls began their exploration for foliage, leaving Todd Bastley sitting on his coachman's seat, a blanket round his knees. They were very fortunate in finding exactly what Victoria wanted in an extremely short time, and so they returned to the coach some half an hour early. Bastley had gone.

'He has just left the coach standing there. It might have been stolen, the horses might have stampeded on their own. Oh, what is he thinking of?' Victoria exclaimed.

'I cannot see him anywhere.' India glanced all round. Only the brave were out in this chilly weather. 'What a stupid thing for the man to do. He has barely been in the job a month and he goes off and leaves the coach untended like this.'

'He is asking to be dismissed. I shall tell Papa what he has done.' Victoria tossed her head. Anyone could have stolen their beautiful coach while it was unattended.

While Victoria patted the horses' noses and spoke to them soothingly, India sped to a little rise nearby which gave her a good view of much of the Park. Far down by a bunch of trees she saw Todd Bastley and another man in deep, fervent conversation. She thought that the other man looked frightened. He kept glancing over his shoulder and huddled his cloak round his cheeks. Todd Bastley's face was gloating and he looked triumphant. Finally, the man handed over a packet and Todd Bastley gave him a sheaf of papers before opening the packet and counting what looked like gold sovereigns.

India's first thought was that Bastley was selling something which belonged to Victoria's father, something which he had purloined from the house, and she clenched her fists in fury. But she could think of no papers which would be worth so many gold sovereigns, and, by this time, she was beginning to realize that she knew the man who had handed over the money. She had seen him not so long ago; he had visited Victoria's father on business. He was an eminently respectable merchant and she believed that he was also a city councillor, too. What on earth could he be doing consorting with such a low fellow as Bastley?

India did not have much more time for speculation, for at that moment Bastley turned round and began to walk in the direction of the coach. Immediately, India hurried down the rise to join Victoria. Rapidly she told her mistress what she had seen.

Victoria thought quickly. 'He is up to something very odd indeed and we must get to the bottom of it. If we are here when he returns he will want to know why we do not question him, why we do not report him to Papa, so I think we should not be here. Quick, let us go back to where we found those last branches. The bushes and trees will hide us from him.' This they did, returning some five or ten minutes later to the coach to find Bastley seated where he should have been before, swaddled in the coachman's rugs, looking every bit as if he had not moved one muscle in their absence. Once in the coach, Victoria whispered to India.

'Now remember, we say not a word to Papa or he will dismiss Bastley immediately, and we want to know what he is up to, do we not? I love a mystery, they do brighten life so.'

Victoria usually gave her coachman plenty of warning when she intended to use the coach so that he could prepare it, fully polishing the bodywork and the horses' harness in preparation, but now she gave Bastley even more warning than usual.

336

What she wanted to do was to catch him herself talking to some man, having left his seat on the coach. She wanted, if possible, to overhear what he said, so that she could get to the bottom of the mystery and surprise her father with the news. She knew that he trusted the merchant who visited him three or four times a year, and that he had money invested in the man's trading ships. He had spoken well of the merchant and he had imparted the information one dinner time that he intended to invest a great deal more money with the man, as he had had such an excellent return for his first investment. If this merchant, Danby Blake, was behaving in a highly suspicious manner and consorting with servants, paying out gold for papers or other objects in mysterious circumstances, Victoria wanted to know what for – and if, as she now believed, Danby Blake was a dishonest man and up to no good, she intended to tell her father before he parted with his gold.

They had some time to wait before catching out Todd Bastley again. Although Victoria had found plenty of foliage on her first visit to Toxteth Park, she invented the necessity for another trip there, she and India wandering off in search of shrub samples. Shortly after disappearing from the view of their coachman, they returned. If he was still in his seat they were going to say that it was too cold for them to remain there that day, but if he was not in his seat they were going to find out where he was and spy on him.

He was not in his seat. Quelling her fury at his negligence, Victoria instructed India to remain by the coach. She then set about finding where Bastley was. From the rise where India had stood on the previous occasion she saw him standing by a clump of trees, talking to George Buscombe, one of the city councillors and a great friend of her father's. She could hardly believe her eyes. Buscombe was standing muffled by scarf and cloak, hat pulled well down over his face, but she would know him anywhere, for he had been a frequent visitor to her house since she was an infant. Bastley's face was alight with malice and anticipation. He had his hand thrust out, palm upwards. Buscombe turned away, as if leaving, at which Bastley spat out some words, making him turn back.

Victoria knew that she must find out what they were saying. On her tiny, dainty feet she sped down from the rise, keeping in the concealment of the copse which began halfway down it, running along for some yards to the clump of trees where Bastley and Buscombe were standing. Avoiding brittle twigs which might snap beneath her feet or stones which might trap her, Victoria hastened down until she reached the clump of trees and there she stood, well concealed, straining her ears to listen to what the two men were saying.

'And if ye don't hand over the gold what is to stop me tellin' them Children o' Liberty 'bout your part in the way all them slaves was thrown to the sharks?' Bastley was rasping.

'Who would believe you?' Buscombe snorted. 'This is monstrous; this whole affair is quite, quite monstrous. I should never have come here. I should not be lowering myself by speaking to such as you. I have my reputation to protect.'

'Yes, and if ye do not give me the gold I will make sure yer reputation is ruined. Ye'll never be elected to the Council again, not when they have found out that ye've been illegally trading in slaves, investing in ships where hundreds and hundreds are crammed together to die on the voyage and be flung over ter them sharks. There be a limit to what men can stand to 'ear 'bout a so-called respectable gennulman like yerself. All this trouble brewed up by them Children o' Liberty 'as made people turn against cruelty ter slaves.'

'Many of my colleagues are similarly involved in slavery, just as I am. They would not dare speak against me while they themselves are involved in exactly the same way. I am not staying here to listen to any more of this claptrap. When I got your note speaking of an important message I thought you had something vital to tell me, not this ridiculous blackmail nonsense.'

'And what about yer part in the profits from selling white

folk?' Exultation illuminated Bastley's ugly face.

Victoria saw Buscombe turn a sickly shade of white.

'How − how did you know about that?' he gasped, before realizing that he had incriminated himself with his shocked reaction.

'My master knows everything there is to know 'bout such things,' Bastley leered. 'He told me yer name. How do you think I knew that ye were involved, why do ye think I'm 'ere now? Ye are not the only witless fool to get involved with my master and then regret it.'

'You mean − you mean that there are others who are b-being blackmailed, that I am not the only one?' Buscombe stammered, pulling at his neckerchief as if it were choking him.

'Many, many more. Some as would astonish yer if ye knew who they were. Important men. They pay me well to keep quiet.'

'And I suppose you take all the gold to your master? Who is he? His name would not be Marshall Atcherley, would it?'

Victoria, who had been temporarily frozen, imagining that when Bastley spoke of his 'master' he had meant her own father, now relaxed, a little sigh escaping her lips. She could not for one moment see her father involved in any chicanery, but nonetheless it had seemed somewhat incriminating that the two men who had been seen with Bastley, Danby Blake and George Buscombe, were both friends of Sheridan Oates. Once she had got over this alarm, there was opportunity for the name of Marshall Atcherley to filter through her mind. Marshall Atcherley . . . That name seemed familiar. Yes, of course; Cassia had told her about the man who owned the Boderley place and other similar establishments in Liverpool. It seemed that his crimes were legion, that he lent his hand to more than child prostitution. Blackmail. Opium smuggling. Illegal slavery. Child prostitution. A weird, nocturnal creature whose odd behaviour could not help but elicit curiosity, especially curiosity as powerful as Victoria's.

Besides, there was something else. With Cassia's disappearance casting a shadow over them all, Victoria and Paul could hardly consider marriage; it would not be seemly. She liked Cassia very much and she had planned to have her at her wedding as her matron of honour, but she could not contemplate that joyous ceremony until Cassia was found. And found she must be. Vincent had been very suspicious about Marshall Atcherley. She remembered him telling her how he had closely questioned the child prostitutes and Mistress Boderley regarding Marshall Atcherley's whereabouts. He would not have done that if he had not thought that there was a possibility the man had something to do with Cassia's vanishing. The man's efforts to evade notice brought notice upon him. His name kept cropping up, so that one was continually reminded of him.

The fraught dialogue between Bastley and Buscombe was drawing to a close. Most reluctantly Buscombe had parted with two gold sovereigns to buy Bastley's silence and then Bastley was grinning, an evil rictus of a grin, and he was telling Buscombe that two gold sovereigns were not going to buy his permanent silence.

'I 'ave proof of your involvement, Buscombe,' he leered. 'I 'ave papers, incriminating papers, with yer name and the part you 'ave played in opium smuggling and the like. Yer fellow councillors would love to see those papers, I 'ave no doubt, and I'll be showing them ter them – unless, of course, ye are generous and pay me not to.'

'You fiend, you inhuman fiend!' excclaimed Buscombe, his pallor vanishing to be replaced by an unhealthy crimson shade, his eyes bulging. 'You deserve a sound thrashing!'

'Then thrash me, if ye have yer wits about ye,' sneered Bastley, 'but when I get up from the ground I shall go straight to yer fellow councillors to inform on yer. That'd be the only right thing fer me ter do in the circumstances, not being a very tolerant man.'

'You despicable swine!' Buscombe growled, but Victoria

could see that he had surrendered the argument. 'How – how much do you want, you knave?'

'Five gold pieces will do me fer a start, sir.' Bastley gave his leering rictus of a grin. 'Yes, five'll do me nicely.'

'Five gold sovereigns for your silence?' Buscombe sounded as if he was being strangled.

'Ye can make it more if yer likes. And the longer I stands around 'ere waiting fer yer to cough up the loot, the more likely I'll be ter raise the figure. I got a job to be doing, cain't be standing around 'ere all day while yer makes up yer mind.'

Victoria saw Buscombe delve into his pocket and count out five gold sovereigns. There was a tight, constricted look on his face and the colour was ebbing from it, so that he was again a sickly white. She thought that he looked ill apart from the experience he had just undergone, and she would have felt sorry for him if she had not just discovered that he had been involved in revolting criminal dealings with poor helpless slaves and opium smuggling. She knew what had happened to poor Nola at the Boderley place because of opium. Once a man or a woman began smoking an opium pipe they were doomed, their lives as good as over from the first inhalation.

Having pocketed the gold pieces and growled that he would be seeing Buscombe again soon, Bastley turned on his heel and made his way back to the carriage. Victoria followed him discreetly so that he did not see her, appearing from another direction in a casual manner, carrying two branches and a shrub sample. Within a few moments they were heading towards home.

As soon as she could get her brother alone, Victoria told him all that she had heard. His eyes glittered with excitement and he slammed his fist into his palm as he listened.

'I think we are onto something here, Vicky. Yes, I do indeed. You seem to have uncovered a nest of thieves, and Marshall Atcherley to boot. That man's name springs up all too frequently for my liking. There is something very odd going

341

on here and we must get to the bottom of it. I shall ride over to Peacock Hall immediately and tell Vincent what we have learned.'

'I shall come with you.'

'Then make haste and get your cloak.'

The first thing Victoria and Charles saw as they rode up to Peacock Hall was a liveried servant taking Joanna's three dogs for a walk. The dogs were muzzled, and Victoria asked her brother if he knew why.

'To stop them from barking. Now that Andrew is recuperating he needs as much peace and quiet as possible. A head wound is a serious matter, you know, my dear. Joanna's dogs have been allowed to romp around and make as much noise as they liked in the past. They say you cannot teach an old dog new tricks, and so muzzles were purchased for them.'

'The poor creatures. They must think that they are in terrible disgrace.'

'I am sure that Joanna will be making it up to them in other ways, sister. Now, let us hasten inside and hope that Vincent is at home.'

He was. He rose at once from his chair on having Victoria and Charles announced. They came into the library, their faces alight, and Vincent strode towards them.

'It is good to see you, Victoria, and Charles. How pleasant of you to visit.'

Victoria thought that Vincent looked much thinner than when she had last seen him. His cheeks were haggard and drawn and there were deep pits beneath his eyes. He had a lost, lonely look and her heart went out to him. However he had erred in the past, it was obvious that he was missing his wife terribly and living only for the day that she returned.

When the servant had brought port for the men and fruit juice for Victoria and delicate slices of honey cake, the brother and sister proceeded to tell Vincent everything that they had

342

learned. At first he looked somewhat mystified at what they were telling him and their reason for relaying this information, but then, as the story progressed, his eyes began to glitter and his face took on an expression of alert interest. Finally he could sit still no longer. He got up and strode to the window and back again, still listening to Charles's story, putting his hands into his pockets and then behind his back and then returning them to his pockets. When Charles had finished he waited for Vincent's response. There was silence for some time as Vincent stared out of the window as if he were alone, and then he turned, his face transformed.

'Yes, Charles, I agree with you. I think we are onto something. We must follow up every lead and, truth to tell, this is the first lead that we have had. We would be fools not to act. We must keep a close watch on Bastley, night and day, every moment; we must know his every move. I am sure that Granville Sharpe will be more than eager to know the names of any men Bastley is blackmailing, for it will mean they have been involved in illegal slave-trading and opium smuggling, and such information will give Sharpe an even greater authority at the hearing.'

'India has been keeping a watch on Bastley,' Victoria put in. 'She says that he often disappears at night. As soon as dusk sets in, if he is not to be asked to take out a carriage that evening, he vanishes. We have never followed him, not late in the evening, of course, for it would not be safe, but now perhaps you can find a man or men who would do so. We must be careful, we must not let him know that we suspect him.'

Vincent nodded his head thoughtfully. 'There is a good possibility he will lead us to Marshall Atcherley, and I must confess that I long to speak to the man. I have a very strong feeling that he is behind much of the worst of the slave-trading that has been going on here. We know that he owns the Boderley place and the Captain's Cabin and other brothels here, which is as good a reason as any for wanting to track him down, but it seems to me that he is involved in just about every criminal activity going on in the city. I get the distinct feeling that he inveigles eminent men into his slave and opium deals, then, when they are fully incriminated, he gets Bastley to blackmail them.'

Vincent found himself filled with a strange sense of urgency. How often that name Atcherley had cropped up and yet he was still a mystery figure. But he must live somewhere. Possibly he had a hideout. If so, Bastley could lead them to him. Charles had the same idea.

'We must follow Bastley; at least two of us, for safety's sake.'

'Yes, the sooner the better. In fact, we start today, Charles.'

'You think it is as urgent as that?'

'I do. We have heard how this man Atcherley is involved in the white slave traffic. What if he saw Cassia at the Boderley place and decided that she would be a prime target for his trafficking?' Vincent frowned, clenching his fists. 'Here, of all places. In England I had thought she was safe but no, it appears we are not safe anywhere.'

'You — you think that Atcherley has kidnapped Cassia, perhaps sold her into slavery?' Victoria stammered.

'That could be so. We must examine every possibility. Who am I to say that he has not when we have no proof that he has not? Everything points to him again and again.'

Victoria was trembling, tears rolling down her plump cheeks. 'Oh, poor Cassia. This is dreadful. Oh, what are we going to do? What if she has become a slave again? Oh, what will Joanna say? She will be hysterical.'

'You go and find Joanna and tell her,' Vincent said quietly, soothingly. 'Tell her what Charles and I plan to do tonight.'

'What of Paul and Andrew?'

'The invalids?' Vincent gave a shadow of his former grin. 'We would not think of their joining us, nor is Andrew fit to and Paul's broken bones are only recently healed. No, tell them they are to remain here and, if necessary, organize a search party if we do not return.'

344

Victoria's trembling hand rose to her mouth. 'You — you think that you might not return? Oh Charles, Charles, be careful.'

'I am sure that we shall return, Victoria,' Vincent said crisply. 'But we must be prepared for all eventualities, it is only wise. Now, go to Joanna and tell her.'

'Yes, Vincent.' Victoria cast them a pleading glance as if to say, take care, take care, then scuttled away on her tiny feet to find Joanna.

Heavily cloaked and muffled, and carrying muskets and swords, Vincent and Charles waited in the shrubbery of the Oates's house, watching the servants' entrance. They had waited some hours and were growing stiff and cold, having seen just about every servant going in and out except the one they wanted, when suddenly Bastley emerged, also heavily cloaked and muffled, looking to left and right of him surreptitiously. Walking swiftly down the path, he went through the kitchen garden and the herb garden, and out through the wicket gate to the road beyond.

Instantly, Vincent and Charles were after him, silently and cautiously.

Bastley walked quickly for his diminutive size, leading them through the streets and alleyways of the city.

'He is leading us towards the moors,' Charles whispered, 'in the direction of the Sisters of Doom.'

'What in God's name are they?'

'They are the twin peaks we shall soon see ahead of us. Looking at them you would think they were joined together in the middle, two indivisible peaks, but in fact they are split by a chasm, a great bottomless crevice, where more than one unsuspecting child has fallen to its doom. Sheep and wild animals, too, and once a whole pack of hounds and the front four riders of a hunting party lost their lives down the chasm.'

'Grisly,' Vincent commented.

'Quite,' said Charles.

'We shall soon be away from cover,' said Vincent. 'It is

fortunate that Bastley does not look back to see if he is being followed.'

'If he does look round we can pretend to be in conversation with one another.'

They continued to follow Bastley for some miles, until well out on the moors. For some half an hour they tracked him, keeping to a circular route so that if he did look round it would not appear that they were directly following him.

Bastley stopped only once, to shift the bundle he was carrying from under his right arm to his left.

Then suddenly, to both the men's astonishment, Bastley disappeared. They had both been looking at him as he vanished and they now pronounced that the dusk must have been playing tricks with their eyes. Following his tracks, they reached the place where he had apparently vanished, and there they found, carefully concealed by shrubbery and branches as if by nature, the entrance to a cavern-like passage leading through one of the hills outlying the Sisters of Doom. Heaving aside the branches and shrubbery, they entered the passage, which was just wide enough for a man to stand upright. Far ahead of them they heard the clink-clink and rattle of stones and pebbles as Bastley made his way through the passage. Having waited for silence, they followed him. Immediately they came out of the opposite end of the rock passageway, they saw a clearing ahead of them, a vale between the hills with the Sisters of Doom hovering nearby. But what immediately occupied their attention was the moorland cabin which met their gaze. It stood almost mid-centre in the vale and a spiral of smoke rose from its one chimney. As they stood at the mouth of the passage they saw the door to the moorland cabin closing behind Bastley.

'What do we do now, Vincent?' Charles said.

'We wait until it is dark and jump them;' Vincent said crisply. 'Use your weapons as deterrents only, for we want these men alive to give evidence.'

The two men made themselves comfortable in the passage's

entranceway, sipping at their flasks of brandy for warmth. Charles had brought a packet of beef sandwiches and they ate half of these, saving the other half for future need. Darkness fell rapidly, for it was December now. Before they knew it, Yuletide would be upon them; an event which Vincent dreaded without his Cassia. She had been so looking forward to her first Christmas in England for three years.

Through the sacking which covered the windows of the cabin they could see that a light had been lit and that fresh logs had been put on the fire, for the smoke from the chimney increased in thickness.

'What happens if Bastley comes out again?' Charles wanted to know.

'We jump him and truss him up, of course. We can leave him here in the passageway. It is Atcherley we want and I believe he is in that moorland cabin ahead of us.'

Charles seemed to find the idea of jumping Bastley highly amusing, for he grinned, took a last nip of his brandy, and then put the flask away in his coat pocket, as Vincent had done with his.

But Bastley did not emerge, and Vincent gestured to Charles to follow him to the cabin.

It was unfortunate that, at that very moment, Marshall Atcherley/Nathan Dash lifted one of the dirty pieces of sacking hanging over a window and peered out into the darkness, ever on the watch, and that at that very second the moon rolled out from behind its shroud of cloud to light the scene. What Nathan Dash saw made him livid with fury, his hands so rigidly gripping the sacking that he had to force himself to release it, otherwise he would have torn it down.

'You fool! You clumsy, incompetent fool!' he snarled at Bastley, who had been sitting at the table drinking from a bottle of wine and munching on bread and pork. 'You blundering, witless dolt! You've been followed! All the times that I warned you to take care, and you've been followed. You blind, stupid, bungling idiot! Dolt! *Fool!*' Dash's curses filled the air as he reached for his dagger and brought it down savagely into Bastley's back – once, twice, three times. Bastley slumped across the table, a strangled sigh issuing from his lips before he died.

Dash looked round him feverishly, then a snarling smile distorted his face. He knew what he was going to do. When he had finished there would be no incriminating evidence. But what of his treasure? How could he leave that? He experienced a sharp twisting pain in the region of his heart as he contemplated being separated from his gold and jewels. Rapidly, he wrenched up the floorboards and stuffed his pockets and the slack tops of his boots with as many gold sovereigns and emeralds, rubies and diamonds as he could manage. Then he went to the fireplace and with the poker he thrust out the burning logs onto the wooden floor of the cabin. Grabbing anything which would burn, he heaped it into the logs, and within seconds there was a flaming pyre in the middle of the cabin floor only a couple of feet from where Cassia was lashed to the bed, semiconscious from starvation and suffering. Dash had flung a blanket over her to conceal her naked body from Bastley, and he now took the blanket and heaped that into the blaze. Then he smashed one of the rear windows, heaved his great bulk through the gap, losing some of his gold sovereigns on the way, and leapt on his horse which was tethered at the rear of the cabin, to gallop off to freedom.

Spirals of grey billowed out from the broken window.

'Look at all that smoke,' Charles whispered to Vincent.

'My God, he's set the cabin on fire!'

It was at that moment that they saw the lone horseman emerge from behind the cabin and gallop off at full speed.

'Atcherley is making a dash for it – or is it Bastley?' But they could see the rider's wild, white hair and beard illuminated in the moonlight.

'It must be Atcherley,' Charles exclaimed. 'Bastley is dark.'

'Watch the direction he goes, Charles. He cannot get far on the moors without being seen. I want to know what is in that cabin. We need Bastley as a witness.'

Muffling his face with his scarf and cloak, Vincent smashed down the cabin door and stepped inside. At first he could see nothing but billows of thick grey smoke which stung his eyes and made them smart, but he was determined to find out if Bastley was still alive and, if so, why he had not ridden out with Atcherley. Almost immediately he saw the body slumped over the table with the three vicious back wounds.

Then turning, as the smoke eddied and cleared for a few moments, he saw the spread-eagled woman lashed to the bed, her Titian hair, although bedraggled and unwashed, spread out around her like a flaming cloud.

'*Cassia!*' Her name was wrenched from him, his heart seemed to stop beating so that his chest was filled with a fiery emptiness. For a few seconds he was so stunned that he could barely move and then he was at her bedside and, in one moment, he had reached for the iron poker which lay in the hearth and smashed at the chains at her wrists and ankles. She barely moved, she did not even open her eyes. He thought that she was dead, and bitter grief engulfed him as he worked.

Fortunately, there was more smoke than flame from the fire for the blanket which Dash had thrown onto the flames had partially smothered them, but the smoke was becoming so dense that it was choking Vincent and he knew that Cassia — if she were still alive — would not be able to survive their inhalation.

A few moments later, lifting her as gently as he could while making haste, Vincent had his wife out in the open air away from the flying sparks and fumes of the cabin. Tearing off his cloak, he tenderly wrapped her in it, resting her head on his folded scarf, while murmuring her name over and over again. When she did not respond, he grew even more frantic. Then he remembered the brandy in his pocket and, carefully lifting up her head, he pressed the liquid to her lips, a drop at a time

349

so that she would not choke. Even so, she coughed and spluttered, moaning his name even before her eyes opened. Then her lids fluttered and he saw in the moonlight the beautiful hydrangea-blue eyes that he adored.

'Vincent,' she whispered hoarsely. 'Oh Vincent, it is you, it is really you? Or am I dreaming? Yes, surely I must be dreaming.' She coughed again, and gently he held some more drops of the brandy to her lips.

'It is I, beloved, it is really your Vincent. You are safe now, that wretch Atcherley has gone.'

'Atcherley –' Cassia whispered. 'That was his false name.' She paused for breath. 'It was Dash, Nathan Dash, with his hair and beard bleached white.'

'*Dash!* You mean –? *Mon Dieu*, you mean –?'

'Yes, Marshall Atcherley is Nathan Dash and this was his hideout.' Cassia's voice was faint but urgent. 'I caught him that morning he was with Sulamee. He recognized me instantly, and knew that I could not go free or I would tell the Justices. He did not know you were still alive, of course – he really believed you were dead. I did not enlighten him. But, all the same, he knew that I was the one person in Liverpool who knew his true identity, and I suppose he thought that I would inform that he was a murderer – that he had murdered you.' Cassia managed a wry smile before collapsing into semi-consciousness with the effort of speaking.

When she had mentioned Sulamee's name, Vincent's heart had missed a beat. He had no intention of telling her of Sulamee's fate while she was in this dreadfully weak condition. Later she would have to know. Poor Cassia, she would take it badly, he feared. But he would be the one to tell her, for the burden was his and the duty, and he would do it out of the great love he bore her, for he did love her. There was no doubt of that. He had been a fool, but a man need only be a fool once in his life to learn his lesson. Whatever agonies Cassia had endured during her imprisonment in Dash's cabin, he, Vincent, would make it up to her a hundredfold. Every day for the rest of their lives he would make it up to her. He would love her, cherish her, adore her, for she deserved no less, and while she was recovering from her ordeal he himself would nurse her tenderly, lovingly. He looked down at her haggard face, the hollowed cheeks and the pits beneath her eyes. She had been in this wretched place for nearly four weeks and it was obvious that Dash had been starving her. God knows what else she had had to endure. But he would help her to forget it, to forget every pain, every agony. He would cocoon her with his love, protect and pamper her, as she fully deserved. Then, when she was better, they would go back to Cornwall, to Penwellyn and Julitta, and, if the Fates were benevolent, they would one day start their family.

Cassia's eyes flew open. She had remembered something. 'Vincent, Vincent, in the cabin. The treasure − your treasure, your gold and jewels. Under the floorboards!'

Vincent knew a moment of exquisite delight. He had forgotten all about the treasure. He had not cared whether it was found or not, all that mattered was that his Cassia was safe. He did not even look round to see if the cabin had burned to the ground behind them. He knew that his treasure was safe.

In his urgent haste in the darkness, Nathan Dash spurred on his horse towards freedom. He knew that across the hills, on the opposite side of the Sisters of Doom, was the city of Liverpool where he would be able to set sail in the first ship leaving port. He had enough gold coins and jewels to pay for his fare over and over. He would start anew somewhere else, somewhere far from Liverpool and England. The West Indies, Jamaica perhaps. He spurred on his horse, directly between the twin peaks called the Sisters of Doom. It was quicker than going round them. On, on he rode, directly between the Sisters. He barely had time to realize what happened next, as his horse crashed into the narrow abyss between the twin peaks

351

and he felt himself falling, falling, down into the bottomless chasm, his terrified cries being added to the ghostly barks of the hunting hounds and the blood-curdling yells of the four hunters, whose dying screams haunted the abyss.